In the Shadow
of a Secret

THE GENTLE HILLS

Far From the Dream
Whispers in the Valley
Keeper of the Harvest
Some Things Last Forever

(All available in large print)

The Bridge Over Flatwillow Creek
In the Shadow of a Secret
One Small Miracle

Lance Wubbels

In the Shadow of a Secret

BETHANY HOUSE PUBLISHERS
MINNEAPOLIS, MINNESOTA 55438

Published by Bethany House Publishers
A Ministry of Bethany Fellowship International
11400 Hampshire Avenue South
Minneapolis, Minnesota 55438
www.bethanyhouse.com

Printed in the United States of America by
Bethany Press International, Minneapolis, Minnesota 55438

Library of Congress Cataloging-in-Publication Data

Wubbels, Lance, 1952–
    In the shadow of a secret / by Lance Wubbels.
       p. cm.
     ISBN 0–7642–2183–3
     I. Title.
PS3573.U39 I5   1999   99–6543
813'.54—dc21   CIP

To
Karen

You made the
difference on this one.
It's easy to say
that I couldn't have
done it without you.
All my love.

LANCE WUBBELS is presently the Managing Editor of Bethany House Publishers where he has worked for the past eighteen years. For many of those years he also taught biblical studies courses at Bethany College of Missions. A naturally gifted storyteller, he is the author of six other fiction books with Bethany House. *The Bridge Over Flatwillow Creek* is a timeless country love story that begins on a quiet summer day in 1901 in southeastern Minnesota and whose two main characters have a role in *In the Shadow of a Secret*. *One Small Miracle* is the award-winning novella about the profound impact of a teacher's gift of love on the life of one of her struggling students. THE GENTLE HILLS series contains four books that capture the heartrending challenges of World War II and the love of family and home.

Combining the skills of a teacher, a researcher, and an editor, Wubbels has also been the compiler and editor of twenty-five Christian Living Classic books with Emerald Books. Having discovered a wealth of classic writings, sermons, and biblical expositions from legendary Christians such as Charles Spurgeon, F. B. Meyer, Charles Finney, Andrew Murray, Hudson Taylor, R. A. Torrey, and George Müller, it has been his desire to present these extraordinary writings in a way that will appeal to a wide audience of readers and allow their ageless messages to be as relevant today as the day they were penned.

Wubbels' recent daily devotional with Emerald Books, *In His Presence*, contains some of the most profound expositions ever given regarding the Gospel of Matthew. It is a finalist for the 1999 ECPA Gold Medallion Award for devotionals.

He and his family make their home in Bloomington, Minnesota.

Prologue

*I*n the dim light of her bedroom, Rebecca Adler ran a slender finger along the gilded edge of the dark walnut vanity and stared blankly into the large oval mirror, lost in a blur of tangled thoughts and broken emotions. Her long wavy brown hair framed the soft lines of her delicate face. Almond-shaped green eyes, bloodshot but holding no more tears, mirrored the agonizing decision she must carry out.

"It's all your fault, you know," she whispered to her reflection, finally blinking her long eyelashes and taking a deep breath of air. "Even love doesn't make this right."

She closed her eyes and gently rubbed them with her fingertips, slowly massaging the strained muscles to relieve the burning irritation, then moved her fingers up around her temples. The sudden chiming of the ornately carved Bavarian clock on her dresser brought out an anxious "Oh no," and Rebecca counted quietly to its rhythm, "Five, six, seven, eight, nine, ten." Opening her eyes, she shook her head and added, "Time to go."

She stood up and carefully straightened the plain black fabric of her long dress, then slid her hands down over the slight bulge in her abdomen and delicately pressed against the new life hidden within. "I will love you ... little one ... no matter what it costs," the young woman declared, pressing her lips together tightly.

Glancing around the elaborately adorned bedroom, everything spoke of the Adler family's opulence and wealth—the solid walnut Paris bed with hand-turned legs and carved corner blocks and white cotton canopy, two huge matching wardrobes filled with Chicago's finest dresses and evening gowns, the priceless antique writing desk that had belonged to her great-grandmother, and the plush velvet settee encased by shelves of her favorite leather-bound books, where she had spent countless hours dreaming of faraway places and adventure.

She reached over and took one last inventory of her precious necklaces and rings, then slowly closed the solid teak inlaid jewelry box and locked it with the worn golden key that she always kept hidden on a wooden ledge beneath the vanity. Placing the key on the top of the jewelry box, it seemed strange that leaving this part of her life behind would feel like the smallest of sacrifices.

Picking up a simple black velvet hat from the vanity, she managed a weak smile in the mirror as she carefully pinned it into her hair. Compared to any of the dozen other hats she could have picked, this was easily the plainest. Indeed, every article of clothing she had packed reflected only the most basic items of her wardrobe. The single piece of jewelry she was taking was a gold heart-shaped locket that held her favorite photo of her mother and father. Where she was going, at least where she hoped she might be able to stay for a while, she was certain there would never be a need for the fancy dresses and immaculately tailored gowns and stylish jewelry that her mother and father had routinely lavished upon her as their only child.

Without making a sound, she picked up her black leather purse, turned, and walked across the lush Persian rug to the bedroom door. Turning off the light, she carefully opened the door to the darkened hallway, then lifted the leather handles of her matching suitcases she had waiting by the door. As her eyes tried to adjust to the darkness, she gazed down the hallway toward her parents' bedroom door. There was neither light nor voices coming from the room, and the door was slightly open.

Rebecca took a deep breath and headed toward the long marble staircase that led down to the front entryway of the mansion. Passing by her parents' door, she did not stop until she got to the wide landing, where she set down her suitcases. Then she reached into her purse and quickly pulled out a white envelope that was tightly sealed with her own wax stamp. Without hesitation she turned and walked silently back to her parents' bedroom door, where she stopped. Stooping down to slide the letter under the door, she caught the scent of her mother's favorite perfumes and paused, caught off guard by the familiar smell.

Slowly standing back up, she leaned heavily against the doorframe. She knew she shouldn't risk it, but her trembling hand reached out through the darkness and lightly touched the brass handle, then cautiously pushed the door open until she could see into the expansive bedroom. She hesitated and stared toward her parents' grand European sleigh bed. In the dim moonlight that streamed in through the French doors leading to a wide balcony, she could easily make out the two familiar forms lying motionless beneath white sheets. A muggy summer breeze filtered in through the open windows, gently tugging back and forth at the long silk curtains.

She stood frozen in the doorway for a few long minutes, breathing heavily, then took a measured step into the room, followed by a second, then a third across the hardwood floor to her mother's side of the bed. Stopping a few feet from the head of the bed until her eyes fully adjusted to the room's dimness, she fingered the letter one more time, then laid it discreetly on the nightstand. As she turned to leave, she hesitated again, glancing at the two figures.

Her father was on his side, turned away from her toward the tall French doors, his wide shoulders and the back of his bald head silhouetted against the white linens. *Seems like this is the way it's always been,* she thought. *Nothing I ever did could get you to turn around and look at me, not even now when I wish I could say good-bye.*

"For the thousandth time, Father," she whispered across the moonlit darkness, "what I did was wrong, but I do love him . . . and I won't give him up . . . or the baby . . . no matter how you feel about it."

A gust of hot wind suddenly rippled the silk curtains, startling her for a second. Outside, the leaves in the huge maple tree that sheltered the west side of the brick mansion began to flutter as an easterly breeze increased. Through the windows she could see the first muted flashes of lightning on the distant horizon, and she knew she had to hurry if she was going to make it to the train station before the storm arrived.

She closed her eyes and wished again that there was the slightest chance she could stay, but could only shake her head at the thought. Her father would never change his mind about her leaving, and the longer she remained in the house, the more her parents would quarrel over her.

"I have to go. . . . Don't you see that, Mother?" she spoke softly as she opened her eyes and gazed into her mother's serene face. "I'll destroy you and Father both if I stay. I'm sorry I let you down. It's no one's fault but my own."

She was close enough to hear her mother's soft breathing, and ever so slowly she took a step toward the bed and started to reach out to touch her mother's smooth cheek, then stopped short. *All the pain I've caused you over this*, she thought. *I hope someday you'll understand.*

The tears she thought she had exhausted welled up again and cascaded down her cheeks to the hardwood floor. She stood there for at least a minute, perhaps two, her hand still outstretched toward her mother, as the tears pooled below her on the floor.

"I love you both" were her last words before she turned and disappeared into the night shadows.

Chapter 1

March 1937

"Christina, relax," Martin Nelson murmured to the young woman standing next to him in a shimmering blue silk halter-top evening dress, lightly touching the back of her shoulder as he leaned in close to her face. "All you have to do is follow my father's lead. Has anyone told you how wonderful you look?"

Smiling nervously as she glanced down at what was easily the most expensive dress she'd ever worn, she reached up and discreetly lifted his hand from her shoulder. "You've told me five times, I believe," she said over the sound of the swing band, flashing her deep blue eyes up at him. "And I'll be a lot less anxious if you keep your hands to home."

"But you're my date . . . on the most important evening of my life!" pled Martin, smiling broadly and gazing around the large ballroom. He reached up and straightened the black bow tie of his tuxedo, then lightly ran his fingers across his dark mustache. "All these lovely ladies and—"

"I'm simply your guest, Mr. Nelson," Christina replied, stepping back and nodding her head. Her shoulder-length blond hair with its natural curl shimmered under the light from the crystal chandeliers overhead. "If you recall, the invitation . . . and the dress . . . came from your mother. My only reason for being here is the painting, and we both know that. I hope you don't feel obligated to baby-sit me."

"I was thinking that *protect* might be a more appropriate word," he said, moving close to her face again. "One of these rich young men might think that a beautiful country girl from Minnesota would make a nice feather in his cap. Some of them don't like it when they don't get their way."

"And that would bother you, Mr. Nelson?" Christina asked, grinning as she studied his golden brown eyes. "My impression is that your list of girlfriends is as long as your shirt sleeve. Would you deny some other man the chance to add to his list?"

"Only if I was considering adding that person to my list first," Martin replied, his face suddenly showing a tint of red. Then he glanced over at his father, who was walking toward the front of the band. "Oh, here we go. It's show time!"

"What am I supposed to—"

"Just do whatever he says."

"Ladies and gentlemen, may I have your attention, please!" Oliver Nelson called out, raising his hands and silencing the swing band. At six feet two and dressed in his well-tailored tuxedo, he immediately drew the attention of the crowd. Every head turned toward the commanding voice, and a hush fell quickly over the 250 or more guests who filled the large ballroom of the Nelson mansion. "Margaret and I would like to thank you all for joining us on this cold winter's evening as we celebrate our son's twenty-first birthday. We consider it something of a miracle that he survived this long, given the torments he suffered from his four older brothers, and it seemed appropriate that we throw him one really big party. Martin, please join me."

Martin smiled and stepped away from Christina to join his father. As he made his way to the front, the onlookers began to applaud, and a few of his friends gave him playful shoves when he passed by them. His mother had stepped next to his father and taken his hand. She reached out and hugged Martin as he arrived.

"Your mother thought your old Ford coupe was looking a little shabby," Mr. Nelson announced, reaching into his pants pocket and fishing out a key, "so she twisted my arm and made me go out and get you a nice new white Jaguar SS100 Roadster." Dropping the keys in his son's hand, he added, "Treat her well. It's the last car we buy you."

To the applause of the crowd, Martin gave a whoop and hugged his mother again, then robustly shook his father's hand and clapped his back. Behind them two of the household servants were carrying out what was evidently a tall, wide painting draped with a covering cloth. They carefully set it up on a wooden easel next to Oliver Nelson, then walked away.

"For your twenty-first birthday," Oliver continued, "I also commissioned a portrait of you from one of Chicago's finest young artists." He looked across the ballroom and beckoned. "Christina Ellington, please come and do us the honor of unveiling your work."

Christina shook her head reluctantly, having clung in vain to the hope that she could hide in the back, then made her way through the audience and stepped next to the eight-foot-tall painting. She smiled warmly and looked toward Martin's father to see what was next.

"This is actually for your mother, Martin," Oliver Nelson declared with pride in his voice. He took his wife's arm and led her around to the front of the painting. "She hasn't seen the portrait yet."

"Neither have I," said Martin, giving Christina a sidelong glance as he came alongside his parents. "Miss Ellington said she'd destroy the canvas if I tried to peek before she finished. She muttered some nonsense about it being an artistic value she wouldn't compromise."

"At least for the paltry bribe you offered me," Christina piped in, her bright smile lighting up her face and releasing the anxiety she was feeling. "I'm certainly glad your father wasn't such a miser."

The crowd broke out laughing, being led by Oliver Nelson, who seemed to delight in the young artist getting the better of his son. His loud, piercing laugh rose above the clapping and other laughter in the room; then he nodded toward Christina and held up his hands.

"As you'll see in a moment," Mr. Nelson called out as the din in the room died down, "Miss Ellington has a marvelous talent and is a worthy student of Chicago's finest illustrator, Carl Langstan." Turning to Christina he continued, "When Carl and I talked, his recommendation that you do this painting was understated, but everything the man does, including his art, is understated. You were the perfect choice, and I would be very pleased if you would now present your portrait of Martin as my gift to his mother in honor of his twenty-first birthday."

Christina nodded, then gracefully reached around the back of the painting and unhooked the cloth that was draped over the front. With a surprisingly dramatic flair, she swooped the fabric off the painting, instantly unveiling the life-sized illustration of Martin Nelson decked out in an expensive black pinstripe suit, wearing a brushed leather hat with a dark ribbon and leaning on a black cane with a golden handle. Every detail seemed perfect, even the tiniest glint of sunshine reflecting from the fine gold chain tie clasp, but it was Martin's face that drew everyone's immediate attention. Something about his expression captured both the man he was becoming as well as the youth he had been. His eyes bore the mark of maturity and clear focus, but his boyish smile was playful and hinted of laughter.

The ballroom was hushed until Mrs. Nelson whispered, "It's perfect," taking her husband's arm but not removing her gaze from the painting. "It's priceless, Oliver."

Around the large room, muffled comments arose and some of the guests began to nod their heads in admiration. Then a tuxedoed gentleman standing near the front called out, "Extraordinary! Bravo!"

An older woman standing next to him joined in with a very loud "Bravo!" which was followed by a chorus of applause from around the room. One by one, people began to move in closer to get a better look at the painting, which only intensified the surge of appreciation for the young artist.

Christina watched with delight as Mrs. Nelson's expression of wonder slowly melted into tears. The stylish socialite covered her mouth with her hand and her eyes spilled over with tears. She tried to regain her composure, but the unexpected emotions held sway until Mr. Nelson rescued her with his handkerchief.

Martin stepped next to Christina and with a sheepish, somewhat embarrassed grin said to her, "You should have upped the price on the old man. I've never seen my mother react like this before."

Christina laughed, releasing whatever was left over of her concern about how the painting would be received. Then she said quietly to him, "Do you like it, Martin?"

Glancing back at the painting, Martin's smile got firmer, and his eyes modeled the same purposefulness of the illustration. "I . . . um . . . I'm very impressed with your work, but I'm not quite sure how to respond to a painting of myself," he said. "I was hoping you'd make me a bit more dashing . . . perhaps thicker through the shoulders and more muscular in the arms. I've always wished that my jawline was—"

"I can only paint what I see, Mr. Nelson," Christina returned, noting that his mother was turning toward her. "I suggest you spend more time in the gym, if that's what you're hoping to see."

"Look at the mess you've made of me," Mrs. Nelson half cried and half laughed as she reached out and took Christina's hands. "You've made me the happiest woman in the world . . . and perhaps the most embarrassed. Whatever will my friends say?"

"I hope they say that you liked the painting," said Christina, her face shining a grin under the ballroom lighting. "I'm so glad you like it."

"Like?" the wealthy mother replied, shaking her head. "I will treasure this painting for the rest of my life, Miss Ellington, and I am forever in your debt. Would you consider coming back again and painting Oliver and myself?"

Christina looked at Mr. Nelson, who nodded that he was willing, then she said, "I would be honored to do so. Let me know when you'd like to start. I can use all the work I can get. Mr. Langstan is a wonderful teacher, and very expensive."

"Martin tells me that on occasion Mr. Langstan actually sat and watched as you were doing this painting," Mrs. Nelson said. "Is that true?"

"Yes, indeed," said Christina, glancing up at the painting. "Do you notice the special lighting around Martin's eyes? It wouldn't have been there except that Mr. Langstan kept stressing to me that I was missing it. He has a marvelous eye for lighting."

Mrs. Nelson nodded her appreciation, then added, "It will probably be a couple of months before we can arrange for a sitting. We'll be vacationing for several weeks on the West Coast, and I'd like to get a special dress made for the painting."

"Mother, you're wearing a beautiful dress that's all of a day old," Martin teased. "Why not do it before you leave for vacation?"

"No, no, no," the older woman replied. "When we do this, we want it done right. I'm not going to rush into it."

"We'll let you know when we can arrange some time with you, Miss Ellington," Oliver Nelson stated. "In the meantime, please receive our heartfelt gratitude for the painting. I've decided that a bonus is appropriate for your work. I'll have our driver drop something off for you in the next few days, if that meets with your approval."

Christina's smile widened and she responded, "Thank you for your kindness . . . and generosity, Mr. Nelson. I'm so happy you're satisfied with my work."

With the crowd pressing against them to see the painting and the congratulations toward Christina mounting, the conversation quickly came to an end. Mr. Nelson turned around and gave a signal to the leader of the band, who promptly picked up their instruments and began to play a popular Benny Goodman tune.

"Let's get out of this mob," Martin said, taking Christina's hand and pulling her away from the guests gathered around the painting. "You owe me a dance, anyway."

"But I can't dance, and I've already told you that," Christina protested, trying to pull her hand loose from his grip. "Stop!"

"Oh, come on," Martin replied, flashing his boyish grin and taking her other hand in his. "There's nothing to it, really. Just follow my lead and you'll be fine."

"That's what you think," she said as he pulled her closer and led her into the dance. "You just want to humiliate me in front of all these people."

"Now why would I do that?" he asked, holding her tight. "See, you've already got this dance down. Wait till they play some swing tunes!"

"No thanks," Christina said, shaking her head. "Not in this dress, and not without some practice first."

"When would you like to practice? There's a place down on—"

"Whoa, now!" Christina protested, relaxing a bit as she swayed to the slow rhythm of the band. "You're confusing me for someone else, I think. Are you forgetting Miss Lofton? Where is she tonight? I haven't seen her yet."

"And you won't," Martin answered. "She's in New York with her father for a couple of weeks. Family reunion or something. Mostly lots of shopping, if you ask me."

"Your mother says you're practically engaged."

"What of it? After all the time we've spent together at the studio, what's a little more time if I take you to some dance lessons?"

"The studio was business that your father was paying me for, Mr. Nelson," Christina said, wrinkling her forehead. "This sounds like you have other intentions."

"And if I did?"

Christina began to laugh and momentarily lost her concentration, causing her to step on Martin's toe. "I'm sorry!" she gasped, laughing even harder and trying to get her feet back into following Martin's lead. "You shouldn't tease me like this. I get befuddled."

"Who's teasing?"

"You're teasing—at least you'd better be," Christina said firmly. "This is another world to me. I feel like . . . like a foreigner who can barely speak the language. I don't think I could ever get used to this."

"Listen, Christina, you're not just a poor little country girl from southern Minnesota," Martin said. "I've never been around a girl who has more style and grace and wit than you. You've never told me your mother's real story, have you? She was no farmer's daughter, I'm sure of that."

Christina shrugged her shoulders and looked away. "I don't know the whole story, and I'm not sure I ever want to know it. My mother would be as comfortable in this ballroom as she is in her little one-room schoolhouse, but there's a part of her life that she almost never talked about."

"And your father?"

"I thought I told you about him. He died a war hero somewhere in France on Thanksgiving Day of 1917, before I was born. I grew up in his parents' home with my mother."

"How long were they married before he left for the war?"

"They weren't," Christina replied, looking straight into Martin's soft brown eyes. "My mother discovered she was pregnant after he left with the army. When her father found out, he told her she'd have to leave home unless she gave me up for adoption."

Martin Nelson showed no change of expression and said nothing.

"So you want to start dance lessons with an illegitimate, poor country girl?" Christina continued. "Try to explain that to your mother and father . . . or Miss Lofton. I suspect they would not share your enthusiasm. Am I right?"

"I . . . um . . . I'm afraid you're correct," Martin replied, glancing over at his parents, who were still admiring the painting with a group of their friends. "I'm sorry. . . . I didn't mean to put you into such a difficult spot."

Christina smiled and said, "It's quite all right, Mr. Nelson. I've been in this spot my entire life. It's just the way it is. There are some things you can't change . . . you just learn to live with them."

"But it's no one else's business," said Martin. "There's no reason why—"

"There may be no good reason, but you know full well everyone makes it their business," Christina interjected. "Our worlds may be very different, but surely we have that part in common. Have you noticed how closely your mother's friends have been watching us?"

"I've noticed the usual gawking. So what?"

"Trust me, there's more than gawking going on. They're waiting to see whether we continue to dance after this song. If you want to minimize the gossip and prying, I recommend that you find another dance partner. I'll spend some time with some of your guests who are looking at the painting, then I'll quietly slip away."

"I can drive you—"

"Thanks, but your mother told me their driver would take me home," said Christina as the band finished the tune and she let go of Martin. "I've enjoyed getting to know you, Mr. Nelson. It was a pleasure to paint your portrait. Perhaps we'll see each other again if I paint your parents. And thank you for the dance."

"I'll call."

"I don't have a phone," Christina replied, stepping away. "And . . . take a look around the room, Mr. Nelson. I'm not a good idea for you. Good-bye."

Christina turned and walked toward the guests gathered around the painting. As the band began to play another song, she glanced back and was relieved to see that Martin had easily found another dance partner. Noting that she hadn't seen anyone she knew except for the Nelsons, she considered leaving immediately.

Her eye went to the large canvas again, though, and she found herself stopping to study the portrait one last time. While she was very pleased with her execution of Martin's face, Mr. Langstan had pointed out that on certain sections of the painting she had gotten looser with her strokes and failed to maintain the same attention to detail. *If I could do it over*, she thought, *I'd go back in and*—

"You have an exceptional talent, young lady," said a tall, slender woman in an elaborate gold-and-black evening gown, breaking into Christina's reverie. The middle-aged woman's emerald green eyes were fixed on the painting, and she lightly rubbed her fingers over a huge diamond wedding ring. "The hands are always the hardest, aren't they? Did they give you trouble?"

Christina glanced quickly up at the woman, wondering how the obviously refined lady could know what she'd been thinking. "Yes . . . well, no . . . not really," she replied, noting the woman's smile. "If anything, I simply didn't take as much time on them as I should have. Looking at his hands now, they're not as finished as I would like them to be. Are you an artist?"

"No, not even close," the woman replied, her thin red lips turning up in a lovely smile. "I'm sorry, I didn't introduce myself. I'm Maria Sikkink, an old friend of the Nelsons. I've known Martin since he was an infant."

"I'm pleased to meet you. I'm—"

"Christina Ellington," the rich woman broke in, "and if I were to believe half of what Oliver says about you, I'd be a fool not to ask you to paint my portrait. What do you say? Would you consider it? I'd like you to do for me what you've done for young Martin."

"What did I do?"

"You've taken all his best features and made them even better. What woman wouldn't want that in her portrait?"

"I don't know if—"

"I'll pay you double whatever Oliver paid you," Mrs. Sikkink said, moving closer to Christina. "And if I'm satisfied, I can assure you that I'll find you several more clients. Have you heard of my husband, Eugene Sikkink?"

"The senator?"

Maria Sikkink nodded and said, "Name your price."

Christina shook her head and rubbed her lips with her right forefinger. "I'm honored that you'd even consider me," she said, "and I really could use the money, but . . . seriously, I've only done a dozen or so portraits like this. You really should talk with Mr. Langstan. I'm sure he could recommend someone who's—"

"Carl is a personal acquaintance, my dear," Maria interrupted, "and you already have his recommendation. How else would I have known about the hands?"

"He mentioned that to you?"

Maria laughed for the first time and crossed her arms. "He said that if I questioned you about the hands, and you admitted they lacked the details of the face, then you were ready to paint me. You passed his test, Christina. I would love for you to paint my portrait."

"But I can't promise that I'll be able to do what you've suggested I did with Martin's."

"Highlight and intensify my best features?"

Christina nodded. "That's asking—"

"Too much. I know, I know, but there's no harm in wishing," Maria declared. "I'm only asking you to do the very best you can."

"But why me when you can afford anyone you want?"

Maria Sikkink pointed to the painting of Martin Nelson and said, "Over the past two years I've looked at the portraits of dozens of artists, some even from New York City, and none of them captured the expression you did in Martin's face. That, according to Carl Langstan, is not something he taught you. He says it's in your heart."

"He actually said that?"

"Twice in one conversation. He also said you're paying your own way through lessons, which is hard to imagine at his rates. So, what do you say? Can you use the money?"

"I certainly can," Christina answered through a big smile. "I'll do my best. That's all I can promise."

Chapter 2

April 1937

Andrew Regan stopped at the office door of the president of the seminary, opened his light jacket, and glanced down over his white Fairway Fine Foods shirt, checking it one last time for any fresh bloodstains he might not have noticed earlier. He felt very fortunate that most of his seminary expenses had been paid for by his job cutting meat, but he wasn't sorry this was his last week of working with the "Choice Meats." "Time for bigger and better things," the store manager had said to him.

Running his fingers over his dark brown hair, he slicked back a few stray hairs, took a deep breath of air, and opened the door. The president's secretary looked up from the stack of papers on her desk and smiled courteously at him. Andrew was surprised to see his father sitting in one of the waiting chairs in the corner.

"Good afternoon, Andrew," Mrs. Turner greeted him. "Thank you for coming down on such short notice. I appreciate your boss letting you out of work. Is he always so nice?"

"Most of the time," Andrew replied, glancing over at his father again. "I've been training a new guy, so they're really not short. What . . . ah . . . why the sudden meeting?"

Mrs. Turner shrugged her shoulders and said, "I have no idea. But you're leaving soon, aren't you?"

"In a week."

"I suspect it's got something to do with that," she spoke softly, tapping her pencil on the top of the papers. "President Williams will see you and your father in just a few minutes. Why don't you have a seat."

Andrew stepped past her desk, shrugged off his jacket, and quickly sat down in the chair next to his father. "What's going on? Did they call you out of work?"

Spinning his heavy wool cap in his hands and leaning forward in his chair, Joseph Regan raised his thick eyebrows and shook his head. A shorter, more muscular version of his son, he had not taken off his waist-length black leather coat with its shiny union buttons of the United Automobile Workers. "No," he said. "I worked the early shift, so I was home. I can't imagine why he asked me to come. I've only met the man a couple of times. I thought you'd clue me in on what this was all about."

"I got called at the store," Andrew replied, glancing down at his watch. "All I was told was that President Williams wanted to meet with me at four o'clock, if I could get out of work. Why would he want both of us here?"

"You paid all the seminary bills?"

"Every dime. Took me ten months since graduation."

Joseph Regan looked away from his son and pursed his lips, still spinning his cap in his thick, callused hands. "Something's fishy here, son. I don't like the feel of this. You'd better be on your toes when we go in there."

"Why?"

"Didn't you say that President Williams wasn't happy with your accepting the pastorate in my home church?"

"I said he didn't seem pleased about it, especially when there were several larger churches that were looking for pastors, but he didn't say anything about it specifically. I guess I read more into it from the way he looked at me."

Nodding his head, Joseph Regan glanced over at the president's secretary and spoke quietly to his son, "I think I know why I'm here now. . . . He's going to—"

Just then the inner office door swung open and President Williams stepped out dressed in a tailored dark wool suit, white shirt, and dark silk tie. Tall and thin and scholarly looking, the fifty-two-year-old man had successfully pastored three congregations before accepting the call to the presidency of the seminary by the board of trustees the year before. "Andrew," he called out, raising his hand in welcome as the two men rose from their chairs, "thank you for coming down so quickly.

And, Mr. Regan, I'm glad you could make it as well. Please come in."

Before either of the men had time to respond, Harold Williams had turned and disappeared back into his office.

Andrew looked inquisitively at his father and stepped around his chair toward the president's office. "What were you saying?" he whispered.

"Just be on your toes," his father said, leaning close to Andrew. "Never . . . ever . . . trust management."

"This is the church, not—"

"Gentlemen, come in . . . come in," President Williams interrupted as the two men stepped into his large office. Two entire walls were lined with shelves holding a vast array of books, many of the rows thick with old leather volumes of Bible commentaries and church history. Motioning to the two oak chairs on the opposite side of his wide oak desk, he said, "Have a seat, please. May I take your coat, Mr. Regan?"

"No, thank you," Joseph replied with a reticent smile as he sat down on one of the chairs. "I wore it through every meeting during the strike. Got so I hardly ever take it off anymore."

"I understand that you were one of the first to sit down at the Fisher Body Plant," President Williams said as he sat down and reached up to straighten his tie. "It must have taken a lot of courage to lead the way into the strike. If it had failed, I imagine the consequences would have been severe for Flint and your family."

Joseph Regan nodded and eyed the seminary president closely. "We'll never know, I guess, but those long months were pretty terrible for all of us. If General Motors would've had a better pulse of the work force, they would have met us at the table a lot sooner. I told them that the strike would spread to the other plants, but do you think they listened? Say, how is it that you're aware of where I work, let alone my involvement in the union? Is this what our meeting is about?"

"No, no. It has nothing to do with the union," the seminarian replied, pushing his gold wire-rimmed glasses back up on the bridge of his nose. "I try to familiarize myself with all of our students' family backgrounds, and I found yours of particular interest with the recent strikes here in Flint. Why do you ask?"

"I figured you wanted to talk to us about Andrew's future," Joseph replied. "Perhaps you're concerned that my relationship with the union might affect him. There are a lot of people who hate what the unions have done here, and I've heard that the seminary doesn't support us. It struck me that you might have something to say about that."

"No, that's incorrect, despite the rumors some have spread," President Williams said with a smile. "Neither the seminary nor the church takes a position on it, although our own personal views occasionally come out in the classroom and in discussions. But that's true of many issues the seminary has not taken a position on. Isn't that so, Andrew?"

"Yes, sir," Andrew replied, leaning forward in his chair. "Several professors were outspokenly opposed to the union and the strike . . . but you were the strongest voice. It seemed strange that none of the other professors ever expressed any support for the strike, even though I'm sure some did support it. My impression was that you were voicing the position of the seminary."

"No, that's not the case," Williams spoke evenly, "although I realize my personal positions are often interpreted that way. I tend to argue strongly when I feel intensely about an issue."

"I've appreciated your strong views, and I hope I can speak as persuasively in my own ministry when I feel the same conviction that you often bring to a subject. But it might be helpful . . . for the students . . . if you would occasionally clarify whether it's your position, or the seminary's, or both," said Andrew. "I was told that Alfred Sloan is a financial contributor to the seminary. If that's true, I couldn't help but think that the president of General Motors might have influenced the seminary's position. Is it true that he is a donor?"

"We have many influential donors who—"

"Who specialize in keeping the company profits from the workers," Joseph broke in, the muscles in his jaw flexing. "Your friend, Mr. Sloan, is making over five hundred thousand dollars a year, while we barely make enough to put bread on our tables. It's hard for me . . . when I read God's Word . . . to imagine that Jesus, with His constant care of the poor, or the leaders of His church in the book of Acts, would support such disparity."

"Alfred Sloan is a good friend of the seminary and a financial contributor, that is a fact," President Williams stated. "But I am at most only an acquaintance of Mr. Sloan, and I opposed the unions long before being appointed to the presidency of this seminary and long before your sit-down strike here in Flint. I know of no influence that he has brought to bear upon this seminary or any of our professors who oppose the unions and the use of violence and strikes to force businesses to—"

"Hold on, now!" Joseph broke in, shaking his head. "Just because violence has tainted some of the strikes is no cause to lump the two together. Ours was a sit-down strike, which is as far from the intent of violence as you can get. But as long as people are involved, there'll be troublemakers on both sides who force things to a confrontation. Tell me that the cops have never attacked or used excessive force on striking union workers whose intention was only to picket a business in a completely legal manner."

"Unions and their ungodly violence are a part of a communistic conspiracy that threatens to infiltrate—"

"I think, President Williams," Andrew declared, standing up and placing his hands on the desk, "that we've gone far afield from whatever it was you wanted to discuss with us. I don't mean to be disrespectful, but I get very angry when anyone associates my father with communism. With your permission, sir, I think it best if we leave."

For a moment Harold Williams looked stunned, but the scowl across his forehead slowly faded and he shook his head. "No, please stay . . . I'm sorry . . . I truly had no intention of discussing the unions, and I apologize for letting my feelings on this matter get me so rattled. And I didn't mean to imply that I consider you a communist, Mr. Regan. But I'm sure you're aware that there are communists involved in your strikes, and that they promote strikes as a powerful force in the overthrow of democracy."

"I'm well aware of their influence, and I have friends who, unfortunately, have embraced communism. But their voice is not driving the union," Joseph said as Andrew slowly sat back down. "If every business and large corporation treated its workers with respect and fairness, what role would the unions play? But when one gigantic business is so committed to squeezing its workers for every nickel of profit, like General Motors is, I don't see an alternative but for the labor force to band together and speak with a collective voice. You can call that communism if you like. I prefer to call it fighting fire with fire."

"Well, your fire was obviously stronger," Mr. Williams said, finally showing a bit of a smile. "When General Motors gave up the battle in February, I suspect that Mr. Sloan was not the happiest man in Michigan. But all this has nothing to do with why I asked the two of you to meet me here. Would you give me another try?"

Andrew looked at his father and said, "Sure. We thought it might have something to do with my taking the call to pastor the small country church in Minnesota where my father grew up. When I told you about it, my impression was that you were less than thrilled."

President Williams nodded, taking off his glasses and carefully setting them on his desk. "It's really more about some of the other pastoral opportunities available to you that you haven't taken since you graduated. I hoped we might discuss it one more time, and I thought it would be good if your father were here."

"You feel that my father might be convinced to try to persuade me in this direction?"

"I thought that with your father's experience in struggling to get the very best for his co-workers, his input would be valuable."

"I've already made the decision and given my word, sir," Andrew replied. "My father would never ask me to break a promise that I've made."

"No, I'm not suggesting that you break a promise," President Williams said. "I'm sure that the small church in Minnesota would understand if you told them that, unbeknown to you at the time of your decision, one of our largest churches here in Flint was considering you for their pastorate."

"Mount Carmel?"

"That's right. As you're aware, Reverend Devries is retiring, and based upon his recommendation . . . and mine . . . they are now moving toward formally calling you as their pastor."

"Me? You're sure?"

President Williams smiled and said, "Why else do you think they invited you to preach there so many times this past year? Many pastors serve their whole careers and never have such a golden opportunity."

"But why would you suggest me? I have no experience and—"

"The consensus among the faculty is that you're the finest graduate to come out of the seminary in several years, Andrew," President Williams broke in, thumping the desk with his finger as he spoke. "We recognize that you're young, but we feel it's a position you would excel in. I say that without hesitation, young man, and I believe you are going to bring honor to this program. What do you think of that, Mr. Regan? Quite an honor for your son."

Andrew's father smiled wryly and stroked the short growth of dark whiskers on his chin. "That's a powerful compliment you've given my son, and I can't tell you how proud it makes me feel. Mount Carmel is a wonderful church, and Reverend Devries is one of the finest preachers I've heard. It sounds too good to be true. What's the catch?"

"There's no catch. None whatsoever," replied President Williams. "Just a wide-open pulpit this church wants to fill as quickly as possible. Here in Flint you'll have direct access to the head office of our denomination, and I'm sure the salary is at least triple that of the Minnesota church. What are they starting you at?"

Andrew shook his head and looked intently at the seminarian. "I . . . ah . . . don't particularly like where this conversation is headed, President Williams. It's an honor to me . . . that you'd consider recommending me to the Mount Carmel congregation, and I'm a bit overwhelmed that they think I might be able to fill the shoes of Reverend Devries. But it's not about the salary, and I have no interest in the denominational headquarters. My interest lies in going where I'm truly needed."

"The need is real at Mount Carmel, Andrew," President Williams stated flatly, tapping his finger again. "Reverend Devries retires this fall, and they'd like to have his replacement in the pulpit for the entire summer."

"Then they'd better start looking harder, because I'm not the man for the job," Andrew replied. "I gave my word and—"

"I'm telling you that the country church will understand if you tell them—"

"No, I don't think they would," said Andrew. "They asked me to seek God's will regarding my possible role in their church's future. I did so, and I told them I felt the Lord was directing me to say yes. I can't take that back."

"But you had no idea about Mount Carmel. They'll understand that you're young and that discerning God's will isn't always easy."

"It certainly isn't," Andrew agreed, "but I have to tell you that I've never felt more sure about any decision in my life. I can't turn away from it."

President Williams raised his eyebrows, then picked up his wire-rimmed glasses, put them back on, and looked from son to father. "Your son has the chance of a lifetime here in Flint, Mr. Regan. I was hoping you might help me here."

"Help you persuade him not to do what he feels is God's will?" Joseph Regan asked. "Coming from your office, that seems like an odd request."

"That's not what I'm asking," President Williams declared. "Even you said this is just too good an offer to be true. It seems to me if anything is an indication of God's will, this surely qualifies. Wouldn't you agree?"

"It might be ..." said the older Regan, taking a deep breath, "but then again, just because a car is bright and shiny when it comes off the assembly line doesn't mean it's the right car for just anyone to buy. This is a decision that's between Andrew and God, right?"

"Sure, but as his father I would think—"

"As his father my only concern is that he does what he feels is right in his heart," Joseph Regan replied. "Whether he pastors a small country church or the largest church in our denomination makes no difference to me. Does it to you?"

"I'd hate for him to waste his talents when a large church is asking him to fill their pulpit today."

"How can I waste my talents if I'm doing God's will?" Andrew asked. "I appreciate your concern as well as your confidence in recommending me, but the peace God gave me when I prayed about the village church was like nothing I've ever experienced. I know you've had such experiences, President Williams. You gave example after example in your chapel lectures."

The president of the seminary nodded reflectively and finally smiled weakly. "You're sure of it, son? I'll press you no further on the matter."

"Yes, sir. I'm sure."

Chapter 3

"Mrs. Sikkink, could you step back about three inches?" Christina Ellington asked as she studied how the midmorning sunlight streaming through the tall window into the den highlighted the woman's face. "There! Right there! Don't move! That's perfect."

"Don't move?" Maria Sikkink replied with a brief laugh. "You actually think I can stay frozen in one spot?"

"No, I'm sorry," Christina said, taking an artist's pencil in hand and stepping up to her large sketching pad that was attached to a wooden easel. "I mean that the lighting is just right where you're standing. If you can keep your face close to where it is right now, it will make a big difference."

"What expression do you think I should have?" Maria turned her shoulders toward Christina and took a deep breath. "Should I be smiling?"

"I'd like you to give me the expression you want me to paint."

"Oh my! I have no idea what the best pose would be. I was hoping you would tell me what looks best."

"First, I want you to relax and move your shoulders back a little bit," Christina replied, looking down as she began to sketch lightly on the paper, then she glanced back at her subject. "I want the focus of your eyes to remain on me at all times . . . but the expression really has to be up to you. What is it you hoped I would capture when you asked me to paint you?"

"I was hoping you'd make me look nineteen again, of course. For starters, I'd like no lines around my eyes. My cheeks should be as perfectly smooth as a baby's bottom, and I was hoping my eyes would sparkle like yours. How am I doing?"

"So far, it sounds easy enough," Christina replied with a laugh, still studying Maria's look. "But who is it you want to see in this painting? Are you hoping others will look at it and say, 'Ah, Mrs. Eugene Sikkink, the loving wife of the famed senator from Illinois. Now, there's one classy lady'?"

"Absolutely not," replied Maria just a little too quickly, shaking her head and twisting her lips. "Every painting I've seen of my friends has them looking like a poor helpless soul who owed everything to her man. Please tell me you hate that mousy look as much as I do."

"It's by no means my favorite pose, and I've painted several women who gave me that look, but I can't say I hate it. How about if you try to give me the same expression you gave me the night we first met? Do you remember?"

"No . . . not in particular."

"You walked up to me so directly, standing tall and strong. Your eyes were intense, calculating. Even your smile said you were in control. Everything about you said you wanted me to paint your portrait, and you wouldn't take no for an answer."

Maria Sikkink laughed and nodded. "Oh yes, now I know what you mean. When my son and daughter were growing up, they called it the 'get big' look. I'm not sure that's what I had in mind for this portrait, but it's worth a try, seeing as it's only a sketch." She stood taller and the expression on her face changed almost instantly. Staring at Christina with a remarkable intensity, she said, "Is this what you are looking for?"

Christina smiled and studied the senator's wife's features. While she was aware that most people would describe the elegantly dressed woman's comportment as stern and almost harsh, Christina saw the regal strength of a woman who had faced adversities and overcome them. "Yes, I think that's just the expression we should go for," she said quietly, as if the sound of her voice might unravel the woman's expression. Glancing back at her rough sketch, she went to the face and began to lightly etch in the first details. "Can you hold that look?"

"Certainly," Maria replied, "but you're remembering that I have to leave shortly, aren't you? You said your preliminary sketch wouldn't require me to pose for very long."

"How long will you be gone?" Christina asked, carefully sketching in the details of Maria's eyes. "While you're away, I thought I might keep working on the sketch and possibly have it ready to put on some finishing touches afterward."

"I just have to help set up and serve at our church's soup kitchen downtown. I'm figuring about an hour and a half. How's that sound?"

"Fine. That'll give me plenty of time."

"If you finish early, feel free to wander around the house or go outside into the backyard. Do you like flowers?"

"Mmm . . . I love them. My mother nearly turned our lawn into one gigantic flower bed."

"Sounds like my neighbor to the south of us. You'll want to visit her backyard and take a look at her gardens. I've never seen anything like it. You won't believe that she doesn't hire a gardener to help her."

"Thanks. I think I'll do that. She won't mind my snooping around her yard?"

"Heavens, no. She loves to talk but has so few visitors. It's really a shame. Her husband is such a sour old miser that he drives people away. I don't know how she can stay in the same house with him."

"Sounds like her garden is a bit of a refuge for her."

"Could be. She's out there from the first day of spring and keeps at it until the first snow starts to fall. Winter must be a miserable time for her."

"I thought winter in Chicago was miserable for everyone," Christina replied, still making light pencil strokes on her pad. "Why should she be any happier than the rest of us?"

"Believe me, that poor old soul has a long way to go before she catches up with us. Whenever I feel a bit melancholy, I think of her. My husband is no prince charming, but he looks like an angel compared to the old man next door."

"I'm afraid you've lost the 'get big' look, Mrs. Sikkink, and I really need you to concentrate on it for a few more minutes. Remember to keep your eyes focused on me. Perhaps we should talk about your neighbors later."

"Certainly," Maria replied, changing her expression almost upon command. "If you meet her, I'd like to hear what your impressions are of her."

Nodding slightly, Christina's full concentration was now on capturing Maria's expression. Glancing from the sketching pad to Maria, then back to the pad, she added light strokes of definition and subtle shadings until the clear image of the senator's wife began to evolve. Then she returned to the eyes, working to catch the intensity they held.

Christina was so absorbed with her sketching that she lost track of the time and barely heard the click of the door to the den as it opened later. But Maria's eyes immediately signaled a change.

"Mrs. Sikkink, I'm sorry to interrupt," the deep, resonating voice of the butler who doubled as chauffeur called out, nearly causing Christina to jump, "but it's time to go. You know how difficult it is for the kitchen when the volunteers come in late."

Maria nodded and said, "Yes, indeed I do. I'll be out in a few minutes . . . after I change my clothes. Have the car waiting, Mr. Jeffries."

"Yes, ma'am," the butler replied as he turned to leave. "It's ready now."

Taking a step back from her sketch, Christina studied her work carefully, then took a deep breath of air as if it were the first one in the past ten minutes.

"Could I be excused?" Maria asked, offering a pleasant smile. "If any of us come in late, it makes it very difficult for the other helpers."

Christina crossed her arms and slowly nodded her head. "Yes, go ahead. I think I've got what I need . . . at least for the moment. But I'll want you to do this one more time when you return. It's coming along nicely, I think."

Maria Sikkink relaxed her shoulders and stepped toward Christina. "Can I take a peek at what you've got?"

"You know my rules, Mrs. Sikkink."

"But it's just a preliminary sketch, not the painting."

"And the rules cover everything. Remember?"

"Yes, yes, yes. You made them clear enough," the senator's wife said as she stopped at the door to the den, still looking at Christina. "I just had to try to see if you were as tough as you sounded."

"Believe me, I am on this one thing," Christina replied. "Until I'm ready to show you what I've got done, don't even ask . . . let alone peek."

Maria Sikkink laughed and waved. "I'll see you later," she said as she exited through the door.

Christina waved good-bye, but the older woman was already on her way down the oak-paneled hallway, the sound of her retreating footsteps giving way to the utter silence of the large room. Stepping back from her sketch, Christina laid down her pencil, closed her eyes, and took in a deep breath of air as she enjoyed the sudden stillness. Between her art lessons, painting portraits to pay for the art lessons, and sharing a small apartment with another girl who had recently dropped out of the art program, there was rarely a quiet moment in her day. She especially relished solitude when she was working on her art, well aware that the heightened focus of her concentration always produced better results.

She went back to work on the sketch and hardly paused over the next half hour. Maria Sikkink's image was clearly in her mind, and Christina knew from past portraits that it was always a race against time to capture the image before it blurred. For most of the time she worked on the lady's elaborate gown, occasionally returning to a missed detail or two on Maria's face or hair. Stroke after stroke, a bit of shading here and there, and the senator's wife slowly emerged.

"Say, you're looking pretty good, sweetheart," Christina finally declared to the image in front of her, setting her pencil down on the easel. Delighted at how quickly and how well the rough sketch had come out, she added, "And I think you're going to love the 'get big' look. It's very becoming."

Satisfied with the overall drawing, except for a few more details that would have to wait for Maria's return, Christina decided to go outside and enjoy the warm spring air and see if the neighbor's backyard was as wonderful as Mrs. Sikkink had described it. She opened a wide French door from the den that led out onto a concrete patio and then followed a sidewalk around to the back of the senator's elegant and highly ornate Victorian house.

With its three floors and high ceilings, the Sikkink mansion was much larger and more striking than the dark brick mansion to the south. But while the senator's backyard was well-groomed with a large variety of roses and shrubs, and a lovely water fountain tucked in the middle of a flower garden, the neighbor's backyard looked like an arboretum. Elaborate garden beds set between winding sidewalks crisscrossed the yard, some surrounded by hedges and others with intricate rock designs. A rich assortment of trees and shrubs adorned the beds and paths. Countless tulips of all colors stood tall and proud in the bright afternoon sunshine.

"Incredible!" Christina whispered, gazing in wonder at the amazing variety and complex planning of the gardens. Almost imperceptibly she continued to walk across the Sikkink lawn to the white picket fence that marked the neighbor's property. "Who could do all this?"

"So, I take it you approve of my gardens?" a woman's voice suddenly spoke, shaking Christina out of her reverie.

Glancing in the direction of the voice, Christina was greeted by the pleasant smile of a frail, white-haired woman who was kneeling in one of the nearby gardens, obviously planting flower seeds. "Yes, I don't know if I've ever seen more beautiful gardens than these," she answered, returning the smile. "I always thought no one could top my mother's gardens, but even she'd be amazed. Mrs. Sikkink recommended that I come out and see your backyard, but I really wasn't expecting anything so grand."

"Oh, it's a bit dull yet, really," the lady replied, slowly standing up and wiping the black dirt from her hands. "The tulips add a wonderful splash of color and drive away the dull winter browns, but if it's grand you're looking for, you must come back in two months when the entire garden explodes with every color you've ever imagined. The fragrances are nearly intoxicating."

"I'd love to see it . . . and smell it," Christina replied as the elderly woman walked over to her. "Actually, I'd love to try to paint it. It's been a while since I've done any floras."

"You're an artist?"

"Yes, well, at least I'm trying to become one," answered Christina, resting her hands down on the picket fence and staring intently at the woman's face. "I've been a student of the painter Carl Langstan for two years now. Have you heard of him?"

"Certainly," the woman said with a nod. "My husband and I met him before he became famous. We bought two large landscapes he painted nearly thirty years ago. I'll bet you'd enjoy seeing them. His painting style has changed so much since then. I think he's the finest illustrator here in Chicago, and I've heard he only takes on a handful of the most promising young artists. You must be very good. Are you a relative of the Sikkinks?"

"No, we're not related," Christina answered, still studying the woman's face. "Actually, Mrs. Sikkink has commissioned me to paint her portrait, and I'm waiting for her to return from helping at her church's soup kitchen so I can finish a preliminary sketch. You know . . . you'll have to pardon my prying, but you look so familiar to me . . . and I'm not sure why. Have you ever been to southern Minnesota?"

"Never. My husband and I seldom get out, and we've never traveled much. You must know someone who looks like me."

"Probably so," Christina said thoughtfully as she crossed her arms. "It's just that . . . where was it? Ah, now I remember. It was a photograph . . . probably taken at least thirty years ago. I used to look at it all the time when I was a little girl. It was in an expensive gold locket my mother kept in a jewelry box in her bedroom. You . . . um . . . can't imagine how much you remind me of the young woman in the locket. She was my grandmother . . . at least that's what my mother always told me. I never met her."

"Oh my, that is odd, but people often tell me I look like someone they know." The kindly smile had disappeared from the older woman's face, and she glanced back at the brick mansion. "If you'll excuse me, I'm afraid I need to go inside and tend to some matters."

Somewhat surprised by the woman's abruptness, Christina stood and watched as she walked quickly toward the house. "Excuse me," Christina finally called out as the woman reached the back door. "My name is Christina Ellington. I don't believe I asked you your name."

The woman stopped and turned around slowly, her face drained white. "Grace . . . Adler. It was nice meeting you, Miss Ellington."

Christina stared in absolute disbelief as the white-haired woman disappeared into her house. She mouthed the word "Grandmother," but no sound escaped her lips.

Chapter 4

As he rounded the last corner through the heavy woods, Andrew Regan pressed down on the accelerator of his green 1929 Ford Leatherback and stretched his back muscles for the thousandth time in the past two days. Having driven alone from Michigan, the sight of open farm country through the native Minnesota forest brought a deep sense of relief. He knew that the second farmhouse down the open lane ahead belonged to his aunt and uncle.

Taking his eye off the road for just a second, he suddenly caught his front left tire in a deep rut in the mushy country road that was more mud than gravel. He braced himself and held the wheel tight as it pulled the car toward the opposite side of the road. "Hold 'er, Nellie," he called out as the car's front end shook hard, then slowly emerged from the rut, and the car began to pick up speed. "That's only the millionth stinking rut between Michigan and here," he mumbled to himself.

Emerging from the shadowy woods into the late afternoon sunshine, Andrew carefully maneuvered the car down the center of the narrow road. Countless ruts lined the edges of the road and huge potholes left behind when the frost went out of the ground forced him to slow down again. Compared to the rolling hills he'd just come through, the farmland before him was relatively flat. Fallow fields of rich dark loam, and greening pastures and hayfields bordered by tightly bound barbed-wire fences, lay undisturbed on both sides of the road.

The first farmyard he passed had a large white house with black shutters and a broad front porch surrounded by at least a dozen leafless sugar maples. A huge red barn, machine shed, and several smaller outbuildings were spread out on the immaculate property. Parked next to the chicken coop was a shiny Ford tractor, the unmistakable sign of a truly prosperous and progressive farmer who had survived and overcome the worst of the Depression years. A sizable herd of Holsteins was gathered on the north side of the barn, waiting for the farmer to open the barn doors for the evening milking.

Even before he had passed this farmyard, he could see down the road to the diminutive buildings that belonged to his aunt and uncle. The white farmhouse was a slender, two-story wooden structure that bore no adornments. The barn was perhaps half the size of the one he had just passed, and even from a half mile away it was obvious that many years had gone by since a fresh coat of paint had graced its sides. An exceptionally large chicken coop was tucked in the back of the property amid several tall elm trees, and in the front yard an ancient pair of nearly identical weeping willows swayed gently in the spring breeze.

As he approached the farmyard, Andrew slowed the car and turned into the beginning of a long and muddy driveway. A large German shepherd came running out of the barn, barking ferociously as Andrew drove past an old rusty truck with its hood up sitting outside the machine shed. Pulling his car alongside the house, he cut the engine and pushed the door open, only to have the dog nearly jump into the car.

"Aw, get outta here, Jack!" Andrew ordered, but then he relented and gently rubbed the dog's face and scratched his ear. "Now, back up and let me out," he finally said, shoving the tan-and-black dog out of his way as he emerged from the car and gave a big stretch.

"That car looks like it's been through a war," his aunt called out, standing behind the screen door of the small enclosed porch attached to the side of the house. "Looks like you made it safe and sound ... and you hauled all the mud in the state of Michigan with you. That the car your father helped you fix up?"

Andrew was well aware that his old car had caked-on mud and grime from bumper to bumper. He had had to stop several times just to wash the windows so he could see. "Yes, ma'am," he said, smiling as proudly as one could at such a dirty mess. "We rebuilt just about everything under the body of that car. She's in fine shape, although she needs a good cleaning. So how are you, Aunt Lizzy?"

"Same as always, but five months older than when you were here to preach last Thanksgiving," Elizabeth Regan replied, pushing open the screen door. "Bring your belongings on in. Harry and I fixed you up a room upstairs. It's the room your father used to share with his brother William when they were boys."

The first sight of his tall and extremely skinny aunt always caught Andrew a bit off guard. "Lean Bean Lizzy," as his father had often called her, was what he considered the classic old maid. Her long salt-and-pepper hair was pulled back tightly in a bun that accentuated the gaunt features of her face. Dark brown eyes and the most pleasant of smiles could not overcome her homeliness. She was wearing a flowery print dress that hung down below her knees, thick white nylons, and black leather shoes with modest heels. "I appreciate the offer of the room," he replied somewhat tentatively, "but I thought you knew I'd be staying at the parsonage. I was hoping you'd ride into Liberty Center with me and show me around the house."

"The place isn't ready for you yet," his aunt stated matter-of-factly. "The preacher's widow hasn't moved out yet, but we got plenty of room here. I think Harry's really looking forward to your spending time with us. Come on in and bring your things."

With a baffled look on his face, Andrew opened his back car door to get out one of his leather suitcases, but then he turned to his aunt and said, "I ... um ... don't mean to sound heartless, but I thought she was going to be moved by the first of the month. Did something go wrong?"

"I'm not going to stand here holding this door open forever. Either you come on in and drink a cup of hot coffee with me, or you can sit out in the car tonight."

Andrew reached into the backseat and pulled out his suitcase, as well as a travel bag that held his razor and toiletries. Slamming the car door shut, he walked up the three wooden steps to the porch and followed his aunt into the house. They went through the doorway into the main downstairs room that served as both dining and living room. The high sheen on the oak flooring and the distinct smell of Johnson & Johnson Wax were strong reminders to Andrew of how notorious his aunt was for a spic-and-span house.

"You may as well take your suitcase to your room while I heat the coffee up," Elizabeth said, heading straight for the kitchen. "Same bedroom as when you were last here."

"Yes, ma'am," Andrew replied, going to the stairway door. "I'll be right down."

The stairway was so steep that Andrew had to duck his six-foot frame in order not to bump his head where the wall came down from above. He climbed the stairs quickly and walked into the first open bedroom at the top. Besides the wooden-framed bed, the sparse room held a large dresser with an attached curved mirror, a white washbasin and pitcher, and a small table and chair. He placed his suitcase on the bed and immediately exited the room.

Down the hallway was a second bedroom that his uncle Harry occupied. The door to the bedroom was open, and Andrew stopped long enough to know that no one was in the room. The metal frame bed was made neatly and Harry's treasured books were stacked in an orderly fashion in the tall oak bookcase in the corner of the room. If Harry had gotten any new books in the past couple of months, Andrew knew they would be the first items his uncle would want to show him.

Descending the stairway, he saw that his aunt was already seated at the table with a small plateful of white sugar cookies. "So, where's Uncle Harry?" Andrew asked as he sat down in the chair across from her.

"Coffee's warmin' up. Have a cookie while we wait," she replied, pushing the cookies close to Andrew. "Harry's out in the fields trappin' gophers. That time of year, you know. Soon as the frost goes out, the pocket gophers get to diggin' somethin' fierce. Harry's always ready for them, though. As long as the man can still walk, you won't find a gopher on our fifty acres."

"He traps them? Why not just shoot them?"

Elizabeth gave a twisted smile and shook her head. "You really are a city boy, aren't you? You don't know the difference between a streaked gopher and pocket gopher?"

"No."

"Have you ever noticed odd-looking mounds of black dirt out in the fields?"

"Sure. I saw some not too far down the road in a hayfield. Six or seven mounds of fresh dirt almost in a line. Some were bigger than others."

"How do you suppose they got there?"

"I guess I didn't think about it. The gophers around our place didn't do anything like that. Neither did the moles."

"Well, at least you're getting closer," Elizabeth said, glancing out a window toward the hayfield. "Pocket gophers stay underground and tunnel deeper than moles, but every so many yards they tunnel up and shove the loose dirt out of their tunnels into the mounds you saw. They love to eat the alfalfa roots, and they can tear a field up in a hurry. The worst part is that if a horse happens to step down and break through the tunnel, it might break its leg. That'll never happen on this farm."

"So, tell me about the parsonage, Aunt Lizzy. Is there a problem?"

"I'll tell you as soon as I check on the coffee," she replied, getting up from her chair and walking toward the kitchen. "Then I'm going to have to get out in the barn and start the chores."

Andrew could hear the rattle of cups and saucers, and in a few minutes his aunt returned with two steaming cups of coffee. "Maybe I can do your chores, if you show me what needs to be done. I don't want to stay here and not pitch in."

"Don't you worry about that," she said, setting the cups on the table and then sitting down. "You'll have plenty to do, getting to know folks here and starting to preach and teach. We do have a couple of calf pens that sorely need a cleaning, though. I reckon it would be good training for you to learn to pitch manure, so you can relate to us country folks better. Don't suppose they taught you that in seminary."

Andrew laughed and took a sip of coffee. "They didn't say much about it, but you're probably right. And I'd like to help you with the chores, if you don't think I'll get in the way. I'd really like to learn how to milk a cow."

"Hmmm," Elizabeth said, squinting her dark brown eyes at him. "You might just be cut out of the right cloth to be a good pastor here."

"You . . . um . . . didn't think so? This started with your letter. Remember?"

"I certainly do, and you showed us last fall what a fine preacher you are. But you realize there's a lot more to pastoring than preaching good sermons. Plus, you got some strikes to overcome. You're a greenhorn, fresh out of seminary. You're city bred, so you don't know what makes a farmer tick. And you're not married, which presents some real problems."

"You think a pastor has to be married to be a good pastor?"

"I think you know full well what I'm talking about," she answered, tapping her finger on the top of the table, "and I'll bet they did talk about this at seminary. Most of the adults in the congregation are married, not old maids and bachelors like me and Harry. You have to admit, it's going to be a bit awkward for you. I've never known a pastor who was single."

"But you voted for me anyway?"

"I did. There are a couple of nice young ladies I'm hoping—"

"Enough on the ladies," Andrew interrupted her. "And don't you go playing matchmaker for me. That's all I need now."

"I think you should give them a chance before you—"

"Don't say another word, and no names. I mean it," Andrew said. "If the Lord wants to work something out here, that's up to Him. He doesn't need your help. Now stop avoiding my first question. What has happened with the pastor's widow?"

"Mrs. Cooper ran into a bit of a problem, but just a temporary one," Elizabeth answered. "She had planned to move in with her oldest daughter, Glenda, who lives in Albert Lea. But Glenda's husband was involved in protests against the American Gas Machine Company and didn't want her mother to come till it was over. Good thing, too. Have you heard what happened?"

"No, seems like there are pickets everywhere."

"Well, this one got ugly. Glenda's husband got arrested in a picket line, then the sheriff and citizens' committee decided to get tough and teargassed the union headquarters. That was a big mistake. Within hours over two thousand unionists swarmed the streets and drove the sheriff and his men back to the jail. They said Albert Lea looked like it was on the verge of a civil war. Fortunately, Governor Benson came down and negotiated a deal before they tore the city apart. It looks like things have settled down and she'll be able to move soon."

"Good."

"She was worried sick about being in your way, but I told her you were in no hurry. Besides, I can see from what you brought that it's gonna work out better for both of you."

"What do you mean?"

"Did you expect that the parsonage came furnished?"

"No. I've got an army cot in the trunk, and some pots and pans," Andrew said, shrugging his shoulders. "I barely could pay for my schooling and fix up this old car, let alone start furnishing a home. I ... um ... figured I'd just try to get along for a while and buy what I need as I can afford it."

"Well, the good Lord is watching out for you," Elizabeth said. "Mrs. Cooper can't take most of her furniture with her and needs to sell it. I talked with her already, figuring you'd be needing most of what she has. It'll make it so easy for her as well as you."

"Just one little problem, Aunt Lizzy. Unless you and Harry have been salting away the dough to lend me, I have no money for Mrs. Cooper."

"Like I said, the Lord's got His eye on you. If you can both agree to a lump price on whatever furniture you'd like, she's willing to take payments as you can afford it. You can't beat that, Andrew."

"You're serious?"

"I thought you realized that I'm always serious, young man. She says she doesn't need the money right away. I suggest you have a chat with her tomorrow."

"Oh man, that would be great," Andrew said. "I really wasn't looking forward to sleeping on the cot or sitting on a—"

The screech of the screen door opening broke in on Andrew's words, and he jumped up and walked to the porch as his uncle entered. A very short man with extraordinarily thick shoulders, Harry Regan glanced up at Andrew in his typical fashion—one eye was nearly squinted shut, his mouth was a funny half smile, and his head with its thick shock of coarse brown hair was nodding. He knelt down and slowly pulled off his muddy boots, using his weak left hand to steady himself against the wall. Then he unbuttoned his coat with his right hand and hung it on a wall hook.

Turning toward Andrew with a limp, Harry gave his traditional little wave of greeting and mumbled something that obviously meant hello. Brown eyes gleaming, despite the squint, he leaned forward and limped quickly to Andrew.

"Uncle Harry!" Andrew cried, hugging the little handicapped man and patting him on the muscular back. "It's so good to see you again. You're looking as fit as a fiddle. I'm surprised Aunt Lizzy hasn't paired you up with someone by now."

Harry shook his head and looked up at Andrew, still squinting and half smiling. Then he poked Andrew lightly on the chest and nodded, then poked him again.

"No, she won't," Andrew retorted, breaking into laughter at the full grin that was spreading across the man's face.

Something of a muffled laugh finally shook out of Harry, more on the inside than the outside, and his shoulders bounced up and down. Even Aunt Lizzy, who was known to frown on levity, broke into laughter at the sight, for it was a rare, rare day when Harry Regan found anything so funny that he could laugh out loud.

Chapter 5

Christina put her silver fork down on the white tablecloth and gazed around the restaurant at the dozens of exquisite cut-glass chandeliers hanging from the high ceiling and countless wall mirrors that reflected the twinkling light. Her fingers ran lightly over the fine silk fabric of her evening gown, and for a moment she wondered if she was dreaming. "That was ... without a doubt ... the most delicious meal I've ever eaten," she said, turning her attention back to Martin Nelson. "And I wouldn't have dreamed that anyone could prepare food to look so beautiful! Thank—"

"Thanking me three times before dessert is your limit," Martin broke in, wiping the corner of his mouth with his linen napkin. He was dressed in a neatly cut dark suit that accentuated his handsome dark features. "Wait till the waiter shows you the dessert cart. You'll think the chef is an artist."

"Oh, I can't possibly eat any more," Christina protested. "I'm sure the lobster was the richest, sweetest meat I've ever tasted. If I eat dessert, I'll never fit into this dress again. Your mother would not be pleased."

"My mother will be pleased just to hear that you wore the gown twice. That's one more time than most of the women in my mother's circle do," Martin replied. "Did I tell you how beautiful you look tonight?"

"That's the third time," said Christina, "but I hate to put limits on compliments." Her deep blue eyes glinted in the light from the candles on their table.

"Here comes the dessert cart," Martin said, nodding in the waiter's direction. "You can't say no, or you'll offend the chef."

"What?"

"I'm telling you the truth. If you don't order a dessert, the chef will be offended."

Their waiter, a distinguished-looking gentleman with graying hair and dressed in black pants and a white jacket, pushed the dessert cart alongside their table and proceeded to show and describe each of the splendidly decorated desserts. With over a dozen selections before them, Christina could not say no to the cherry cheesecake, and Martin ordered a baklava rich with honey and finely crushed walnuts.

"Does this ever bother you, Martin?" Christina asked as the waiter pushed the cart back toward the kitchen.

"Does what bother me?"

"All of this?" she answered, waving her hands and glancing around the restaurant. "All the wealth . . . and luxury . . . and mansions . . . and fancy cars. With so many thousands of people who've lost everything . . . still so few jobs . . . the lines of people waiting for food at the missions, do you ever feel guilty about this?"

Martin shrugged his shoulders. "Not really, but I guess I don't think about it very often. There have always been poor people around—homeless bums, alcoholics, gypsies, crazy people. When I was little I saw them sleeping in the alleys and wandering around downtown. Just because there are more today, why should I feel guilty about it?"

"Last year the government estimated that there were eight million people without jobs. You never talk about it with your parents?"

"About the poor? No, but my father's business employs hundreds of people," Martin replied. "My parents were hurt when the market crashed, and they had to tighten the belt for a while. But my father mostly talks about all the opportunities he has. Last year was fantastic for him. This year, with another crash, he hasn't fared as well. But it's nothing like in '29. I was thirteen that year, and one of my best friends lost his home. Do you remember how bad it got then?"

Christina shook her head and said, "No, not then. It took a few years to really make an impact out in the farm country. But it had been bad for several years before that, so it was more like one setback on top of another. There were a lot of farms that went bust, and my mother wrote me that she just had another student leave school because their family lost their farm."

"My father thinks it's going to end soon."

"Everyone said that last year, if you recall," Christina said, taking a sip of her dark coffee as the waiter brought their desserts. "Thank you very much," she said to him as he set before her the cheesecake covered in a rich cherry sauce. "It's lovely."

"Thank you," said Martin as the small china plate of baklava was set before him.

"You got me sidetracked, but I wasn't finished with my question," Christina said as the waiter left. "Even though a poor family could probably feed itself for a week from what you're spending on this meal, it doesn't bother you?"

"No. They'd be just as poor the following week. Besides, you don't look too guilty yourself."

"Just because I'm thoroughly enjoying this doesn't mean I've figured out how I feel about it," Christina replied. "When you told me you'd watched the South Chicago police shooting and beating the strikers on Memorial Day, I was surprised that it didn't seem to trouble you. Those men who were striking were earning next to nothing, you know."

"I ... um ... didn't enjoy what I saw ... not at all," Martin said uneasily. "The whole thing was a dreadful sight. After the police moved in with their guns and clubs, ten strikers lay dead and scores more were injured. Some of the injured were policemen, by the way, so this was no sit-down strike. But those people had jobs that provided income, despite the conditions and the pay. They should have felt lucky just to have work. It was their own fault."

Christina shook her head. "You don't really believe that."

"I believe ... last week ... the police attack was unwarranted and ruthless," Martin replied, looking down and pushing the thinly layered pastry around his plate with his fork. "But anyone who strikes has to know that he is putting himself in harm's way."

"And if the owners won't negotiate fair wages or working conditions, what do you suggest workers do rather than strike?"

"If they don't like it, they should quit and find another job."

"It's as simple as that?"

"It's a free country. Nobody's forcing them to stay."

"Well, well, well," Christina said, setting her fork down beside her partially eaten cheesecake. "I'm glad we got that cleared up. I've been in so many wealthy people's homes, and I've never dared ask them how they felt about their position in life. What you've said helps me put several things in perspective. Would you mind my asking you another personal question?"

"Ask me, and I'll tell you whether I mind."

"It's none of my business, of course, but I'm curious whether you attend church . . . regularly. Do you mind my asking?"

Martin raised his eyebrows and stared into Christina's eyes. "No, I don't mind. You shouldn't confuse me for an altar boy or a deacon, but I usually make it to church on Sunday. Why do you ask?"

Christina pursed her lips and ran her fingers along her chin. "It's probably just a pet peeve, but I think it helps me understand what makes people tick."

"So, you're religious?"

"No, not in the least. I've not been to church since I moved here."

"So why does it matter to you if I go to church? Do you find it offensive?"

"No," Christina answered, then laughed at the confused look on Martin's face. "My mother is a deeply religious person, and I love her with all my heart. I just . . . find it confusing."

"How so?"

"I see so many apparent contradictions, and I don't know what to make of it."

"Such as?"

Taking a deep breath, Christina replied, "Well, does it seem like a contradiction to you that some church people have no compassion for the poor . . . when Jesus Christ was so obviously consumed with meeting the needs of the poor? I don't know what to make of that, and I've seen so much of it here."

"Our church helps support a mission—"

"I'm sorry. I probably shouldn't have brought this up," Christina interrupted. "But I don't mean a program that a church participates in. I mean how people actually feel about something . . . and what they do about it. I'm wondering why so few wealthy people seem to actively do something to help the poor, even if most of them are church members."

"I'm sure some do."

"Do you know any?"

"No. Not in the way you're talking about."

"And you don't feel there's a contradiction?"

"I ... um ... don't take it that literally, I guess."

Christina nodded and looked away, then she sat back in her high-backed chair and looked around the restaurant at the dwindling dinner crowd. "My mother always told me that I was a little bit too serious for my own good. I tend to believe that everyone else thinks in the same way I do, and I often push people too hard. I'm sorry if I've spoiled your evening."

"No, it's fine. You've challenged me to think in new ways. Who knows, maybe I'll be working in the Salvation Army soup kitchen next week." Martin laughed in his good-humored way and shrugged his shoulders again. "Who knows, right? And, being with someone as lovely as you are—you'd really have to push it to spoil my evening. Just being with you again is a delight."

"You flatter me, Mr.—"

"Martin. You have to stop switching to Mister every time I start getting too close."

"And how close are you proposing to get?" Christina asked, leaning forward again and resting her elbows on the table. "I've enjoyed this evening so much ... to experience a dinner at Rudolph's is beyond my dreams. But what of your Miss Lofton? Surely she's returned from New York."

"She has."

"And you are engaged?"

"Not formally. But plans are being made."

"And still you take me to dinner? Isn't this a bit risky on your part?"

"Yes. If she finds out, I'll have some explaining to do."

"And you'll tell her what?"

"I'll tell her that ... this was my way of thanking you for making my mother so happy."

"Is that what this is?"

"It's whatever you want it to be."

49

Christina laughed and looked around at some of the other guests. "Mr. Nelson," she said, turning her gaze back on him, "with your handsome looks and charm and money, I'm sure you can have just about any young woman you want. If your choice has been Miss Lofton, tell me plainly what your words mean. Do you not love her?"

"Hmmm," Martin sighed, taking a sip of his ice water. "I was hoping that you might just enjoy being with me . . . in these surroundings, and that you might want to continue seeing me from time to time. Miss Lofton, Mary, is very nice and comes from one of Chicago's richest families. She's very pretty, but quite frankly, she bores me to tears."

Shaking her head and rubbing her forehead as though she were massaging a giant headache, Christina smiled and said, "And I was worried I was going to spoil your evening. I hope my stomach can keep that lobster down after what you've said."

"I didn't—"

"No, no, you've said all I need to hear," Christina broke in. "I may be a country girl, but I've heard a line or two in my day. The other day, while I was painting Mrs. Sikkink, she told me about a friend of hers who just found out that her husband has had a mistress for several years. She said that it's not uncommon at all, and that many women she knows quietly put up with it. Is that true?"

"It happens all the time, Christina."

"And that's what you'd like from me?"

"I said it can be whatever you want it to be. If it only means spending time together talking, I'd like that. I could help you get a better apartment and—"

"Thank you again for the dinner," Christina spoke evenly as she stood up. "I'll be on my way now. No, please stay seated, Mr. Nelson," she said as Martin started to stand up. "If you don't want me to make a scene, just let me go now. I'll take a Yellow Cab home . . . with my own money."

"Here, at least let me pay your fare," Martin said, reaching into his pocket and pulling out a ten-dollar bill as the waiter approached, obviously noticing that Christina was leaving.

"For our waiter. You're so generous!" Christina exclaimed, taking the bill from Martin's hand. "This is for you, compliments of Mr. Nelson," she said to the waiter, whose face lit up when she handed him the money. "And good night."

She made a quick exit without looking back and got straight into a cab that was waiting alongside the curb on the street outside the restaurant. Silently gazing out the window as the taxi passed endless rows of buildings, she had all she could do to quiet the anger she felt welling up inside. Martin's offense, though deep and degrading, was not a new experience for Christina. As a teenager, certain young men seemed to think that her illegitimacy meant that she was also a "loose woman," as she had been referred to on occasion. Since coming to Chicago as an aspiring artist and mingling in art circles, she had encountered several men who seemed certain that anyone with an artistic nature was bent on romantic affairs. But Martin had seemed different, and though she felt no romantic attraction to him, she had enjoyed his company.

"Just goes to show that you can't trust any man," she whispered to herself as the Yellow Cab pulled to a stop in front of her old apartment building. "He fooled me once, but never again."

Stepping from the cab and paying the fare with her own hard-earned money, Christina felt the satisfaction of at least a measure of dignity being restored. Glancing up at her apartment windows and seeing the light on, she realized that she might not have much, but at least no one else owned or controlled her.

As she walked to the front door of the apartment building, Christina heard a voice behind her calling her name. Turning around, she saw a tall, elderly man dressed in a chauffeur's uniform stepping out from behind the wheel of a large black limousine and coming toward her. She had been so preoccupied with her own thoughts that she had failed to notice the rare presence of such an expensive vehicle in her neighborhood.

"Miss Ellington, I'm so sorry to inconvenience you at such a late hour," the man called out in a deep voice, approaching her with long strides, "but I was asked to deliver this note. And I was told that if you were not home, I should await your arrival . . . as well as your response to the note. May I?" He held out a white envelope, which she took immediately from his hand.

"Who are you?" Christina asked, looking at the note. "Who sent this?"

"I am the driver as well as the butler of the William Adler family," he replied. "I believe you met Mrs. Adler in her garden on a previous occasion. My orders to deliver the note to you were directed from her."

Christina felt the same sudden weakness sweep over her that she had felt when the woman next door to the Sikkinks had stated her name as Grace Adler. She had still not come to terms with the shock of her chance encounter with her grandmother, whom she had never desired to meet and thus had never sought out.

"Might I persuade you to read the note?" the uniformed man asked. "I do not wish to detain you."

"Um . . . certainly, I guess," Christina mumbled, tearing the wax seal from the envelope and pulling the note out. She opened the note and held it up to the dim streetlight and slowly read the words:

My dearest Christina, long ago I gave up the dream that one day we might meet you and see your mother again. She, and you, have every reason to hate my husband and me for how we treated her . . . how we failed her. I can hardly force myself to write these words. It seems unthinkably wrong of me to even ask you, but since we met, my darkened heart pleads with you to meet with me again. My husband, your grandfather, will be gone on Monday of next week, and we can only meet when he is gone. Would you be willing for our driver to pick you up before noon and join me in our home for a short luncheon? I am not expecting your forgiveness, but there are things that belonged to your mother that I want you to have.

Christina stared blankly at the signature, "Grace Adler," then closed her eyes and rubbed her forehead.

"Perhaps you'd prefer some time to consider the matter," the driver finally broke into her reeling thoughts. "I could stop by tomorrow night and inquire of your decision, Miss Ellington. Or, if you prefer to leave a note on your apartment door, I can simply pick it up without disturbing you."

"I'm sorry . . . I can't respond so quickly," Christina said, looking at the older man. "I need at least all of tomorrow to think about it. I never . . . ever . . . thought this day would come. I'm just so shocked."

"I understand, miss. We were all shocked."

"Did you know my mother?" Christina asked, eyeing the man closely.

"Your mother was three years old, I believe, when I started my service to the Adler household," he answered. Then he looked away from Christina and continued, "I drove her to the train on the night she left, and my heart has never mended." That said, he immediately turned around and walked toward the waiting limousine, his head bent slightly down.

Christina wanted to call out his name to stop, but realized she hadn't learned his name, and when she opened her mouth to ask, the words all stuck in her throat. She watched as the limousine slowly pulled away from the curb and glided quietly down the street . . . soon to disappear into the darkness.

Chapter 6

Wiping the sweat away from his face with the sleeve of his flannel shirt, Andrew stood at the barn door and leaned his pitchfork against the wall, having finished cleaning out the worst and the largest of the two calf pens. A cool breeze cut through the doorway, and he took in a deep draught of its earthy odors. Over two weeks of sunshine and these same nearly constant breezes had dried the soggy soil, allowing the farmers to get into the fields and get much of their spring work done.

He watched as his uncle Harry drove the shiny steel blade of the plow into the edge of his aunt's large garden and then call out for Big Jim, one of the farm's two huge workhorses, to pull. Effortlessly, the chestnut-coated Belgian took up the charge and stepped down the garden lane with the ever-limping Harry holding the plow as straight as an arrow to the watchful eye of his aunt Elizabeth. She had her potato seed cut from some of the remainder of the last fall's potato crop and was anxious to plant, although she and Harry had disagreed on whether the ground was really warm enough yet.

For a man with a clubfoot and a deformed left arm, Harry was a constant source of amazement to Andrew. While it was obvious that nearly every task took him longer to do than the average man, nothing seemed to deter him, and his stamina appeared inexhaustible. And although he had little strength in his left hand and could only use his left arm for pushing and bracing and holding things down, Harry's right arm was incredibly strong. He had challenged Andrew to an arm-wrestling contest, but the match was anything but a contest. Andrew's arm had been snapped down so fast, his shoulder still ached.

Yet even more amazing to Andrew was Harry's rapport with the farm animals. With some coaching from his aunt during the two weeks of his stay at the farm, Andrew had picked up on several of what he had thought were Harry's unintelligible words and phrases. But the animals had no problem understanding Harry's mumbled words, which came as a result of his cleft lip and palate. A gentle and patient master with all the animals, Harry was constantly shadowed by Jack, the big German shepherd, who was now trailing along behind Harry in the garden.

"I think I've pitched enough manure for one day. What do you think, Morgan?" Andrew turned and asked the other heavily muscled Belgian, whose stall was by the barn door where he was standing. The stout horse with a head that seemed too small for her massive body blinked her mirrorlike black eyes in complete disinterest. "You get to lie and rest while Big Jim is working. Wait till next week when old Harry gets you out in the fields. Then we'll see what kind of shape you're in."

Hearing his aunt call his name, Andrew walked out of the barn and headed toward the garden. She was at the wooden picnic table under an elm tree, pouring a couple of glasses of lemonade. The table did not appear to have been painted within the last decade, like most of the farm buildings.

"Harry, come and take a break," Elizabeth called out as Andrew approached, but the short little man simply waved her off and shook his head.

"You'll never need a tractor as long as you have Harry around here," Andrew said as he sat down at the table across from his aunt. "He puts me to shame."

"Go, go, go," she said, shaking her head and handing Andrew one of the tall glasses of lemonade. "He's been like that since he was a baby. When he was first born, he was so weak and sickly, nobody but my mother thought he was going to live, including the doctor. But your grandmother was seldom wrong, and by the time Harry was nine months old, he was shaking the baby crib so hard at night you could barely sleep. In his sleep he'd get up on his knees and his good hand, and he'd rock back and forth, back and forth. I was four years old at the time, and his crib would be banging the walls so hard that my father finally screwed the crib to the floor. Harry hasn't stopped since."

"How old were you when Grandmother died?"

Elizabeth took a drink of her lemonade and gazed up at the tiny green leaves that had just sprouted on the tree. Taking a deep breath, she said, "I was . . . fourteen at the time. Harry was ten; your father had just turned eight. Seems like forever ago, but I can see her working this garden. She'd have the whole thing planted by now."

"Pa says you raised him and Harry, Aunt Lizzy."

"Didn't have much choice, did I?" she said with her pleasant smile. "Fortunately, I was pretty much done with school. Your father was so young, and I always felt bad that he had to grow up so fast. I had to give so much attention to Harry, there wasn't much left for your father. Your grandfather was a good man, but he could be hard on the boys at times. I expect this is where your father got the inner strength to stand up for the unions against General Motors."

"You're probably right. During the strike, he used to say, 'Pop was the toughest boss I ever had . . . next to Lizzy. If I could come to terms with her, I can come to terms with anybody.' "

"What?" she sputtered. "He said that?"

"No, I'm just kidding."

"You brat! Your father was just like you."

"That . . . I consider a compliment," Andrew replied. "So, tell me how you discovered that Harry wasn't . . . um . . ."

"An idiot?" Elizabeth spoke matter-of-factly. "At the time he was born, anyone in his condition was considered an idiot . . . retarded. I still wonder how it could have taken so long for us to believe that Harry was a normal person locked up inside a broken body. If you watched his eyes, you knew he wasn't missing anything. And he tried so hard to respond to us, but we didn't get it.

"Then one day, when I was playing cards with your father, it finally happened. Whenever we played, Harry would come and watch and watch and watch. Harry was sitting next to me that day, and it was my turn to play. Your father had laid down a six of hearts, and Harry suddenly pointed to the seven of hearts in my hand. It was unbelievable at the moment. He knew both the right number and the suit to play. How we all failed to realize what was going on inside his head before then, I don't know."

"So you taught him how to read and write and do arithmetic?"

"Yeah, I did," she said softly, pushing her glass of lemonade to the side, then resting her elbows on top of the table. "It took forever ... but ... I've never regretted it. If you ever meet anyone who loves books more than Harry does, I'd like to meet him. Harry never got very good at writing, which I couldn't figure out why. But at least he got the reading down. We couldn't send him to school, of course. People made you feel that folks like Harry were supposed to be tucked away in a locked room at home, like we were supposed to be ashamed of him. Your father got in a lot of trouble at school over it."

"He apparently didn't like it when anyone called his brother an ... idiot."

"That's an understatement. If someone called Harry that, or something worse, it didn't make no difference who it was, how big or small they were, your father would fight. I never heard of him ever backing down on it. He understood Harry even better than I did. They were great friends who were also brothers. Did your father tell you that he was really responsible for helping Harry with math?"

"No, you're kidding."

"I don't kid, and you know that. Your father would bring his math problems home, and he and Harry would sit at the table and work on them together. Turns out Harry can figure sums in his head faster than most people can do on paper. And he's the best cardplayer I've seen, but then you know that, too."

Andrew laughed and shrugged. "I haven't won a game since I got here. I swear he stacks the deck, but I can't figure out how he's doing it."

"Rest assured, Harry'll never cheat you in cards ... or in life. What you see in Harry is what Harry really is. There's a possibility you'll meet someone who loves books more than Harry, but I have a hard time believing you'll find someone who loves God more than he does. He's the saint on this farm, let me assure you. If I suddenly got possession of his faith, I think the Lord would take me home before I messed it up."

Andrew nodded and took the last sip of his lemonade. "He's just about worn out that Bible of his, that's for sure, and his library is better than what I've gathered. I feel really bad that he doesn't go to church, Aunt Lizzy. Don't you think that—"

"No," she broke in. "It's just too hard on him. Can you imagine what it feels like when he walks down the sidewalk in Liberty Center or Bradford, and people actually cross the street to avoid him? Kids stand and gawk at him like he's a little monster. It's just too hard."

"But the church is—"

"Just as bad any day of the week. Mother used to take Harry to church when he was little, and it wasn't just the other children who made fun of him. Some of the parents acted like he had a disease their child could catch. When Mother died, Harry refused to go to church, even though our father didn't like it."

Andrew looked over at Harry as he finished turning over the dark brown soil of the garden, then directed Big Jim toward the machine shed so he could put the plow away. "That . . . Aunt Lizzy . . . makes me really upset to hear. The church should be—"

"A whole lot different than it is," Elizabeth broke in again, standing up and moving toward the garden. "But it isn't going to get any better by us sitting around here chewing on it like an old bone. How about you grab one of these spades and help me get the soil ready to plant?"

"But I just finished cleaning out the big calf pen. Do you know how deep the manure and straw was?"

"You only got the big one done?" she asked, then smiled, picking up a spade that lay in the grass alongside the garden. "If you want any supper, wrap those fingers of yours around this here spade and help me out. The sun is still shining, city boy."

Andrew jumped up and walked over to where his aunt was already digging in the soft dirt, breaking up clods and smoothing out the surface. "You are just as tough as my father said you were."

"Baloney!" Elizabeth railed, shoving her spade down and breaking up a big dirt clod. "You don't know what tough is. Look at this perfect soil—it's so rich and damp it nearly crumbles at the touch. Five years ago I put this garden in and I didn't get one thing out of it the whole summer. Harry got the crop planted early that spring and the whole works was shriveled to nothing by the Fourth of July. In the fall we actually went out and gathered in the weeds so the cattle would have some bedding during the winter in the barn. Now, that was tough. Tremendous heat and no rain. The dust was so thick you could almost choke. Harry used to lie on the floor in the cellar to cool down. That was the year, the only year, I thought we'd lose everything."

"That was a bad year wherever you went," Andrew replied, taking a spade and starting to help his aunt dig. "I've wondered how you ever survived it, too. From the Crash in '29, hadn't farm prices dropped in half by that summer?"

"At least in half," she replied. "Got so bad back then that a county courthouse in Iowa burned corn for fuel one winter because it was cheaper than coal. I read that a county elevator in South Dakota listed the price of corn at minus three cents. *Minus* three cents a bushel! If you wanted to sell a bushel of corn, you had to bring in three cents. They couldn't afford to even handle it. I don't know if it could get much worse. That's when you heard about farmers committing suicide.

"I'll tell you the secret that got us through. Before our father died— God bless his soul and memory—he switched us over from dairy cattle to that fine herd of beef cattle you see out in the pasture. See 'em?" She pointed out in the pasture to the cattle with the red bodies and white faces that were grazing lazily on the spring grass. "Polled Herefords. Prices on beef have stayed relatively good, so we've done all right. Guess all those auto workers in Michigan have to eat something."

"What made him switch you over, do you think? Did he see it coming?"

"No, he died five years before the Crash. But he told me why. He said that when he was gone, he didn't think it'd be fair to leave Harry with all the Holsteins to milk with his bum arm. Besides, we got a fair amount of untillable land, and those Herefords thrive on it."

"Why'd you call them polled Herefords?"

"They're a separate breed of Herefords that doesn't have horns, which my father also preferred," she answered. "Some man in Iowa crossbred them that way. Too bad we can't do the same thing with people. You know, find a way to get rid of pointy horns and mean attitudes and sinful natures."

"That would be good," Andrew replied with a chuckle, smoothing out the surface of dirt where he had just loosened the soil, "except I'd be out of a job. Which reminds me, you cut off our discussion of the church. I don't want you to think I'm asking you to bad-mouth the church, but . . . you obviously have strong feelings about the church's spiritual health. I'd appreciate knowing your thoughts, and knowing what you feel I'm up against."

"Oh, I guess I don't feel I know enough to say much. I'm not sure I've ever been in a healthy church ... least if it's supposed to be anything like some of the ones you read about in the New Testament," Elizabeth replied, stopping to lean on her shovel and stretch her back muscles. "But it is the reason I felt the Lord might want you to come here."

"What is?"

"I got the impression you weren't the type to just let what's been in place for so many years continue," she said, "if indeed it needs to be shaken out. My feeling is that we've got an old wineskin the Lord wants to make into a new one. That's not going to happen unless somebody is willing to take a stand and tell the truth."

"Sounds like a big challenge for a greenhorn, as you've so lovingly designated me."

"Green is good, I think. We need something new to sweep the old cobwebs out of the church. We got all these dry bones lying around that need life breathed into them, you know? Harry's got me reading some books by R. A. Torrey of the Moody Bible Institute. Are you familiar with him?"

"I've not read his books, although Uncle Harry keeps putting them on my desk as a subtle hint that he thinks I should be reading them," Andrew answered, breaking into a laugh. "But Torrey was well-known for his revivals and his worldwide preaching tours. I think he was a bit radical for me, though."

"Is he still alive?"

"No, I'm sure he died several years ago."

"That's a shame."

"Why's that?"

"We could use him here. Radical is good, Andrew."

Chapter 7

Christina spent most of the long night sitting in her cushioned rocking chair, staring out the window into the star-filled spring sky. By the time her roommate arose and headed off to work, she was ready to give Grace Adler the answer the older woman was hoping to hear, and she was ready to go to bed. Fortunately, while she had intended to go to the studio and work on a landscape she had been painting with Mr. Langstan's supervision, there was no set time that she had to be there.

The actual decision of whether to visit her grandmother was not as difficult to make as she had anticipated, although the emotions surrounding it were like a nightmarish seesaw of agony that seemed beyond her control. Until she had walked away from the Adler backyard, she had never had to deal with her feelings toward the unknown grandparents who had treated her mother so shamefully because of her. Indeed, she had seldom been aware of her feelings toward them. Now she finally had a real person with a real face to despise. But, despite an overwhelming surge of anger and contempt, Christina's encounter with the elderly woman had proven somewhat disarming. It was difficult to hate the friendly white-haired lady whose love for gardening—and her almond-shaped green eyes with long eyelashes—mirrored her mother's.

And while her mother's past had always been shrouded in mystery, suddenly the door of discovery was wide open before her. Just to know that the limousine driver had known her mother since she was a little girl, to know that he knew things about her mother that she might never know unless she talked with him again, and to see his brokenness at the mention of her mother's long-ago departure were all the incentive Christina needed to want to uncover more. As difficult and as painful as this encounter might be, she would not deny herself an opportunity she had never expected to have . . . or even to desire.

During the troubled night, one of Christina's recurring thoughts was that she had few memories of her mother ever talking about her home. Although her mother had said she grew up in a well-to-do family and with the best of private schools, Christina had never imagined her mother living in a stately brick mansion among the elite families of Chicago. It suddenly put into perspective why her mother had always stood out in their rural setting. Her impeccable manners, her love of classical literature and music and the arts, and her refined sense of class and style—all of which she had imparted to Christina—now made perfect sense. Yet her mother was free of the arrogance and snobbishness Christina often saw among the rich families whose homes she visited. To think that her mother had completely left behind this cultured life among the wealthy and influential and never shown anything but contentment and joy as a poor country schoolteacher and single mother seemed unimaginable.

Leaving a note on her apartment door for the Adlers' driver, Christina left her apartment midafternoon, feeling somewhat refreshed by five hours of sleep. She looked forward to staying late at the studio and putting all of her energies into the landscape painting and hoped she could keep her focus on the canvas. After all the hours she'd already worked on the large oil painting, she could not afford mistakes. If she had one wish, it was that her scheduled meeting with her grandmother was not so distant.

✦✦✦✦✦✦✦✦✦✦✦

As his note had stated, the Adlers' driver pulled the shiny black limousine next to the curb in front of Christina's apartment building at precisely 11:30 A.M. on Monday. Christina was waiting anxiously in the front entrance to the apartment, shielded by a thick glass door from an ice-cold rain off of Lake Michigan that made it feel more like winter than spring. The butler immediately came to the door with a large umbrella and escorted her through the pounding rain to the leather-seated warmth of the limousine.

Pulling away from the curb, Christina had all she could do to resist the urgency she felt to engage the driver in conversation about her mother. Having been touched by the man's sensitivity to the matter, she feared that any words spoken might lead to an avalanche of emotions that would leave her unprepared for her meeting with her grandmother. She also felt that if things did not go well with her grandmother, there was still the strong possibility of meeting with the driver at a later time to talk.

The blocks passed in a blur with Christina preoccupied with thoughts of her grandmother Adler. Over and over again she had contrasted the woman she met in the garden with the grandmother in whose house she had been raised and in whose house her mother still lived. Gentle and extremely reserved, Grandma Ellington had welcomed her mother into her small home, even though their only connection was Christina's father—a connection that had brought their family public shame. When Christina's father was killed in battle, shortly after her mother moved into the Ellington house, and when Grandpa Ellington was taken in the terrible flu outbreak of 1918, Grandma Ellington's love and provision had never wavered. Together, through their poverty and need of each other, this grandmother and her mother had survived through the worst of times and beaten the odds. Grandma Ellington's passing, when Christina was twelve, had been the deepest loss of Christina's life, a greater darkness than that of the Great Depression that soon followed and refused to go away.

"What is she like?" Christina blurted out suddenly.

"Excuse me, ma'am?" the driver asked, glancing into the rearview mirror, then looking back to the road.

"I'm sorry," Christina replied, immediately embarrassed by her question. "I haven't even asked your name."

"It's Edgar, ma'am. Edgar Mitchell," he replied. "I'm sorry, but I didn't hear your question."

Christina fidgeted in her seat, unsure of whether to ask again. "I . . . was wondering what Mrs. Adler is like."

"Your grandmother, ma'am?"

"Yes . . . my grandmother."

"She's not the person you think she is, ma'am. Nothing is ever that simple."

Somewhat stunned by the driver's comment, Christina glared into the mirror, feeling offended and yet sensing that there was truth in his words that required consideration. Her immediate reaction was to tell "Edgar" he had no idea what she was thinking, yet she was quite sure that he did. She swallowed the words that were burning on the tip of her tongue and finally said, "You think I hate them, Mr. Mitchell?"

"Edgar, ma'am. Everyone calls me, Edgar," he responded. "Given what I know, it would be difficult for you not to hate them, ma'am."

Christina shook her head, unsure of what the driver really knew, and stared out the window at the transformation that had occurred from the crowded apartment buildings and factories where she lived to the palatial neighborhood of her grandparents. As if thinking out loud as the limousine turned into the dark brick mansion's half-circle entrance, she asked, "Why should I give them a chance, Edgar?"

"To end the darkness, ma'am," he said, gazing into the rearview mirror intently as the limousine came to a stop underneath an extended white portico in the front of the mansion that kept out the rain on such a dreary day. "A pot of gold in a pitch black dungeon doesn't make the dungeon any less dark. Someone must open the door to the light."

As Edgar Mitchell stepped out of the car and walked around the vehicle to open Christina's door, she grasped at his profound words, wishing the limousine would pull back into the street and allow her the time she needed to sort out his meaning. Slowly, her door opened, and she forced herself to take the first step out. Standing next to the driver, she looked into his perfectly serene face and said, "My mother knows nothing of darkness, Mr. Mitchell."

"Edgar, ma'am," he said with a nod. "And your mother ... is an angel reclaimed. I did not mean to imply that the darkness lies within her."

"What am I supposed to—" Christina began, but was interrupted as one of the adjoining heavy wooden doors to the dark mansion creaked open and the slight form of her grandmother emerged, looking more frail than Christina recalled from their meeting in the garden.

"Thank you for coming, Christina," the white-haired woman said, her voice edged with emotion and sounding nothing like what one would expect from the matron of such a regal manor. "Please, come in."

Christina glanced at Edgar, who had already turned away to attend to the limousine. She yearned that he might come along as her spokesman, but it was obvious she was on her own. Approaching the woman, she found her own false words of greeting stuck in her throat as her personal sea of spite and anger and fear suddenly surged to the surface and threatened to spill out. She could only nod to her grandmother as she passed through the door, feeling almost faint with dizziness for a moment and wishing desperately that she had never agreed to any such meeting.

A uniformed maid stood attentively in the marble-floored entryway and greeted Christina, then took her coat and scurried off to a separate coatroom to hang it up, but Christina hardly noticed the woman. She stepped from the entryway into a high-ceilinged room whose long marble staircase had tall pillars at the bottom. To her left, through an arched doorway with Greek-style columns and elaborate scrollwork, was a sprawling sitting room that had tall windows adorned in golden curtains, a huge wall mirror rimmed with fine gold metalwork, high-back furniture with golden fabric, and a Persian rug that nearly covered the marble floor from wall to wall. An exquisite glass chandelier hung from the arched ceiling, but most impressive were the three enormous windows at the far end of the room that were framed in the same Greek columns and scrollwork as the doorway, the center window reaching from floor to ceiling.

However, it was not the lovely re-creation of an English country house that held Christina's attention, for she had painted portraits in several mansions that far excelled this one in size and extravagance. It was the shock of thinking that her mother had grown up in this very house, had called this home, only to be forced to leave it, that gripped her heart. She covered her mouth with her hand and closed her eyes, imagining her mother's lovely voice filling what now felt like a cold, lifeless mausoleum, almost hearing her mother's footsteps on the stairway in front of her. Suddenly the years of pent-up anger and shame came thundering in upon her with a sense of panic.

"I'm sorry!" she finally gasped, spinning around and stepping toward the door. "I can't do this!"

"Please stay!" the elderly woman pleaded, grabbing Christina's arm. "Please try! For Rebecca's sake!"

Christina easily shook herself free from the feeble grasp and gazed into the woman's green eyes, the mirror of her mother's. "Who are you?" she screamed, her jaw muscles clenching. "What kind of a monster are you, anyway? You dare to call yourself a mother, or to call the man you married my grandfather? I was the reason you drove her away. Me! I was the reason. Look at me! Do you know how much I hate you? I *hate* you! I hoped I would never *ever* see you as long as I lived, and now that I have, I never want to see you again."

Wheeling around, Christina marched out the front door and slammed it behind her, the sound thundering down the marble corridors inside. A cold breeze slapped her in the face and she stopped, realizing she had left her coat inside and that it was raining too hard to walk back to her apartment. Then she started to tremble, not from the cold, but from all of the repressed emotions she had finally released. She leaned against the huge white door, shaking and wanting to cry or scream or run, but it was then that she felt the stirrings of her own heart. Though Christina had expected to feel some vindication from condemning the woman with the pleasant smile, instead she felt horrible . . . even evil. She had wondered at Edgar Mitchell's reference to darkness, and now she fully comprehended his meaning. She was inside the circle of darkness, just as surely as were the couple who had given birth to her mother.

From inside the entryway came the distinct sound of a woman's sobs—at first soft, so that Christina barely heard them above the spring wind and rain, but the sobs soon swelled into loud, agonizing cries. Edgar's words, "She's not the person you think she is," accompanied the gut-wrenching sobs, tearing at Christina's raw emotions, anger and contempt flaring up inside of her again, seemingly fueled by the pitiful lament. "Suffer, you old witch," she hissed, clenching her hands. "I hope you suffer till your last breath."

Her bitter words, so fierce and cold-blooded, escaped her lips and instantly shocked Christina. The thought of how her mother would have reacted in this same situation, and how her mother would feel if she had witnessed what Christina had just said and done, brought a numbing shame. Rebecca Ellington was only full of tender mercy and compassion, even toward those who treated her badly. Rebecca Ellington would never leave her broken mother alone in her tears, even if her mother had left her to struggle for twenty years.

How could I ever call my mother's mother a witch? Christina relented, wishing to recover the ill-spoken words and banish them forever. The grief echoing through the stony mansion did not sound like the cries of a witch, but sounded more like the cries of someone who had already suffered long and acutely. On and on it went, giving Christina the distinct impression that the woman inside, her grandmother, would prefer to be dead rather than live on with the consequences of what she and her husband had done.

Slowly, Christina pulled the heavy wooden door open and saw the white-haired woman collapsed in a heap on the cold gray marble floor with no one to comfort her, with no one who cared. From somewhere deep inside of her came the words, *"Open the dungeon door, Christina. Don't you see what the darkness has done?"*

"Yes, I see," Christina whispered to her heart, and her words were true. Whatever terrible things had happened in the past, the affluent lady lying on the floor was still her grandmother. This was a woman dearly loved and deeply missed by her mother, and she was a woman who had been robbed of her daughter and her granddaughter. This woman deserved a chance.

Something within Christina's heart started to melt, and a cooling trickle of pity began to seep into the hot sea of her anger and contempt. Slipping through the doorway, she stepped toward the suffering soul, and with each step came another surge of pity. A pool of tears glimmered on the marble floor beneath the woman, who seemed to not even be aware of Christina's presence. "Oh my," Christina gasped, catching her breath at the poignant sight.

Kneeling down beside the grieving woman, Christina's trembling hand reached out and touched her shoulder, which for the moment stilled the sobbing. In the silence, Christina found the words she thought she could never say. *"Grandmother—"* she choked out the words, "please forgive me."

Chapter 8

Christina wrapped her arms around her grandmother and held her for the longest time. The older woman remained in the same collapsed heap on the floor and made no attempt to get up. While the intensity of her tears diminished, her sobs continued to rise and fall in waves. And with each round of tears, Christina felt the pity in her heart changing to compassion for the poor, broken soul in her arms.

"Grandmother," she whispered a second time, tears beginning to splash down her own cheeks, "please forgive me for my horrible words. I'm so sorry. . . ."

Grace Adler tried to clear her throat, then spoke in a nearly inaudible whisper, "Your words . . . are true . . . truer than you know. . . . Go now. It was wrong of me to ask you to come."

"No, please, let me try again," Christina said soothingly, all of the contempt having drained out of her voice. "I got overwhelmed . . . thinking of my mother in this house. What I said . . . was shameful. I wanted to hurt you back. I'm so sorry. Please let me stay."

"Words never hurt a dead person, Christina, and I died long ago," her grandmother said in a muffled voice. "I don't deserve your sympathy. Just leave me."

"No, I won't go," Christina persisted, taking her grandmother's hand. "It would break my mother's heart if I left you like this. We both have to try . . . if only for her sake. Please. . . ."

Grace Adler remained in her crumpled repose for a while, taking shallow breaths, then she seemingly willed herself to move. She slowly pushed herself to a sitting position, her white hair tousled and wet with tears. She glanced at Christina through bloodshot eyes, still brimming with tears, then wiped her wet face with a white silk handkerchief that she pulled from her dress pocket. "Some welcome to Grandma's house, eh?" she whispered, closing her eyes and taking in a deep breath. "I'm sorry you had to see me like this. I didn't think . . . after all these years, that I would still react like this. When I hear your voice, I hear Rebecca. . . . I shouldn't put you through this."

"How about we try to start over again . . . maybe put this behind us," Christina replied, taking a deep breath as well and wiping the tears from her own eyes. "I know this is probably just as hard for you as it is for me, but I really want to find out what happened."

"You don't know?"

"My mother never wanted to talk about it. She only said that she hurt you terribly . . . as a result of her pregnancy, and that her father had disowned her. She always said it was better for me to know as little about her past as possible. I knew your names, but little else."

"You didn't know who I was when you came to the backyard?"

"No."

"She never told you where she lived? About our wealth?"

"No, just that her family was well-to-do," answered Christina, leaning back on her hands. "Seeing all of this explains a lot about her . . . things I guess I took for granted. She's an extraordinary woman . . . everyone loves her. You taught her well."

Grace Adler shrugged her shoulders and gave the slightest hint of a chuckle. "She had the best teachers money could buy here in Chicago, but . . . I take no credit for the person she's become. She never told you what we did? She's not bitter?"

"No. I've seen her upset with people before, but I never saw her bitter. And people gave her plenty of reasons to be bitter."

"I can't understand her not hating us. Can you explain that?"

"No, although she'd say it was because of her faith."

"She wrote me about that."

"She did? Did you write back?"

"No. At the time . . . I didn't believe her. And I couldn't write her back. Do you believe as your mother does?"

Christina shook her head. "No, but not because of my mother. If others were like her, I think I could believe."

"Would you help me up? My old bones are about ready to crack into pieces," Grace said, trying to get her feet straightened out in front of her. "Would you like some lunch?"

Standing up and taking her grandmother's hand, Christina pulled and helped her to stand. "No, maybe later. My stomach is still in knots. I'd rather talk, if you're up to it."

"Certainly. How about I let you look around your mother's room while I make myself a little more presentable?" her grandmother asked, stepping toward the marble staircase. "Would you like that?"

"Her room? You kept her room?" Christina asked, following the older woman.

"Yes," Grace said, the word filled with emotion as she climbed the steps. "It's exactly as she left it. I could never bring myself to get rid of anything that was hers. I keep hoping . . . she'll come home soon. How foolish can that be, Christina?"

Christina did not respond but silently followed her grandmother to the landing at the top of the stairway and then down the hallway.

"I thought . . . perhaps you might want to take some of her things," Grace said as they passed a bedroom door. "She left nearly everything behind. I hoped, when I asked you to come, that there were things you'd want."

"That's why you invited me?"

"Yes," her grandmother replied, stopping at a second bedroom door and pushing it open, a gray light spilling out into the dark hallway. "I'm going to my bedroom to see if I can put myself back into some sense of order. You look around and see if there's anything in this room that you'd like. If it belonged to your mother, it's yours for the taking."

"I couldn't—"

"Just look around and think about it," Grace broke in, stepping aside from the door. "There's no hurry. If you need me, I'll be in the bedroom toward the stairway."

Her grandmother looked away and walked back down the hallway as Christina stood frozen at her mother's doorway. In the dim light filtering through the bedroom's large windows, she could see a beautiful walnut hand-carved canopy bed, the likes of which she had never seen before. On each side of the bed were huge matching wardrobes. In the corner of the room was an antique writing desk and a plush velvet settee surrounded by shelves of leather-bound books.

At first, it was too much to take in, but slowly the reality that this room had been her mother's began to sink in. Stepping across the threshold and onto the room's lush Persian rug, she noticed a dark walnut vanity with a large oval mirror next to a dresser with an ornately carved Bavarian clock on it. She walked over to the first wardrobe, then pulled open one of the tall doors. Hanging inside were the most elegant clothes she could have imagined—what had obviously been Chicago's finest evening gowns, dresses, blouses, and skirts. Running her fingers through them, feeling the expensive fabrics, and noting the fine tailoring, she smiled as she pictured her mother decked out in such apparel.

Walking back across the room to the vanity, she couldn't help noticing a jewelry box on it. A gold key had been left on its solid teak inlaid top, which seemed odd to her. Sitting down on the vanity's matching chair, Christina took the key and held it in her hand, noticing how worn it was. She wondered how many times her mother must have sat at this very vanity and how precious the contents of the jewelry box must have been to her. Slipping the key into the keyhole, she turned the lock and slowly opened the lid. Inside were dozens of gold and silver brooches and necklaces and rings, some plain and others exquisite.

A gold dove-shaped pendant caught her attention, and she carefully lifted it from the box. Holding it up to the light, she turned it around and noticed the inscription on the back: "To My Wonderful Daughter, Dad." The words sent a chill down her spine, and she glanced back at the bedroom door before she quickly deposited the pendant back in the safe confines of the jewelry box. She felt a fresh wave of anger rising up inside, but it was not nearly as intense as before. Closing the teak inlaid top, she locked the box and placed the key where she had found it.

"There's a special hat that I'd like you to try on," her grandmother's voice suddenly sounded from the bedroom doorway, causing Christina to jump in her chair. "I'm sorry, I didn't mean to scare you."

"You just caught me off guard. What did you say about a hat?"

Grace Adler walked into the room and went to a long shelf that held several hatboxes. Pulling down one of the boxes and opening the round lid, she said, "Your mother loved this hat. I don't understand why she left it here. It's a bit out of style, I suppose, but I think you'll like it." From the box she carefully lifted a blue hat with black feathers on the sides and stepped toward Christina. "It was her favorite. Try it on, please."

"My mother wore this?" Christina asked, staring at the lovely hat as her grandmother placed it in her hands. She held it gingerly, running her fingers along the soft velvet and black-and-red ribbon. Then she raised it up and slowly set it down on her head, all the time staring into the mirror. "I love it," she whispered, noting how on the sides and back of the hat the bottom curled out and up, showing a black underside that matched the ribbon and feathers.

"Your blue eyes are a perfect match for the hat," her grandmother said, crossing her arms. "I didn't think anyone could look lovelier than Rebecca did in that hat. I was wrong."

Christina glanced up and could see the tears spreading down her grandmother's face again. "I'm sorry, I shouldn't have—"

"She was wearing that hat . . . the day she met your father . . . and on the day he left," the older woman continued, despite the tears. "He loved her in that hat. Whyever would she leave it here, Christina?"

Her grandmother's words suddenly sounded like thunder that threatened to take her breath away. Christina quickly slipped the precious hat from her head and set it on the vanity, then stood up and walked over to the window. The mention of her father—by her grandmother—was followed by an eruption of clashing emotions. Rather than react wrongly again, she determined to keep her mouth closed and let the swirling currents die down. She gazed blankly out the window at the cold spring shower and tried in vain to identify what she was really feeling.

Christina could sense her grandmother pass behind her as she went to sit down on the settee. She thought about why her mother had left the hat behind, and she finally said, "Perhaps she left the hat because she knew it would recall too many memories . . . too much loss. Whenever she spoke of my father, the tone of her voice always changed . . . it got real soft and tender. You had to listen very close or you couldn't understand the words."

"She loved your father from the day they met," her grandmother said, staring at Christina. "He was a bright young man—filled with lots of ideas. He'd just gotten a job in my husband's office, and apparently no one warned him that he was out of line talking with the boss's daughter. By the time William discovered they were in love, it was too late. Your father couldn't be bribed to stop, and firing him didn't change anything either."

"He wasn't good enough for my mother?"

Grace Adler bit her lip and shook her head. "Rebecca is our only child. He would never consider anything less than the best of families for her."

"*Best* meaning *richest*?"

"Yes. He did everything he could to chase your father away, but it took a war in Europe to separate them."

"And then you discovered she was pregnant . . . with me?"

"She didn't tell us until your father was in France," her grandmother stated. "By then, she was already showing. How she disguised it, or how we didn't notice it, I can't imagine."

"How—?" Christina began to say, turning to look at her grandmother, but the swirling emotions choked her throat and cut off her words.

The older woman ran her fingers across her forehead and closed her eyes, then she said, "The whole thing turned into a nightmare. I was caught somewhere in between my daughter's remorse and my husband's anger. He . . . couldn't forgive her. He felt that if people found out about it, she'd bring shame upon herself and upon us, so he threatened to disown her unless she went somewhere, secretly had the baby, and gave it away. He never thought she'd leave us instead."

"And you let it happen?"

"Your mother left without asking me, Christina," her grandmother said. "But did I fail her? Yes, terribly. I could not persuade your grandfather to forgive her or to relent of his threats. The more I tried, the worse it got. Finally, he became unbearable toward her. Your mother had no choice but to leave. She loved your father too much to give you up. You were a part of him . . . she could never have parted with you."

"How could you . . . put up with it?"

"Why didn't I leave with her, you mean?"

"Or refuse to let it happen."

Her grandmother shook her head and said, "I don't expect you to understand my answer, but even though I believe what your grandfather did to your mother was terrible, I still loved him. And I had vowed ... before God ... to be faithful to him, submit to him, obey him, honor him ... in good times and in bad ... until death parts us. I'm still breathing, Christina."

"No, that's not right," Christina protested, although she had treasured the words of the wedding vows since she went to her first wedding as a little girl. "There's something wrong with this. By going along with it, you've joined yourself to his wrongs."

"To his sins, you mean," her grandmother replied. "Yes. We're one flesh. I hate what he did, but I'm joined to him. I promised to submit to him, which the Bible clearly commands I must do. But I know it sounds wrong. I really mean it when I say I don't expect you to understand it. I've never understood it myself. But I had to do what was right."

"Is that why you said you *couldn't* write to my mother when she wrote you years ago? Did he forbid you to write to her?"

"Yes."

"To ever see her again?"

"Yes."

"Are you disobeying him today ... by meeting with me?"

"No. He's never specifically forbidden this."

"But if he knew...?"

Grace Adler rubbed her eyes and stood up, then walked to the other tall window and stared out. "If he knew, he would be very angry. As far as I know, he has no idea that you're here in Chicago."

"So help me understand. You say you're not disobeying because our meeting has not been outlawed yet. Right?"

"Correct."

"But aren't you dishonoring him, aren't you *not* submitting to him, if you do something you know he would condemn?"

"I'd rather not talk about it."

"I'm sure you wouldn't. My mother says it's always easier to run from the truth than face it. Maybe you've just been running from the truth all these years."

Her grandmother looked at Christina as if stunned by these words.

She nodded and replied, "I don't think I have any idea what the truth is anymore. I don't know—"

A sudden knock on the bedroom door interrupted Mrs. Adler, then the maid who had taken Christina's coat earlier stepped into the doorway. "Excuse me, Mrs. Adler. You asked me to interrupt you . . . no matter what."

"He called?" the older woman asked, visibly shaken.

"Yes, ma'am. His business concluded early. He's on his way home."

Glancing out the window in a panic, Grace spoke firmly to the maid. "Call Edgar, and tell him he must drive Miss Ellington home immediately."

"Yes, ma'am," the maid replied, turning quickly to go.

"Wait! Is our lunch still on the table?"

"Yes, of course. We held it thinking—"

"Clear the table!" Grace ordered. "He must not find out Christina was here. Do you understand?"

"Yes, ma'am. Perfectly. The table will be cleared as soon as I've notified Edgar."

"Good. Now go."

As the maid departed, Christina studied her grandmother's cowed expression. "This can't be right, Grandmother. And you know it."

"I don't know that, Christina. But I do know you have to leave, or this will be our last meeting. Do you want this to end now?"

"No, but it's wrong . . . it's wrong."

"Please go," her grandmother urged, then stepped toward Christina.

"I'm taking the blue hat," Christina stated as she walked toward the vanity.

"What?"

"You said I could take whatever I wanted that belonged to my mother. I only want the blue hat," Christina said as she reached out and took it in her hand. "I'll treasure it for the rest of my life. May I take the box as well?"

"Yes, of course," her grandmother agreed, picking up the box and handing it to Christina. "Take the jewelry too. Your mother loved her jewelry. I don't know why—"

"No, thanks. I think I know why she left it here, and I don't care for it either. Just the blue hat," Christina said as she closed the box with a smile. "Oh, and a hug, too. Did my mother learn to love hugs from you?"

Grace Adler's troubled expression changed to a momentary large grin. She nodded and said, "Oh yes. It's been years...." Then she reached out and embraced Christina, holding her as though it might be the last chance she'd get.

Chapter 9

Andrew shoved the rotary lawn mower into the last thick section of grass in front of the parsonage until its blades jammed, then backed up and hit it again. The mower's dull blades made it nearly impossible to get through the wiry thatch. With one final push he clipped the remaining green stubble and leaned the mower against the white wooden slat wall of the house, then wiped the sweat from his face.

"You look like you could use a cold drink," Rebecca Ellington called out behind Andrew as she walked across her lawn onto the parsonage lawn with two tall glasses of lemonade. A warm June breeze tugged at her blue dress and long wavy brown hair. "It got hot in a hurry, didn't it? A few weeks ago we were wearing jackets." She set the taller of the two glasses down on the arm of one of the heavy redwood chairs that Andrew had moved into the front yard, then sat down in the other chair and took a sip of her lemonade.

"And I picked the hottest day so far to mow," Andrew lamented, picking up the glass and taking a big drink, then sitting down across from Rebecca. "Thanks for the drink. It really hits the spot. I still have to do the backyard. I'm thinking about buying a billy goat and letting him range around back there. What do you think?"

"I don't mind, as long as you keep him out of my gardens," Rebecca answered with a twinkle in her green eyes. "Otherwise, I hope you like goat meat."

Andrew laughed and took another drink. "I hate goat meat, but don't tell anyone. Some of the church members keep bringing me portions when they butcher. Why do they do that?"

"Same reason that other folks bring you eggs and strawberries and beef. They don't have any money to give, but they can give you what they're raising on the farm. The only way most of them have kept their farms is to live off the produce."

"Don't I know," Andrew replied. "With all the chickens in her hen-house, my aunt Lizzy turned every meal into an egg feast. It's nice to have a little variety, now that I'm settled here."

"Variety!" Rebecca exclaimed, sitting back in her chair and laughing heartily. "Since you moved in here, how many supper meals have you fixed? That's not counting your five-course peanut-butter-on-anything meal. If your sweet aunt Lizzy didn't invite you out nearly every evening, you would turn into a straw. What are you fixing tonight?"

"Mmm, I guess I haven't had time to think about it," said Andrew, shrugging his shoulders.

"I've got some fresh garden peas, last fall's potatoes, and a small ham," Rebecca offered. "I won't twist your arm, but . . ."

"I really shouldn't. I owe you about twenty meals already. Maybe I could—"

"Six o'clock, same as always," Rebecca stated. "I'll make you a deal. You keep on dishing up those fine sermons, and I'll keep on dishing you up an occasional meal . . . at least until you figure out the difference between a frying pan and a cooking pot."

Andrew gave a crooked smile and nodded, then sat back into his chair. "I'll take you up on your offer, but I don't know that it's proper to call them 'fine' sermons. Maybe they will be someday."

"You don't listen very well, Andrew. I'm afraid you'd have had a hard time in my classroom. I expect my students to hear what I say to them and to act on it."

"I know . . . for the tenth time, you're telling me to be as patient as you are with your flowers. And Aunt Lizzy reminds me that the farmer must patiently wait for the seed to yield its crop. Lesson learned."

"Lesson assented to; lesson not learned."

"You're right. I wouldn't do well in your classroom."

Rebecca laughed and said, "I wish you'd believe me when I say that your sermons are excellent. Reverend Cooper was a kind, compassionate pastor, but his preaching was so disjointed and disorganized. You have a wonderful gift of teaching with your preaching. I know . . . because I have a teacher's heart, and I can spot it in a second when someone else has it. It's in you, Andrew. Just let it keep doing its work."

"You're very kind . . . too kind, perhaps. . . . I just don't understand why there's so little response from the congregation. I study and pray and—"

"It'll come, believe me. Pastor Cooper was here for seventeen years. It's going to take a while for people to open up the way you'd like. And, Aunt Lizzy might be right when she says the church has gotten lukewarm, but she's been saying that for years."

Andrew laughed, realizing that Rebecca knew more about his aunt . . . and the church . . . than he did. "All right, I'll be patient for another five minutes. So what's the deal with the dress? Not exactly your work-in-the-garden duds."

"Oh, I drove down to Bradford and had lunch with my best friend, Annie Anderson. Have you met her?"

"No, but I know her husband, of course," Andrew said. "I met Doc Anderson the night that Mr. McCormick passed away. Actually, he helped me to comfort the wife. What an outstanding physician he is. He sort of reminds me of my father."

"Do you have plans for lunch on Sunday?"

"No, not yet, anyway."

"That's great!" Rebecca exclaimed, standing up and gathering the empty lemonade glasses. "Annie and Stuart are coming to church first, then to my house for lunch. It's time that you met Annie as well. She has been . . . God's gift to me, and I don't mean anything less than that. She stepped into my life when I thought every reason to live had died. And she's done the same for dozens of others, but . . . she's my best friend!"

"I'd love to meet her," Andrew said as he stood up.

"By the way," Rebecca said, turning around, "before Stuart decided to go into medicine, he had intended to pursue the ministry. You may find his story interesting."

"I'm sure I will. He obviously made the right decision."

◆◆◆◆◆◆◆◆◆◆◆

"It's hard to compare this backyard to the parsonage's," Andrew said to Stuart Anderson as the two men walked through Rebecca Ellington's vast array of colorful gardens. Both were dressed in black suits with white shirts and black ties, and they were waiting for Annie and Rebecca to finish the lunch preparations. "It's like we're in another world here. Rebecca tells me you've known her for several years."

"Ever since she moved here," Stuart replied, pushing back his bifocals to inspect a variety of flowers that he wasn't familiar with. His black eyes flashed as the noonday sun suddenly emerged from behind a large puffy cloud. "She's a wonder, isn't she? You've never met anyone like her, have you?"

"You do know her well," Andrew said, noting how the sunlight contrasted the gray from the black in Stuart's hair. "She's easily the most encouraging person I've ever met. Since I started here, she's been a constant source of inspiration. At first, I thought she was faking it, always seeing the positive side of things. It didn't take long, though, before she dispelled that idea. Has she always been like this?"

"No," said Stuart, sitting down on a wooden lawn chair under the one large dark maple tree in the backyard. "There's something you should probably know about Rebecca. You're likely to hear it soon enough anyway, and it's best you get the story straight."

Andrew sat in a lawn chair next to Doc Anderson and waited for him to go on, wondering what it was the doctor felt he needed to know.

"When Rebecca came to live with the Ellingtons, she was four months pregnant and had just been disowned by her parents in Chicago for the illegitimate pregnancy. Soon after that she was grieving the loss of the child's father, whom she loved deeply."

"They didn't marry?"

"No. James Ellington was inducted into the army at the beginning of the U.S. involvement in the war in 1917, and Rebecca's parents refused to let them marry before he left. He was in France when he discovered that Rebecca was with child. He pledged to marry her upon his return, but he was shot and killed soon after he wrote the letter. Rebecca changed her name from Adler to Ellington, but her grief and the stigma of illegitimacy stuck."

"That explains a few comments I've already heard about Rebecca," Andrew said.

"You'll hear more, although it's often subtle," Stuart continued. "Some people are so incredibly petty, and others get downright mean. There were people in this community who treated her like dirt, especially after the baby was born. Others just wouldn't talk to her. As if she needed more shame put on her."

"Her parents made her leave home?"

"The options were to leave or to give the baby away. The Ellingtons, not knowing that, had already invited Rebecca to come live with them. They were a wonderful Christian couple, who felt responsible to help her in any way they could, despite their own grief over the loss of James. She came, thinking it would only be temporary, until—"

"Stuart, what are you two talking about without me!" Annie Anderson broke in, her brown eyes giving him a mock tease as she stepped around the garden behind them and sat down in a lawn chair next to her husband. Her pale blond hair looked golden in the muted sunlight. "Rebecca kicked me out of the kitchen . . . as usual."

"I was just telling Andrew about Rebecca's difficult past," Stuart continued. "He wondered if she had always been such a source of encouragement."

"Hardly," Annie said, her face suddenly shadowed with troubled memories. "Go ahead with the story, Stuart."

Stuart looked back at Andrew and said, "As if things weren't bad enough, the following year Mr. Ellington contracted the horrible Spanish influenza and died within a matter of days. We lost a lot of people in this community in 1918. Rebecca had come to love John Ellington very much. For those first six months after the baby came, he'd been the world's best grandfather. Suddenly, there was a widow and an unmarried mother in this house, a tiny baby, no income, and almost no savings. That was about as low as things could get."

"And you were her doctor, I take it?" Andrew asked.

"I'm the only one around here," Stuart replied with a smile. "Folks don't have much choice. Yes, I'd delivered the baby . . . with Annie's help."

"You're a nurse, Mrs. Anderson?"

"Please, call me Annie, and I'll call you Andrew, Reverend," she said. "And, no, I'm a schoolteacher in Bradford. But little Christina came breech, and Stuart needed an extra hand. I came out again when Mr. Ellington was dying. It was . . . so dreadful, that flu, and you were helpless to stop it. Mrs. Ellington seemed to cope with her grief, but Rebecca slid into a depression so deep and grim that I thought she wouldn't be capable of taking care of the baby."

"She mentioned there was a time when you helped turn her life around," Andrew said.

Annie's bright smile drove away the brooding darkness. "I did precious little, other than to stay by her side for a few days. And I told her my story . . . of how God sent Stuart to rescue me when I was trapped beneath the wreckage of the old bridge that spans the Flatwillow Creek in Bradford in 1901 . . . and of how Stuart and his wonderful mother introduced me to the Scriptures and helped me to discover faith. I told her how God stepped into my own fragmented family and changed my parents' lives. My father was so cruel, especially when he got to drinking, that he nearly drove us away, but even his life was changed by God's grace. And I told her about how close I came to marrying the wrong man, a debonair deceiver, and how good the Lord has been to Stuart and me. She kept listening, and I kept talking."

"And she came to faith."

"She did"—Annie's smile was infectious—"though it wasn't without a battle, and it wasn't like there were no struggles that followed. Nothing about her painful circumstances changed, except her coming to believe that God loved her and that He would help her through it. Given her life at the time, I've often wondered if I could have believed the same."

"So how did the two women survive?"

"Together is how," Stuart stated. "There's no other way to describe it. The local schoolteacher here in Liberty Center had taken a job offer in Minneapolis, leaving the school without a teacher in the fall session, and Annie recommended that Rebecca be offered the position. Some school-board members were up in arms about hiring an unmarried mother, of course—things like that just aren't done even now—but there was no one around with Rebecca's educational background, especially with her training in music and art. So cooler heads prevailed and Rebecca got the job. A couple of board members resigned over the decision, but things eventually settled down and people pretty much accepted it. Mrs. Ellington took care of Christina during the day. It wasn't perfect, but they managed."

"You'll never meet a better teacher in the entire world," Annie said, staring at Andrew. "More children from her little school have gone on to pursue their education than any one-room school that I know of. Did you notice the artwork in Rebecca's house?"

"Are you kidding?" Andrew replied. "It's wonderful ... and it's on every wall, I think. Between the plants and flowers and paintings, there's something interesting in every room. Her daughter must be as gifted as she is."

"As gifted and as beautiful," said Annie with a nod. "Her mother had her painting when other children were learning how to read. Unfortunately, it seems like Christina's the one who's suffered the most over the years. Don't you think so, Stuart?"

Stuart nodded, his forehead wrinkled in thought.

"How so?" asked Andrew. "The grandmother was—"

"No, no," Annie interrupted. "Her grandmother was wonderful, and Rebecca never neglected Christina ... never. But this is, as I'm sure you're discovering, a small community where everyone knows everyone else's business. The fact of Christina's illegitimacy traveled with her, particularly among the other children in the area. We all know how cruel children can be to each other, and with Christina's gifts and intelligence making her the envy of the other children, it became a weapon that some of the children tormented her with. Remember the slip of paper that she brought home from church once, Stuart?"

Stuart shook his head and sat forward in his chair. "Some child had stuck a piece of paper in her Bible that said, ' "A bastard shall not enter into the congregation of the Lord" (Deuteronomy 23:2). We all hate you.' Of course, she had many friends, but still, it's hard to get that out of your head. It still makes me as mad as fire."

"And no one even tried to correct it?" asked Andrew.

"No," Stuart replied. "Like a lot of important things, everyone hoped it would just go away, even though no one did anything about it. And, of course, it never went away. So Christina did, when she got old enough."

"To Chicago ... to study art, Rebecca tells me," Andrew stated. "She also asked me to remember to pray for Christina. Apparently she's not a believer?"

"No," Annie replied. "Not surprisingly, considering the way she was treated by—"

"But, goodness," Andrew broke in, "how you can have a mother like

Rebecca and remain an unbeliever? I don't understand that."

"How can you have a brother named Jesus and not believe? That's the one I don't understand," said Stuart.

Andrew threw up his hands in surrender. "Point well taken. If you—"

"Time to eat," Rebecca called out as she stepped out onto the back porch of the small white two-story wooden-slat house. "And take off those somber faces. The sun is shining, if you hadn't noticed."

"She never quits, does she?" Stuart declared and then laughed.

Chapter 10

"I think I'm going to have to stop for the day," Christina said, setting down her paintbrush and pushing back a strand of hair. Her eyes lingered on the canvas a moment longer. Then she looked over at Maria Sikkink still posed near the same window in the den. The sun was about to set and shadows played on Maria's face. "I'm afraid my powers of concentration are about exhausted, but I'm very pleased with how this is coming along. I think, if things go well tomorrow, I should be able to finish it up . . . at least so you can get your first peek at it."

"Ah . . . that's wonderful!" Maria exclaimed as she stretched her back muscles and arms. "I'm dying to see it, believe me. If it wouldn't have been for that unplanned trip to Washington, you could have been finished with me weeks ago. I'm sorry for all the delays on my part."

"It hasn't been a problem, really," Christina replied. She had stepped back and was studying the painting, her hands rubbing her arms. "I've had the one other portrait to work on, so I've kept busy in between times. I just hope you like what you see . . . and if not, I can hopefully make the improvements necessary. But I am pleased." She turned to look at Mrs. Sikkink.

"As long as I look like I'm nineteen," she breezed, "I told you I'd be happy." Maria started toward the door of the den. "And thirty pounds lighter would really help."

"Mrs. Sikkink, do you mind my asking you something else . . . about my grandmother?" Christina asked hesitantly, picking up the variety of paintbrushes she had used and setting them into a tin of mineral spirits. "You've been very kind to listen to me all the while I've been painting you, but you never made any comments. I'm wondering what you think about it. It all still bothers me a lot."

Maria stopped and turned toward Christina. "To tell you the truth, I guess I'm still in shock that Grace is your grandmother . . . and that the two of you met for the first time in my backyard. But . . . why do you ask me what I think about it?"

"I thought that . . . well, you seem to be very involved in your church," Christina said. "I think there's something right about what my grandmother said about honoring and obeying my grandfather, but there's something wrong about it too. I mean, I don't know anyone who's religious enough to ask what they think. You're the only person I've really discussed it with, and I'd appreciate knowing what you think about that—honoring and obeying to such a degree."

"Certainly, if you consider my opinions worth listening to," Maria responded. "I've thought about it as you've talked, and I think I've learned something that might help your grandmother. But with my husband's political career, I have to ask you to keep this information confidential."

"Yes, ma'am. I hope I've given you reason to trust my word."

"You have, and I do trust you." Maria smiled and nodded. "Years ago—actually it wasn't long after we got married—my husband had some business matters that he asked me to lie about. I went along with it for a while, but it bothered me every time I thought about it, and I could see that to keep that lie covered was going to require more lies. I finally got up the nerve to talk with my husband and tell him I couldn't do it again . . . ever."

"Were you afraid of his reaction?"

"I was nervous, sure. My lie had helped to seal a land contract he was negotiating. There was a lot of money changing hands then, and we were poor at the time. He could have easily felt like I was refusing to support him."

"So what gave you the courage to take a stand on it?"

"It had bothered me long enough that I finally went to talk with our pastor," said Maria. "I thought he'd tell me that I simply needed to believe I was forgiven, but what he showed me in the Scriptures ended up making a huge difference in my life. I wish Grace could have met him before he passed away. I'm sure he could have helped her too."

"I know this is asking a lot . . . much more than what's proper,"

Christina spoke softly, "but if I could talk my grandmother into coming over here, would you be willing to tell her what he told you? She obviously believes the Bible supports her submitting to my grandfather's treatment of my mother, but I don't know Scripture well enough to reason with her." Christina's eyes held Maria's.

"Oh, I don't know, Christina. I'm not a Bible teacher, but this was one lesson I feel I really did learn." Maria rubbed her forehead and said, "Tell you what. I don't want to stick my nose into your family's business, so you have to make it clear to her that you're the one who is making the request. You have my permission to tell her what I found myself confronting and that I'll gladly discuss how I resolved it. But she has to know that it's completely up to her. Is that a deal?"

"Yes! It's a deal. Thank you!"

"You'll probably find her in the backyard. Meanwhile, I'm going to change out of these fancy clothes," Maria said, pulling a long pin from the dark hat she had worn through each of the sittings and then lifting the hat from her head. "If your grandmother wants to talk, let's meet back here in . . . twenty minutes. If it doesn't work out, you and I can discuss it."

◆◆◆◆◆◆◆◆◆◆◆

Christina found her grandmother in the garden as Maria had suggested. But when she tried to explain the matter, she got so nervous she trembled almost uncontrollably. She was amazed that her grandmother listened, and when she heard what Maria Sikkink had gone through, she quietly assented to the meeting. Rather than offending her grandmother, as she feared might happen, Christina soon found herself back in the den seated at a large table with the two other women. One of the housemaids had delivered a glass pitcher of iced tea and three tall glasses to the table.

"Mmm . . . this tea is so refreshing," Grace Adler said after she'd taken a long second sip from her glass, then she leaned back in her chair and looked from Christina to Maria. "So, my granddaughter tells me she's confided our family's story to you, and you've confided back some of your own story. You realize, Maria, that I dread anyone knowing something like this about our personal lives. We're very private people. But let me try to put you at some ease. I've lived with this for twenty years, and I've never dared talk with anyone about it." She set her glass down and wiped her fingertips on the cloth napkin. "Seeing Christina ... whom I'd given up hope of ever seeing ... has changed something inside me, and I'm not sure what to do with it. Truthfully, it frightens me, but I'm willing to listen. What convinced you that you could no longer lie for Eugene?"

Maria sat quietly, her hands folded over a leather Bible she had brought to the table when she joined them. "Before I tell you, Grace, I want you to know that what I say is about me, something that God helped me see about myself. I don't pretend to know your situation well enough to say it applies to you. And I know this is extremely difficult to talk about. You're brave to be here."

"No, perhaps desperate, but not brave," Grace replied. "Christina is the brave one, and I'm thankful she's here."

Christina reached over and took her grandmother's hand, feeling tears forming at the corners of her eyes.

"I also want you to know," Maria continued, "that I believe in what you said to Christina. The Bible is very clear about a wife having a submissive heart, honoring her husband, loving him, supporting him, helping him. What I'm going to say helps define what that means, but it isn't meant to contradict it. Are you familiar with First Peter three, verses five and six?"

"No, not offhand," answered Grace as Maria opened her Bible to a page marked with a purple ribbon.

"I wasn't either until our pastor showed it to me," Maria said, glancing down at the Bible. "Let me read it through. 'For after this manner in the old time the holy women also, who trusted in God, adorned themselves, being in subjection unto their own husbands: Even as Sarah obeyed Abraham, calling him lord: whose daughters ye are, as long as ye do well, and are not afraid with any amazement.'"

"Sounds like what we talked about—submission," Grace said. "But I've never called my husband 'lord'! That sounds a bit extreme."

"Did you catch the last part of the sentence, though?" asked Maria. "Listen closely to the words. 'Whose daughters ye are, as long as ye do well, and are not afraid with amazement.' That didn't make any sense to me at first. But my pastor translated it this way: 'You are her daughters if you do what is right and do not give way to fear.' That made it much easier for me to understand."

"Meaning what?" Christina asked. "It sounds like Sarah is the model of submission to her husband. What does she have to fear?"

"You have to start back in the book of Genesis and carefully follow the story of Abraham and Sarah," Maria replied. "Do you remember that over the course of many years God spoke to Abraham several times, promising him an offspring who would bless all nations? Yet the years went by and Sarah remained childless."

"And eventually Sarah gave her personal maid to Abraham," Grace added.

"She did. But there's nothing to indicate that her motive was to produce the promised child," Maria stated. "There's no hint that Abraham had told Sarah of the promise from God. Her stated reason for giving Hagar to Abraham was 'to obtain children by her,' meaning that she felt they could build their family through Hagar. Childlessness was a cultural grief and reproach, so what Sarah did was in keeping with the practice of the day."

"They seemed to do a lot of strange things back then," Christina said. "No Sunday school teacher I ever had was very fond of explaining concubines and polygamy."

"So," Grace said, "they had Ishmael, but you're saying he wasn't necessarily the promised offspring. Ishmael was the result of Sarah's desire to have a family—a desire that Abraham went along with. With a younger woman involved, I would guess that he was probably more than happy to comply, don't you think?"

"Probably," Maria agreed with a smile. "Then thirteen years go by, and Abraham is ninety-nine when the Lord speaks to him again. This is the first time the Lord specifically tells Abraham that *Sarah* will be the mother of nations, clearly indicating that the promised child would come through her. It appears that Sarah knew nothing about her role in this, and even on this occasion, it wasn't Abraham who told her, but she heard this news herself while she was eavesdropping on Abraham and three heavenly visitors. Can you imagine the shock she got from such a promise at her age? It's no wonder she laughed and laughed. I would have screamed. It was ridiculously crazy, unless God intervened and made it happen."

"But she did conceive and have Isaac," said Grace. "She also forced

Hagar and Ishmael to leave, if I remember it right, which always seemed malicious to me. She was the one, after all, who gave Hagar to Abraham. They had both done what Sarah wanted and then she turned on them once she had Isaac."

"Okay, this is where the verse from First Peter applies," Maria explained. "After Sarah heard God's promise for herself and miraculously gave birth to Isaac, she truly understood the unique blessing of God that was on her son. When she saw Ishmael, who was around sixteen, threatening and mocking Isaac's position at a special birthday feast, she went to Abraham and demanded that he get rid of Hagar and her son; specifically, Sarah said that 'this bondwoman shall not be heir with my son.' Ishmael, she said, must not be allowed to threaten the special promise of God. But this deeply grieved Abraham. How could she demand that he send his oldest son away?"

"Which Peter seemed to indicate was the right thing for Sarah to do," Christina said. "How could he be sure it was the right thing?"

Maria turned the pages of her Bible back to Genesis twenty-one and pointed down at verse twelve. "Peter can say it because the Lord backed Sarah up. 'And God said unto Abraham, Let it not be grievous in thy sight because of the lad, and because of thy bondwoman; in all that Sarah hath said unto thee, hearken unto her voice; for in Isaac shall thy seed be called.' To 'hearken' means 'to act on what you hear.' Basically, God tells Abraham to obey Sarah's word."

"That doesn't sound much like a wife who's in submission," Christina reasoned. "Sort of sounds like the other way around. Abraham was to submit to Sarah."

"But it really wasn't," Maria said. "Isn't it clear that what was important here was to obey God? Sarah realized that Ishmael absolutely had to go, and Abraham didn't see it. But God spoke to Abraham and told him she was right. Sarah was standing for the right thing, even though it was a very difficult stand to make. She could not allow her fear of Abraham's reaction to get in the way of her doing what was right."

"My goodness, that's a bit overwhelming," Grace said, taking a deep breath. "In all my years of going to church, I've never heard anyone present Sarah like this."

"Fortunately for me, I did. But I don't want you to misunderstand

Peter's point," stated Maria. "Sarah still called Abraham 'lord,' which was the common term of respect in their culture. Although she fearlessly stood for the stated will of God—against Ishmael, Hagar, and her own husband—she still loved and honored her husband. The two weren't exclusive in this case, and they don't have to be exclusive in our cases. The fact is, we fail to honor and love our husbands if we go along with them in their sin. Rather than help them to know God's will, our disobedience simply aids their disobedience.

"The day came for me to confront Eugene and tell him that I could no longer lie for him," Maria continued. "I refused to allow his sin to be my sin. Even if he got mad at me, my place was to fearlessly obey God. If a clear command from God means that I must oppose my husband, God expects me to do so, and yet to do it with respect and gentleness."

The three women sat in silence for a few minutes, obviously pondering the story of Sarah and Maria's commentary. Grace stared absently into her nearly empty glass of tea while Maria's eyes seemed to be rereading some of the verses she had quoted from Genesis.

Christina was the first one to break the quiet. "I don't mean to labor the point, but all of this brings another Bible story to mind," she said, glancing at her grandmother. "It's another one that seemed strange to me in Sunday school class—bizarre, really—but I get the feeling it fits here, and perhaps it isn't strange at all. In the story of Ananias and Sapphira, if it was the right thing for Sapphira to lie because she was submitting to Ananias, that lie should not have cost her her life as it did Ananias. God should have commended her for obedience, right?"

"It would seem so," Maria responded. "Sapphira . . . and I . . . could not hide behind our husbands and say that it was good and right to lie because we were acting in submission. That is completely preposterous and irrational, and it's no surprise my conscience was killing me over it."

"How did your husband react?" Christina asked.

Maria shook her head and said, "He . . . didn't get mad, and he never asked me to do it again, but I wish I could say that he eventually said he agreed with me. Sarah fared better on that point than I did. But I had to be willing to face the worst—which, it turned out, I didn't have to."

"I . . . um . . . think I've been given more to consider than I thought possible," Grace said, pushing her chair back and slowly standing. "If you don't mind, I'd like to get back to my garden. Maria, thank you for sharing with me. I want to read through Genesis and get a better sense of Sarah's story. I honestly am not sure what to think of all this, but I find it deeply unsettling."

"Thank you for listening," Maria said. "Again, I wasn't meaning to imply that this story applies to your situation, but it surely did to mine. I'm not sure what my marriage would be like today if I had continued down this road."

"Is that the painting you've been working on, Christina?" Grace asked, glancing across the room at Christina's easel. "Do you mind if I take a look at it?"

Christina looked over at Maria and asked, "Do you mind?"

"No," Maria answered, "as long as you promise me I can see it tomorrow."

"I promise," Christina said as she followed her grandmother to the painting.

Grace Adler stepped around the canvas and immediately registered a smile of delight and surprise. "My, oh my, oh my!" she exclaimed softly, glancing from the canvas to Christina to Maria. "This is phenomenal. My, oh my! To think my granddaughter can paint so exquisitely. Oh my! Maria, you're going to love this!"

Chapter 11

*T*he village of Liberty Center had a total of thirty-three homes, a church and graveyard, one general store, combination garage and feed mill, and a one-room schoolhouse that was joined to a community softball field and park. Slender, dusty roads from the north and south and east and west split the village into four nearly equal sections. An occasional car or truck came rumbling to a stop at the village's main intersection, but for many of the local farmers, their sole mode of transportation was by horse and buggy and their fieldwork was still done with workhorses.

Andrew was walking from the parsonage to the general store, enjoying the cool breeze under a huge burr-oak tree that stood close to the road. He was still adjusting to rural life in the tiny Minnesota town as compared to the big city of Flint, Michigan, where automobiles and heavy machinery reigned supreme. And the transition from a meat-cutting job to the pastoral duties of a small church was a far bigger shift than he had anticipated. It wasn't the sudden change to the unsupervised work of the pastorate that challenged him, for he was strongly self-disciplined, but it was the guilty feeling that always seemed to stalk him whenever he was out on visitation. No matter what he tried to tell himself, visitation always made him feel like he was slacking off.

Crossing the road to the Wilson General Store, Andrew bounded up the four concrete steps to the wide concrete walkway in front. Walking past the store's row of tall windows, he pulled the screen door open and stepped inside. As usual, he was immediately greeted by the store's unique blend of odors—a strange combination of smells from a rich array of products that ranged from fresh and dried foods, coffees, and teas to leather workshoes and mothballed fabric that looked as if it had been there several years too long.

"Good day, Reverend," Vivian Wilson greeted him, stepping out from behind a long glass display case that she appeared to be cleaning. In the bright sunlight streaming in through the windows, her white dress with wide black buttons was almost dazzling, highlighting her short dark hair. "I appreciate your coming this morning. I'm sure you had plenty else to get done. I hope I didn't call too early and wake you."

"No, I'd been up for a few hours," Andrew replied. "Friday mornings I like to start early, preparing my sermon. It takes me a lot longer to get a sermon ready than I wish it did."

"I can tell that you put a great deal of time into your messages," said Vivian as she pushed her gold-rimmed glasses back up higher on her nose. "When I lived in Minneapolis, I visited a lot of churches, and I never heard anyone preach a better sermon than what I've heard from you. I so look forward to your Sunday messages and the Wednesday evening teaching, Reverend Regan."

"Thank you," Andrew replied, glancing toward a door behind the store's main counter. "I . . . take it that your mother is back in your apartment? She didn't go out to the house, did she?"

"No. She's lying down on my davenport, just like last time you were here," Vivian answered. "You can go right on back. I really should stay out here and tend the business."

"That's fine," said Andrew as he walked past her. "I can't stay long anyway."

"Reverend," Vivian called out, stopping Andrew just as he was reaching for the brass doorknob, "I hate to ask you this, but could you move these sacks of flour for me? My daddy could do it later, when he gets home from work—"

"No reason to wait," Andrew replied, walking back to where Vivian was standing. "Where would you like them?"

"Um . . . if you could put them on the corner around from the door, I think that would be better," Vivian replied, pointing to the spot at the front of the store.

Andrew tipped up the first one-hundred-pound sack of Pillsbury flour, lifted it with one swift motion, and toted it around the corner of the door and set it in the designated spot. "You're sure you want it here?" he asked, looking back at Vivian. "Seems a little close to the floor traffic, don't you think?"

"No, that should work," Vivian said with a warm smile. "With all your experience at Fairway Foods, we should have you come in and help us reorganize the store."

"All they let me do was cut meat," Andrew replied as he walked back and picked up a second sack. "If you're going to open a meat market, give me a call."

"Lifting all that meat must have built up your strength. You toss those big sacks like they're nothing."

"I think it was helping my uncle Harry out on the farm that did it," Andrew replied, not quite sure how to respond to Vivian's comment. He lifted the third bag onto his shoulder and turned to finish the task. "Aunt Lizzy was a slave driver. I had to move to town to get some rest."

"She's a nice old lady," Vivian said. "But your uncle is really strange. When I was younger, he'd come into the store with your aunt, and I'd get scared of him. I always thought he looked like the Hunchback of Notre Dame. One time I heard him say something, which was really spooky. Can you understand him?"

"Pretty good, since I've had the chance to work with him and heard him repeat certain phrases over and over," Andrew replied. "And he is, without a doubt, the least scary man in the world. He spends as much time studying Scripture and reading spiritual books and praying as anyone I know, including my seminary professors. He may not look like it, but he's smart as a whip and as gentle and strong as any man I've ever met."

"So, why doesn't he ever come to church?"

"I'm hoping I can talk him into coming someday. We've talked about it several times, but, quite frankly, he doesn't feel welcome in the church. That has to change. Harry has a cleft palate, a deformed arm, and a clubfoot, which doesn't qualify him as a monster. I'll tell him, though, that you asked about him. Maybe that'll help get him to come."

"No . . . I mean, I was just curious," Vivian sputtered, stepping back to the glass display case and picking up a cleaning rag. "If people gawk at him and children are scared of him, maybe it's best for him to not have to go through that. I wouldn't want to, if I were him."

"But he's our brother in Christ . . . with gifts from God to share with all of us," Andrew argued, turning his full gaze upon her soft brown eyes and delicate face. "As long as he stays home, he is deprived of what we're meant to give him as members of Christ's church. It also deprives him of what he can give us, and so we all lose out. That's what I'm saying has to change. Don't you agree?"

"Perhaps. I really haven't thought about it," Vivian replied. "But you may be expecting too much from people. If he weren't your uncle, you might not feel as strongly about it."

"If that's the case, I should resign the pastorate . . . immediately," Andrew stated, feeling an angry fire starting to rise up inside of him. "From my heart I hope my feelings have nothing to do with the fact that Harry Regan is my uncle."

Vivian looked away from the glow in Andrew's dark eyes and said, "So, you would wish the same for Mrs. Watson's daughter, Clara? I'm not so sure you'd care to handle her disturbances."

"Clara is severely mentally retarded," Andrew said, his fingers tightening into fists. "If I thought that Clara could understand anything of what was being said in church, I could tolerate a lot of her screams. And wouldn't it be nice if Mrs. Watson could get out of the house on Sunday morning and mingle with folks at church? Clara is a tremendous burden for her mother."

"She should be institutionalized," Vivian said. "It's too much for anyone to bear."

Andrew sighed and rubbed his forehead. "I can't imagine how difficult it is—every day, around the clock. But have you ever visited an institution for the retarded and insane?"

"No, but—"

"You really should see one for yourself first, and then try to imagine that it's your daughter whom you're committing there," Andrew broke in. "I have seen it . . . and you can't compare it to the life that Mrs. Watson is giving her daughter at home, as staggeringly hard as it is."

The scrunching sound of thin rubber tires on gravel and the rattling fenders of an old truck as it pulled to a stop in front of the general store interrupted their conversation, which Andrew was only too happy to conclude. He glanced out the window, then turned and said, "I should be moving along. I'm sure your mother is waiting for me."

"Yes, I'm sure she is," Vivian replied as he walked past her. "Go right on in. Thanks again for moving the flour."

"You're welcome," Andrew replied with a nod, then turned the brass handle and opened the door that led from the store to an attached apartment on the store's south side. While not large, it had an abundance of windows, which gave its small kitchen and combination dining and living room a cheeriness and warmth.

"Ah, Reverend, you made it," Gertie Wilson called out from the long davenport, where she was lying underneath a quilt with several pillows propping up both her head and legs. She set down the book she'd been reading. "I thought I heard your voice out there."

"Yes, Vivian and I had a bit of a chat," Andrew replied, stepping across the dull brown linoleum floor, which was worn through in several spots. He sat down on a wooden chair next to the davenport.

"Oh, I'm so glad the two of you like to talk," Gertie said, smiling at Andrew and then giving a sniffle. Her dark brown eyes were magnified behind the lenses of her reading glasses. "You realize that she's only a few years younger than you."

"Yes, I think you've told me that a few times."

"And she loves your sermons.... My goodness, how she raves on about your sermons. Did she ever tell you that?"

"She just mentioned it, surprisingly enough."

"Good ... that's good. She's a beautiful girl, isn't she?"

Andrew began to nod but didn't get a chance to answer.

"Can you believe ... I still can't believe ... with all the single men in Minneapolis ... that she never fell in love up there. Can you believe that?"

"I guess she never met the right one, don't you think?"

"Absolutely ... absolutely. That's going to happen one of these days ... *soon*, I think. I get excited just thinking about it."

"What ... ah ... seems to be the problem, Gertie?" Andrew asked, leaning toward her. "Working yourself to the bone again?"

"You got that right, Reverend," Gertie agreed. "I was busy sweeping the floor, which is the very first thing I do every morning, and all of a sudden my head started to spin and I thought I was going to faint dead away. I don't know what I'd do without Vivian here. I was sorry when she lost her job in Minneapolis, but I surely couldn't run this store without her. She's going to make some man very happy sometime soon."

"Have you been to see Doc Anderson?"

"No, why?"

"Well, I mentioned it to you the last time you called," Andrew answered. "This is the . . . fourth fainting spell you've had since I moved into the parsonage. Doesn't that concern you? It could be serious, you know—high blood pressure or something. Maybe I should talk with Lloyd and—"

"No, no, no. He's got enough on his mind trying to work in the bank in Bradford and still balance our books here. I'll be fine in no time. Nothing that a good prayer won't take care of."

Andrew nodded and scratched the back of his head. "Well," he said, "I'll be happy to pray, but I really do want you to talk with the doctor. Biblical prayer was never meant to be separated from using the best medical care available. Doc Anderson is a fine doctor, and a believer as well. I'm sure he prays with and for his patients."

"But it's not the same."

"What?"

"It's not the same," Gertie repeated, wrinkling her forehead. "You're the preacher, and he's doctor. You're the man of God."

"I am . . . at most . . . a young man of God . . . who has a lot of maturing to do," Andrew said slowly, hoping not to get into another disagreement. "Stuart Anderson is what I consider 'a man of God,' in the full sense of the word. But in God's sight, every believer who prays is on an equal level. Being the church pastor does not make me a man of God who is more qualified to pray for the sick than any other Christian. But being the pastor puts me into more situations like this where I can pray, so why don't we pray? I'll—"

"Oh, I was also wondering, before you pray, if you could join us for lunch after church on Sunday. We so enjoy having you. Vivian was just saying—"

"I'm sorry, but you just had me for dinner on Monday night . . . and I'm afraid I already have a commitment."

"Rebecca Ellington?"

"Why, yes," Andrew answered, feeling his stomach muscles tighten. "Does that matter?"

Gertie's already large eyes opened wider. "Reverend, you're new here, and I realize there are some things . . . some real unpleasant things we'd rather not talk about . . . that you're going to discover. If I were you, I'd stay out of Rebecca's house as much as I could. People tell me she has you over regular. That true?"

"Since school got out, yes, you could say it's been fairly regular," said Andrew, wishing he'd never left the parsonage that morning. "She's been teaching me how to cook, which I should have learned long ago, but my mother always kicked us out of the kitchen. I . . . ah . . . can't tell you how thankful I am for her. She's been wonderful to me."

"That's nice, but . . . just remember that this is a little town, and people talk."

"Are you referring to the fact that when Rebecca moved here, she was pregnant and not married?"

"She told you?"

"We've talked about it. It's about as sad a story as I've ever heard. The Ellingtons must have been wonderful people to take her in. I assume you knew them."

"Yes, they were fine people, and so was their only son. She must have corrupted—"

"Hold it, hold it," Andrew interrupted, shaking his head. "Two young people fell in love . . . and also fell into temptation and sinned. Rebecca would never deny that, if you've talked with her. Have you discussed this with her?"

"No. It's not my business—"

"Then it's not our business to judge her as if she were the temptress, or even if she was, that we somehow stamp her life with her indiscretion. Some of Jesus' closest friends were prostitutes and tax collectors, which was as low as you could get in that society."

"We're not Jesus."

"No, not even close. But we're to become like Him, aren't we? Isn't that what our lives are all about?"

"That's a nice thought, but let me tell you for your own good, you're only harming yourself by befriending her. People *never* forget some things, no matter what."

"Meaning you?"

"Meaning a lot of people in this community ... and church. Not everyone here corrupted themselves in such a manner."

"Mrs. Wilson," Andrew stated, rising to his feet, "I cannot ... and will not ... abide you speaking in this manner. If God could forgive Rebecca for her sins ... and if He could forgive me for my sins, I overwhelmingly must forgive others for their sins, even if they sin against me. I treasure Rebecca Ellington as my friend, and I feel honored to have been welcomed into her life. I suggest, if you want someone to pray for you, that you give her a call. My guess is that you'll find her a good deal more gracious than I am."

Andrew spun around and walked quickly to the door, feeling the intense burning of two large brown eyes focused on his back. As he turned the doorknob, he turned to the storekeeper and said, "Good day," then walked out, knowing full well that he'd not heard the last of this discussion.

Chapter 12

Christina stood on the hot downtown Chicago street and watched people coming and going through the large revolving glass door of the office building next to the Palmolive Building. Had she heard from her grandmother in the past two weeks since their talk with Maria Sikkink, she perhaps would not even be contemplating whether to follow through with her plan. But with every passing day, the urge to finally meet her grandfather had grown to a compulsion that dominated most of her waking hours. Having discovered that her grandmother was not the monster she'd suspected, Christina was now determined to meet face-to-face with the man who had disowned her mother and never made one attempt to contact her in twenty years.

She took a deep breath, willing her nerves into a calm that kept her from turning back, then stepped from the street corner and headed straight for the revolving door. Edgar Mitchell had given her the address of her grandfather's office when he drove her back to her apartment the last time. He had also told her that, should she attempt a meeting with her grandfather, she must find a way to do so without implicating her grandmother in any way. William Adler, the chauffeur had said, would surely be furious if he found out that his wife had promoted the contact with their granddaughter in any manner.

Passing through the revolving glass doors into the refreshingly cool air-conditioned lobby, Christina walked purposefully to the elevator and took it to the fourth floor. She then followed Edgar's instructions and went down two hallways and came to a glass door with the neatly painted inscription, Adler Enterprises. Surprised that her nervousness had turned to resolve, she opened the door and stepped into the modest-sized office suite that included an open area for a receptionist and four secretaries, and seven or eight enclosed offices.

"Good afternoon," the receptionist said, appraising Christina as she came through the doorway. Fifty or so years old, dark featured with short, wavy black hair sprinkled with gray and a large nose, she presented herself in a manner that gave no doubt that she was in charge of all newcomers to the office. "May I help you?"

"Yes, ma'am," Christina replied as she stepped to the woman's desk. "I have a two-o'clock appointment to meet with Mr. Adler."

The receptionist glanced down at her appointment book, then looked back up at Christina with a bit of a glare in her eye. "Miss Baxter?"

"Yes. I'm here to interview Mr. Adler for a story I've been working on for a long time. I'm hoping he can fill in some of the details I'm still missing."

"Is this for a newspaper? I didn't take your call, and my note didn't indicate what this was for."

Christina squeezed her notebook tightly and managed a smile. "I'm actually still in school, and this is one part of a very large project I'm working on, but I thought I'd cleared all of this information in my previous call. Is there a problem?"

"No, but Mr. Adler can't afford to waste his time on—"

"Young women who should keep their noses out of the business world—"

"No, he's not like that," the woman broke in, holding her hand up for Christina to stop. Then she stood up and said, "Let me check and see if he's available."

"Thank you," Christina said, relief washing over her.

The receptionist took a couple of steps toward Mr. Adler's office, then turned to Christina and asked, "Have I met you before? You look very familiar."

"No, not that I know of," answered Christina. "How long have you worked for Mr. Adler?"

"Twenty . . . six years," the lady replied, still eyeing Christina closely. "Why?"

"Oh, nothing. Just curious. Perhaps I remind you of someone."

The receptionist nodded and shrugged her shoulders, then moved quickly on to Mr. Adler's door and knocked. A muffled voice answered, and the woman opened the door and said, "A Miss Baxter to see you, sir. She's writing a story that includes you."

"Send her in" came the sharp response.

The sound of the strong voice from inside the office caught Christina off guard, and she felt a sudden urge to turn around and run out the door. Swallowing heavily, she gathered all her courage and stepped forward as the receptionist signaled for her to come. She managed a weak "Thank you" as she passed the woman, who was still studying Christina's face.

Walking to the door, she thought of her grandmother's life, and much of her own nervousness then fell away. She told herself that whatever this man may have done to her grandmother and her mother, she wasn't about to shrink away in his presence. He may have held sway over their lives, but she was free. Indeed, she brought with her the element of surprise, which bolstered what little confidence she had.

"Come in. Come in," the bald-headed executive with black wire-rimmed glasses and brown tweed suit said from behind his large walnut desk. He did not stand up but motioned for Christina to sit in one of the large leather chairs in front of his desk. He gave her a wide, friendly smile as she moved to the chair. "What's this all about, Miss Baxter? No one's ever asked me for an interview for an article. How do you know who I am?"

Christina settled in the green coolness of the leather chair and glanced around the large office with its tall windows, heavy draperies, and dark wood paneling. Across the room stood a large table with several piles of business ledgers, but her grandfather's desk was perfectly neat. A framed picture of her grandmother stood on the right side of the desk, and on a credenza to his side she was surprised to see a picture of her mother when she was about sixteen.

"I've been researching a story, Mr. Adler, and your name came up as someone whom I should consider interviewing," Christina replied, pulling out her pen and opening her notebook. "I was told that you'd have an interesting perspective on it, and looking around your office, I'd say they were correct. Very impressive."

"Oh, it's fairly modest, actually, but it's more than adequate for a man who's going to retire soon," William replied, raising his eyebrows and gazing around the office. "What's the nature of your story?"

"It's primarily about interesting people," Christina replied. "Tell me about your work. What does Adler Enterprises represent?"

Her grandfather sat back into his tall leather chair and said, "Our business is not all that interesting, so I'm not sure what you're looking for. For the past thirty years I've bought up broken-down businesses, primarily those with heavy machinery, then I go in with some of my associates and we assess whether it's best to liquidate the assets or to try to save the business. Some people have called me a scavenger, which is a term that probably fits."

"You see how interesting you are," Christina said, doing her best to pretend that she was taking notes in shorthand. "Who else would admit to being a scavenger?"

William Adler simply smiled and nodded to her.

"Tell me what your business has been like since the Crash," Christina continued, looking up again at this man who represented the greatest pain anyone could inflict on a daughter. It seemed a bit unreal that she was actually here before him.

"As you might guess, the Depression has been a boom for me," he stated. "Are you familiar with Beardsley Ruml?"

"No, sir."

"He is an advocate of the theory: progress through catastrophe," William said. "He said that in all catastrophes, there is real potential of benefit. In my case, there seems to be no end to it. After the Crash, I particularly watched for businesses owned by the banks. Many banks made the mistake of taking over failed companies and putting in their own men to run them. Bankers, believe it or not, are the worst operators of businesses, and in the end, they lose everything. When I step in, they're just tickled to get these businesses off their backs."

"And you turn those businesses around and take the profits."

"Five years ago I bought a business for $33,000," her grandfather said. "Today, if I wanted to sell, it's worth nearly half a million dollars. We don't always win like this, but most of the time we come out in the black."

"Did the Crash hurt you?"

"As I said, it was a boom for my business. Personally, I got hurt, like most investors. I got caught up in some of the heavy speculation that was going on, and I got burned. I had cigar stock that was selling for $110 a share and dropped to $2. I learned my lesson, kept working hard, and it's paid off. Have you heard of William Benton?"

"The advertising tycoon?"

"That's him. I met him when he and Chester Bowles were just opening their first office shortly before the Crash," her grandfather said. "He convinced me to put money into Pepsodent, and that money has doubled and quadrupled. Four years ago, he talked to me about what they were going to do through radio with Maxwell House Coffee, and that's been a superb investment."

"Through the *Maxwell House Show Boat*, I take it," Christina replied, continuing to scratch imaginary notes on her pad.

"The number one program in broadcasting."

"So would you say you hardly knew the Depression was going on?"

"Every time I see a man smoking a cigar, I recall there's a Depression going on," William answered, another warm smile crossing his face. "But you look for where you can profit through the catastrophe, and I can't complain. We've made a lot of money out of this thing."

"Tell me about the cigars," Christina asked, looking up. "Was that about greed?"

"Greed ... yes—" he nodded, "and stupidity. I should have seen it coming. The overspeculation was so rampant, it couldn't help but collapse. Anybody could buy $500,000 worth of stock with $500 down. I got greedy, and the market made me pay. But I had more than enough to cover my losses, which was not the case with most investors."

Christina took a few moments to jot down markings on her pad, then nodded and said, "I'm impressed with the business side of your life. Sounds like your life could be characterized as conservative and yet opportunistic. Is that an apt description?"

"I'd say so."

"I'm curious if you'd mind my asking a few personal questions to sort of correlate with your business life?"

"I'm a very private person," William responded. "I'd prefer to stick to the business side, if you don't mind."

"How about if I ask a question or two, and if you're not comfortable answering, we'll just leave it alone."

"Fine, but ... I have some pressing matters that don't allow for much more time."

"I realize you're a busy man, Mr. Adler," Christina said. "I was wondering if that's a picture of your wife?"

"Yes, this is Grace," he said. "We've been married forty-three years."

"And the other picture"—she pointed to the credenza—"who is that? A daughter? Granddaughter?"

"That *was* my daughter."

"I'm sorry. Is she...?"

"No, I'm sorry. It's a private matter, but she is alive."

"And her name?"

"Rebecca."

"Adler ... or Ellington?"

William Adler's no-nonsense smile instantly turned sour. "What is this all about, anyway? Where did you learn—?"

"Any other children?"

"No, but—"

"Any grandchildren ... to love and to cuddle and to cherish?"

"Like I said, I'm really not comfortable with these questions. I'd like to end this interview, please."

"I'm sure you would, Mr. Adler," Christina said, setting her pen and note pad down and leaning forward in her chair, "but I've waited twenty years for this interview, and I've not gotten the least bit private yet. Do your associates know that you sent your daughter away because she was pregnant and unmarried? I need to know ... and you're the only one who can tell me ... how it's possible for someone who fathers a child to treat his daughter like that. Was your father that heartless to you?"

"That's none of your business. I'll ask you to leave this once, and then—"

"Or that you have never attempted to contact your daughter or to meet your granddaughter? You were content to leave them on their own after the man your daughter loved was killed. I'm really struggling to understand how anyone could do that, and live with himself. If I told you that about one of your associates, would you want that person working in your office?"

"Who do you think you are coming in here and—?"

"And who do you think you are doing what you did to my mother?" Christina railed, standing to her feet. She leaned over his desk and stared into her grandfather's disbelieving face. "Are you so blind that you don't know who I am? Even your receptionist could see the resemblance, but then maybe you were so busy buying cigar stock, you never noticed what my mother looked like."

Her grandfather sat motionless, doubt giving way to clear recognition, yet no hint of a breakdown in his composure. His eyes were squinted, and he ran his index finger across his lips, all the time continuing to stare at her. "Your mother," he said coldly, "could have stayed, but she chose to leave in the dark of night. She . . . and her lover . . . would not heed my counsel, choosing instead to break the moral commands of God, and then she broke her mother's heart. Judge me as harshly as you wish, but I warned her, then I gave her a second chance, but she was so bent on her own way, she would not comply. What happened to her was entirely her own doing, and I bear no responsibility for it."

"It's as simple as that, eh?" Christina responded, shaking her head, her blues eyes still sparking. "If she would have just gone away for a while and gotten rid of me, everything would have measured up to your moral standard. You would never have had to face the shame of others knowing that the family had been stained. How nice for you! And what about me?"

"What about you?"

"You would have preferred that I not be raised by the most loving mother any child has ever had?" Christina sputtered. "You would have denied me my mother for the sole reason of protecting your own image. I hoped it wasn't true. I hoped you could give me *one reason* not to hate you . . . but you've given me just the opposite. I hate what you've done. I hate what you are. And I'm ashamed to call you my grandfather, but I will anyway, because my mother will still call you her father."

"Close the door when you leave," he said, his face still not showing any emotion.

"That's it?" Christina said, staring hard into his pale blue eyes. "Twenty years, and this is the best you can do?"

"What is it that you want? Money?" he asked, smiling a tight smile and reaching into his suit coat pocket and pulling out a thick wallet.

"I was hoping you'd want to know about my mother's life, or maybe even say my name out loud."

Her grandfather opened his wallet and pulled out several green bills, then handed them toward her. "Why don't you mosey along, now. I don't care to know about your mother's life, or yours, for that matter. This should pay your bills for a while."

Christina's glare turned to an icy steel, then she smiled slightly, took the bills, and flipped through them. "I could put every one of these dollars to good use, but . . . I'd rather starve than let you pay my way out of your life. You're a shrewd man, Grandfather. Surely you can't believe that I'm about to let you off this easy. I can be as nasty as you are. Just watch me."

That said, Christina took the green wad of bills and gave them a kiss, still evoking no response from him. Then she threw them up into the air and let them flutter down all around her grandfather. "Easy come, easy go, eh? We'll be seeing you around. I need to have a little chat with your receptionist before I leave, though. Good day."

"Don't you dare—" William ordered, but Christina was already nearly to the office door.

"Oh, I dare," Christina responded as she pulled the door open and waved to him. She turned and pulled the door shut with a loud *bang* that snapped the receptionist and four secretaries to immediate attention. Then she walked quickly to the receptionist's desk and spoke loudly, "I'm sorry, but I lied to you. My name is not Baxter but Ellington. I got the impression when I walked in that you knew my mother . . . and my father."

"Rebecca's daughter?" the woman gasped, taking her face in her hands. "Oh my word. I never thought I'd see this day! You're just as beautiful—"

"Don't say another word to her!" William Adler's voice roared from his office doorway, wiping the joyful expression from the receptionist's face.

"Good-bye, again, *Grandfather*," Christina called out as several other office doors opened and heads poked out to see what was going on. Then she turned around and walked slowly from the office.

Chapter 13

"Thank you for the fine sermon, Reverend," Vivian Wilson said, shaking Andrew's hand as her mother and father waited behind her after one Sunday evening service late in the summer. "You make the Sermon on the Mount so clear that I could almost imagine being there and listening to it. That's a gift, isn't it, Papa?"

Lloyd Wilson, tall and gaunt with long arms draping down and tired eyes, nodded and said, "Been a long time since this church heard anything like it. It's a gift all right. And I understand that you're coming to supper on Tuesday night. We're looking forward to that."

"Thank you," Andrew replied, shaking the older man's hand, then turning toward his wife. "How have you been feeling, Gertie?" Andrew's relationship with the Wilsons had been somewhat strained the last few months since his angry outburst at Gertie, but he had tried to put his own feelings aside and maintain his concern for the family.

"Just fine . . . just fine, thank you," she replied. "Vivian makes me rest more, and that seems to have made the difference. She's gotten me through a hard summer. And your prayers, of course."

Andrew looked into the woman's large brown eyes, which seemed to reflect only sincerity, but he couldn't believe that the remark wasn't a slur. "I'm sure the resting has helped," he said.

"Couldn't make it without her," Lloyd added, nodding toward his daughter. "Just wasn't enough profit in the store to support us when the hard times hit. Nearly closed our doors after I had to take that bank job in Bradford. Just too much for one woman to run."

Andrew smiled and nodded. He was curious to ask how Gertie had survived for the year that Vivian had worked in Minneapolis, but his only wish at the moment was to say good-night and get out of his hot suit and tie. "Well, I'll see you on Tuesday evening," he said, pushing open the big wooden front doors of the church. Although the late summer sun had set, there was still at least a half hour of light left before the twilight would be overtaken by darkness. "I've got another commitment yet this evening, so I need to move along."

"Going over to someone's house for a snack?" Gertie asked as they made their way through the door.

"No, not tonight," Andrew replied.

"You have a commitment, but not to see someone?" Gertie persisted.

"Gertie, you're meddlin' again," Lloyd reprimanded, taking his wife's arm.

"I'm not meddlin'," she returned. "Just trying to understand what the commitment is."

"Which is not your business. Now, let's go home."

"Good night," Andrew said with a smile, noting the frown on Gertie's face.

"See you Tuesday night," said Lloyd as Andrew closed the church door.

Andrew quickly gathered up his Bible and preaching notes, then walked to the door and shut off the lights. Pushing open the door, he exited the church, crossed the lawn to the parsonage, and went straight inside. He took off his suit coat and hung it over a chair, breathing a sigh of relief as he undid his tie. Picking up his Bible, he walked through the kitchen, went out the back door, and plopped down in one of the wooden lawn chairs.

"Oh God, where are you?" he asked aloud, lightly fingering the gilded edges of his leather Bible. Exhaling deeply, he stared out across the empty hayfield into the pasture beyond with its thick oak trees and dark clusters of prickly gooseberry bushes. "Whyever did you send me here, God? Did you really want me to come here, or was I just being stubborn?"

"Who you talking to?" Rebecca Ellington called out from her backyard, where she had been watering some of her treasured red rose bushes. "For a minute there, I thought you were Mr. Henderson."

Andrew burst out laughing as he imagined the old man who lived in the tiny house on the south side of the village and never seemed to stop talking to himself. He nodded to Rebecca as she came across the lawn toward him. "The only difference between me and good ol' Mr. Henderson is that he makes more sense than I do. Did I interrupt you there—breaking the Sabbath again? I thought we'd talked about that."

"The sun has set, if you notice," Rebecca continued the bantering as she sat down in the chair across from him. "And I pumped the water into the bucket yesterday, which allows me to pour it today. Does that fit the code?"

"Close enough, I guess," Andrew said. "Maybe we should check in with Gertie. She could clarify it, I'm sure."

Rebecca grew serious and studied Andrew's expression. Then she said, "Is Gertie giving you a hard time? Is that what's got you so frustrated?"

"What makes you think I'm frustrated?"

"The way you flopped down in that chair and then started carrying on a conversation with yourself. I've seen cheerier souls in my day. Gertie's been known to get under people's skin from time to time."

"Ah, I shouldn't have said anything about her. I'm just frustrated with everything." Andrew sighed deeply, squeezing his Bible between his hands and looking over at Rebecca.

"I guess I don't understand," she replied, concern spreading across her face. "Both of your sermons today were excellent. I was just thinking, while I was watering my roses, about what you said about 'compassion' being the key word of the Savior's life. I even jotted down your exact words: 'It gave a wondrous expression to His eyes; it caused the subtlest tones to enter into His gentle yet all-pervasive and all-penetrating voice; it was the secret and the very inspiration of His life.' I loved that."

Andrew nodded, barely smiling. "Thanks. If you weren't in the congregation, I'm not sure I'd bother to preach. Looks to me like half the place is falling asleep, and the other half are bored stiff."

"That's not true, and you know it," Rebecca handed him her gentle rebuke. "I've heard all kinds of great comments about your preaching."

"Comments, yes. I've visited every family in the congregation this summer, and I've heard over and over how much folks appreciate the preaching. That's nice, and I hope they were sincere remarks, but you have to figure that a lot of it is just buttering up the preacher. It's just that there's nothing happening here.... Week after week ... nothing changes."

"What are you expecting to happen?"

Andrew swatted a mosquito on his arm and pondered Rebecca's question. "I'm not sure, but whatever it is, it's not happening now. Don't you think ... if I'm faithfully preaching and teaching the Word of God that the result should be changed lives ... or people being caused to search for God ... to repent of their sins? When you teach children how to read, don't you expect to see changes? Isn't it measurable?"

"Yes, it's measurable. But children learn at different speeds. I see many children who don't seem to get it, and don't seem to get it, and then all of sudden, the lights go on and they're on their way. It's amazing at times."

"But they learn to read, correct?"

"Yes."

"You see, that's the difference. I've been here nearly a half a year, and I can't name one significant change that's happened in anyone's life. There's either something wrong in my life, or maybe I wasn't supposed to come here."

"Are you sure that's what your Boss says?"

"Who?"

"Your Boss," Rebecca repeated, pointing to the Bible in Andrew's hands. "What's He got to say about this?"

"I don't know."

"May I read something to you?" she asked, reaching for his Bible, which he handed to her. She turned the pages to James five. "Here it is, verse seven. 'Be patient therefore, brethren, unto the coming of the Lord. Behold, the husbandman waiteth for the precious fruit of the earth, and hath long patience for it, until he receive the early and late rain. Be ye also patient.'" Then she handed him back the Bible and stood up, cupping her hands over her mouth and lowering her voice. "What if the Boss is saying, 'Andrew, be patient like my husbandman who waits for the precious fruit of harvest. The rains will fall, but you must be patient.'"

Andrew laughed at her bit of role-playing and nodded in agreement as she sat back down, then he said, "And the Boss, as you've named Him, might be saying what He spoke through Jeremiah—'The prophets prophesy lies in my name: I sent them not, neither have I commanded them, neither spake unto them.' Who knows? That's why I came out here. I thought maybe the Boss would clue me in."

"Well, I best be getting on home and letting you have some time alone." Rebecca paused, glancing off across the field. "Do you have anyone you could talk with about this? Another minister? Someone wise and mature? When I first started teaching, I had Annie Anderson to help guide me through the struggles of my early years."

"No, I haven't met anyone like that yet."

"How about Stuart Anderson? He's very mature."

"Yeah, I respect Doc Anderson a lot, but . . . I don't know him very well."

"Well, give it some thought, and I'll be praying about it, too," Rebecca said, standing up. "I do have one piece of advice for you, though. The Lord sometimes speaks through people whom you wouldn't expect . . . and at times when you least expect it. That's the way He's worked in my life anyway. Be on your toes, Andrew, and be humble. God hears the cries of our hearts, and He answers."

"Thanks," Andrew replied softly. "I appreciate that."

"Good night."

"To you, too."

◆ ◆ ◆ ◆ ◆ ◆ ◆ ◆ ◆ ◆ ◆

"You're just as impatient as your father was," Elizabeth Regan declared, pouring both Andrew and his uncle Harry a second cup of coffee. "Isn't he, Harry?"

Harry shook his head no, squinting his right eye tightly, then giving his crooked smile.

"Oh, he is too!" She gave Harry a stern look. "If he planted a potato eye, he'd be out in the garden digging it up every day to see if it was growing. Let me tell you what I know for certain: things are not going to change overnight in this church, Andrew. We're too set in our ways for that, and you have to accept the fact that you're new here. It's going to take a while for folks to warm up to you and really take you seriously, whether you preach a fine sermon or not. What did your father say in the letter you got?"

"He said pretty much what you've been saying . . . and what Rebecca keeps hammering me over the head with."

"See, there. How many folks d'ya need to get your head screwed on tight?" Elizabeth asked. "You listen real good to Rebecca's advice. She's the godliest woman I know, and what she says comes from a woman who's lived through some extremely hard times. When Mr. Ellington died, Rebecca and Mrs. Ellington hardly had a penny between 'em. They faced the Depression long before it arrived for others."

"Rebecca's past doesn't trouble you, Aunt Lizzy?" Andrew asked.

Elizabeth's eyes held Andrew's for a moment, then she smiled and shook her head. "So . . . you heard, did you? Like I said, we're real set in our ways here. Rebecca Ellington has lived in this community for nearly twenty years, I reckon, and has done nothing but pure good to everyone she meets, and some folks still speak behind her back like she's a loose woman. No one has ever dared to gossip about her to me, but I know there's still talk. It's a wonder she ever stayed after Mrs. Ellington died. I suppose she's told you that she's been offered teaching positions in some of the finest private schools in the country?"

"No. She hasn't mentioned it."

"Figures. She's not one to toot her own horn. My guess is that she could go almost anywhere and get triple the pay that our little school offers. She hasn't stayed because she had nowhere else to go, that's for sure. You listen when she tells you something."

"So, Uncle Harry, what do you think about my situation?" Andrew asked, glancing across the oak table. "You don't concur with Rebecca and Aunt Lizzy that I simply need to be patient?"

Harry shook his head no as he set his coffee cup back into its saucer with a bit of a rattle. The sunlight streaming in through the window behind him highlighted his thick, coarse brown hair and wide muscular upper back and neck. The sinewy muscles on his right forearm bulged beneath his long blue shirt sleeves.

"This isn't a game, Harry," Elizabeth said. "So tell us what you think young Andrew's problem is."

Harry held up one finger, then stood up and limped across the room to his rocking chair in the corner. He sat down and picked up the small chalkboard that was leaning against the wall, then took a piece of chalk from the wooden stand by his chair and began to write on the board.

"You just remember that you asked for this," Elizabeth said to Andrew, watching her brother scratch the letters down with agonizing slowness. "He never writes on that board unless he means business. Something's got his motor cranked up, but he hasn't said a word to me about it."

Harry finished writing, then sat and studied his letters before putting the chalk back on the wooden stand. Satisfied, he stood up and limped his way back across the room and gently set the chalkboard down on the table in front of Andrew and Elizabeth. The poorly scrawled script read "you need power from on high."

The words struck Andrew with a significant force—the gut-wrenching feeling one gets when confronted with absolute truth that you don't understand, when the words ring true but you have no inner sense of comprehending their meaning. His immediate reaction was to pretend that he did understand. After all, he was the one who had gone through seminary, and he should be able to define these scriptural words with exact clarity. But knowing the meaning of the words by the book did not equal knowing the meaning of the words in his heart.

Andrew simply nodded his head, then looked into Harry's brown squinting eyes that seemed to be peering into his own soul. "You've been reading Moody and Torrey again, I bet."

Harry smiled and nodded, then he waved for Andrew to follow him as he started across the room toward the stairway.

"Well, I did ask for it," Andrew said, turning to his grinning aunt. He followed his uncle up the steep stairway, past the guest bedroom at the top of the stairs, and down the hallway to Harry's sparse room.

Pointing to the other chair beside his desk, Harry sat down in his chair and quickly began flipping open the pages of his Bible. As Andrew sat down, Harry found the verses he was looking for in Luke twenty-four and handed Andrew the Bible, pointing to verse forty-five. As he had done on many occasions with Harry while he stayed in the guest room, Andrew read the words out loud:

" 'Then opened he their understanding, that they might understand the Scriptures, and said unto them, Thus it is written, and thus it behooved Christ to suffer, and to rise from the dead the third day: and that repentance and remission of sins should be preached in his name among all nations, beginning at Jerusalem. And ye are witnesses of these things. And, behold, I send the promise of my Father upon you: but tarry ye in the city of Jerusalem, until ye be endued with power from on high.' "

Andrew stopped and looked over at the ever-squinting Harry, who pulled the Bible back and turned the pages to Acts, chapter one. Then he handed the Bible back to Andrew and pointed to verse eight.

" 'But ye shall receive power, after that the Holy Ghost is come upon you,' " Andrew read, " 'and ye shall be witnesses unto me both in Jerusalem, and in all Judea, and in Samaria, and unto the uttermost part of the earth.' "

Before Andrew was even finished, Harry had pulled one of his books down from a shelf and was fingering through it. Andrew could see that it was from a biography about Dwight Moody, the great American evangelist who founded the Moody Bible Institute. Harry nodded finally and handed Andrew the book, pointing to the top of one of its pages.

Andrew took a few moments to read the paragraphs in front of where Harry had pointed, then he started in, " 'Moody continued to hunger for a deepening of his own spiritual life and experience. He had been greatly used of God but felt that there were much greater things in store for him. The year 1871 was a critical one with him. He realized more and more how little he was fitted by personal acquirements for his work, and how much he needed to be qualified for service by the Holy Spirit's power. This realization was deepened by conversations he had with two ladies who sat on the front pew in his church. He could see by the expression of their faces that they were praying. At the close of the service they would say to him, "We have been praying for you." "Why don't you pray for the people?" Mr. Moody would ask. "Because you need the power of the Spirit" was the reply. "I need the power! Why," said he, "I thought I had power. I had the largest congregation in Chicago and there were many conversions. I was in a sense satisfied. But right along those two godly women kept praying for me, and their sincere talk about anointing for special service set me thinking. I asked them to come and talk with me, and they poured out their hearts in prayer that I might receive the filling of the Holy Spirit. There came a great hunger into my soul. I did not know what it was. I began to cry out as I never did before. I really felt that I did not want to live if I could not have this power for service." ' "

Andrew skimmed the page before coming to this part, which he again read out loud for Harry's sake: " 'I was crying all the time that God would fill me with His Spirit. Well, one day, in the city of New York—oh, what a day!—I cannot describe it, I seldom refer to it; it is almost too sacred an experience to name. Paul had an experience of which he never spoke for fourteen years. I can only say that God revealed Himself to me, and I had such an experience of His love that I had to ask Him to stay His hand. I went to preaching again. The sermons were not different; I did not present any new truths; and yet hundreds were converted. I would not now be placed back where I was before that blessed experience if you should give me all the world.' "

Andrew closed the book slowly and slid it across the desk to Harry. Harry handed him another book, this one entitled *The Baptism of the Holy Spirit*, by R. A. Torrey.

"I'm sorry, Uncle Harry, but I really can't handle any more," Andrew said, pushing the Torrey book back across the desk. "What you pointed out is more than enough for me. Maybe when I come out next time we can look at it."

Harry shook his head and pushed the book back to Andrew, then he pointed at Andrew with his forefinger.

"You want me to take this one home," Andrew acknowledged. The grin on Harry's face widened and he nodded. "Maybe I should just go back to being patient? Do you think?"

Harry puckered his lips and slowly shook his head no. "S . . . seek," he whispered.

Chapter 14

*E*dgar Mitchell had pulled the limousine over to the curb, obviously intent on hearing every word that Christina had to say about her meeting with her grandfather. Christina had assumed he would enjoy her story, especially how she set up the sting and thoroughly embarrassed him in front of the entire office, but the expression on Edgar's face never changed. If anything, Edgar's mood only seemed to grow more somber as she ended the story.

Tipping his driver's cap back and rubbing his forehead, Edgar looked like he was going to say something, but instead started the car back up and pulled away from the curb without a word. Christina watched the older man's eyes in the rearview mirror but could not tell whether he was sad or angry.

"I thought you might find my story humorous," Christina finally spoke up. "My roommate laughed until the tears were rolling. She thought I did pretty good."

"She obviously doesn't know your grandfather, Christina," Edgar replied, glancing at her in the mirror.

"Meaning what? Did he get angry with Grandmother? I never mentioned—"

"Not to my knowledge," Edgar cut her off. "He said nothing to me, but the receptionist at the office, Mrs. Guild, told me what she knew. He was obviously furious after you left, but he made no attempt to undo the damage. Apparently, he went back into his office, and that was the last of it."

"But you aren't even a little amused?"

The chauffeur's eyes held Christina's in the rearview mirror. He finally said, "No. This is no game, Christina."

"I never said it was a game," Christina stated, her temper immediately flaring. "He had it coming, and you know it. When he threw his money at me, that did it."

Edgar said nothing but looked straight ahead as he drove, which only irritated Christina more.

"Tell me he didn't have it coming," she demanded.

"That's hardly in question," he stated. "But if you're going to shame someone in public, you best be prepared to face the consequences. My fear is that you were dreadfully shortsighted."

"My only fear was for Grandmother," Christina replied. "And I gave no hint that I had contacted her, so she is spared. I don't see where the damage can come."

"Because you don't know your grandfather."

"What more is there to know?"

"Whatever you may think about your grandfather," Edgar said as he turned the limousine into the Adlers' wide driveway, "you should have known that it was the shame of your mother's pregnancy, and the pride of the family name, that caused him to react as he did. You shamed him, though, in a way that your mother never would have. No one has ever done that to him. I can't imagine what thoughts have been going through his head since then. He may have deserved it—he may have deserved something far worse—but let me assure you there will be consequences. You drove a spike into his pride, and unless something changes his heart, he will strike back."

Christina's heart seemed to flutter erratically. She gripped her hands together in her lap and they felt moist. She managed to breathe out, "How so?"

Edgar pulled the car to a stop under the white portico in front of the Adler mansion, then turned around to look at Christina. "I don't know, but you will need to keep your eyes wide open. Anyone with as much money and as many connections as your grandfather can pull a lot of strings in this town. The nature of his business is to discover the other guy's weakness and then to exploit it. For your sake, I hope he doesn't stoop so low. But if I hear something, I'll let you know."

"Like what, though?" Christina questioned, still a bit stunned. "What do I have that he would go after?"

"I don't know, but he has ways of making it very hard on people," Edgar said, then opened his door and got out.

Christina looked out the window and saw her grandmother standing at the mansion's large double door. Edgar came around the limousine and opened Christina's door. She exited the car and walked toward her grandmother.

"You weren't followed?" Grace Adler called out.

"What?" Christina asked.

"No, ma'am," Edgar answered from behind Christina. "And as far as I could tell, there was no one watching the apartment."

"Good," Grace replied.

"Grandmother, what's—"

"Mrs. Adler, the situation is far graver than the way Mrs. Guild described it," Edgar Mitchell broke in. "I am quite sure, based on what Miss Ellington has told me, that there will be consequences."

"Oh no!" Grace gasped. "What do you suggest we do?"

"I think it would be wise, for a time at least, to not meet like this," Edgar answered. "Hopefully, nothing will come of this. But better to be safe than sorry."

"You're right," Grace replied. "Thank you, Edgar."

"This is just a little bit crazy, isn't it?" Christina said to her grandmother. "Next thing you're going to tell me that my grandfather is linked to organized crime."

"Come on in," Grace said, holding the door open as Christina walked past her into the spacious entryway to the mansion. "And, no, your grandfather is not a gangster, just a hard-nosed businessman who is not known to show mercy."

It took a few seconds for Christina's eyes to adjust from the late summer sunshine to the relative darkness inside the mansion. She followed her grandmother across the marble-floored entryway, past the long marble staircase, and into the sprawling sitting room with its three huge glass windows framed in Greek columns and its lofty chandelier hanging from the arched ceiling. Her grandmother led the way across the Persian rug to high-back chairs with golden upholstery.

Christina sat down next to her grandmother, who started to pour coffee from a white English stoneware teapot into cups. On her first visit to the mansion, Christina had only had a chance to glance into this room, but now that she was inside, even a casual look around easily distracted her thoughts from her grandfather. She took a few moments to study the many details and fineries of the room. Everything was perfect, each detail fitting together precisely, all the colors and shapes and spacing of the room's furnishings in harmony.

"This room is a decorator's dream come true," Christina breathed, her eyes drinking in its serenity. "I've been in a lot of expensive homes, but this room rivals anything I've seen. Who was the decorator? Let me guess. It reminds me of a room I saw in the Stafford home when I was painting their twin daughters. Let's see. They told me the decorator was Jerome ... Hamill ... Hamilton. Am I correct?"

"No, not even close," Grace replied, handing her a cup and saucer. "But I appreciate the comparison. I'll tell the decorator your exact words."

"Theodore Mecklenburg?"

"No. You'll never guess it in a million years," her grandmother answered, her soft smile breaking through and erasing a serious frown. "I put this room together myself many years ago. Your mother was probably around sixteen years old at the time. I had great hopes for this room—hopes that we'd have lots of people over to entertain—but look at the fabric on these chairs. It's faded a bit over the years, but it's hardly been sat upon."

"You decorated this room?"

"The whole house, my dear. What else did I have to do?"

"But where did you learn all this?"

"I read a lot. I studied different room layouts whenever we visited other people's homes, and I experimented a bit," Grace replied. "It took me a few tries to get it right."

"That's a wonderful talent," Christina said. "You could have been a designer."

Her grandmother shrugged her shoulders. "I suppose, but William would never have considered that a possibility," she said. "I guess I preferred gardening, anyway. I couldn't see any reason to keep redesigning the inside of this house, so I took my interests into the backyard. With the plants and flowers and shrubs and trees, everything is always changing out there. I enjoy making the most of it."

Christina sipped her coffee and wondered at the white-haired woman. "And your backyard is living proof of that," she said. "What else don't I know about you? You're a poet as well, I suppose?"

"No, not me. Your mother was the creative writer of the family, but I'm sure you're aware of that," Grace replied. "Which reminds me, I've got something to show you before you leave today."

"My mother writes well, but what do you mean by a 'writer'?"

"A novelist. She used to tell me the most wonderful stories. And I'll bet she always told you stories when she would put you to bed at night."

"She did. And I've never read those stories anywhere else."

"That's no surprise. She probably made most of them up in her head while she was putting you down. Has she ever written the stories out?"

"No, I don't think so," Christina answered, "but then again, it seems like there's a lot I don't know about people these days ... like my grandfather. Do you really believe he'd have someone follow me?"

Grace shook her head and said, "I really don't think so, but Edgar knows more about how he operates. My husband rarely talks with me about his business dealings, and I never ask. Edgar says it's not unusual for him to hire private investigators when he's looking for ways to close a sale. You're certainly better off if he doesn't know that you and I have met ... and so am I."

"So, he didn't say anything to you after I went to his office?"

"No, but he came home early, which he seldom does," Grace said. "And he was brooding all night, pacing around the den and muttering to himself. I knew something was disturbing him, and it had nothing to do with work. I hoped that he hadn't found out about you, but Edgar told me what Mrs. Guild had told him. I should have warned you to not go to him, but I never dreamed you'd do it. Why did you? What did you hope to gain?"

Christina looked into her grandmother's green eyes, a constant reminder of her mother, and said, "Over two weeks had gone by since I heard from you, and I guess I figured that our discussion with Maria had gone nowhere, even though I thought she gave you some excellent advice. Hearing what you've said about him, I ... just couldn't take it any longer. If I had never met you, if I didn't know anything about the past, I would not have bothered. But ... now that I'm involved, I couldn't stand by without confronting him. I don't care if he comes after me. I did what I felt I had to do. He tried to pay me off, to keep my mouth shut."

Grace set her coffee cup down and swallowed hard, then she closed her eyes and ran her fingers across her forehead. "Oh, I'm so sorry," she said softly. "I should have contacted you, but I haven't known what to do about this. Even at the worst, though, I can't imagine what's happened. You must have really scared William terribly."

"I scared him? He wasn't the one who was shaking."

"I've never understood this about your grandfather," said Grace, taking a deep breath. "But despite all appearances, deep down inside, he's an extremely insecure man. He's always feared that the day he shows a sign of weakness will be the day his success ends. He has spent his life making sure that never happens—even if it meant losing his only child. It wasn't that way when your mother was younger, but the older she got, the worse it seemed to plague him."

"And you just sat back and let him get worse?" Christina blurted out, regretting the words even as she said them. "I'm sorry, I didn't—"

"No, don't be sorry. You're more right than wrong," her grandmother stated. "For years I did try to talk with him about it, especially when he began to pull back from other people so no one could really know him. We did fight bitterly over your mother, but when she left I . . . ah . . . I gave up hope. I couldn't save my own daughter, so why try to save him?"

"What did you conclude after talking with Maria?"

Grace frowned and twisted her mouth, then she looked at Christina and said, "I concluded that I have done a great job of lying to myself for well over twenty years. How I interpreted my wedding vows was a convenient way of excusing my cowardice. Did I say your grandfather was insecure? Well, I look in the mirror and see his equal."

"So what does that mean?" Christina felt like screaming. She stood up feeling frustrated and suddenly helpless, then sank back down into the cushions. "Your daughter, who never said anything bitter about her past, has not heard from you in all these years. You can't mean to tell me that you would allow him to stand in the way of your loving her . . . and I know that you love her deeply. Loving and honoring your husband does not mean not loving your daughter."

Grace looked away, her hands folded in her lap.

"You let him take away your only daughter ... and now you'll let him take me out of your life as well," Christina railed, wanting to give her grandmother a good shake. Tears welled in her eyes. "I hate it! I wish I had never known this."

"I don't know what to do or where to start, Christina. It's such a terrible mess, and I am so afraid. I can't just run into his office and shame him like you did."

"Why not! Why not?"

"Because it could crush him," Grace said. "If he sees himself for who he really is, I fear his reaction. I'm hoping something will happen— somehow a way will open for him to take the first step. But confronting him, as you did, can only make it worse. I'm sure of it."

"So you want me to sit around and twiddle my thumbs?"

"I didn't want you to do anything," Grace answered. "But after talking with Maria that day, I've started to pray about it again. You could pray with me."

"No, that I can't do," Christina said, shaking her head and standing up. "You'd best ask Maria for help in that department. God makes no sense to me, and I'm feeling like I need to leave. The longer I'm here, the more I want to head downtown and have another chat with my grandfather. It makes me so angry that I'm not sure I care how crushed he feels."

"I'd really like you to stay."

"I can't. I can't stay and keep silent."

Grace finally stood and put her hand on Christina's arm. "I was hoping you'd go up to your mother's room and go through it thoroughly," she said. "I know you'll find other things that you'll treasure ... like the blue hat. We may not have another opportunity to do this, so, please, I want you to take whatever you'd like."

"No, I can't do that either."

"Why?"

"Because the room belongs to my mother, and until she comes to claim it, I really don't have a right to go through it and take what I want," Christina stated. "I haven't even been able to write my mother about having met you. It doesn't seem fair to tell her until you decide what you're going to do regarding her. You have a chance, Grandmother, to do something about this. But if you won't, all the treasures will have to stay trapped in that room with your memories. Please, if you could call Edgar, I'd like to leave."

"Just let me get you one thing, that's all I ask," Grace said, holding up her hand and walking toward the door.

"What is it?"

"Just one thing," her grandmother answered. "It's up in Rebecca's room. I'll be right back."

Christina walked out of the sitting room and stopped at the bottom of the marble staircase, looking up at the landing. She could hear the light tap of her grandmother's shoes across the upstairs hallway.

"Here it is," Grace said, carefully holding a thick black leather pouch with a zipper across the top as she made her way down the wide staircase. "I found this in one of her drawers. She was writing this at the time she left, but she never told me she was doing it. You have to have this, Christina."

Her grandmother's last sentence was delivered as a command, and when Grace handed Christina the pouch, she took it without resisting.

"What is it?" Christina finally asked, fingering the old leather sides.

"It's a book," her grandmother whispered. "A wonderful story . . . that's unfinished. I'm sure it's meant for you."

Chapter 15

"I'll bet you'll never stop by for another quick chat," Andrew said, leaning back against the front bumper of Stuart Anderson's car with his arms crossed. A light fall breeze rattled the leaves in the maple tree in front of the parsonage. "I really didn't mean to unload my frustrations on you, but you came by at just the right time."

Stuart smiled and said, "It's really not a problem, Andrew. With my crazy schedule, it's been years since Annie tried planning a suppertime. She's not going to mind if I'm a little late tonight. But why discuss this with an old country doctor like me rather than someone in the ministry?"

"Truthfully," Andrew replied, "I'm still getting to know some of the local pastors, and based on what our seminary professors taught, I don't think I'd get much of a hearing from them on this if I wrote them. Rebecca told me about how you felt God calling you into medicine, although your original plans were to go into the ministry. I thought there might be something from your experience that would be helpful."

Stuart nodded and loosened his black tie as he sat down on a wooden lawn bench. "Perhaps, but I doubt it," he answered. "As a young man, I dreamed of becoming a pastor like my grandfather, who became recognized as one of the finest Presbyterian ministers in the nation. But that was not to be. After my first year at the university, God used a tragic accident, followed by the shocking advice from the elderly doctor in Bradford, to show me my true gift was in medicine. At the time it happened, I'd never considered becoming a doctor. It took a fair amount of convincing for me to believe it was the thing I was to do."

"I understand that an old iron bridge in Bradford collapsed, trapping Annie in the water beneath the bridge, and that you saved her life. Is that what did it?"

"It was at the bridge, but it was actually helping the other person who was injured that day that caused me to consider becoming a doctor. You must have met Walter Sorenson by now?"

"The tall, gangly man who owns the drugstore in Bradford? The one with the bum arm?"

"That's right. That arm was pinned beneath one of the bridge's iron beams when my father and I pulled him out of the wreckage. It's hard to describe how his shattered arm affected me, but the fact that I stopped the bleeding and helped save his life set the tone for the rest of my life. I simply knew this was what I was meant to do."

"Any regrets?"

"No, not one." Stuart grinned at Andrew. "As my mother often pointed out to me, I lack several basic traits that make for a good pastor, and I'm sure I would have been very unhappy in the ministry. God made me to be a doctor, and because I've been faithful to the calling He put on my heart, I believe I've been able to make more of a difference in the lives of people than had I gone into the church ministry."

"You've certainly had a big impact on this community. Everyone speaks highly of you, but it's much more than just your doctoring. People tell me how you've prayed with them about their problems, how you've comforted them, and how you are generous to them in terms of paying or not paying their bills in these hard times. It's very impressive."

"Thank you, and I appreciate their saying so," Stuart said. "I've simply been a Christian who has enjoyed his practice as a doctor. But my experience . . . I don't see it as all that relevant to what you're going through."

"What?"

"I don't see how the redirection of my life relates to your situation. Nothing you've told me suggests that you doubt whether God called you into the ministry, and coming from one who is a lifelong observer of pastors, I'd say that God has given you all the gifts you need to do the job. What I hear you saying is that you're not satisfied with the results of your ministry. Correct?"

"Yes, I suppose you're right."

"And what is it that you want to see happen that's different? I've only heard a few of your sermons, but they were outstanding."

"Thank you," Andrew said. "Coming from you, I take that as a real compliment. But as important as it is to have a good sermon, I want to get beyond that. I feel like . . . a doctor who sits in his office all day, dispensing wonderful theories of medicine but never actually making contact with his patients. It's like everything is in place except the most important part. I want to see changed lives."

"So you think your uncle Harry is right?"

"I hate to admit it, but I do. I've spent a lot of time reading and praying about it, and I've concluded that when Jesus told His disciples to remain in Jerusalem until they had received power from on high, He meant the power to prevail with God and men, the power to impart saving impressions on the minds of men. The disciples were not lacking in knowledge or love or sincerity, but they needed God's power to make the truth as transforming as Jesus had promised it would be."

"That rings true," Stuart agreed. "I've often felt that we treat the church like a piece of machinery. We will preach, pray, teach, and give as machines . . . unless the Spirit of God is with us. Have you ever read any of the sermons of that famous British preacher, Charles Spurgeon?"

"No, but I probably should. Maybe Uncle Harry will be passing me copies of Spurgeon next, now that I've read Torrey."

"Spurgeon is wonderful to read, I can assure you. My grandfather had a favorite quote from him that you might appreciate. Spurgeon once said, 'How much there is of church work that is nothing more than the movement of a galvanized corpse. If the Spirit of God is absent, all that the church does will be as lifeless as the rustle of leaves above a tomb, like the congregation of the dead turning over in their graves.' Isn't that profound!"

"Yes, and it's exactly how I feel."

"And you've been pastoring how many months? Think of spending a lifetime feeling that way."

"No thank you. I need to solve this soon."

"But how?"

"That's what I'm asking you. You seem to have a real spiritual influence on your patients. What can you tell me about the Holy Spirit in your life?"

Stuart raised his eyebrows and blew out a breath of air. "Attempting an answer to that question makes me a little nervous. You weren't here when the supposed miracle worker came through a few years ago talking unceasingly about the Holy Spirit. He did so much damage to people's faith that just talking out loud today about 'Holy Ghost power' makes one a suspect. Despite the discredit he did to the Holy Spirit, I do have some definite beliefs regarding Him. If I share them with you, you won't brand me as a heretic, will you?"

"No, but I'm aware of the dangers of going too far."

"Too little . . . or too much—both are problems," Stuart said. "The only safe place is believing what the Word of God clearly states, but discovering that took me a long time and involved a lot of searching. It started with the simple truth that God's promise of the power of the Holy Spirit was given to every believer, not just to ministers. Do you agree with that?"

"Certainly. That's absolutely clear in the book of Acts. Every believer is called to preach the gospel, whatever their profession might be."

"Once I believed that, then I struggled to come to terms with the person of the Holy Spirit," Stuart continued. "For years I only thought of the Holy Spirit as an influence, but when it dawned on me that He is a person—a person as real and as dynamic as Jesus Christ—dwelling in my heart, that changed everything. The Holy Spirit is a wonderful, gracious person, who loves us and desires to work in us. The day finally came when I understood that He desired to be the God of my life— personally . . . inside me. That was revolutionary to my faith."

"I understand that much . . . I think," Andrew said, taking a deep breath. "But as I've opened my heart to the Holy Spirit, it's like He's been shining a light on the deepest parts of my soul. I can't tell you, though, how awful it is . . . the sin that He's revealed. When I started praying about this, I thought it was because I wanted to glorify God more, but He's shown me that my real motive was to elevate myself. It's so ugly, Stuart, I'm almost too ashamed to admit the truth. I want my ministry to affect lives in such a way that I'll be recognized as a great pastor and church leader. It's about me, and not Jesus Christ."

"That's exactly what the Holy Spirit does, as painful as it is. When He reveals sin in our lives, it's never a pretty picture," Stuart added. "We all have to die, but we don't die easy."

"Say that again."

"I said that if we truly want to live for Christ, we have to die—to selfishness and sin," Stuart said. "We have to utterly surrender ourselves to Him, and that sounds a lot easier than it is. Jesus said that apart from Him we can do nothing—absolutely nothing. But we don't believe that. We keep thinking that we can do it, if we just try harder, or pray more, or say just the right words in just the right way. Look at how powerless the disciples were to make an impact upon Jerusalem before the Holy Spirit came upon them; then look at them afterward. Who would have dreamed that such an insignificant little group, hiding behind closed doors, could suddenly be impassioned with a message that would transform not only the city of Jerusalem but the whole world?"

"This is where I seem to be stuck. I think I'm surrendered, but then I see more of my selfishness, and it seems like there's no limit to it. What do I do?"

"Seems to me that you do what the first disciples did. Continue to wait upon God, asking the Holy Spirit to search your heart and reveal any other sin that He desires to cleanse from your life," Stuart offered. "There is absolutely no use asking God to give you power from on high if you're holding back parts of your life and will not surrender your will to Him. In my life it even involved letting go of control over how I wanted God to meet me. I tried to tell Him exactly when and how He should pour out His spiritual power. God will come in His own way, and one must never limit His working."

"This is agonizing," Andrew muttered, dragging his fingers through his dark hair. "I don't know if it'll ever end."

"I know the feeling, but don't rush it," Stuart urged. "God knows what He's doing. When you're truly ready, believing God's promise will be the easiest step of all. By faith you need to receive the Holy Spirit in His fullness, but it starts with a heart that's ready. We always want to run ahead, and when we get there, we mess things up. Then God has to start the lesson over again. Better to wait for His timing and refuse to dictate the terms. Not everyone gets to hear a mighty rushing wind or have a tongue of fire rest on his head."

"Well, either one sounds pretty good to me right now."

"And it might happen that way. But remember: all you need is a spark to set a forest on fire. A spark is sufficient to begin with, for fire multiplies itself until nothing can put it out. If God can take a reluctant prophet like Jonah and bring all of Ninevah to repentance by one simple sentence repeated over and over, think of what He can do through your preaching of His gospel. He can carry the words of truth that you speak and fill them full of life and fire. If the Holy Spirit rests upon you, other souls will be set ablaze with a desire for God. It happened for the disciples, and the Holy Spirit is no less present today."

Andrew raised his eyebrows and nodded, then he stood up straight and stretched. "You'd never know it, based on the response I got to my last sermon. I can't see much point in going through the motions and getting nothing but nice smiles at the end. I'm not much good at pretending things are all right when they're not. But I appreciate your advice. You should offer your teaching services to our seminary. No one there ever spoke of the Holy Spirit as you have."

"Perhaps they've never struggled to understand Him as I have," Stuart said as he stood up slowly from the wooden bench. "If you're taught that the power of the Holy Spirit diminished after the death of the apostles, why would you seek for it? It's a shame, both in our churches and in our personal lives, that we give so little place to the Holy Spirit. Try to read the book of Acts or the various epistles and imagine what they would be like if the early church had limited the role of the Holy Spirit as we have."

"There wouldn't be much there to talk about, that's for sure," Andrew replied, reaching out to shake Stuart's hand. "Thank you again for your counsel. I may call upon your services from time to time."

"You're welcome, and call me whenever you want to talk," Stuart offered as he shook Andrew's hand. "And don't count out your uncle and aunt. Sounds to me like Harry has some real insight and wisdom, Andrew. Perhaps he's able to hear God's voice better because he's not so busy talking all the time like we do. If I were you, I'd enlist him as my prayer partner."

"I'm quite sure I already have," Andrew said, "and he's not going to let me off the hook until I get this right."

Andrew leaned back in his chair and gazed over the shelves of books that his uncle had managed to collect over the years. "Uncle Harry, I came here today simply to ask you to pray with me, not to give me more information to think about. I don't think I can preach Sunday if God doesn't give me some inner peace. Could we skip the reading this time?"

Harry looked up from behind the Bible and other books that were on his desk and squinted at Andrew, shaking his head, then raised two fingers.

Taking in a deep breath, Andrew sighed and nodded in surrender. He picked up the Bible and looked down to the twelfth verse of Hosea ten where Harry was pointing, then he read, " 'Break up your fallow ground: for it is time to seek the Lord, till he come and rain righteousness upon you.' Now, that sounds familiar. I don't think there's much left inside me that's not been broken up."

Harry's twisted half smile was beaming across his face as he reached over and pressed his finger against Andrew's heart. Then he slid a book across his desk and pointed to the top paragraph of one of its opened pages.

"Charles Finney," Andrew said with a chuckle. "Not a favorite evangelist around our seminary. You're going to get me into trouble if you keep insisting that I read from these dubious sources, Uncle Harry."

Harry shrugged his shoulders and pointed again to the paragraph.

"Okay, I'll read it. 'In breaking up your unplowed ground, you must remove every obstruction. Don't put it off; that will only make the matter worse. Confess to God those sins that have been committed against God, and to man those sins that have been committed against man. Don't think of getting off by going around the stumbling block. Take them up out of the way. Things may be left that you may think little things, and you may wonder why you have not broke through to God, when the reason is that your proud and carnal mind has covered up something that God has put His finger on. Break up all the ground and turn it over. Do not balk at it, as the farmers say; do not turn aside for little difficulties; drive the plow right through them, beam deep, and turn the ground all up, so that it may be mellow and soft and ready to receive the seed and bear fruit a hundredfold.'

"I think . . . I hope . . . that the plow has done its work, Uncle Harry," Andrew continued, still gazing at the page. "Every time I've gone to pray in the past few weeks, the Holy Spirit seems to bring something different to my attention—a bad attitude, a sin, a lie I've believed. The conviction seems to have finally come to an end. What's the other Scripture you want me to read?"

Harry took the Bible and opened it to Matthew three, then pointed to verse eleven as he handed the Bible to Andrew.

"John the Baptist," Andrew mumbled as he looked at the text. " 'I indeed baptize you with water unto repentance: but he that cometh after me is mightier than I, whose shoes I am not worthy to bear: he shall baptize you with the Holy Ghost, and with fire.' That doesn't leave much room for wondering what the role of the Holy Spirit is, does it?"

Shaking his head, Harry lifted one finger and took down a commentary by Alexander Maclaren from an overhead shelf. He turned the pages and came to where he wanted, then he slid the thick book to Andrew.

" 'Fire purifies,' " Andrew began. " 'When the love of God is shed abroad in our hearts by the Holy Spirit, His love will purify us and sever us from our sins. Nothing else will. Moralities and the externals of religion will wash away the foulness that lies on the surface, but stains that have sunk deep into the very substance of the soul and have dyed every thread in warp and woof to its center are not gotten rid of so. God be thanked, there is a mightier detergent than all these—even the divine Spirit that Christ gives and that divine forgiveness that Christ brings. There, and there alone, we can lose all the guilt of our faultful past and receive a new and better life that will mold our future into growing likeness to His great purity. Do not resist that merciful searching fire that is ready to penetrate our very bones and marrow and burn up the seeds of death that lurk in the inmost intents of the heart! Let Him plunge you into that gracious baptism as we put some poor piece of foul clay into the fire, and like it, as you glow, you will whiten, and all the spots will melt away before the conquering tongues of the cleansing flame.' "

Andrew closed the commentary and bowed his head. "I am the foul clay, Uncle Harry," he whispered. "I am stained to the depths of my being. God have mercy on me."

That said, Harry wrapped his strong right arm around Andrew and held him tightly. Andrew closed his eyes and opened his heart to the heavenly Father as the gentle man began to pray in fervent words that only heaven could understand. And in that moment, the sweet presence of Jesus filled the room with an intensity so real and so bright that Andrew was afraid to open his eyes. Joy and peace swept through his soul as one word from Harry came through with absolute clarity: "Jesus."

Chapter 16

Christina stepped back from the canvas and gazed over her most recent illustration with a subdued sense of pleasure. The painting of a local banker's daughter and her huge Saint Bernard walking down a snowy Chicago street had come out far better than she imagined, although she wished now that she had put more color variation into the girl's coat and hat. But having successfully made up the snowy environment and wintry sky without any strong visual references was an achievement that brought Christina great delight. And she was thrilled with the carefree expression she had caught on the little girl's face as she followed the lead of her gigantic protector.

Christina's teacher and mentor, Carl Langstan, stood next to her, rubbing his chin and observing the painting as well. Slender and tall with a thick shock of unruly blond hair that crowned his gaunt Nordic face, Carl's most noteworthy feature was his deep-set blue eyes. Whatever came under the focus of his eyes also came under his analytical scrutiny, like a sky-born predatory bird that has eyed its prey.

"I really don't understand," he finally said, shaking his head. "This is not nearly up to your capabilities, Christina. Actually . . . your past three paintings lacked your earlier promise. Has something got you distracted?"

Totally unprepared for this comment, Christina's deep blue eyes went immediately to her teacher's eyes, but he did not look away from the canvas. While he always had specific instructions on what he felt she could do better, he had never been critical of her overall work. "Yes," she was quick to respond, desperately scanning the canvas for what it was that her teacher was seeing that she had missed. "I've had some personal matters that have been a distraction. But ... I didn't think it was affecting my painting. I thought ... by way of your comments ... you were quite pleased with my last three paintings, especially the landscapes. You said that the lighting—"

"You must have read more into my comments than I intended," Carl interrupted her, finally glancing at Christina momentarily. "I've told you repeatedly that your palette has gotten far too restrictive, that your attention to lighting has diminished to amateurish, and that the integrity of your compositions is breaking down. This is your poorest attempt yet. I cannot tolerate such inferior work."

Immediately fighting back tears, Christina struggled to maintain her composure as her mind reeled at each of the accusations. "I'm sorry ... but ... you've never even hinted that you were displeased with my work," she gasped. "You never said any of those things. If I had—"

"Are you calling me a liar, Christina?"

"No, I ... ah ... I just don't recall your ever saying what you just said," Christina objected, talking with her hands. "You said my landscape was a brilliant—"

"I said your landscape was a brilliant setting, but that your painting lacked focus and definition. A strong layout does not overcome a lazy man's painting, and you've been cheating on the details. You're not seeing the shadows or adding in details that take a painting above the ordinary. I'm afraid you've become just another painter who'll be painting rich people's children for the rest of your life."

With a disgusted grunt, Carl Langstan turned and began to walk away.

"I don't believe you, Professor Langstan," Christina blurted out, stopping him in his tracks. "I don't know what's gone wrong, but this is not like you."

"I told you ... in the beginning," he replied, turning around slowly, "that any student of mine has to be prepared to receive instruction and criticism. It sounds to me like you're having second thoughts."

"I was prepared for both, and I've received both in the past ... without objection," Christina said, still groping to understand her instructor's strange behavior. "But what is this? You turn away from my painting without anything but a general disapproval. Professor Stanley walked by and told me it was the most refreshing illustration he's seen in this studio in months."

"Professor Stanley is not your instructor," Carl snapped back with a sharp glare in his eyes. "And I find it offensive that you would play his comments against mine. Either receive my review as I gave it, or find another teacher. I don't have time for students who feel they know more than I do."

"Such a thought has never crossed my mind," Christina pled, holding her hands out in appeal. "But I've worked on this painting for over three weeks, and I think it deserves a closer look. Dr. Stanley said that the composition was extraordinary. How can he be that wrong?"

"I warned you not to play him against me," her instructor said flatly. "Given your attitude, please take whatever belongs to you here and leave. Unless Professor Stanley wants to pick you up as one of his students. But I'm afraid his style and yours are hardly compatible. Good-bye, Christina."

"No, this isn't right!" Christina protested, her voice cracking. "You owe me more than this. I earned every dollar for these lessons, and you can't pull out of it before we've finished. There's still—"

"I can pull out of any arrangement I have with any student, and I owe you nothing," the professor railed. "Why don't you go to Paris to study. Perhaps the painter from Vichy would take you under consideration. You're one of his ardent admirers, and they say he likes to work with attractive young women."

Christina stood silently in disbelief with Carl Langstan's last words ringing in her ears as the blond-haired man turned and exited the art studio. All at the same moment she wanted to cry, scream, and run away. During the countless hours she had spent with him in the past two years, he had never even joked in such a manner as this. When the door clicked shut, she was left in utter silence and shock.

Her immediate thought was to follow Langstan to his office and make her appeal, but his final words were so repugnant, she never wanted to see him again. "How can it end like this . . . with a man whom I've admired for so long?" she whispered to herself, gazing around the studio for the limited number of items that belonged to her. She slowly gathered up her brushes and paints, then carefully rolled up the canvas of the girl and her dog. Nearly every canvas she had painted had been sold to pay for her classes, so it didn't take long to gather her belongings into a tall, skinny cardboard box that someone had left behind.

Carrying her materials out of the studio and down a long inner stairway to the street, Christina stepped out onto the sidewalk in a bit of a daze, hardly noticing the picture-perfect fall day. A cool breeze rippled the yellow and red leaves in the maple tree above her, but she saw little except the haunting memory of the strange expression on Carl Langstan's face. As she continued on down the street toward her apartment building, it began to sink in that it really was over, and that whatever had triggered the sudden reversal in her instructor's opinion of her was not about to change.

She took her time on the walk home. There was no reason to hurry to her apartment, because there would be no class the following day to prepare for. She recounted their conversation over and over, wondering why Langstan had suggested she consider going to Paris. It was something the two of them had discussed many times, and Langstan was well aware of her fear of the extreme nationalism of the Nazis in neighboring Germany. With Hitler's vow to avenge Germany's defeat in World War I and his violation of the Treaty of Versailles by sending German soldiers into the Rhineland during the previous year, she would never consider going to France. The thought that her father had died on French soil from a German bullet was sufficient to keep her on American soil.

It was all too strange for Christina to comprehend. None of the pieces fit together in any way. Approaching her apartment building, she opened the front door absentmindedly, plodded softly up the wooden stairway to the second-floor hallway, then turned to the right and nearly crashed into her landlord. "Mr. Goodwin! I didn't see you standing there!" she cried, pulling herself backward to avoid him. "My mind is elsewhere. Sorry."

"No, it's my fault," the elderly man said. "I heard you coming and should have stepped aside."

"Why is our door open?" Christina asked, looking past the landlord to her apartment. "Is something wrong? Where's Josie?"

"She's gone already," Mr. Goodwin answered coldly. "Read the notice on your door. I'll give you till tomorrow afternoon to be out as well."

"What are talking about?" Christina protested. "We've paid our rent on time every month since I've been here, and we're paid through the end of September. You can't just force us out. Where did Josie go?"

"Read the eviction notice before you tell me what I can't do. It's perfectly legal," the landlord growled as he began to walk away. "Everyone living on this floor signed the complaint against your apartment. And I have no idea where mousy little Josie went. She gathered her stuff, called a taxi, dropped off the key, and is long gone. Didn't even close the door when she left. You make sure you only take what belongs to you, and give me your key before you leave. I'll be watchin' the front door for when you go."

"Mr. Goodwin," Christina said, "Josie and I never did anything the least bit questionable in this apartment. We didn't even allow men we dated to come up to our room. What could anyone complain about?"

The landlord sighed and turned around slowly. "It don't matter to me what it was," he spat the words, "but I believe the notice states that the two of you were involved repeatedly in drunken and lewd behavior with several men that spilled out into the hallway and offended your neighbors. I can't have that in this building. This ain't no dive, and I won't let you give it a bad reputation."

Christina burst out laughing at the ridiculous charge, which only lengthened the scowl on the landlord's pie-shaped face. "You can't possibly be serious," she sputtered, setting down her box of art supplies and taking the legal notice from the door. "Mr. Goodwin, we're the quietest residents you have in this building, and we've never brought a bottle of liquor into our room. You know this is a lie."

"You don't get it, do you?" he replied. "I don't care whether it's the biggest lie ever told. I want you out of this building by tomorrow afternoon or else I call the police. They delivered the notice, and they'll be stopping by to enforce it if you have a mind to disobey. I've heard some of Chicago's finest can get real nasty when it comes to eviction deadlines."

As the footsteps of the heavyset man clomped down the wooden stairway, Christina stood in the hallway studying the eviction notice. Mr. Goodwin's words proved to be absolutely accurate. The document was clearly legal and binding, enforceable by the county sheriff's office, and only allowed them one day to move their possessions. A quick glance inside the apartment confirmed that Josie had taken her belongings and was gone.

A door down the hallway opened, and a young married woman stepped through the doorway. She started to lock her door, but when she noticed Christina, she pulled her key back out and reopened the door.

"Helen!" Christina called out, walking toward the woman. "Can you tell me what's going on here? This notice has your signature on it. It accuses Josie and me of—"

The apartment door slammed shut, cutting Christina off, and the lock on the inside of the door clunked heavily into position. Christina stood staring at the painted wooden door, hoping that her cordial relationship with Helen Sommerly would prevail and cause the woman to reopen the door and talk, but a minute of silence eroded that as a mistaken notion. Eviction notice in hand, Christina turned and went into her own apartment and closed the door behind her.

She set the legal document down upon the kitchen table and glanced blankly around the apartment, certain that Josie would not have left without at least writing a good-bye note. But she could find nothing, and it appeared that Josie had packed in a hurry, for she had left behind some of her books. Walking over to the window, Christina shook her head in disbelief and wondered what in the world was going on. She had no idea what she would do or where she would go. Then she heard a familiar child's voice out in the hallway.

Going quickly to her door and opening it, she glanced down the hallway and saw the ten-year-old daughter of one of her neighbors coming toward her. "Sally," she called to the girl, "have you been home all day? I was wondering if you happened to see Josie moving out?"

"Yes, I saw her," Sally responded, nodding her head.

"When?"

"This morning . . . before the police came and put the paper on your door," the girl said. "They were very big men. Did you do something bad?"

"No, sweetheart," Christina replied. "Josie left before the police came?"

"Yes, ma'am."

"By herself?"

"No. The tall man was with her. He carried her clothes and a few boxes down to a taxi."

"Did you know the tall man? Had you seen him before?"

"I don't know his name, but he was the man who came to our door a few days ago," the girl answered knowingly. "Mama sent me to my room, but I peeked."

"Did you see something?"

"I saw Mama sign a piece of paper, and then the man gave Mama some money. Mama's been real happy since then. We don't have much money."

"Grandfather!" Christina whispered to herself. "So he's the one behind all this. No wonder."

"The tall man was your grandfather?"

"Was he bald? Broad shoulders?"

"No. He had thick brown hair and was real skinny. He looked sick."

"It wasn't my grandfather, then, Sally," Christina replied. "But there's no doubt who his employer is. Thank you for your help, Sally. I hope the money helps your family."

The girl said a polite "You're welcome" and continued on down the hallway. Christina turned around and went back into her apartment, closed the door behind her, and leaned back against it.

"Edgar was right," she whispered to herself, closing her eyes and regretting the day she had stepped into her grandfather's office. While she had thought herself so poor that her grandfather would find nothing worth taking from her, she never considered how devastating it would be if he cut her off from her art instructor. "I had no idea whom I was dealing with, or just how hard he was willing to play."

A sudden loud knock on the door behind Christina nearly caused her to scream, but she quickly recovered and said, "Yes, who is it?"

"A friend of your grandfather," a deep voice sounded from the other side of the door.

Christina felt a chill go down her neck and debated for a few moments whether she would respond at all. Then she turned around and slowly opened the door. The tall man with the thick brown hair did not look the least bit intimidating, which restored some of Christina's confidence. "I didn't know that my grandfather had any friends," she said. "I heard that you've spread some early Christmas cheer to the entire second floor. How much did it cost between Professor Langstan and the folks here in this building?"

"Not much, actually," the man replied. "Even your silly little roommate grabbed the few bucks I offered her. If she's one of your better friends, you don't have much to brag about."

"With the eviction notice, it doesn't look like you gave her much choice but to move on," Christina replied. "You probably mentioned to her that your intention is to drive me away, and that other evictions will follow me until I go wherever it is that my grandfather wants. I assume that you didn't knock on my door to see how I was doing."

"You're a smart girl . . . just like your grandpa," he quipped sarcastically, tapping on the door with his bony fingers. "Tell you what," he said as he reached into his pocket and pulled out a hundred-dollar bill, "let's cut to the chase here. It's as simple as this: you leave town immediately, and I give you this bill. There should be plenty here for your transportation and next apartment. Every month you stay away, you'll get a twenty-dollar bill in the mail. That should buy you an art lesson or two, don't you think?"

Christina shook her head and then burst out laughing. "You are without a doubt the icing on the cake," she declared. "It's not enough for him to take away the art lessons that I treasure and the small apartment I call home. No, now he's got to insult me on top of it all. That, Mr. Friend of My Grandfather Whom I'd Rather Not Know Your Name, was a big mistake, and I think you'd best mosey on back and tell him so. Tell him my price is a lot higher than that."

"Like this much?" he asked with a sickly smile, pulling another hundred-dollar bill out of his pocket.

"Deeper."

Without blinking he pulled out three more bills and handed her the five hundred dollars. "He wants you out of town and no more problems. Understood?"

Christina began to reach out her hand, then smiled and shook her head. "Tell my grandfather that I'm sorry I did what I did in his office. Tell him that my mother would be ashamed of me, even though he deserved it. And tell him that because my mother would never take the money, I can't take it either. I may pay him a visit one of these days, but I promise not to make a scene."

"You stay away or he'll find another way to get at you," the tall man warned. "Did anyone ever tell you that you're an idiot?"

Christina shook her head at him in disgust and then answered, "You're doing my grandfather's dirty work, then you call *me* an idiot?" And with that, she slammed the door.

Chapter 17

"Aunt Lizzy, I can put these away," Andrew said, picking up two glass Mason quart jars of tomato juice and setting them onto one of the upper shelves in the parsonage pantry. Just then Harry came into the pantry lugging a third large crate of canned goods. "Whoa! How much are you giving me? I can't take all of your garden produce!"

"You hush, young man," Elizabeth replied, barely glancing at him. "Look at these empty shelves! Goodness. Don't you realize it'll soon be winter? You planning on getting by without food?"

"I think I'll find a way to survive," Andrew answered. "Now, how much is Uncle Harry bringing in?"

"Twenty quarts of tomato juice," said Elizabeth, "fifteen quarts of applesauce, fifteen quarts of stewed tomatoes, twenty pints of green beans, and thirty pints of corn. Harry has never cared much for tomatoes, so he's pleased to make a donation to the starving pastor drive."

"I can't take this much—"

"We got one hundred and eighty-five quarts of applesauce and pie apples," Elizabeth broke in as she and Andrew continued to stack jars on the pantry shelves. "You let me know when you start running low. My cellar's about ready to burst. We may not have any money, but we eat like a king and queen."

"Queen Lizzy and King Harry. Doesn't quite fit you. Are you finished with your canning?"

"Nope, not yet. Still got some tomatoes to ripen, and we can't eat them fast enough. Harry's bringing in a chicken we butchered this morning. You know how to roast a chicken, don't you?"

"Um . . . I think I'll probably just fry it up. Unless you've got some extra time on your hands and you'd like to roast it for me."

"No time . . . no time at all," Elizabeth said as Harry came into the pantry with the last crate of canned goods and the freshly butchered chicken in a pan. "Harry's anxious to get back home and keep working on his field corn." Harry shook his head no and smiled, then she continued, "You don't get it into the crib by sitting around reading all day. Andrew, don't go letting that chicken sit too long and spoil on you."

"I'll jump right on it," Andrew replied, glancing at Harry and giving him a wink.

"Good. Say, every time I go into the store, that Vivian Wilson talks about you like the two of you are courting. You takin' a shining to her? She's a pretty girl. I was hopin' you might get interested—"

"I'm not taking a shining to anybody right now," Andrew interrupted her. "She claims to enjoy my sermons, but that's it."

"Yeah, she talks about that, too," Elizabeth explained. "But then she mentions what you talk about when you come over for all those meals, and how good you've been to her mother, and how you help her with arranging the store."

"Oh, come on!" Andrew railed as he stacked the emptied crates on the pantry floor. "I move a couple bags of flour and I'm suddenly re-arranging the store? What am I supposed to do when she asks me to help?"

"She is pretty and smart."

"Yes, she is. But I'm not the least bit attracted to her. You want me to propose to her anyway?"

Harry started laughing, then so did Elizabeth.

"Got your goat, didn't I!" Elizabeth teased, still laughing. "I just want you to keep your eyes open to what's going on around you. Remember me telling you it was going to be real tricky for you to be a bachelor pastor? I was right, you know. Vivian might not be right for you, but she's smitten with you, and there's something about her that makes me real nervous. She's the type who can make it awful tough on a young man. Do you know what I mean?"

"Look, I'm not blind, but there's not a lot I can do about it, other than stay away from the store whenever possible," Andrew replied. "And I'm not doing anything to warrant her romantic interests—nor do I have any plans in that direction."

"Just being friendly is enough in some cases," Elizabeth stated, closing one of the upper cabinet doors that she had filled with quarts of tomato juice. "Sometimes it doesn't need a good reason to get stirred up. I'm just telling you to be extra careful."

"I appreciate that, and I will be," Andrew said. "But I have to treat her like others, and I hope that nothing comes of it."

"Me too," said Elizabeth. "Harry, grab the crates and let's get moving. Andrew looks like he's anxious to throw that chicken in the frying pan."

"Wait a minute," Andrew interrupted her directive. "You got me so distracted, I almost forgot to ask what you're thinking, Uncle Harry. Would you be willing to start coming to church?"

"I don't think that he—"

"Forgive me, Aunt Lizzy, but I want to talk to Uncle Harry about this," Andrew stated. "Something is starting to happen in the church. I've had more than one person come up and ask me to pray with them about their spiritual lives. I don't know if it's because of the time Harry and I spent praying together, but I sense an urgency in my heart that he come and be a part of it. I would really like you to come, Uncle Harry. I believe that your presence and your prayers are important, especially to me."

Harry rubbed his weak hand and wrist with his strong right hand, then moved up to his stubbly chin. He stared at Andrew through his squint but gave no expression either way.

"He's really not—"

"Please," Andrew again broke in upon his aunt, "let it be Harry's decision. If he's not comfortable with it, or if doesn't feel that the Lord is directing him this way, that's fine, and I'll give up on this for a while. But I can't squelch what I hear in my heart just because I think it could present some problems. What do you say, Uncle Harry?"

Slowly nodding his head, Harry tightened his lips and the word formed into a slurred "yes."

"Yes!" Andrew cried out, nearly tripping over the chicken pan that was sitting on the hardwood floor as he lurched to give his uncle a hug. "This is great!"

Elizabeth stood by watching, straight and tall, with tears forming at the corners of her brown eyes. "Yes," she whispered. "Oh yes."

"I'm so sorry to trouble you, but I didn't know who else to call," Christina said as she opened her door and Maria Sikkink entered the apartment. "I have to be out of here by tomorrow, and I . . . just thought that . . . perhaps . . . with your husband being away . . . that you might rent me a room . . . until I can decide what I'm going to do. If I try to find another apartment, I'm sure my grandfather will find another way to get me out."

"Is that tall drink of water with the dark hair the delivery boy?" Maria asked, going to the window and looking down on the street. "The guy down at the bottom of the stairs?"

"Yes. I'm sure he's going nowhere until I make my move."

"He offered you the money to leave?"

"Five hundred dollars."

"Not bad," Maria said, sitting down on a chair by the table. "Your grandfather must really be troubled. You could go a lot of places with that much money these days. I admire you for saying no."

"I just couldn't give in, and I see now how foolish I was to provoke him," Christina replied, pacing methodically across the floor. "But it shouldn't end like this. I'm sorry I had to involve you, but I couldn't call my grandmother, and you've been so kind—"

"You're welcome to stay with me as long as you like," Maria broke in. "Did you say that you have some more portraits lined up to do?"

Christina nodded and said, "Yes, I've got two more, and I'm in the process of finishing another one now. When I finish this one, I could pay you—"

"I don't want to be paid," Maria stated firmly. "If you take my offer, I want you to come in as my guest. We don't need the money, and you do."

"But I can afford it, and I'd be paying it if I lived elsewhere."

"In my house you're my guest, plain and simple. If you feel you must do something, you can make a donation to the soup kitchen I work at. There's never a time when they don't need money."

"You *still* work at that soup kitchen?"

"I'm doing three mornings a week now," Maria replied. "Does that surprise you?"

"Well, yes, I guess it does," Christina answered. "I thought it was strange when you mentioned it before. It's just that I haven't met any-one—"

"Wealthy who seems to care about the poor," Maria finished Christina's sentence. "You'd be surprised at how many wealthy people help through our church's soup kitchen. And you're welcome to come down there with me anytime. But right now we need to get you out of here."

"How can we do that without the delivery boy following us?"

"We won't. Now, how much of this stuff is yours?"

"But we can't let my grandfather discover where I am. He's—"

"Not to worry, Christina," Maria assured her. "I have nothing to fear from your grandfather, and I don't particularly care what he thinks of me. This is my business, and he knows enough to keep his distance from a senator's wife. Two can play his game, you know."

"You're sure?"

"Without any doubts. It is a bit ironic, though, isn't it? He gets you tossed out of your apartment, and you end up in a room that overlooks his mansion. He's not going to be the happiest man in Chicago, that's for certain." Maria broke into laughter, and it was warm and contagious.

"I can wave when he goes by," Christina added, laughing for the first time all day.

"This will be interesting, but I don't suggest waving at him," Maria added, winking at Christina. She then surveyed the furnishings around her. "Now, you look exhausted, and I think we should get you out of here right away. Is everything here yours?"

"No, it's a furnished apartment," Christina said. "My roommate and I had almost nothing of our own. Just the suitcases and clothes on hangers that are against the wall. And the boxes, and the rocking chair. And the canvases and paints and brushes."

"Tell you what," Maria replied. "Let's take your clothes and art supplies with us now, and then I'll send my driver back down to get the rest. You can give him the key, and he'll have you moved by evening."

"No, I should help—"

"You are going to take a nap before you fall over," Maria ordered. "And he needs no help. He gets paid handsomely to drive me around. It's not going to hurt him to do a little manual labor for once. By the way, I assume you were paid up through the end of the month here. Correct?"

155

"Yes. Why?"

"And your landlord is in on this?"

"Yes."

"Well, it seems to me that if he's in such a cooperative mood, he'll be happy to cooperate with me as well. He owes you your rent money back, and I'm going to see to it that you get it."

"He could care less about being fair with the rent."

"You forget that there are some advantages to being a senator's wife," Maria said, suddenly changing her expression to the "get big" look. "I think your landlord's suddenly going to become very careful about being fair with you. Now, you hand me an armful of those long hanging clothes, and I'll have Robert come up for your suitcases. You should look around the apartment for anything else that might be yours. You're not coming back here."

✦✦✦✦✦✦✦✦✦✦✦

It had been three days, and Christina could still hardly believe where she was when she woke up in the mornings. Maria had given her the use of the most spacious guest suite in their extraordinary, grand mansion, rooms that overlooked her grandparents' home. An abundance of tall windows filled the lavishly furnished bedroom with morning sunlight. The canopy bed was so large that it would not have even fit into her bedroom back in Liberty Center. The suite's bathroom shone with sunlight reflecting off the white claw tub and chrome accessories, and the neutral tones brought a sense of peace.

Christina's heart was filled with gratitude, and she went to work on a painting that she hoped would make an appropriate "thank you" gift to Maria for her grand hospitality. In the Sikkinks' den, Christina had noticed a darling photo of Maria and her daughter when the girl was about six years old. She had found out the girl's hair and eye color from the butler and was progressing well on her painting of them.

A sudden knock on the bedroom door shook Christina out of her intense concentration, and she quickly turned the easel so the painting could not be seen from the doorway. "Come in," she called out, glancing at the mirror on the dresser to make sure her hair was still in place.

"Good morning, Christina," Maria's cheery voice called out as the door opened. "I've got a visitor who's come to see you. Do you have a few minutes?"

"I've got a visitor?" Christina asked, staring at the doorway. "The only one I've told is my mother, and I just wrote her yesterday."

"Not your mother, but close." Maria's smile was warm, and she reached her hand out to the guest, who was not yet visible to Christina. "Your grandmother's made the long trip across the 'Great Divide' and would like to see you."

Grace Adler stepped gracefully into the room with a warm smile and said, "You didn't call and tell me we were neighbors. Now we can get together whenever we want." She walked across the room to Christina and hugged her warmly, then stepped back. Her eyes briefly took in the lovely furnishings of the guest room and then came to rest on her granddaughter's face.

Christina's eyes spoke utter surprise. She was taken totally off guard and needed several seconds to comprehend Grace's presence in her bedroom. "How did you find out I was here? What about Grandfather?"

"Oh, I knew something was up two nights ago when William came home from the office," Grace replied. "He was thrashing around in the den and finally came out and told me about you, although he didn't tell me you had moved in with the Sikkinks. He said he was quite sure you'd be contacting me soon, and that I should be ready. It wasn't until this morning that Edgar told me where you were. I guess he and Maria's driver talked about it."

"Grandfather didn't forbid you to see me, then?"

"He told me that you would probably cause us some trouble . . . and that I should do everything I could to stay away from you." Grace took Christina's hand. "Looks like I'm not doing so well in complying."

"Sounds like you've been doing some thinking about it," Maria piped in from the doorway. She had not followed Grace into the room.

"Months . . . and months of thinking," Grace sighed deeply. She closed her eyes while pressing her fingers to her temples. "Over and over again, I've replayed it in my mind and done nothing with it." Her eyes opened then, and they held Christina's. "This morning, when Edgar told me that you were here and that William had driven you away from Carl Langstan and had the police chase you out of your apartment, my decision became crystal clear. I love my husband, but I won't let him interfere with my loving my own granddaughter."

"And if he finds out?" Christina's voice was a whisper as she reached for her grandmother's hand and held it tightly.

"He'll just have to be mad, I guess." Grace grasped Christina's other hand and pressed it possessively. "What he's doing, and what he's done, is wrong. It's . . . immoral . . . unconscionable, and I should have taken my stand years ago. I can't tell you how much better I feel. I almost feel alive again!"

But Grace's whole body was trembling, her words having been spoken with extreme conviction when she said the last sentences. She stood silently working at composing herself, then pulled Christina into an embrace, but this time she burst into tears. These were not like the tears of grief she had shed in their first meeting, but were a poignant mixture of joy and anxiety. Christina held her grandmother tight, breaking into tears herself, feeling something of the liberation and hope that her grandmother was experiencing.

Maria crossed the room and embraced both of them, stretching her long arms around the two women and joining in the celebration of life. "God can work all of this out for you, Grace," she whispered softly to the white-haired woman. "I know He can. He did it for Sarah, and He did it for me. Never be afraid if you're doing the right thing."

"Thank you, Maria. I could never have done this without you."

"Oh, my goodness!" Maria suddenly cried and abruptly let them go, stepping around the two women toward the turned easel where Christina had left the photo from the den lying exposed on the table. As Maria lifted the photo up, she said, "This is my favorite photo in the world. Why is it here, Christina? Are you—"

"Wait!" Christina felt her throat choke with tears. She followed Maria's eyes from the photo to the easel. "Please, it's not ready to . . ."

But it was too late. Maria had already stepped around the easel where she came to a dead stop. "Oh, Christina!" she gasped, her hand flying up to cover her mouth. And then, as she stared with delight at the nearly completed painting, tears streaked her face and she whispered, "It's so perfect!"

Chapter 18

*A*ndrew hesitated at the screen door of the Wilson General Store, wishing he didn't have to go inside for some basic kitchen supplies he had run out of. He felt only a little guilty that he'd actually driven to the stores over in Bradford on several occasions simply to avoid Vivian and Gertie Wilson. He hoped these out-of-town excursions would not be observed and would thus go unreported to the mother and daughter. But he couldn't remember a single conversation where the three of them didn't end up in some sort of disagreement, which he found extremely annoying.

"Here we go again," he whispered under his breath as he pulled open the screen door and stepped into the store. Seeing Vivian behind the counter totaling a bill with a customer, he nodded a greeting and went quickly to the shelves in search of his supplies. It didn't take him long to find a tin of Folger's coffee, a box of A–1 graham crackers, some Manchester biscuits, a ten-pound bag of C&H sugar, and black shoelaces and shoe polish.

"Good day, Reverend," Vivian called out with a bright smile as Andrew approached the counter. "It's been a while since you've been in. Looks like you're running low on some things at the parsonage. We're so close that I don't understand why you wait so long."

"Just too busy, I guess," Andrew replied as he placed his goods on the counter, glancing behind Vivian and noting that the door to her apartment was open.

"Do you like my new dress?" Vivian asked him, stepping out from behind the counter and modeling the dark floral-patterned dress for him. "I bought it at The Dress Shop in Bradford. Isn't it a dandy?"

"Very nice," Andrew said genuinely.

"Thank you!" she exclaimed, her eyes sparkling at his comment. "It's the first new dress I've bought in ever so long. I probably should save it for church, but I get so tired of my old ones."

Andrew smiled and reached into his back pocket for his billfold, hoping that she would quickly tally up his bill. But Vivian never seemed to be in much of hurry when he was there, and in the delay Andrew could hear movement from back in the apartment. Just as he pulled the dollars from his billfold, Vivian's mother emerged through the apartment doorway.

"Reverend Regan," she greeted him, pushing her reading glasses up on her nose. "I thought I heard your voice. I can tell your voice anywhere."

"Good day, Gertie," he replied as he handed Vivian the money. "How are you?"

"Doesn't she look gorgeous in her new dress?" Gertie asked. She put her hand on Vivian's arm and smiled.

"Very pretty," Andrew concurred, knowing that every word he said would be repeated and scrutinized the minute he stepped out of the store.

"Prettier every day, I say," Gertie said. "Don't you think? Prettier every day?"

Andrew nodded, hoping that a nonverbal answer might suffice.

"Reverend," Gertie continued, causing Andrew to flinch at what was coming next, "Vivian and I have been talking, and we wonder if you can explain to us what's going on in the church."

"I'm sorry"—Andrew's eyes held surprise at Gertie's remark—"but I'm not sure what you're alluding to."

"Come now. It's the talk of the church," Vivian stated as she handed Andrew his money and a written receipt. "You're surely aware of that."

"If you mean, can I explain why so many people are staying after the services to pray, no, I can't explain it," Andrew answered. He took the change from Vivian's hand and dropped it into one of his front pants pockets. "I don't think I'm preaching any different, or doing anything else different. Do you?"

"Not that I've noticed," Vivian responded. "But we thought you might be able to explain it."

"The only explanation I can offer is that God is working in the church in a way that we're not used to Him working," Andrew answered, noting Vivian's quick glance over at her mother. "But if that's the case, it seems to me that time will show the truth of it. You . . . um . . . seem a bit troubled by that. Is there a problem?"

"I'm not comfortable with it," Vivian replied. "I get the feeling that everything's getting out of hand."

"Because people are staying after a service to pray?" Andrew queried. His stare went from Vivian's pretty face to Gertie's large brown eyes. "I would think that if people are truly seeking God and want to remain in the church to pray about what they've heard in the service, we'd be delighted. I appreciate your concern, though, that our services remain orderly, and I've changed nothing in that regard."

"What about Vera Gartner?" Gertie snapped. "That was disorderly, don't you think?"

"When she started crying?"

"Yes. She carried on something fierce."

Recalling his time of prayer with Mrs. Gartner, Andrew smiled at the suggestion that her recommitment to her faith might be considered disorderly. "Gertie," he said, "it wasn't even during the church service, and she didn't make a scene. She was dealing with an issue of her heart that easily touches the emotions, but it's really not appropriate for me to discuss what that was. But it was hardly disorderly."

Gertie took a deep breath, as if she were going to disagree, but she stayed silent. She did continue to stare at him, though.

"What about your uncle?" Vivian asked.

"That he's coming to church?" From her previous comments, he knew this was a powder keg that only needed a spark to get him to blow sky-high.

"No, that he's coming is nice for him, I'm sure," answered Vivian. "But we don't think it's right for him to get involved in praying for those people who stay after church."

"Why is that? Do you think he's not a believer?"

Vivian smiled and ran her finger along the seam of her dress collar. "No, I didn't say that." She couldn't quite look into Andrew's eyes and seemed to be choosing her words carefully. "I do know that he's neither an elder nor a deacon, and I don't know anything about your uncle's faith. But that, I would think, is reason enough why he shouldn't be praying for people. We don't know him well enough to trust him."

"He shouldn't pray for people when they specifically ask him to pray with them?" Andrew pressed. "He didn't volunteer for this, and I didn't ask him to do it."

"But you've been telling people that he is a man of prayer." Gertie's comment sounded more like an accusation. "And I was told that you even had him pray for you, of all things."

"Which is absolutely true," Andrew confirmed. "He stopped coming to church when he was young because he felt rejected, and for forty years he's stayed away and studied Scripture and developed an amazing prayer life. I did ask him to pray with me, and God answered those prayers."

"Why didn't you ask the elders to pray for you?" Gertie persisted.

"I always ask the elders to pray for me. Just ask them." Andrew could feel tension building in his throat. "But this was a personal matter, and I'm not sure they would have understood it. Uncle Harry gave me a lot of time and counsel on it. I am deeply indebted to him."

"He can't even talk, and you say he counseled you?" sputtered Gertie. "That's rich!"

With every statement from the mother and daughter, Andrew's face had gotten redder and redder. "I'm sorry," he finally spoke as calmly as he could, hoisting the sack of goods into his arms, "but you're insulting my uncle, who can pray and talk and give counsel like no one I've ever met. If you'd like to get to know him, give me a call and I'll see if I can arrange something for you."

"I heard that a church member actually went to your uncle's farm and asked your uncle to pray with him," Vivian spoke, as if she hadn't heard Andrew's last statement.

"That's true," Andrew confirmed, turning around and starting to walk toward the door. "Aunt Lizzy gave the person a cup of coffee as well. Is that wrong, too?"

"It's getting out of hand," Vivian stated heatedly. "You will need to do something about your uncle."

Andrew did not turn around but continued to the door and a welcomed exit. "If you can show me in Scripture that it's wrong for a believer to pray for other people, I'll gladly listen. Good day."

Christina sat silently in the back of the Sikkinks' dark limousine, staring blankly out the window as it cruised noiselessly toward downtown Chicago. It was a cloudy Wednesday as the limousine passed the church where Maria attended. Christina glanced back and watched as it faded from view. Out of curiosity, she had gone with Maria to the Sunday church service as well as to the church's soup kitchen on Monday, and her curiosity had turned to mild shock.

The first surprise came when she discovered that the church members represented a true blend of society. Some of Chicago's most affluent people, such as Maria and now Christina's grandmother, called this their church home, but so did some of Chicago's poor and middle-class folks. The other surprise came at the soup kitchen, where Maria acted and was treated like one of the regular workers. From the moment they arrived, Maria put on an apron and worked as hard as anyone there.

At first Christina had thought that the wealthy Maria was simply a fiercely independent woman who was doing exactly what she wanted to do in exactly the way she wanted to do it. But the more she got to know this woman, the more Christina knew that here was another person, like her mother and Annie Anderson, whom she could not understand apart from their faith. And although she had been able to rationalize away much of the role of faith in Annie's and her mother's lives, Maria was not so easy to dismiss. Indeed, with every passing day the validity of Maria's faith chipped away at Christina's mountain of skepticism.

Turning around in her seat and looking straight down the street ahead, Christina's thoughts swung back to the task at hand. She was glad that Maria had not asked her where she was going when offering the use of her limousine and driver of five years, Mr. Sanders, for she assumed that neither Maria nor her grandmother would approve of her resolve to talk with her grandfather again. Even now, her own heart told her she had to try, but her head was shouting that it was hopeless to think she could prevail with him. After all that had happened, why should she believe he would listen to her now?

Lost in her swirling thoughts, Christina grew oblivious to her surroundings, and was unaware that they were approaching her grandfather's office building until Mr. Sanders announced their momentary arrival. She lifted her mother's blue velvet hat from her lap and stroked the ebony feathers, then gently placed it upon her head. Somehow, this remnant of her mother's past brought her a sense of courage. As the limousine cruised past the Palmolive Building and came to a stop, Christina opened the streetside door by herself and jumped out with a "thank you" to Maria's driver. It was already settled that he would park the car and wait for her, despite Christina's protest that he go back to the mansion and wait for her call.

Passing through the revolving glass door into the building's expensive lobby, Christina took the elevator to the fourth floor and followed the mazelike hallways to the glass door inscribed with "Adler Enterprises." She paused at the door, her heart pounding furiously, and tried to rein in her fears and disjointed thoughts, but to no avail. She had no plan or specific agenda to implement this time, and she had no idea what might happen. Nevertheless, she took the brass doorknob and turned it, pushing the door to the office open just enough for her slender frame to pass through. She hoped that her grandfather did not have anyone in his office with him.

All four secretaries and the receptionist recognized her immediately as she came through the doorway and hushed their conversations. The receptionist slowly stood up as Christina approached her desk, clearly unsure of how to handle the situation, despite her air of professionalism.

"Mrs. Guild," Christina said softly, taking the initiative, "I'm here to see my grandfather. Is he alone?"

"Yes," she responded, holding up her hand for Christina to stop, "but he's ordered us to call Security if you come into the office. Why don't you leave now, Miss Ellington? I don't want you to get into trouble, but I have strict orders."

"You knew my mother, didn't you, Mrs. Guild?"

"Yes, very well."

"For her sake," Christina appealed, "would you let me pass as if I rushed to the door, then call Security as you're ordered . . . but give me five minutes before you call . . . and ask them to take their time? I promise you I'll never do this again."

Mrs. Guild turned around and looked at the four staring secretaries, who all nodded their approval and pretended to go back to their work. "Fine," she whispered, "but don't expect more than ten minutes. And good luck."

Christina nodded and walked straight to her grandfather's door.

"Miss Ellington, stop!" Mrs. Guild called out as Christina opened the door. "You can't go in there!"

William Adler looked up from the paper work on his desk, instantly bemused. Then, in clear recognition of the blue hat, a degree of shock registered on his face.

"I'll call Security," said Mrs. Guild. "I tried to stop—"

"No!" William ordered sharply. He stood then and moved around to the front of the desk and sagged against the edge. "No Security. I'll take care of this. Please close the door."

"Yes, sir," Mrs. Guild spoke a little too brightly, and she quickly pulled the door shut behind Christina.

Her grandfather was speechless for the moment, a deep frown wrinkling his brow. He took off his black wire-rimmed glasses and set them down on his walnut desk, still staring at her. His bald head reflected the morning sunshine that poured in through the large picture window behind him. "What do you want?" he asked in a subdued tone. "Did you decide to take the money after all?"

Christina shook her head no. "May I sit down?"

"Sit."

Christina continued gazing into William Adler's face. She could tell his eyes were focused not on her but on the hat, and she wondered fleetingly if he was envisioning her mother in another time. She lowered herself into the same large leather chair she had sat in before and shifted her gaze to the photo of her mother that still sat on her grandfather's credenza. "Grandmother told me that my father loved to see my mother in this hat." She paused, continuing to stare at the photo. "You loved to see her in this hat, too, didn't you?" She spoke quietly, almost reverently.

William Adler's wide shoulders seemed slumped beneath his dark wool suit coat, but he did not respond.

"She still loves you."

"Why are you here?" William Adler's voice sounded forced.

Christina smiled and pondered his question briefly. "I've thought about this for several weeks. . . . Actually, I've thought about my *mother* for several weeks and what she would think of my behavior. When I came down here before, I hoped you were the type of person I could despise and strike out at. What I did was wrong, and I've decided I need to apologize to you face-to-face. My mother would be crushed if she ever found out how shamelessly I treated you, playing games with you and then humiliating you in front of your employees." Christina looked down at her hands and found them moist and clasped tightly to each other.

Her grandfather's expression did not change, nor did he speak as she paused.

"For what I've done," she continued, "I want to ask you to forgive me. I don't understand how you can despise a daughter who loves you so much, and I hate what you've done to me, but I can't hate you. I love my mother too much to let you make me hate you. And I've come to love my grandmother, too. For her sake as well, I will not hate you."

"You've corrupted her," he stated without any hint of emotion.

Christina studied her grandfather's expression, then almost broke into laughter, all of her pent-up fears and anxieties wanting to spill out. "*I've* corrupted her?"

"You and that Sikkink woman."

"You don't like it that she's not obeying your command to stay away from me?"

"That's between Grace and me."

"Well, if you claim that's the source of your problem," Christina stated, "you're actually blaming the Bible as the corrupter, as I understand it. And seeing as I don't particularly believe the Bible, I can't imagine my sharing in the blame. Do you believe the Bible, Grandfather? The verses in First Peter seem clear enough. Can you refute them?"

"Those aren't the only verses to consider. And, yes, I believe the Bible is the Word of God."

"All right, toss those out and try a few others," Christina suggested. "What about the two I heard last Sunday? One said something like unless you forgive others for their sins, you won't be forgiven yourself. The other one said that charity covers a multitude of sins. When you say you believe in the Bible, do you include those? The pastor didn't seem to think these were optional."

"What do you know about the meaning of forgiveness?" her grandfather retorted.

"Very little ... almost nothing," Christina admitted. "But I know this much: if unforgiveness makes a person as bitter as you are, I hope I can learn to forgive."

"Get out. Now," William demanded.

Christina nodded and stood. "I didn't come hoping that you might suddenly welcome me into your life, but I thought you might be interested in this. I found it in my mother's jewelry box, and it's got your name on it." She pulled a gold pendant out of her purse and held it up into the light, turning it so she could read the inscription. " 'To My Wonderful Daughter, Dad.' " Setting it on the stack of papers he'd been looking at on the desk, she continued, "Those may be the truest words you ever spoke."

"I said get out. You've said enough. Now go." His voice was lower and very controlled.

Christina started for the door, then turned and spoke quietly, "Because you said that about my mother, I think there's still hope for you."

♦ ♦ ♦ ♦ ♦ ♦ ♦ ♦ ♦ ♦ ♦

Andrew took one last look around the church to make sure it was empty, then he turned off the lights and went out the wide front doors. "Man, am I tired," he muttered to himself, yawning as he sauntered down the front steps. Although the evening service had ended over an hour before, a number of people had stayed afterward for prayer, and a few had asked for counsel. His uncle Harry was the only person whom he'd been able to enlist to help, although he was hopeful that Rebecca Ellington would soon join in. But for the time being, all of the counseling matters came to Andrew.

Crossing the road to the parsonage, Andrew thought it odd that Rebecca's house was completely dark. He recalled seeing her after the morning service, when she had mentioned how much she was looking forward to the evening message. "This is odd. She never misses a service," he observed, staring at the house. Then he got a strange feeling in his stomach that he should check on her. "Naw," he told himself, figuring she had simply gone to bed early. "She's probably getting rested up for a big day of school tomorrow."

But while he was walking up the sidewalk to the parsonage, he got another strong sense that something wasn't right. He turned, determined to find out for sure, even though it might cause him some embarrassment. Going to Rebecca's front door, he was surprised to find that it was not closed. She never left it open at night, not even during the worst of the summer heat.

Gazing into the darkness, Andrew knocked on the door and called out, "Rebecca, are you home? It's Andrew."

Rebecca's bedroom was on the first floor but was situated toward the back of the house in a hallway that split off from the kitchen. If she had gone to bed and closed the door, Andrew knew she might not hear him. Pulling open the screen door and stepping into the entryway, he paused so his eyes could adjust to the dark shadows, then peered into the living room and called out loudly, "Rebecca, are you here?"

In the silence that followed, Andrew heard what he thought was a tap against a wall, then another tap. "Rebecca!" he hollered, reaching for the light to the living room and turning it on. Another tap followed.

Andrew walked quickly through the living room and kitchen, then into the hallway. He turned on the hallway light. Reluctantly, he went to Rebecca's open bedroom door and called out "Rebecca," and looked in through the doorway. He could see her form in the bed.

"Andrew!" Rebecca's voice was but a whisper.

Hurrying to her side, he could see beads of perspiration on her forehead even in the dark shadows. It was evident that she was feverish. He took her hand and found it clammy and trembling. Andrew leaned over her. "Rebecca, what's wrong? How long have you been sick?"

"What took you so long?" she murmured. Her eyes seemed to struggle to focus on his dim face. "You know I wouldn't miss one of your sermons unless I was dying."

"This is no time for jokes," Andrew urged, reaching out his hand and touching her forehead. "You're burning up, Rebecca. When did you get sick?"

"Right after church." She opened her eyes extra wide. "My head ached so bad during church that I should have left. By the time I got home, I had a nosebleed I couldn't stop for the longest time. Then I got this fever and the shakes."

"Why didn't you call me or someone else?"

"It's just the flu. My schoolchildren love to pass it along to me."

"What's your temperature?" Andrew asked, noticing a thermometer on the nightstand next to the bed.

"Not that bad."

"Baloney!" he cried and picked up the thermometer. Stepping back toward the light from the hallway, he held it up and read it out loud. "One hundred and two . . . point four! I'm calling Doc Anderson."

"No, it's just the flu," Rebecca protested. "Don't trouble the man with my little problems. But I'm afraid they'll have to cancel school tomorrow."

"Isn't there someone who fills in for you . . . someone I can call?"

"There was last year, but she moved. I have no one who can do it."

"Well then, they'll just have to enjoy the day off. I'm calling the doctor."

When Rebecca did not protest again, Andrew knew she felt worse than she was letting on. He turned quickly and left the room, heading straight for the wooden crank telephone in the kitchen.

Chapter 19

Andrew stepped out the front door of the parsonage into the cool morning air and stopped on the front steps to rub his eyes. It had been well past ten P.M. before Annie and Stuart Anderson arrived, and some time after midnight before Andrew had plopped into bed. The few hours of sleep he'd gotten were troubled by the anxiety that he read on the doctor's face. Andrew hated to think the worst, but it seemed obvious that Rebecca was suffering from more than the flu.

He crossed the lawn and climbed the front steps of Rebecca's house, knocked on the screen door as he was opening it, and stepped into the entryway.

"Come on in," Stuart's voice called out from the kitchen.

Andrew went through the living room and into the kitchen where Stuart was sitting at the kitchen table. "Good morning, Doc," he said. "Looks like you found the eggs and bread."

"And coffee," the doctor added, lifting his coffee cup toward Andrew. "You look like you could use a cup. Have you eaten breakfast yet?"

"No, but I usually don't eat right away in the morning." Andrew breathed in the aroma of freshly brewed coffee and stepped toward the stove. "I think I'll try the coffee, though. Did you get any sleep?"

"Oh . . . some," Stuart replied. "I'm not sure that Annie did. I lay down on Christina's bed and slept for a while, but Annie stayed with Rebecca all night."

"Is she in there with Rebecca now?"

Stuart nodded. "She should be out soon. I've got a full schedule of patients today, so I need to get going soon."

"Annie's staying, right?"

"For today, yes," Stuart answered. "She called one of the other teachers in Bradford, who agreed to juggle her classes with Annie's for today. But finding teachers around here is a real problem. Annie has had a substitute in the past, but the woman just had a baby and won't be available again for some time."

"What about tomorrow, then?"

"Annie wondered if your aunt might be able to come tomorrow?" Stuart queried, putting down his fork and taking a sip of his coffee. "If the severity of Rebecca's symptoms continues today, we're going to call Christina and see if she can come home from Chicago."

"I'm sure Aunt Lizzy will be glad to help for several days, if she's needed. But it sounds serious, Doc. What do you think is wrong?"

Stuart glanced away, staring out the window and rubbing his day's growth of whiskers. "I hope what I think is wrong," he said, turning his dark eyes on Andrew. "It may be a while before we know for sure. Her temperature went down a bit last night, which is good."

"But what do you think it is?"

"I fear it could be rheumatic fever," Stuart said gravely. "But I don't want that broadcast around until we're certain."

"Rheumatic fever...?" Andrew gasped in disbelief. "How can that be? I thought it was just children that got it. What makes you think so?"

"All the general symptoms are there—fever, headache, rapid pulse, especially the unexplainable nosebleeds," Stuart replied. "Then in the night she started getting pains in her elbows, wrists, knees, and ankles. She's definitely got inflammation of the joints. That's not good."

"But ... you could say the same for some flus ... or meningitis, right?"

"Yes."

"Why think the worst, then?"

"Well ... she never gets nosebleeds, and that sets it a bit apart from some of the other possibilities," Stuart stated as he pushed away his coffee cup. "But ... do you remember about a month ago, she had a strep throat?"

"Yes. She had me tend her gardens for a few days when she was down with that."

"Attacks of rheumatic fever are usually preceded by a streptococcal infection, whether it's strep throat or impetigo or scarlet fever. That usually occurs within one to five weeks. Rebecca's case certainly fits the pattern, although rheumatic fever does occur primarily in children."

"I had a friend who got it when he was about eight years old," Andrew said. "It damaged his heart. They said he'd have a heart murmur for the rest of his life."

"It's a very serious condition," Stuart explained. "The heart valves can become damaged so they no longer open and close properly. The passage of blood around the valves produces a sound called a heart murmur. If the heart is severely damaged, it can lead to heart failure."

"If it is rheumatic fever, how bad do you think it is?"

Stuart shrugged his shoulders and said, "It's impossible to know. You simply don't know the severity until it's run its course."

Andrew stared down at his empty coffee cup, hardly noticing that he'd never gotten around to filling it. "I can't tell you how much I hope you're wrong. She is—"

"Stuart," Annie interrupted, suddenly stepping into the kitchen doorway, "you should take a look at Rebecca's back before you leave."

"Why?" Stuart jumped up from his chair and quickly crossed the kitchen.

"She's got a large red patch on her skin," Annie said as Stuart passed her and disappeared down the hallway.

Andrew poured himself a cup of coffee, then went to the kitchen table and sat down to wait. Stuart and Annie were in Rebecca's bedroom for a few minutes, then came out into the kitchen together. "Not good news, I take it," Andrew remarked, noting the same solemn expression on both their faces.

"I'm sure it's rheumatic fever. I've seen that dreadful ring-shaped rash too many times before," Stuart said. He pulled out his pocket watch and checked the time. "I wish I didn't have to leave, but I've got appointments, and there's not much I can do here."

"How do you treat it?" Andrew asked.

"Aspirin, lots of rest, and lots and lots of prayer," Annie replied in a very weary voice, then she kissed Stuart good-bye. "See you tonight, love. Try to catch a nap today."

Stuart smiled and shook his head. "I haven't had a nap in thirty years, but today might be my lucky day. You get some sleep, Annie. There's not going to be a lot you can do for her. Give her plenty of liquids. See you after six o'clock."

Annie nodded as Stuart turned and walked out the kitchen door, then she poured herself a cup of coffee and joined Andrew at the table. "You look tired and worried, Andrew," she stated, rubbing her forehead and eyes with the tips of her fingers. "Suppose I look about the same, only worse."

"Did you sleep at all?"

"No. I ... um ... I keep thinking that at any minute something could go wrong," Annie replied. "I don't think I'd survive long if I were a nurse. Every time Rebecca moaned, I jumped out of my chair like a jack-in-the-box. I believe I popped up one time too many."

"I can listen for Rebecca this morning if you want me to," Andrew offered. "You really should sleep."

"We'll be fine, and I'm sure I'll sleep," Annie said. "Now that we're pretty sure of what it is, I think it'll help me rest. At least we know what we're up against."

"I'm still in shock, I guess," said Andrew. "I'll drive out later and check with my aunt about tomorrow, but I'm sure she'll be happy to help. I didn't realize that finding substitute teachers was so hard."

Annie took a sip of her lukewarm coffee and said, "It's nearly impossible. Most of the night I was trying to figure out what we could do for the school here in Liberty Center. It could be weeks before Rebecca is able to teach again, if at all, and there's no one here who can take her place. I know that Rebecca will torment herself over the school situation, and it concerns me that it could slow her healing processes down."

"There's not even a retired teacher around?"

"Rebecca's been the only teacher in this town for twenty years, and the teacher before her moved away from the area," Annie replied. "We need the Lord to bring someone along *fast*. I know that Rebecca has her lesson plans laid out like clockwork, so it's not like whoever fills in will need to start from scratch. We mostly need someone who can carry out what she's already got prepared."

"I'll get my uncle Harry to pray about it." Andrew forced a tired smile. "Things seem to speed up when he gets involved."

Annie nodded. "That's what I've heard. And a speedy answer would be nice. Pray, too, that I'll be able to reach Christina today. If we can get her home, she'll be a tremendous comfort to her mother."

❖❖❖❖❖❖❖❖❖❖❖

Christina jumped out of the limousine. Mr. Sanders had been sent to get her from the home of a local judge where she was painting a portrait of the children. She ran to the front door of the Sikkinks' Victorian mansion, which Maria opened before she could reach for the doorknob. "What's wrong? He wouldn't tell me what's wrong. Is it my grandmother?"

"No," Maria spoke soothingly, but the look in her eyes did nothing to assuage Christina's concern. "We received a call from a friend of your mother's, Annie Anderson. She'd like you to come home . . . as soon as possible. Dr. Anderson thinks that your mother has come down with rheumatic fever."

Christina stared into Maria's face, momentarily frozen like a statue, trying to comprehend the words. She knew several people who had had rheumatic fever—and survived—with varying degrees of long-term complications. And she knew one boy who had died. But this was her mother, the one who was always strong, the invincible one, who almost never showed a hint of mortality. She searched for words that would capture her disbelief but could only come up with, "Is she all right now? Did Annie say how bad it is?"

Maria put her arm around Christina and embraced her warmly. "She said that your mother's fever had gone down, but that she had a lot of pain in her joints. There's no way of telling just how bad it's going to be. That's why you need to get home as fast as possible. I've called the railroad office, and there's a train you can catch at four o'clock. Otherwise you have to wait until tomorrow morning."

"Four o'clock!" Christina exclaimed, glancing down at her watch. "I've only got a little over an hour to get there!"

"It's only twenty minutes to the station," Maria assured her. "You go get packed. Edgar will drive you."

"My grandmother knows?"

"Yes. She wants you to take some things to your mother, too. Hurry!"

"Thank you for your help," Christina whispered, hugging Maria tightly. Then she pulled away and raced up the stairway and down the long hallway to her room. As quickly as she could, realizing she could be gone for weeks, she loaded her suitcase with the clothes and personal items she thought she'd need. She carefully tucked her mother's old manuscript on top, then closed the suitcase and strapped it tightly with its leather belts.

Pulling on a khaki coat that Maria had bought for her, Christina looked into the tall dressing mirror and noticed her mother's blue hat on the dresser. With a slight smile, she picked it up and gently turned it in her hands. "I think you might be just what the doctor ordered," she said. Then she placed the treasured hat on her head and hurried out of the room with her suitcase in hand.

Racing down the stairway, she saw Maria coming through the front door and called out, "Where's Grandmother?"

"She's right outside," Maria answered, giving Christina another hug. "Godspeed, Christina. My prayers go with you, as will our church's. If you've forgotten anything, let me know and I'll send it."

"Thank you, Maria," Christina said, stepping away and opening the front door. "I'll write or call."

Edgar Mitchell was standing beside the Adler limousine with the engine running as Christina came outside the mansion with her large leather suitcase. He quickly came across the driveway and took it from her as Christina turned to her grandmother, who was cutting across the Sikkink front lawn toward her. One look at her grandmother and Christina immediately began to cry.

"Grandmother!" She reached out to the white-haired woman whose green eyes were bloodshot and wet with tears. The elderly lady sank into her arms and began to sob. "She'll be all right, Grandma. I'll take care of her for you. Don't worry."

Christina's words seemed to bring comfort to her grandmother, who managed to stop her sobs and catch her breath. With a tremble in her voice, she whispered, "I want to come with you."

"There's no time, Grandma," Christina spoke softly. "I've only a few minutes to get to the train station. Maybe I can return when Mother's back on her feet, and I'll take you to visit her. But I have to go now."

"Would you do that for me?" Grace's voice was pleading. She looked up into Christina's face with the first hint of hope breaking across her expression.

"Oh, I'd love to do that, Grandma!" Christina's tears welled up again. "And I promise I'll do it just as soon as Mother is better. Goodbye. I have to go."

"I packed a suitcase of your mother's things," Grace called out as Christina ran to the limousine, where Edgar stood with the door open. "And I called your grandfather. I think he's on his way here."

"What?" Christina asked, stopping and turning toward her grandmother. "Why?"

Grace shrugged her shoulders and said, "He's . . . her father."

A car's engine roared into the Sikkinks' driveway and Christina turned to see a Yellow Cab roll into the driveway. As it pulled to a stop behind the limousine, her grandfather paid the driver, stepped out of the cab, and stood still as it drove back out onto the street. His expression was grim as he looked from Grace to Christina, but he did not speak or move.

The silence was overwhelming as Christina and her grandfather stared into each other's eyes. Then Christina slowly walked over to him and put her hand on his crossed arms. Her voice, fraught with emotion, hardly registered as a whisper as she said, "Now I know . . ."—squeezing down on his forearm—"you still love her . . . and I'm going to tell her that."

William Adler did not blink as she spoke, and his jaw muscles did not relax, but neither did he protest as Christina walked away. She went straight to the limousine and stepped into the backseat as Edgar shut the door behind her. A large suitcase was lying on the seat in front of her, and she wondered what her grandmother might have put into it that had belonged to her mother.

As the black limousine began to move, Christina glanced out the window and waved. The sight was almost surreal. Maria had joined Christina's grandmother and had her arm around the elderly woman. Her grandfather remained exactly where he had been when he stepped out of the taxicab. And only Maria returned her wave.

"Do you believe in miracles, ma'am?" Edgar Mitchell's voice from the front of the car broke the spell that had fallen over Christina.

Christina turned around as the limousine exited the Sikkink drive and pulled onto the street. "Do I? No. Why do you ask?"

"You just saw one, ma'am, whether you believe it or not," he said, glancing up into the rearview mirror at Christina. "In twenty years, your grandfather has never shown one glimpse of concern over your mother's welfare. Someday . . . hopefully soon . . . you'll tell me you believe in miracles."

Christina stared back, still dazed by it all.

"You saw it in his eyes, didn't you?" Edgar continued. "It's been there all along, burning like a fire in his soul, and he can't put it out. What else could make him so miserable? You said something to him. What was it?"

Closing her eyes, Christina could see something of the flame burning in her grandfather's eyes. "I told him . . . that I knew he loved my mother, and that I was going to tell her so," she said, then sighed and leaned her head back on the leather seat. "And that's exactly what I'm going to do."

"You tell her," Edgar said, his voice suddenly cracking, "that I've prayed for her for twenty years . . . every day. Tell her, for me, that the people who walked in darkness have seen a great light, and those who dwell in the land of the shadow of death, upon them hath the light shined. The light is greater than the darkness, Christina."

Chapter 20

"What I can't figure, Andrew, is how you seem to always know what time we're going be eating supper," Elizabeth Regan said as she finished filling three cups with coffee and sat down at the table with Harry and their guest. "Now, how could you know we were going to eat early tonight?"

"I didn't know, and you know I didn't know," Andrew replied with a grin. "I only wanted to make sure you could come in tomorrow to help with Rebecca. It was good timing, though."

"Doc Anderson's wife has to teach tomorrow, isn't that right?"

"Yes. She's pretty exhausted, but she wants to follow through on this commitment."

"Seems to me it would be better if I was to ride back in with you and take over for her tonight," Elizabeth said. "Don't seem fair to have her on call all night and then have to teach all day. Harry can take care of himself for a day or two, can't you, Harry?"

Harry squinted and nodded.

"Well, I'm sure Annie would appreciate it." Andrew lifted his coffee cup and took a sip. "I'm going to be picking up Rebecca's daughter tomorrow at Bradford, so that should make things a little easier."

"Been quite a while since she's been home ... least I haven't seen her for ... probably two years," said his aunt, tapping absently on her dessert plate with her fork. "It'll be wonderful for Rebecca to have Christina at home instead of having friends and neighbors hanging around the house."

"Like me?" Andrew joked.

"Yes, like you ... or like me tonight," Elizabeth said seriously. "How would your mother like it if she was sick and folks like us were tromping through her house?"

"Not so good . . . well, not at all," Andrew conceded. "Yes, I have no doubt she'll prefer having her daughter there."

Elizabeth glanced over at Harry, then back at Andrew. "They're in a real pickle, aren't they?"

"Who's in a pickle?"

"Rebecca and Christina, of course," Elizabeth said, giving Andrew a bit of a disgusted look, as if to say he should know better. "If neither one of them are working, how they gonna pay their bills? Even if Rebecca recovers quickly, it could be weeks before she teaches again. What are they gonna do? With her salary, I can't believe she's got any savings."

"Goodness, I guess I hadn't thought that far ahead," Andrew replied. "I don't know how they'll get along without some income. I've just been relieved that Christina would be there to care for her."

"I think the doc's wife is right about the school, too," Elizabeth commented. "Those children are Rebecca's life. If the school has to shut down, it's gonna eat away at her something fierce. There must be someone around who can fill in."

Andrew nodded and added, "Annie said Rebecca's lesson plans are so thorough that most of the hard work is done. She thinks that even someone with limited teaching experience could handle it. I told Annie I'd ask Uncle Harry to pray about it."

Harry rubbed his chin and nodded back, but then he opened his right eye funny.

"Here we go again," Elizabeth warned as Harry got up and walked over to his chair in the corner and picked up his little chalkboard. "You stirred up something."

"All I did was ask him to pray."

"That's all it takes."

Harry brought the board over to the table, bent over it with his chalk in hand, and started to slowly scribble down his letters. Andrew drained his cup of coffee while his uncle pressed the chalk against the board and seemed to struggle unusually hard to get the letters right.

"There," Elizabeth spoke for Harry as he handed the board to Andrew. "What's it say?"

Andrew studied the letters, glanced at Harry, and shook his head in his aunt's direction. "Looks like he's written 'open door' with a question mark after the 'door.' What's that supposed to mean?"

Elizabeth tapped her dessert plate some more and said, "Let's see. He wonders if something is an open door. Right, Harry?"

Harry smiled his crooked smile and nodded.

"What's an open door?" Andrew asked, staring down at his uncle.

Harry held up his hands as if he were holding a book and pretended to be reading; then he picked up his chalkboard and pretended to be writing across it.

"Teaching school?" Elizabeth asked her brother, who nodded again. "He wonders if teaching in the school may be an open door."

"For whom?" asked Andrew, still bewildered at where his uncle was taking them.

"You," Harry mouthed the words and pointed at Andrew. Then he repeated it.

"Me!" Andrew exclaimed. "You wonder if teaching in the school is an open door for me?"

Harry smiled and nodded several times.

"You must be kidding!" Andrew sputtered, but Harry puckered his lips and shook his head no. "Oh, come on. I can hardly keep up with pastoring the church, let alone try to take Rebecca's place. This is something we need to pray about, Uncle Harry."

Rubbing away the words from his chalkboard with his arm, Harry glanced up at Andrew and pointed at him again. Then he took up his chalk and started to scrawl out another word.

"You don't need to remind him that you asked him to pray about this," Elizabeth commented. "He's praying all the time. But he's not finished with you yet."

Andrew watched as Harry finished the one word and handed the chalkboard to him. " 'Servant,' " he read, staring down at the word, then glancing up at Harry. "You want me to be a servant?"

His uncle nodded emphatically.

"But I am a servant," Andrew pled. "You know that, Uncle Harry. I study for and plan out my sermons, I visit the sick, I teach in the Sunday school and on Wednesday nights, and I pray all the time for the people of the church. You know that, Harry. You and I have prayed about it as well. What more can I do to be a 'servant'?"

"I don't think he's suggesting that you aren't a servant, Andrew," his aunt spoke up as she often did, interpreting what her brother meant. "He's wondering if teaching in the school might be an open door for you to serve the Lord in a new way."

"And just add it on to everything else I'm doing?" Andrew didn't try to hide his growing frustration.

Harry shrugged his shoulders.

"He doesn't know," Elizabeth reminded Andrew. "He's simply wondering about it. If it is an open door of service, you don't want to miss it, do you?"

"No, but it's crazy."

"Yes, it sounds crazy. I'll give you that much," Elizabeth agreed. "But . . . when you think of it, there are a whole lot of times in the Bible when the Lord told someone to go do something that didn't make much sense."

"That's true, but this is different. I've got all kinds of responsibilities I can't just drop."

"I agree," his aunt said, "but you have to admit that you have the education and teaching background to be able to step in for Rebecca. That part makes sense. If God wanted you to serve Him in this way, you are more qualified than anyone around here. I think that's where Harry is coming from."

Harry nodded, then held up his hands to pray and pointed again at Andrew.

Andrew felt a wave of irritation well up inside of him, but he bit his lip and looked away from his uncle's pointing finger. He could not argue against Harry's logic, but neither could he imagine even considering such a daunting task. Taking a deep breath, he sighed and reluctantly said, "Well, if it'll make you happy, I will pray about it. But that's all."

✦✦✦✦✦✦✦✦✦✦

Standing on the wooden platform outside the small train depot in Bradford, Andrew pulled out his pocket watch for the third time and muttered, "How can it be so late? They said—"

"They said at approximately two-thirty but that the train was delayed in La Crosse," Stuart Anderson broke into Andrew's grousing, seeming to appear suddenly out of nowhere. "It's only fifteen minutes late."

"Doc, I wasn't expecting you." Andrew laughed, feeling sheepish at being caught grumbling. "Annie thought you'd be delivering a baby today."

"She was right, only the big boy surprised everyone and came early," Stuart replied somewhat triumphantly. "So I could have picked up Christina after all. I thought, seeing as I had some time, that I'd at least greet her now and try to calm her fears about her mother. And I thought you might prefer being introduced properly."

"I appreciate that," Andrew conceded. "Annie told me to look for a beautiful twenty-year-old woman who said she'd be wearing a tan coat and a blue velvet hat. I did see her picture at Rebecca's, of course. Sort of . . . made me a little nervous."

Stuart burst out laughing and patted Andrew on the back. "Good to know you're human," he said. "I check the pulse of any young man who says he doesn't get nervous when he meets a pretty girl. I remember being a twenty-year-old and taking the train from Minneapolis and pulling into the station with Annie standing on the platform here. Man, my heart was pounding out of my chest."

"Annie told me she was eighteen when she married you."

"Eighteen, and almost as beautiful as she is today. I'm fifty-five, and my old ticker still gets revved up when I see her," Stuart said, then he looked down the tracks to the south and pointed. "There's the train now. Not so late as I thought it might be."

Andrew turned and saw the black cloud of smoke rising up behind the oncoming passenger train. Surrounded on both sides by rolling golden hills tinted with red and yellow, the train rolled down the tracks toward them and then slowed as it neared the station. Andrew waved at the train's engineer as the engine passed them, then he stood and waited as it came to a halt.

"There she is!" Stuart called out to Andrew above the noise of the train as a blond-haired woman in a tan coat and a striking blue hat appeared on the steps of the passenger car in front of them. She waved to Stuart and then gracefully stepped from the train as a porter followed behind her carrying two large leather suitcases.

Stuart ran up to Christina and gave her a long hug while Andrew stepped around them and quickly tipped the porter. Andrew turned and could see by the way that Stuart was talking with Christina that the two of them needed some time together, so he picked up the heavy suitcases and headed for the car. He lugged the suitcases around the depot to where he was parked and loaded them into the backseat. Then he decided to wait for the two of them beside his car, feeling that the best way not to rush them was to stay out of sight.

He stood there a good ten minutes before Stuart and Christina came around the corner of the depot toward him. Much of the concern that had been written on Christina's face was gone, and as they approached Andrew, Christina broke into a bright smile at something Stuart said. Andrew was immediately struck by how pretty her face really was, especially her deep blue eyes, which were in such contrast to her mother's green eyes.

"Andrew Regan," Stuart said as they reached the car, "may I present Christina Ellington, lately of Chicago, whom I claimed long ago as my second daughter. Christina, this is Reverend Andrew Regan, lately of Liberty Center, who has been a great help to your mother and is your chauffeur for the day."

"Reverend," Christina said, her eyes sparkling in the autumn sunshine as she shook Andrew's hand, "I'm so pleased to meet you. My mother often mentions you in her letters. I can't tell you how grateful I am that you checked on my mother Sunday night. Doc says that getting her fever down that night may have made a big difference in her recovery. Thank you."

Andrew found himself caught off guard by Christina's sincerity and gratitude, her gracious manner so similar to Rebecca's. "It's . . . um . . . it's a pleasure to meet you, Miss Ellington," he bumbled the words through an embarrassed smile. "Your mother is—" He choked up suddenly, surprised by his unexpected emotion. "Your mother is the kindest, most godly woman I've ever had the privilege of meeting. She has helped me more than anyone else in my first five months as pastor here. I am very glad that you could come home and care for her."

"Well, sweetheart," Stuart said, taking Christina's arm, "I have some patients who are probably getting impatient. Annie and I will drive out tonight and see how your mother is doing. Don't bother to cook. We'll bring—"

"No, don't bring anything," Andrew broke in. "Aunt Lizzy is there, and she's working her magic on a beef roast from one of her treasured polled Herefords. There'll be enough to feed an army, the way she was going at it."

"That's even better!" Stuart exclaimed as he started down the sidewalk toward his downtown office.

"You don't want a ride?" Andrew called out.

"No!" Stuart answered, patting his stomach. "Gotta make some room for that roast. See you tonight."

"Good-bye!" Christina called to Stuart, who nodded and waved. "Tell Annie I can't wait to see her."

Andrew turned and unconsciously found himself looking directly into Christina's eyes, holding his gaze a moment longer than he should have. "Um . . . we should be going," he said, stepping around the side of the car and opening the passenger door for Christina. "I hope you don't mind riding in this old clunker of mine. Your mother says you often get to ride in limousines in Chicago when you're painting portraits."

Christina laughed and stepped into the car. "Riding is one thing," she said as Andrew closed the door, "and owning is another. I couldn't afford to pay for the leather on the seats. It was simply a privilege that came with painting portraits of Chicago's elite. If it hadn't been for my art instructor, I would never have had access to them."

Jumping into the driver's seat, Andrew started the car and backed away from the train depot, then moved out into the street. "I've admired your paintings around your mother's house. You have a wonderful talent."

"Oh my." Christina didn't hold back a delightful laugh rising up from deep within her. "I'm so embarrassed that she still has those old things up on her walls—all her walls, as a matter of fact. I think it's time to retire some of the them. If I'm home long enough, perhaps I can do some new things. I hope that my two years of art lessons will show a difference. Did you know that my mother taught me to draw and paint?"

"How else would you have learned?" Andrew asked with a smile.

"Liberty Center is not exactly the artistic hub of the Midwest. It's your mother who's made that country school into a learning center that has few rivals."

"My mother wrote that you grew up in ... Michigan?"

"Flint, Michigan. Car Town, America."

"Whyever would you leave the big city for a place like Liberty Center?" Christina gazed out the window down at the gentle, swirling water of Flatwillow Creek as they crossed the steel bridge that exited the city limits of Bradford. "I know your aunt and uncle are here, but this must have been a shock for you."

"It ... ah ... took some getting used to," Andrew agreed. "Why did I come? I've wondered that myself at certain difficult moments, but it comes down to something pretty simple. When my aunt wrote and asked me to consider being the pastor here, I thought it was sort of humorous. I knew I was going to have some good opportunities for a large city pastorate when I graduated from seminary. Liberty Center was hardly on my list of choices. But my aunt asked me to pray about it, so I did, and so I'm here."

"It was that simple?"

Andrew chuckled. He glanced at Christina and found her extraordinary eyes looking at him. He focused his own eyes back on the road in front of them, slowing the car for a sharp corner at the edge of a dark woods. "It wasn't so simple. The president of the seminary thought it was a really stupid move, and I know that's what it looked like. But when I prayed about it, I got such an overwhelming sense of peace about this being the direction I should take that I couldn't dismiss it. I've never sensed anything like it before, and I hesitate to say that God sent me here, but I do feel He wanted me to come."

"You sound like my mother," she said quietly.

Andrew felt her gaze upon him again and said, "Any comparison of me to your mother is stretching things too far. 'Sound like' is about as close as I get. Your mother is ... a saint."

Christina was quiet for a minute. She took off her blue hat and set it in her lap, then ran her fingers through her curly blond hair. "A number of people in the church," she finally said, tapping the hat lightly, "do not share your estimate of my mother's spirituality, do they? They ... um ... seem to appreciate her ability to teach their children at school, but I recall the whispers that she wasn't worthy to teach the Holy Bible."

Andrew swallowed hard and shook his head, unsure of how to respond to what he knew had been said in the past. "I wish I could say it isn't true," he said, "but I have encountered it, and it's ugly ... it's sinful ... and if I could drive it out of the church, I would. I hate it. Amazingly, your mother has never once spoken to me about it."

Christina smiled and said softly, "She never will either. I think it must have something to do with sainthood, as you've mentioned. This is one point of our lives where my mother and I have nothing in common. I cannot look at the church and pretend not to see what's there. There's much to be despised."

"Yes, there is. There's nothing more despicable than religious hypocrisy," Andrew replied without hesitation, his hands squeezing hard on the steering wheel. "But what if a lot of it isn't the true church—only a poor masquerade that carries the name and not the inner reality?"

"It's universal, Reverend," Christina countered. "I saw it as clearly in Chicago as in Liberty Center."

"It's alive and well in Flint, Michigan, to be sure. But I'll bet you saw the reverse too, didn't you?"

"What do you mean?"

"I'll bet you met people like your mother there," Andrew suggested. "People whose lives matched what you thought the church should be."

"Yes, I did ..." Christina said thoughtfully, "but there weren't many."

"What if those few are what the true church is," Andrew continued, "and everything else is either dross that needs to be purified or just plain old tares among the wheat?"

"What's your point?"

"My point is that I'm afraid the disfigured image the church often projects is nothing like God himself," Andrew answered. "Sometimes it's exactly the opposite of what God is like. I believe that, Miss Ellington, with all my heart."

"And I cannot believe *anything* about the church, Reverend Regan."

Andrew felt the sting of her words and considered his response carefully. "That ... I do not believe. You may have dismissed much about the church as untrue—and often with good reason—but you are too honest to consider your mother's faith as anything less than based on absolute truth."

Christina opened her mouth to protest, but she was suddenly struck by the rightness of Andrew's words. Maria Sikkink, Stuart and Annie Anderson, her mother, her grandmother Ellington—she could not dismiss the reality of their faith, despite the dozens of other people she knew whose beliefs seemed like nothing more than wishful thinking. She turned away and gazed out on the pastureland and fields that were so familiar, and for the first time she felt good to be home again.

Chapter 21

Christina left her suitcases to Andrew's care and went straight to her mother's bedroom after finding out from Aunt Lizzy that her mother had been sleeping most of the day. She left the blue hat on a small corner table in the hallway, then knocked softly on the bedroom door and entered. Rebecca stirred but did not seem to awaken as Christina came alongside the bed and bent over her.

With the shade pulled down over the room's only window, Christina's eyes needed time adjusting to the shadowy light. Even in the room's dimness, she could see the swelling in her mother's wrists and elbows as well as the skin nodules that ran up her arm. Rebecca's long wavy hair was matted and unkempt, and the usually soft face had taken on a gaunt look.

"I love the smell of your perfume," Rebecca suddenly whispered, barely opening her eyes. A fragile smile crossed her lips and she said, "I could hardly wait for you to get here, baby girl."

Christina's anguished expression transformed to a hesitant joy mixed with instant tears. "Mother!" She tenderly wrapped her arms around her mother's shoulders as she kissed her cheek. "I came as fast as I could. How bad does it hurt?"

Rebecca's smile grew larger with every splash of Christina's tears upon her face. "I feel better already, but I'm afraid I might drown if you keep this up."

Christina burst out laughing, doing her best to mop back her tears with a handkerchief she had grabbed from her mother's nightstand. "What do you expect from me?" she asked, shaking involuntarily from the contrasting emotions. "I've never been so afraid in all my life. I love you so much!"

Tears began to roll down from the corners of Rebecca's eyes, and she shook ever so slightly as well. "And I love you more than anything in this world, Christina. Give me another hug," she whispered, raising her hands as Christina wrapped her arms around her again. "Mmm, I think I'm going to need a lot of these."

"Doesn't this hurt?"

"It's worth it. It hurts anyway."

"Doc says it could be painful for a long time."

"Which will give us a lot of time to catch up on each other's lives," Rebecca said as Christina pulled away again. "How is this going to affect your lessons with Professor Langstan? I was glad to know that you were coming home, but I'm concerned about your schooling. Were you able to work things out on such short notice?"

"It won't change anything regarding my lessons with the professor," Christina responded truthfully, hoping to avoid the bad news for a while. "That's all set for now."

"Good." Rebecca's eyes brightened. "I hated the thought of your losing your place with him. By the way, could you open the shade? Elizabeth thought the sunlight was too hard on my eyes, but I can't stand this cheerless drab."

"But you didn't have the heart to tell her so, did you?" Christina reached over and pulled the shade by its string, carefully letting it up.

"That's why it's so nice to have you here," said Rebecca. "Even having Annie, whom I love like a big sister, is a bit awkward. I'm just not used to having other people in my house."

Christina reached out to lift several damp strands of hair from her mother's forehead. "You're so hot. What's your temperature been reading?"

"So far it's been between 100 and 101, which could be a lot worse," answered Rebecca. "Then there's the swollen joints. Check out my ankles. I won't be swinging to any Jimmy Dorsey or Glenn Miller songs in the next few days."

Christina pulled back the lower part of the bed sheet and nearly gasped. Both of Rebecca's ankles seemed to be doubled in size and her skin was very red. "Oh my!" she whispered and moaned in sympathy. "This is bad."

"No, not really," Rebecca countered. "The swelling and the fever will pass, and the aspirin is helping. I'm just tremendously tired, which I'm told will continue, so you'll have to put up with all the naps I get to take. It's my heart that's their big concern, and the long-term possibility of arthritis setting in. It's all in God's hands. He knows what's best. I feel so completely helpless."

Christina caressed her mother's warm cheek. It wasn't like her mother to sound so discouraged. "I have some good news. Doc told me that he and Annie will help us with paying bills if we need it. Isn't that great? With neither one of us working, unless you've got some savings, I don't know what else we'll do. I thanked them for both of us. They're so good to us."

"I hate to borrow"—Rebecca grimaced—"but maybe we'll have to. Since I moved into this house with your grandma Ellington, I've never had to borrow a cent. What I'm more concerned about is what will happen to the school. Annie says not to worry about it, but I know there's no one to take my place. I've been praying about that too. I need God to take care of those children as well."

Christina took a deep breath and sighed. "It's too overwhelming for all of this at one time. But Annie's right. You can't worry about the school or the money. And we have you to be concerned about, and the others don't compare. If we can get you better, we can do something about all the other stuff."

Rebecca nodded slightly and yawned. "Can you tell me about your change in address? Are you still with your roommate in this new place you wrote about?"

"No, we parted ways. It was a bad situation. I've got a room to myself." Christina patted her mother's hand. She stood and stretched, suddenly realizing how tense her back seemed.

"Sounds like you've got a fantastic deal with the senator's wife," Rebecca mused. "You said that you'd painted her portrait and that she took a real liking to you."

"Yes, she did. In fact, it's her house I'm staying in right now. She's a great lady, but I'm hoping it's only a temporary arrangement. My roommate left so suddenly, I didn't have enough time to find a suitable place. Mrs. Sikkink has been very kind."

"Hmmm. So, how many days do you think it'll take me to squeeze the whole story out of you?" Rebecca smiled weakly at her daughter.

"What story?" Christina responded innocently. "I just don't want to take advantage of Mrs. Sikkink's kindness."

"I'm your mother, Christina," Rebecca reminded her. "Your letters over the past months . . . there's something you've not been telling me. You and your roommate never had a problem in the two years you shared the apartment, and suddenly it's a 'bad situation'? Then there's your new address. You did give me the address, you know."

Christina suddenly got busy, straightening the blue quilt on her mother's bed. She realized she'd never thought about the address. "Maybe we should talk about this later. You really should rest."

"I've slept all day," Rebecca spoke as purposefully as her illness allowed. "I think I can last awhile yet, and my curiosity's just about killed me since your last letter. Do you know who lives in the house next to the Sikkinks?"

"You're pressing really hard for this, Mother." Christina could feel her face flushing. "I had no intention of hiding anything from you, but I'd hoped to wait some days before we got into it. Are you sure you feel up to this? We've got lots of time."

"You do know, don't you?"

"What I know could be upsetting for you. It has been for me. Can't you wait at least another day?"

"No! I don't think I'll be able to sleep again until I find out."

Christina shook her head at her mother and frowned. "I should have asked Doc about this. I'll never forgive myself if your condition weakens after this."

"Don't worry about my condition. You keep me in suspense and it will really bring me pain. Now what do you know that you're not telling?"

"Give me a second, but take some deep breaths, because you're going to need them," Christina replied, turning around and stepping out of the bedroom into the hallway. She got goose bumps as she reached out for the blue hat, then held it contemplatively in her hands, finally reaching up and placing it on her head. Glancing at her reflection in the hallway mirror, she got the chills again.

"Ready?" Christina called out from the hallway.

"Yes" came the answer from within the bedroom.

Christina pushed the door open and slowly walked into the room, stopping only when her mother's startled face took on the expression of one who is about to faint. All of the reddish blotches in Rebecca's face turned white, and she moaned as she laid her head back on her pillow and closed her eyes. Tears formed at the corners of her eyes and began to stream down her face.

"Mother, are you all right?" Christina fell on her knees at Rebecca's bedside and grasped her mother's left hand. "Oh, Mother, I'm sorry. I shouldn't have shown it to you. I brought it home thinking it might help speed your recovery. I'm really sorry. I'll take it out."

"No, no!" Rebecca's eyes were still closed, and her right hand with its swollen wrist covered her mouth. "You warned me. . . . I just never thought I'd see that hat again. . . ."

Christina began to cry again, but softly. She took the hat off and set it on her mother's chest. "I know how much this hat meant to my father, and so I knew how much it must mean to you."

Rebecca opened her eyes and took the hat into her hands, lightly running her fingers over the blue velvet sides and stroking the delicate black feathers. "Your father loved to call me the 'Lady in the Blue Hat,' and I loved to hear him say it. How did you ever get it, Christina? It was in my room, but that was twenty years ago. Did you go to my room? You told me that you would never look for my parents, that you never wanted to meet them."

"It's a long story, Mother, and it's going to take days on end to tell." Christina felt very weary all of a sudden. "But, yes, I was in your room . . . with your mother, Grace Adler, my grandmother. When I was leaving to come here, she sent along a whole suitcase of your things. I'm not even sure what she packed."

Closing her eyes again, Rebecca smiled and continued to run her fingers over the precious blue hat. "How is my mother?" she whispered, pain edging the corners of her lips.

"Your mother . . . my grandmother . . . is still heartbroken over what happened, over what she allowed," Christina replied, choking up again. "At first I wanted to hate her, but I came to love her. Why didn't you ever tell me what you went through? Or what you left behind?"

"Oh my," Rebecca heaved a sigh. "It took me so long to forgive them, and to finally believe that they weren't going to change their minds and let me come home again. I guess I hoped to spare you the extra pain of knowing the details. You suffered enough without all that. Besides, God gave us a wonderful new family and a new life here ... a good life."

Christina pulled herself up from her knees and sat on the edge of the bed. She shook her head gently and spoke more reprovingly, "Still ... I would have liked to have known. You never told anyone here, did you? You kept this secret for all of this time?"

"No," Rebecca replied, looking sheepishly at Christina. "After your grandfather Ellington died, I told Annie my whole story, but I don't think she even told Stuart about it. She walked with me through the darkest, lowest time of my life, and she led me to the light. I don't know what would have happened to me if she hadn't been there. Shortly after my father forced me out of my home, your father was killed, and then your grandfather died a year later. Life didn't seem worth living to me, except for my beautiful baby." Rebecca tweaked Christina's cheek. "You were the only reason I had to keep going."

"Goodness, I can't imagine your ever feeling that much despair. I've never seen you dark or melancholic or anything like that. My room-mate was at times, you know, despairing of life, and nothing I said seemed to help her."

"I'd never experienced anything like it, before or since," her mother stated. "It was like traveling through a black fog with dreadful voices calling out their haunting agonies all around me. I could not bear it, and it drove me down, down, down in a spiral of loathsome pity. Annie would not let me go, though. She planted herself between me and what appeared to be death's door—at least that's what it felt like at the time."

"Grandma would feel even more terrible if she heard this," Christina mused. "I won't tell her—ever."

"You actually plan to see her again?"

"Certainly. I've been with her half a dozen times ... at least."

Rebecca shook her head. "I can't imagine it, although I've never totally given up hope that something like this might happen. But I never thought it would be happening to you rather than me. What about my father? He doesn't oppose it?"

"Your father . . . my grandfather, although that is still a hard word for me to say . . . does oppose it, and made it as difficult as he could for me and for Grandmother," Christina replied. "But he's in good health, still works all the time, still makes a lot of money, and he's tough as nails. He and I do not feel any warmth toward each other."

"He talked with you?"

"Sort of."

"Meaning?"

"I said it was a long story, and he's not the part I'd like to talk about now."

"If he opposed my mother's talking with you, you're saying that she continued anyway? What happened? Did you do something to him?"

Christina burst out laughing and crossed her arms. "Whatever would make you think that I would—"

"How about your senior year when you blackmailed your world history teacher at Bradford High? Then there was—"

"All right already," Christina broke in. "So I've given you good cause to wonder. You have my word that I did nothing like that to your father, although it's still worth considering. Grandma kept seeing me because she finally determined it was wrong for him to keep us apart, and she wasn't going to comply with it any longer."

"After all these years. . . ? How did she finally get up the courage to do that?" Rebecca wondered out loud.

"I guess I challenged her about her lack of courage," Christina answered. "But it was studying the Bible that did it. The story of Sarah telling Abraham to send Ishmael and Hagar away from their camp seemed to make a point with Grandma."

"You studied the Bible with my mother?"

"No . . . well, yes." Christina laughed again. "I brought Grandma over to see Mrs. Sikkink. She showed Grandma several Bible verses that made it clear that submitting to your husband doesn't mean you should let your husband cause you to sin. It took a while for Grandma to understand, but when she did, she stuck with her decision."

"I'm getting confused . . . and real tired." Rebecca let out a moan as she rolled over on her side to find a more comfortable position. "Some of what you're saying almost sounds true, but I think I'm going to sleep on it for a while. Maybe I'll be able to believe it later on. It all sounds like a biblical miracle to me. I'm afraid if I hear any more of the story, I might wake up and discover that none of it was true."

"Somebody else you know was just talking to me about miracles, Mother."

"Oh. . . ? Who was that?"

"Edgar."

"Edgar Mitchell!" Rebecca's tired face lit up at the name. "He's still there? Isn't he the most wonderful man?"

"He . . . intriguing. I take it . . . from the way he talked . . . that he believes just as you do."

Rebecca nodded her head. "He believed long before I did. I just never understood what he was talking about. Why did he speak to you about miracles?"

"He . . . um . . . said we'd just seen one," responded Christina.

"When?"

"When I was leaving for the train depot . . . your father came home after Grandma called him . . . to see me off, I guess. Actually, I'm not sure why he came," Christina said. "Edgar said it was the first time he'd seen your father show any interest in you since you left twenty years ago."

"Oh my," Rebecca spoke softly, moving her head back and forth. "Father told me that I was no longer his daughter, and that if I left, he'd never have anything to do with me again. Did he say anything?"

Christina took her mother's hand again. "He didn't have to, Mother. I could see it as clear as crystal in his eyes, and I told him so. I told him I was going to come home and tell you that despite everything he's done . . . he still loves you. I saw it burning in his eyes, and he didn't deny it. He loves you, Mother."

"No."

"Oh yes. He surely does. I have no doubt he's more troubled in his soul about it now than he's ever been. I think the change in Grandma is doing something to him as well."

Rebecca's eyes were closed, and she was silent, but there were no more tears. Christina held her mother's hand until her breathing grew heavy and she quietly fell asleep.

Chapter 22

Andrew stood outside Annie Anderson's classroom and waited as the last student came through the doorway and headed down the hall. Stepping to the door, he could see that Annie was busy with paper work at her large wooden desk. He rapped twice on the door and entered the room.

"Andrew, what a pleasure!" Annie called out, looking up from the tests she was correcting and then leaning back in her chair. "Come on in. What brings you to Bradford on such a dismal day?"

"Mostly to see you," he replied, pulling off his wet trenchcoat as he walked across the room and draped it over a student desk, then sat down on a chair next to Annie's desk. "I hope you have a few minutes to spare. I thought it would work best to catch you right after school let out."

"I've got as much time as you need," said Annie. "What's up?"

"Well, last night at dinner with Christina, you know we were talking about what was going to happen at the school in Liberty Center."

"Yes. By the way, your aunt's beef roast was wonderful. I could hardly get to sleep. I indulged a bit too much."

"Aunt Lizzy is a wonderful cook. I'll tell her you mentioned it," Andrew said. "About the school deal, though, I need your advice . . . and your help, I think."

"You want *my* advice?" Annie asked. "This is a bit of a reversal of roles."

"Not really," Andrew replied. "I'm way out of my league here, and I need you to tell me what to do. I know this is going to sound a little crazy at first, but I've . . . ah . . . had this brewing on my heart for a couple of days, and it just gets stronger and stronger. You said that

Rebecca has her lesson plans laid out like clockwork, and that mostly what's needed is someone who can carry through on what she's already got prepared. Right?"

"Yes, that's true. I've never seen another teacher as thorough in her plans as Rebecca."

"What if I stepped in . . . at least temporarily, and we got the school going again?" Andrew asked. "The children have already missed a week, and it would be unfortunate for them to miss any more if this goes on. I could be ready to open the doors on Monday morning. What do you think?"

Annie's brown eyes never shifted from Andrew's face, and her thoughtful expression did not lighten. She rubbed her forehead, brushing her fingers against her golden hair, and then smiled. "I know your intentions are good, Andrew, but have you truly thought this through?"

A big grin spread across Andrew's face, and he nodded his head. "Yes, I think my brain has pretty much exhausted the subject. I know I can't cut back on my pastoral responsibilities, but my intent would be to teach only the basic classes for the children. If I don't attempt the art and music lessons that Rebecca has made legendary in her school, I think I could limit the time to four hours a day. The children could be sent home at noon, and I'd still have most of the day for pastoring."

"If you only did the basic lessons, which is fine, and if you're very disciplined to stick with the lesson plans, I'd say you could be done by noon," Annie responded. "But you still have grading and paper work and preparation for the next day to do. You're not looking at just four hours, Andrew."

"So, maybe I stay up later at night," he countered. "I'm young . . . I've got the energy to do it . . . at least for a while. I honestly am not thinking that I can do both jobs over a long stretch of time. But perhaps for a few months I can fill in. Maybe by then Rebecca will be better, or another teacher will have been found. But the school shouldn't be put on hold."

"You really have thought it through, haven't you?" Annie said. "I can't imagine how you even came up with the idea."

"I didn't, actually," Andrew replied. "My uncle Harry told me I should pray about it. He felt it might be an open door for me to serve. To tell you the truth, he kind of irked me. It seems like all I do is serve. But when I prayed about it, I started to get the same sense in my heart that I did when I prayed about taking the call to the church in Liberty Center. There were a lot of reasons not to do it, but it was like God was saying to do it anyway. That's the way I feel about this."

"Have you talked with the church board yet?"

"No, that's next." Andrew grimaced a bit. "First I wanted your advice on whether you thought I could do it. What do you think?"

Annie glanced out the window as the rain pelted the glass heavily. "Well . . . this is really difficult. Rebecca tells me that you're an excellent teacher, and that the children like you. You've had plenty of education, and you would have Rebecca's lesson plans to work with. I'd have to say yes, I think you could do it . . . at least it's worth a try . . . and we'll have to see how much time it takes you. I'm amazed that you're willing to attempt it, Andrew. Rebecca will be thrilled and so grateful."

"I hope it eases her mind and helps her recuperate a little faster," Andrew said. "Would you be willing, if I can clear this with the church and with Rebecca, to gather the school board and see if we can get their approval?"

"If you clear it with the church, I assure you the school board will follow. They have no other options," Annie reasoned. "You know . . . there might be a way to work in the art and music lessons. If—"

"I really can't," Andrew protested, holding up his hands. "I was useless at art, and no one ever asked me if I sang in the choir. I have zero sense of rhythm."

"If you could just hold on to your horses for a second, I'll explain what I mean," Annie said. "There's no reason why Christina can't take a few hours per day to help you out. She's tremendous with her art, and she's nearly as gifted with her music. Rebecca's not going to want Christina sitting around the house every minute of the day. Christina might even be able to help you with the paper work and grading." She paused and clapped her hands together. "Hey, this really could work!"

"Mmm, I don't know. I'm not sure that Christina would be comfortable working with me. She's not too keen on the church."

"Don't you worry about that. I think you should ask her to help. It'll be good for her and for Rebecca."

Andrew sat quietly for a moment, studying his hands. "Only if you think so."

"I do. But what about the church? I've heard that things are stirring all of a sudden. Aren't you afraid you won't have the time you need to study and prepare for whatever is happening?"

"It concerns me, yes. But if it's God who's working in church members' lives, He can help me accomplish what I need in my preparation and in my preaching. If this is the right thing to do and I'm obeying Him, I don't see any reason to be concerned."

"And what if the church board doesn't think you should do it?"

Andrew stood up. "That's what I'm going to find out now. I'd appreciate your prayers."

✦✦✦✦✦✦✦✦✦✦✦

"I can't speak for the board, Andrew, and you know that," Arden Walton said as he pushed his wool cap back on his bald head and leaned his shoulder against the wooden side of the grain wagon he'd been working on in the machinery shed. His dark, contemplative eyes studied Andrew carefully.

"But you're the chairman, and I've been to enough board meetings now to know that when you're convinced on an issue, the other elders follow you," Andrew reasoned. "It doesn't seem fair to ask the board to consider this when I haven't talked with Rebecca about it yet. And I really can't talk to Rebecca without having a sense of whether the board's going to approve. What I'm asking is whether you'll support me before the board if Rebecca gives me permission to teach the classes."

Arden rubbed some of the dirt from his large hands and wrinkled his forehead. "Well, it makes a lot of sense, if you can do both jobs, and it's a shame the school is closed. How many of the children are from our church families?"

"Twenty-one out of the twenty-three. That seems like a good enough reason to do it right there."

"That's reason enough for me," the blocky farmer agreed. "Matter of fact, it's important enough that I'd be willing to support you if you find you can't keep up and you need to cut back somewhere on your church work. I know that all of the families with children are going to be in favor of this."

"I appreciate it, and I think you're right about the support," Andrew said. "But I'll do everything I can to maintain my responsibilities in the church."

"You do realize that some folks are going to criticize you for this, no matter how well it goes," Arden said. "And they'll be waiting for anything that looks like you're slacking in your commitment to the church. There's already some talk going around that our services are getting tainted with emotionalism."

"And that my uncle shouldn't be involved with praying for people," Andrew added. "I'm all too aware of that. A few of them aren't shy about letting me know either. Are you concerned, Arden? I'm not doing anything different in the services, and all I know is that my uncle has a very effective prayer life, and that several people have gotten help when they've asked him. Whether he's my uncle or my barber, I can't imagine anyone in the church opposing what God seems to be doing through him."

"I'm only concerned about the rumors that get to flying around," Arden responded. "What happened with Edith Schuppert on Wednesday night? I've never seen her get so upset as long as I've known her."

Andrew crossed his arms and looked out the door of the machinery shed at the cold rain that continued to fall. "I can't give the specifics, of course, but . . . she had something that's been on her heart for a long time and she finally knew she had to bring it to God. It was no easy matter for her, but I think she got it resolved."

"This type of thing is getting to be a pretty regular occurrence."

"Not just after the services, though," Andrew said. "I've had a couple of men stop by the parsonage for prayer, and Uncle Harry actually had someone stop him along the road and ask for prayer. Nothing like that has happened in the six months I've been here."

"Nothing like it has happened as long as I've gone to the church." Arden smiled and rubbed his hands together as if they were getting cold. "I get a little excited about it myself, but I am concerned that it not get out of hand. Just keep in mind that people are watching, and some of them don't like to have their feathers ruffled."

* * * * * * * * * * *

Andrew pulled his car into the parsonage driveway, turned off the engine, and looked through his rain-streaked window at the Ellington house. Feeling a weariness deep in his bones, he pushed the car door open and got out, then closed it and walked across the soggy parsonage lawn to the Ellingtons' front door. He took a deep breath and knocked.

Christina quickly came through the front entryway and opened the door. "Reverend Regan, hello. Come in." She stood aside, holding the screen door open for him. "You look like you could use some hot coffee and soup."

"Hello, Christina . . . Miss Ellington." Andrew nodded his assent to her offer as he stepped into the entryway. "That would be wonderful. This cold rain feels like it's gotten inside my bones."

"Here, let me hang up your coat," Christina offered as Andrew unbuttoned it and handed it to her.

"Thanks," he said, returning her bright smile. He took off his boots, placed them by the door, then followed her into the living room.

"Well, well, well, you're just in time to indulge in some beef stew with me," the weak voice of Rebecca piped up from her semi-inclined position on the long velvet davenport. She was draped in a cream-colored wool blanket. Her wavy brown hair had become flattened to one side. In her hand she held a steaming mug filled with the homemade goodness.

"You're up!" Another big smile broke across Andrew's face. "I wasn't expecting you to be out here. This is very good!"

Rebecca smiled gamely and said, "That Chicago slave driver, who has made herself quite at home, has kicked me out of my bed and said I needed to get a change of scenery. I hadn't even complained. I'm still not persuaded the scenery's all that much better out here. I may need some rescuing."

Andrew's gaze followed the object of Rebecca's complaint as she crossed the living room.

Christina stopped at the kitchen door, looked at Andrew, and rolled her eyes. "Mother, stop your bellyaching," she spoke playfully. "Andrew, I'll bring you a big bowl of beef stew and some buttered bread and a cup of coffee. Anything else?"

Andrew chuckled. "No, that should be plenty, thanks. I didn't mean to stop by during your sup—"

"He knows exactly when I'm going to eat, Christina," Rebecca teased. "You may as well plan the meals around him."

Christina laughed and disappeared into the kitchen.

"How's the fever, Rebecca?" Andrew changed the subject. He walked over and sat down in the big oak chair across from the davenport and studied her face.

"About the same, I'm afraid, although I didn't ache as badly today," Rebecca answered. She took a tiny spoonful of the stew. "The first few days were murder. I hope it doesn't come back like that. I guess there's no rhyme nor reason to it, unless you get up and try to do too much."

"Which is exactly what you're likely to do, if I know you."

"No, I don't think so this time," Rebecca spoke slowly. "I've seen too much heart damage from rheumatic fever over the years. I'm not going to push it, and Christina would never let me loose even if I did get such a notion. The only thing that's really bothering me is the school. I just wish I could put my shoes on tomorrow morning and open the doors again."

"Which is precisely why I stopped over, even though you falsely accused me of only wanting the food," Andrew joked as Christina came back through the kitchen door, carrying his meal on a metal tray. "I spent most of my day finding a way for the school to get under way by Monday morning. How do you like that?"

"You did what?" Rebecca nearly dropped her mug of stew. "I may look like the picture of health to you, Andrew, but I assure you I'm in no mood for joking around about the school." Her eyes were firm but had relaxed in anticipation of an explanation.

"You found someone?" Christina paused midway in her placing the tray of food in Andrew's hand. Her eyes searched Andrew's. "I've understood that there is absolutely no one who could fill in, Reverend."

"Well, I think someone has been found." Andrew took the tray from Christina, sitting up straight, and carefully straddled the tray in his lap. "And, Christina, you have to call me Andrew. Give me twenty more years and perhaps I'll feel comfortable with the 'Reverend' part." He smiled somewhat shyly up at her. "Please sit down. Looks to me like your supper is getting cold."

"It's okay," Christina said as she sat down on the other large oak chair that was closer to the davenport and gathered up her supper tray, which she had set on a coffee table at Andrew's arrival. "I can always heat it up. Please, you've got to tell us who was found to fill in for Mother."

"Me."

Christina glanced over at her mother, who was staring at Andrew.

"What did you say?" Rebecca's voice squeaked with utter shock. "I thought you said something silly like 'me.'"

Andrew swallowed a big spoonful of the beef stew and nodded. His eyes were twinkling, thoroughly enjoying the moment. "Keep an open mind here, Rebecca. Isn't that what you're constantly telling me to do? This is something I've been thinking and praying about for several days. I've talked to Annie, and she's willing to help me with your lesson plans. And I've talked with Arden Walton, who says he's willing to support me before the church board. If you—"

"Just a minute, I've got to lie all the way down," Rebecca said, setting her mug down on the end table and slowly swinging her legs up and over the edge of the davenport, then gingerly slipping her body down to a fully inclined position. "There," she continued, still holding a dazed expression. "Now, try again. You're saying that *you* could take my place?"

"Yes."

"And who would take your place?" Rebecca searched Andrew's face.

"I would do both," Andrew replied, feeling Christina's blue eyes riveted upon him. He continued to look at Rebecca. "Annie says that your lesson plans are excellent and that if I follow them diligently and only teach the basic lessons, I can probably wrap up my part by noon."

"This is Annie's idea?" asked Christina.

"No, it's my idea ... well, actually it's my uncle Harry's idea, but that's another story," Andrew replied. "I'm saying that it's not right for the children not to have school if I can do it. Rebecca, you know I'm a good teacher, and I do well with the children in the church. I've got the educational background, and I want to do it, so I say it's worth a try. What do you say?"

Rebecca closed her eyes and tugged her blankets tight up under her chin. "I'd say I must be dreaming. Andrew, it's a wonderful offer, and you're a fine teacher, but you can't pull away from the church. Mrs. Schuppert stopped by today and apologized to me about some things she'd said in the past—many, many years ago. I could barely remember it, but it had been very hurtful at the time. She said your messages have been going straight to her heart, and she had to clear her conscience. Were you aware of that?"

Andrew nodded and took a sip of perfectly brewed coffee. "I talked with her after the Wednesday night message. I'm glad she got up the nerve to come talk with you. She was deeply troubled by her memories of it."

"You can't do it, Andrew," Rebecca stated flatly. Her face struggled to hold a firm look. "You can't pastor the church and try to run the school at the same time. Both take a tremendous amount of energy, and I can't let you do it. If the good things that are happening in the church diminished because of it, I'd feel worse than if the school stayed closed. I won't let that happen."

"Rebecca...if I feel this is God's will, are you going to try to prevent it?" Andrew spoke soothingly. "Like I said, this idea didn't start with me, and I wasn't too keen on it when my uncle told me he thought I should pray about it. But since then, it's come very clear to me that it's the right thing to do. I am deeply concerned about how it may affect the church, but if I'm in the will of God, we have to believe that He can keep working in the church. Right?"

"You're saying that from the heart?" Rebecca's voice was filled with emotion. "Andrew, I have to know that."

"Yes, absolutely," Andrew assured her. "And I'm realistic enough to know this isn't something I can keep doing long-term. But until you're better, or until another teacher is found, I believe I can do it, and I believe God will help me with the church."

Rebecca shook her head. "I can't believe it, Andrew. I would never ask you to do this, and I think you're going to make me cry. I couldn't have even dreamed this up. It makes me think that it must be God's idea."

"I'm not quite finished yet, and I was hoping to do this without your crying." Andrew smiled. "I wanted to reassure you that as long as I fill in for you, your teaching salary will continue to come to you. I—"

"Oh no, Andrew, that's not right," Rebecca protested. "If you do the work, you're the—"

"I won't do it unless the money goes to you," Andrew stated firmly. "This isn't for the money, Rebecca. Uncle Harry said it was to serve God, and that's what I'd like to keep it as. Besides, I have a salary coming in, and you don't. If I'm going to keep having all these free meals, I have to do my part. You can't argue with that."

Rebecca could only shake her head as the tears began to flow. Christina's eyes were teary as well, but she got up and took her handkerchief to her mother, who made no attempt to respond to or even look at Andrew.

"I think she means to say thank you," Christina said quietly, turning to Andrew, "and ... I can't believe you're doing this for us, Rev ... Andrew. I keep asking myself why you're really making this offer. I accept your explanation, but I am stunned by it ... and I don't understand it."

Andrew had anticipated Rebecca's reactions to his offer, but even so he was moved by her tears. That he could finally offer something meaningful back for the many kindnesses she had shown him was overwhelming, but there was something about Christina that he found especially unnerving. He looked away for a moment and tried to regain his composure.

"There is one more thing," he spoke again, looking at Christina this time rather than Rebecca. "And this was Annie's recommendation, not mine. I told her that I could cover all of the basic courses, but not music or art. She told me I should ask you whether you'd be willing to take those ... and perhaps help me with some of the grading and paper work. It would probably take a couple of hours a day."

Christina stood motionless beside her mother with her deep blue eyes fixed on Andrew's face. He met her gaze and held it, unsure of her response, but certain that he had never looked into a lovelier face.

"It really was Annie's idea," Andrew urged, suddenly realizing that she must be doubting his intentions. "I'm not meaning this as—"

"I'm sorry," Christina broke in. "It's just that there have been others ... oh, never mind. Yes, yes, I'd be happy to help you in any way possible. Mother's already complaining about never having a moment's rest with me banging around the house. I love children, and it sounds ... well ... fun. I'm not the teacher that my mother is, but I think I can do in a pinch. When should I start, Andrew?"

"If we get the school board to approve this, Annie said she'd meet me on Saturday morning to go over the lesson plans," Andrew answered. "Would you be available then?"

"I'll be there."

Chapter 23

Christina had dreaded this moment from the time she arrived home, but she had delayed her trip to the Wilson General Store as long as she could. Lifting a box of oatmeal from one of the store's shelves and placing it in a basket with other staples for her mother's kitchen, she turned and approached the counter where Vivian stood waiting. For reasons Christina never understood, Vivian had seemingly despised her since the two of them were little children. The near sneer on Vivian's face told Christina that little had changed in the two years they had been apart.

"Vivian, how are you?" she asked as politely as she could, stacking her purchases on the counter, hoping to pay quickly and head out the door. "It's been a long time. You're looking as lovely as ever."

"Miss Christina Ellington, newly returned from Chicago where she studies under a world-renowned painter," Vivian announced loudly, although there was no one else in the store to hear her. She began to write down the items of Christina's bill but was going about it as slowly as she possibly could. "I'm surprised you could take time out of your cosmopolitan lifestyle to return to your humble roots. We're all so sorry to hear about your mother, of course. How's she doing?"

"Doc Anderson says she's doing well, and she hasn't shown any symptoms of apparent complications." Christina smiled politely. "She still has a recurring fever, and she sleeps a lot, but that's typical. Thank you for asking. And if you had seen where I was living in Chicago, or the size of my apartment, you would never call it cosmopolitan."

"I heard you were hobnobbing with some of the richest families in Chicago," Vivian responded. Her tone sounded almost accusatory as she continued jotting down another item on the bill. "Don't tell me your mother was lying."

Christina bit her tongue, feeling all the old bitterness rise in her toward Vivian. "I worked for several very rich families, painting portraits, but I don't believe that qualifies as hobnobbing. It was a great help in paying for my art lessons, and I did meet some interesting and powerful people. But that's pretty much the extent of it."

"When are you going back? I know how much you hate our little village. It must be miserable for you here."

"I came home to care for my mother, and I'll be here however long it takes for her to get back on her feet." Every word from Vivian grated against Christina's soul. "My mother told me you spent a year working in Minneapolis. Did you enjoy it?"

"Like you're actually interested?" Vivian spoke sarcastically, shaking her head. "I got laid off, and I never met anyone remotely rich or powerful. I came home to pursue my dream of working in my father's store. Maybe someday it'll all be mine. What do you think of that?"

Christina felt her composure slipping, but she spoke calmly, "If this is what you want to do, then it's a good thing. At least you have a job. I saw hundreds of people who—"

"You think I can't find a job somewhere else?"

"No, I didn't say that. I just meant that these are mighty hard times for most people, even people who are willing to work hard. To have a job is a wonderful thing. If a company is laying off people, there's nothing the employees can do about it."

"You do have money to pay for this, don't you?" Vivian asked, staring up through her gold-rimmed glasses. "I don't extend any credit."

"Certainly, I can cover the bill," Christina replied. "Is it almost tallied?"

"Almost." Vivian's eyes dropped back down to her figuring. "With no income coming in, I was afraid you and your mother might be broke. I suppose the Andersons are helping you. They're rich."

"Rich!" Christina gave a short laugh. "Annie is a schoolteacher. Do you know what teachers get paid? And my mother tells me that Doc doesn't charge half of what his services are worth, and often he doesn't charge at all. They're not rich by any means. And, Vivian, it's really none of your business where we get the money to pay our bills."

Vivian gave a twisted smile and stopped writing on her pad. She looked up through narrowed eyes. "You'd be surprised at what I consider my business. How long have you and Reverend Regan been teaching at the school together?"

Christina looked at Vivian. She was clearly not surprised by Vivian's ability to meddle. "Everyone knows how long it's been. It was announced in church. Why?"

"Don't you think it's an unseemly relationship that the two of you share?" Vivian accused. "A single man and woman spending most of their day together in a schoolhouse with no other adults around? Sounds a bit scandalous to me."

"Andrew is there for four hours in the morning, and he leaves when I get there at noon." Christina was aghast at this kind of thinking. "That is scandalous?"

"You call him Andrew now? And he always leaves when you arrive? You can prove that?"

"No. On a few days he's stayed to help me, and I've helped him as well. What is the problem, Vivian? What are you trying to conjure up in your mind?"

Vivian's look was the picture of innocence. "I'd just hate to have a rumor start, that's all. It looks like the two of you have pushed the door open to a juicy one, though. Wouldn't it be a terrible thing if you were to ruin the pastor's good name? I guess it runs in your family, though. Bad blood, loose living, some folks say."

Christina clenched her jaw and wanted to grab Vivian by her short dark hair and give it a good yank, but their past history reminded her it wasn't worth it. "I'd appreciate your finishing the bill, Vivian, or I'll leave this stuff on the counter and take my business to Bradford," she said in a controlled tone. "And I don't know why you'd want to threaten the reverend's reputation. You certainly can't damage mine worse than you already have in the past." Christina paused, searching Vivian's face. "Are you and Andrew interested in each other?"

Vivian returned a smug stare. "We've spent several evenings together, and he stops in to talk all the time." She held Christina's gaze evenly.

Christina let out a short laugh. "Surely you don't consider me as your competition? The last person in the world I'd want to marry is a minister. You know that."

"I know that you've always wanted what was mine, and you're not afraid to try to ruin what I have."

"Oh, for Pete's sake, Vivian, I've never done anything like that to you." Christina was clearly tired of continuing the conversation. "Threatening to start a rumor that could ruin Andrew's career sounds very bizarre, if in fact you really are interested in him. Sounds more like you dislike him, or are grasping for some dirt on him. Which is it? Do you really want to hurt him?"

"I just want you to stay away from him," Vivian demanded. "And I'm watching what you do. I'll hurt *you* if you get in the way."

Christina raised her eyebrows in shock at Vivian's declaration, then shook her head in disgust. "You go ahead and keep on watching, but you have no way of hurting me, Vivian, unless you plan to attack me physically. You and your mother have slandered me and my mother for years. There's nothing new that you can add to that. And if you're suggesting that you have some dirty laundry you could use against me, just keep in mind that I know things about your past no one else knows. I'm sure—"

"Here's the bill," Vivian interrupted, handing Christina the slip of paper. "And let me assure you, I will find a way to keep you away from *Andrew*."

Christina pulled some currency from her small leather hand purse and counted out the exact change, then slapped it down on the counter. "Well, Vivian, this has been an enlightening conversation that I wish we never had. Next time my mother needs sugar, I won't think twice about taking my business to Bradford."

Vivian smiled almost pleasantly. "Say, by the way, did my eyes betray me, or did I actually see you in church on Sunday?"

"You never know what surprises might pop up in Liberty Center, do you?" Christina said, picking up her staples. "Perhaps I'll become a regular. Andrew is a fine preacher, isn't he?"

◆ ◆ ◆ ◆ ◆ ◆ ◆ ◆ ◆ ◆

"I warned you not to let her get your goat," Rebecca called out to Christina as she marched through the living room and disappeared into the kitchen. The slamming of cupboard doors followed, then a couple of drawers banging shut, and finally silence. "After all these years, how can you continue to fall into her traps? You know she loves to torment you, and she'll stop at nothing to get you rattled. Are you still in one piece?"

"Yes, I'm in one piece . . . as you can see." But Christina was visually agitated by the encounter. She stepped through the kitchen door into the living room, past her mother, who was sitting up on the davenport with a book on her lap, and moved to one of the big windows that faced the front lawn. "I was prepared for the usual banter, but she's either gotten meaner or I've gotten softer. I've never met anyone like her. She makes me so angry. . . ."

"What was it this time? Did she comment on your being in church Sunday?"

"That was brought up at the end, but only briefly," Christina sputtered as she turned around and plopped down into the large cushioned rocking chair in front of the windows. "I don't want to talk about it. All you need is a little fire on top of your fever to get you feeling sick again. Do you have any idea why she hates us so?"

Rebecca shrugged her shoulders and said, "I don't think her mother ever liked me, although I don't think I ever did anything to offend her. She's never let me forget that your father and I never married. I'm sure that's influenced Vivian. And I think that being in the same classroom with you was always hard for Vivian. You were so talented and bright that you got most of the attention, and you always had a way of getting the boys to turn their heads your way. Vivian made no bones about how unfair that was, and Gertie was always there to support her negative attitude."

"I'll never understand how you ever put up with those two people." Christina sat back in the rocker and felt herself begin to calm down. "You had so many teaching opportunities that would have taken us away from all of this. Why did you subject yourself to it?"

"At first I stayed because Grandma Ellington could never have made it on her own, and she had sacrificed so much for us when we first came. I owed her that much," Rebecca reminisced. "But she helped me to see that if I couldn't forgive the few people who treated me like dirt, I would never be happy no matter where I went or what I did. When you can't forgive, you can't help but get bitter."

"So why didn't you leave after Grandma died?" Christina asked. "You had several more wonderful teaching offers, and you'd obviously perfected forgiving the local stone throwers. I would have appreciated some new scenery as a teenager."

"I ... um ... maybe for your sake I should have left here," Rebecca suggested. "I guess I so thoroughly loved the school and the children— and I still do—that I felt like I couldn't leave. Why go somewhere else to teach when I've got these children to teach right now? You get attached to the kids, and it's not so easy to walk away. You've only been doing it for a few weeks, and you know what it feels like already, don't you? Besides, we would probably have become acquainted with others just like Vivian and Gertie no matter where we went. As soon as they learned the truth, they would treat us the same way. Folks here in Liberty Center knew about your father and me right from the start, so there was no hiding it. Then after I'd become a Christian, it would never have entered my mind to lie and say I was a widow, even if we moved elsewhere."

Christina nodded her head and said, "You're right about falling in love with the children. It doesn't take long, that's for sure. It's so much fun to see one of them actually catch on to how to draw a figure or to see the expression on their face when they sing their part really well. I have to admit that I like this more than I would have dreamed." Christina paused and looked away from her mother, fastening her gaze on the scenery outside the window. She spoke very softly, "I know I would have let people believe I was married. It would've made life so much easier."

Rebecca did not respond to this but continued on with her favorite topic. "I can tell every day when you come back from the school." Rebecca's voice was warm with admiration. "I'm thrilled. I'm glad you have the opportunity to experience what I've loved all these years. See, maybe there's a reason for all of this."

"Vivian thinks I'm out to steal Andrew from her," Christina blurted out, not having intended to talk more about her encounter in the store. "She calls our teaching together an 'unseemly relationship' and 'scandalous'! Can you believe that?"

Rebecca burst out laughing and was immediately joined by Christina. The idea seemed so preposterous that the two of them laughed and laughed until tears appeared at the corners of their eyes. Rebecca finally had to lie back down on the davenport to rest. This burst of emotion had quickly exhausted her.

"Vivian was never all that perceptive of what people thought about her, but she's sadly mistaken about Andrew," Rebecca stated. "I think he has all he can do to act civil around her. She sees everything through a different pair of glasses than he does, I can tell you that."

"Well, I hope Andrew and I can keep our relationship from getting any more 'unseemly.'" Christina laughed out loud again.

"It's easy to understand why Vivian would be attracted to Andrew, though," Rebecca mused. "He's charming, conscientious, caring, and he's so handsome. If I was fifteen years younger, I think I'd be jealous of anyone who got to spend as much time with him as you do."

Christina nodded her agreement. "He seems a catch, that's for sure, but he's a lot more than how you've described. I can't believe he refuses to take any money for his teaching. I've never met anyone like that. It's pretty incredible."

"And it's possible you may never meet another person like him."

Christina became quiet in the rocking chair. Looking down at her hands, she seemed to be checking the pink polish on her nails. "I'm still embarrassed about my reaction when he first asked if I would help with the art and music. I was so certain that the only reason he was volunteering to take your place was to get at me. I've experienced so many men attempting to make me feel guilty into spending time with them. And I did such a lousy job of masking my reaction to Andrew's innocent and generous proposal that was anything but a come-on."

Rebecca gazed with understanding at Christina's perfectly proportioned features. "Oh, he seemed to understand, if I recall it correctly. And from the way he talks about working with you, I think he might consider a ploy or two if it meant getting to know you better. He told me the other day when he stopped by that he'd never met anyone like you . . . that you constantly amaze him. What do you think of that?"

A touch of red spread across Christina's cheeks. "That could mean anything really. It might be a compliment . . . or an insult."

"I think it means that you've charmed him right off his feet, and he's—"

"Now you're sounding just like Vivian," Christina cut in. "Rest assured, there's nothing cooking between the good reverend and the ... ah ... pagan neighbor, as Vivian and her mother used to call me. No scandalous affair is occurring in the schoolhouse, although the scenario might make a great storyline for a novel. Perhaps you could write it."

"Me write a scandalous story? Now that will be the day!" Rebecca was clearly amused.

"Have you never thought seriously about writing novels?" Christina asked. "I've finished reading the partial manuscript you had written when you were...?"

"Fifteen ... or sixteen. I can't remember. It's a silly story, I—"

"It's a wonderful story, and don't ever call it silly again!" Christina was adamant. "The little girl who's lost her mother is absolutely a delightful character, and her father, who reminds me of your father with his aloofness and coldness, is perfect. Some of the storyline needs help, but I'm sure it's a reflection of how young you were when you wrote it. I'll bet if you reworked the story, a publisher would be very interested."

Christina's enthusiasm took Rebecca a bit by surprise, but she was not so convinced. "No, it should have stayed in its drawer where—"

"Mother, how were you going to end the story? You can't just leave the child where she is. What was going to happen?"

Rebecca laughed and pushed her long brown hair back out of her face. "Oh, I'm not sure. Maybe that's why I tucked it away in the drawer. You know as well as I do that the little girl lives for the day when her father will return and take her home."

"That sounds like the ending I'd like to read."

"And I'm sure that's the ending I wanted to write. Unfortunately, every story doesn't have a happy ending," Rebecca stated. "I'm still cheering for the little girl, though."

"So am I. And I'm cheering for you as well. I would really love for you to take some time to retell the story. And I would love it if you would take the time to write out all the other wonderful stories you used to create for me when I was little. Even if they never get published, I want to have these stories for my children, and for their children, because they came from you."

The look in Rebecca's eyes said she was touched by Christina's sincerity and her recollection of very wonderful times together. "You keep talking about grandchildren, and I might just start writing tomorrow."

"What's wrong with today?"

Rebecca leaned her head back against the davenport's cushioned arm, turning her head toward Christina. "Today ... I'm too tired, sweetheart. Besides, I just finished writing a letter, which has totally sapped me of what little energy I had gained from my nap earlier. It actually has taken me four days while you've been off to the school. I was hoping you might get it in the mail for me."

"Certainly," Christina answered. "Where is it?"

"Right here on the end table."

Christina uncurled herself and stood up. She crossed the room and reached for the letter. "Oh my goodness!" she cried, scooping it up and staring at the address. "Is this really to your father?"

"Whose name is on it?"

"You're writing to your father?"

Rebecca closed her eyes and said quietly, "It's time, Christina. I believe it's time."

Chapter 24

"Mother, your fever is up again because you overdid it yesterday," Christina reasoned as Rebecca slowly slid back into bed and allowed her daughter to pull the comforter up around her chin. "I should have never let you go outside and start rooting around with the flowers. I can't imagine what you were thinking. And today you're paying for it."

Rebecca's expression was that of a rebuked child, and she attempted a defense on behalf of her actions. "But it felt so good to get out in the warm sunshine and the fresh air. I think it was worth it. Besides, there's so much work to get done out there if my gardens are going to be ready for winter."

"You let me worry about your gardens, and if I don't get them as perfect as you're used to having them, that'll give you more incentive to be ready for spring," said Christina, sounding very much the parent as she looked at the wooden clock on the dresser. "Oh dear, I'm late. I've got to dash over to the school right now. You stay in bed and sleep for a while. If somebody knocks on the door, don't answer it. You need to rest."

"You're going to the school dressed in slacks?" Rebecca's voice expressed alarm. "You really should change and—"

"Didn't I mention that Andrew promised the whole school we'd have a special softball game this morning if every class was caught up to your lesson plan?" Christina replied. "I'm in slacks because I'm going to play with them. Doesn't that sound like a great way to reward them for their hard work? The children are thrilled."

"You didn't tell me because you knew what I would say, didn't you?"

"You're right. You were purposely kept in the dark, and I told Andrew these exact thoughts that just crossed through your mind," Christina answered with a laugh. "You think the reward is excessive for the fact that they simply accomplished your preset goals. You would want them to far exceed your goals before such a prize was given. Correct?"

"You got it," Rebecca replied sheepishly. "If you give them—"

"Listen, Mother, I'm late for the game already," Christina interrupted. She brushed Rebecca's forehead with a kiss and stepped toward the bedroom door. "And you're wrong about the prize. That the students have kept up to your rigorous lesson plans without your school-mistressing is remarkable, and they deserve a little time off. See you later, and sleep tight."

"I will," Rebecca promised in a soft voice, but Christina was already out the door and down the hallway to the kitchen.

Christina picked up her blue sweater and put it on over her white blouse, then headed out the front door into the bright morning sunshine. The smell of wet fallen leaves awakened her senses, and she deeply breathed in the still, crisp air. The muted sounds of the children playing beyond the school yard caused her to quicken her pace.

As she approached the school building, she couldn't help but smile at the strange realization of how delighted she was to be here, going to play softball with children and the local pastor. Her artistic dreams, which had been so close to being realized, no longer consumed her waking hours but seemed content to take a backseat to the moment. The quiet gravel road seemed a pleasant exchange for the noisy streets of Chicago, and the dark-haired reverend seemed an even more pleasant exchange for the likes of Martin Nelson and other young men who had sought her attention in Chicago. Such musings, even a month previous, would have been unimaginable.

Christina came around the corner of the school and was greeted by the calls of several of the children, all of them wanting her to be on their team and some of them reminding her that she was late. Andrew was up to bat, and he smiled warmly and waved.

"Good morning, Christina. Are you really up to this?" Andrew called out, resting the end of the wooden bat on the ground as she approached.

"Are you kidding?" Christina answered and laughed. "I'm raring to go. Did you think I might not play?"

"Well . . . you don't seem like the ball-playing type," Andrew replied. "I . . . ah . . . guess we should have waited for you. Our team has jumped out to a three-run lead, I'm afraid."

"So that's your strategy! Try to beat us when the best player isn't here!" Christina exclaimed, looking out in the field at her team. Only two children had small leather gloves—an older girl who was pitching and one of the boys who was playing first.

"Why don't you play second base?" Andrew suggested. "There's a little hole there you might be able to plug."

Christina pointed at Andrew in fun and said, "We're going to show you how to play ball today, Reverend. You hit anything my way, you're out of there."

Andrew patronized her with a nod and raised his bat toward her as she ran out toward second base to the cheers of her team. "What do you say, team?" he called out, turning to the children standing off to the side. "Let's bat around!"

"Yes!" yelled his young team members. "Let's go!"

"How many out?" Christina asked, taking her position and glancing around at her teammates.

"Two out and no strikes," Andrew offered, lifting the bat over his shoulders and getting ready for the next pitch.

Eleanor, the tallest girl in the school, pitched the ball in a high arch, and Andrew swung hard and missed, which was followed by hoots and hollers from Christina's team.

"Nice whiff!" Christina crowed, clapping her hands together. "You swing like a rusty beer sign!"

Andrew laughed at the picture her words created, and he hollered his excuse. "The ball got in the sun and I couldn't see it. This one is coming right at you, Miss Ellington. I suggest you prepare to get out of the way."

"Bring it on," Christina yelled as the pitcher let the second pitch go.

Andrew waited for the ball, then swung and skipped the ball into the gap between Christina and the first baseman. Christina got a good jump on the ball, moved quickly to her left, and dove for the ball, knocking it down. From her knees she scooped the ball up and made an easy toss to the boy at first base, just beating Andrew's step on the base.

"I warned you!" Christina exalted as she jumped to her feet and joined the celebration that was already under way as her teammates ran off the field.

Andrew was completely taken aback and could only shake his head as he and his teammates exchanged places on the field.

"You bat, Miss Ellington," one of the younger boys said as she joined the team behind home plate. "We need some runs."

"Okay," she puffed, picking up the bat and walking past the catcher. That bit of exertion clearly pointed to her need for more exercise. "Let's bat around and show these guys what we're made out of."

"Back up! Back up!" Andrew joked as he waved his outfielders deeper into their positions. He stood at first base and started shaking his knees like they were trembling. "It's Babe Ruth's sister!"

"Time to teach you a little respect," Christina threatened as Andrew's team laughed and cheered. She stepped to the plate and took a nice, fluid practice swing. "Just meet the ball," she said to her teammates. "You don't have to kill it. We'll whip them one run at a time."

Christina glanced toward Andrew, who was moving up the first base line toward home and smiled at him. "You're asking for it," she warned. "You get any closer and I might loosen a few of those white teeth."

"Any time," he countered.

The pitcher went into his motion and pitched the ball high toward the plate. Christina waited patiently, then drove the ball deep down the third base line, only to have it slice foul before it landed.

"Whoa!" Andrew exclaimed along with just about every child on the field. Then he backed up almost all the way to first. "Not bad ... for a girl."

"Knock it out of here!" one of the boys on Christina's team called out as the ball was thrown in to the pitcher from the left fielder.

The pitcher readied, then tossed the second pitch again in a nice high arch that got up into the direct sunlight. Christina squinted to see it, then struck it softly to the right side and took off on the run for first base. The ball was spinning sideways toward the first base line, and the pitcher, an athletic eighth-grade boy, was on it quickly. He picked up the ball, spun around, and just missed tagging Christina as she raced past him, then he raced after her down the first base line.

"Throw it!" Andrew shouted from first base as the pitcher reached the ball toward Christina, who remained just out of his stretch. Finally realizing he couldn't catch her, he tossed the ball over her head to Andrew.

As the ball floated through the air past Christina, time seemed to go into slow motion. She saw the ball land softly in Andrew's hands just as she reached the base, but he had made the mistake of standing directly behind the base. Lowering her shoulder, she drove her body into his stationary form and knocked the ball loose, then felt the two of them falling, falling, falling through the air, his hands coming around her sides to protect her. She felt him thud on his back, then crunched down directly on top of him, her face against his face, his strong arms wrapped tightly around her.

Christina heard Andrew's deep moan and her nose caught the faint traces of shaving cream on his cheeks as the two of them lay motionless for a moment. Stunned, it took her a few seconds to recover, and when she did she found she was in no hurry to move away. "Are you all right?" she whispered, pushing herself up with one of her arms and gazing into Andrew's dark eyes.

"I'm not sure," he responded softly, rolling his eyes but not moving a muscle as some of the children gathered around them. "What happened?"

Christina burst out laughing and noticed that one of Andrew's arms was still holding her tight. "I warned you," she said, wiping some grass from his face and then pulling away. "Not bad for a girl, eh?"

Andrew slowly sat up and flexed his back muscles. "Lesson learned, Miss Ellington."

◆ ◆ ◆ ◆ ◆ ◆ ◆ ◆ ◆ ◆ ◆

"So you like teaching together with Rebecca's daughter?" Elizabeth Regan shot a glance at Andrew, who was leaning against the doorjamb between the kitchen and living room. She was sitting at the farmhouse table, skillfully stitching a patch on the knee of one of Harry's overalls.

"It's great . . . well, it's a lot of work, but it's been enjoyable," Andrew replied, looking out the living room window and watching his uncle limp toward the barn and the evening chores. "I think I've been an adequate replacement, but Christina is fantastic with the children. She's got them doing things that even her mother is surprised to learn about. I think I might have enjoyed music and art if I had had Christina for a teacher."

"Don't hurt none either that she's as pretty as the paintings she draws." His aunt sent an amused look in Andrew's direction. "I . . . ah . . . didn't actually think this arrangement would work very well. She never had much time for religion once she reached her teen years. I thought the two of you might knock heads over it."

Andrew laughed at the literal truth of her words and found the reminder to be a pleasant memory. "You thought I would try to get her to join the church on the first day?"

"No, but I got the impression she was a porcupine around anyone who got too lathered up about the church." Elizabeth continued to watch Andrew's face with interest. "Maybe she's lost some of her quills over the years."

"I don't know what she was like before, but I haven't had any confrontations with her, if that's what you mean," Andrew stated, returning his aunt's gaze. "Working with her—she's actually taking over some of the basic classwork for me now—is nothing but a pleasure. I've got some church members who I wish were half as pleasant."

"She's a charmer, that's for sure, just like her mother," said Elizabeth, snipping her blue thread and tying a knot. "You and her . . . are the two of you hitting it off?"

Andrew's expression was of complete surprise at the notion. "No, goodness, no," he protested a little too pointedly, looking back out the window toward the barn. He calmed a bit. "I enjoy working with her. It would be hard to dislike her."

"So you *like* her."

Andrew looked over at his aunt and frowned, then walked over to the table and sat down. "I said I *like* her. Don't you *like* her? Should I not *like* her?"

His aunt picked up her thimble and started back in on another side of her patchwork. "Just because I never got married don't make me blind, Andrew. You're walking on thin ice, and you know it, don't you?"

"What is it about stopping by here for a nice chat with my aunt and uncle?" Andrew asked. "I hardly get my foot in the door and one of you, or both of you, seem to have me pegged about something. Maybe I should stop coming out so often."

"You'd starve if you stopped." Elizabeth gave him a blank look. "I saw you peeking into the kitchen, trying to figure out what I got going on the stove. Now, tell me the truth. You're skating on thin ice with Miss Christina Ellington, ain't that so?"

"No, Aunt Lizzy, I'm not skating with anybody," Andrew said. "I know exactly what you mean, and I'll admit that there have been many moments when I've wished I could put the skates on. But I know better, and I'm being extremely careful."

"You think she's lacing up the skates, too?"

"No, the last person on earth she'd fall for is a pastor. That's what I've heard, and you know that."

"Now you got me scared again, young Andrew," his aunt said. "When it comes to love, the last person on earth may be the best candidate. She was in church again on Sunday—both services. I saw her wearing that lovely blue hat. It's very striking."

"Which is good, don't you think? I mean her being in church."

"Certainly . . . but hopefully it's for the right reasons."

"Certainly . . . but neither you nor I can determine that."

"No, but I'm telling you the skates are hanging on the wall, so you better be careful."

"And I said I will be," Andrew answered. "Now, you tell me what Uncle Harry is so happy about. I've never seen him so animated."

"I don't know, and no one knows him better than me," Elizabeth replied, setting her sewing down on the table to take a break. She leaned back in her chair and smiled. "He would never tell you this, but we've been having some church people stop by from time to time. This morning we had a husband and wife over here."

"For prayer?"

"No, not exactly, although Harry still has some people stopping by for prayer. These people came to apologize to us."

"About what?"

Elizabeth let her arms and hands relax in her lap. "Well, I've known them since I was a kid, and Harry knew them back when he still went to church. They've been feeling real bad about how they treated Harry back then . . . me too, I guess. Seems that they liked to refer to me as the 'idiot's sister,' a fact that your father wouldn't have appreciated. When Harry started coming to church again, they said it made them mad that the idiot was back. Apparently, one of their grown-up children asked Harry to pray for them, which truly humbled them."

"They told you all that?"

"In between crying—both of them. It ... um ... it was ... a ... difficult, but good, morning ... rewarding ... really. Didn't get much work done, though."

That explained to Andrew why Harry was hurrying so fast toward the barn this time of day. "And others have stopped by to do the same?"

"A few." Elizabeth looked straight out the window. Tears had welled at the corners of her eyes. A blink would cascade them down her gaunt cheeks. "I never expected to see Harry this happy ... at least in this lifetime. I always figured it wouldn't be until he was walking on the golden streets of glory that I'd see him really, truly jubilant."

"Did he know before that these specific people thought of him this way? Is that what's making him so happy?"

"He knew of these two people, but I'm quite sure he wasn't aware of the others," Elizabeth said. "But that's not what's making him so happy, although he's happy that they are dealing with this sin in their lives."

"So what is it?"

"You're the pastor, and I have to tell you?"

"I'm not God. Maybe Harry's happy for the sake of the church."

"He's happy for the individuals and for the church, because both are going to be better as a result of these confessions and pleadings for forgiveness. But what makes him most happy is the overwhelming sense that he belongs to the Church of Christ. And it's not because people are apologizing and shaking his hands, which is very wonderful. It's because the truth is dawning on Harry that he really belongs to the eternal family of God, which starts here on earth and is far grander in glory. He's so thrilled, I'm afraid he's going to pop the buttons on his shirts and make me do some more mending."

More than a few tears streaked down her thin cheeks and dropped to her lap. Andrew choked up at the sight, feeling overwhelmed by the wonderful changes that were showering in blessings on these lives whom he had come to love and treasure. He closed his eyes and silently thanked God from the bottom of his heart.

He remained still for a moment, willing the emotions that seemed lodged in his throat to subside. "I'm so glad that I didn't give up trying to talk him into coming to church," Andrew was finally able to say. "Everything changed at that time for him."

"No, son, that wasn't it exactly, although that's been very good," Elizabeth countered gently. "Everything changed the day you let him pray for you to receive the gift of the Spirit. Something inside of Harry changed that day, and something inside of you changed. I don't think we'd be where we are today, if both things hadn't happened."

"You think I changed?"

"Yes!" Elizabeth's eyes shone and she laughed a joyously bright laugh that shook her bony shoulders beneath her flower-print dress. "Oh yes, you changed. But not in a way that everyone sees."

"How do you see it?" Andrew's voice held the same excitement as a small child questioning the contents of a birthday package.

"Simply, Andrew. I see everything simply. Your words didn't change, your sermons are not better prepared, and you look the same, but you have this new kind of *power* behind your life and message. The difference may seem subtle, and yet it's a world apart. You're not the same young man who first pulled in this driveway with half the mud of Michigan on his car."

Chapter 25

Seated at his desk in the den with his opened commentaries spread out around him, Andrew heard the engines of two cars turn off, one right after the other, at the front of the parsonage, followed by the sound of several car doors slamming. He stepped over to the window to see who had arrived. Vivian and two other church couples walked purposefully up the sidewalk. From the look on their faces, he knew he was in for trouble.

When the knock on the front door came, he thought for a moment about simply not answering it, pretending he wasn't home. But he remembered that his car was parked alongside the house, which clearly signaled his presence. He slowly walked through the living room to the front door and could hear their muffled voices but could not make out their conversation.

Groaning inwardly, he pulled the wooden door open and stepped up to the screen door, not opening it but resting his hand on the handle of the screen door. He forced a smile and spoke brightly, "Vivian, good morning. George, Maude, Bill, Harriet, how are you? What brings you folks by so early?"

Vivian didn't give the others a chance to speak. "Reverend, we're sorry to bother you on a Saturday morning, realizing you're probably busy with preparing for tomorrow's services. But we're here to speak with you about your involvement with the school, as well as some other disturbing matters about our church services. As church members, we feel it's our duty to first speak with you directly. May we come in and talk?"

Andrew's smile had disintegrated at her abrupt announcement and request, and for a moment his expression went blank. "No, I don't believe so," Andrew replied flatly, which registered an expression of shock on Vivian's face. "I'm willing to discuss any matter that concerns you, but I think it would be best if I ask one of the elders to join us. I would like to call Arden Walton."

Glancing back at the others, Vivian again spoke for the group and said, "That is acceptable, but I recommend you meet with us alone and hear us out first. You might say something in front of Arden that you'll regret later."

Andrew seemed to ponder her comment. His gaze swept over the group. "I'll take my chances with him here. Now, if you folks would kindly wait in your cars, I'll give him a call and see if he is able to come immediately, unless you prefer to meet at another time?"

"No, we're here to talk now," Vivian sputtered, her voice bristling. "You're not going to invite us in?"

"Not until Arden arrives," Andrew responded in a controlled manner. "Excuse me while I call. If he can't make it, I'll come out and let you know when a better time for him might be."

Andrew closed the door and could nearly feel its paint blister from the glare in Vivian's eyes. He knew it wasn't safe to say anything to her without having an elder close by to back him up later. Given the look on her face, anything he said could and would be used against him, if it served her purpose.

He went into the kitchen to the phone and felt fortunate to catch Arden at home during the midmorning. If he hadn't been able to get ahold of Arden, he wasn't sure which of the other elders he would have called. None of the others seemed to have the same convictions, and Arden was without question the most sensitive to spiritual things. Andrew was relieved to hear that Arden would be there within ten minutes.

Andrew went and stood by the living room window and could see the party of five huddled together in one of the cars. Almost without hesitation, he went back into the kitchen and directly to the back door of the house. Pushing it open, he circled down to the lower part of the lawn, where he couldn't be seen from the road in front of the parsonage. He then cut through Rebecca's gardens and came to the Ellingtons' back door, which was off their kitchen. He knocked hard and waited.

Christina opened the door with a look of pleasant surprise and said, "Andrew, how nice to see you. Come on in. What brings you to the back door?"

"I got problems at my front door," he said calmly, stepping into the kitchen. "Could I speak with Rebecca?"

"Sure. She's in the living room." Christina closed the door behind him. "Go right in."

Andrew wiped his shoes hurriedly on the floor mat and then stepped quickly across the kitchen and paused in the doorway of the living room. "Rebecca, do you have a minute?" His tone gave a sense of urgency to his presence. "I need your help."

Rebecca had been reading. She raised her head, noting the troubled look on her neighbor's well-featured face. "Andrew, what's wrong?" She sat up a bit taller and brushed back a strand of hair from her forehead.

"I need your prayers, and I need them fast." Andrew rushed his words as Christina went to the front windows and peeked out at the two cars parked on the road outside. "Vivian and two other couples from the church want to grill me about my involvement in the school and some of the things that have been happening at church. Arden Walton is on his way to be at my side, but this could get nasty. I knew it was coming, but I didn't think it would be this soon."

"Oh my, I'm so sorry," Rebecca said softly. "I've got you into trouble over this and—"

"It's me she wants out of the way," Christina cut in, turning around and staring at Andrew. "I'm the problem." She moved to stand on the other side of the doorway to the living room.

"What do you mean?" Andrew's face registered bewilderment.

"She's jealous of me," Christina replied simply. "She thinks I'm out to steal you away from her, and this is her way of blocking it. Unfortunately, I was in the store the other day and she warned me. I just didn't think she'd do it." Christina's eyes reflected sadness and concern. "I'm sorry. I should have told you."

A dawning of understanding began to clear away the frown from Andrew's face. "She told you this?" he questioned further.

"Yes. She hates me . . . always has ever since grade school." Christina's tone was clipped. "She admitted that she can't stand the thought of you and me teaching together, and she hinted at scandal. This is the way she's going to stop it. She threatened she would do something. Andrew, why don't you tell them that I've decided I can't help you any longer. If Vivian gets that much out of this debacle she's created in her mind, perhaps she'll back off the other stuff. There's no reason for me to be the cause of a problem that—"

"You're not the problem, and I'm not giving her anything," Andrew declared. "Those schoolchildren love you, and I'm not about to allow her to take you away from them. Vivian's the problem, and we just have to hope that she steps over the line and shows her true colors. Please pray. I have to get back over there."

Andrew turned to go, but Christina reached out and grasped his arm. "Andrew, please! Don't let me get in the way. The children need you more."

Andrew smiled at her and covered her outstretched hand with his, giving it a gentle squeeze. He released her hand and shook his head. "I don't think so. If you give the devil an inch, he'll take a mile. Vivian's not the devil, of course, but she won't stop there. It's time to stand for the truth, no matter what it costs. But I'd sure appreciate your prayers as well."

Christina dropped her hand as Andrew exited the room alone and closed the kitchen door behind him. She watched him go, then turned to see her mother slip off the davenport and kneel on the floor. Although she had seen her mother kneeling in prayer many times through the years, this was the first time since Rebecca had gotten sick, and at the moment the sight was compelling. For the first time in years, Christina actually felt an urgency to join her mother. She took a step, then hesitated, and in her hesitation thoughts took over of how foolish it was for her to do such a thing when she could not believe it mattered.

✦✦✦✦✦✦✦✦✦✦✦

Andrew heard Arden Walton's old Ford truck pull up and stop outside. He went to the front window and observed Arden getting out of his truck and being followed by the five dissident church members. The sight of the six of them walking up the parsonage sidewalk made his heart sink, and he prayed again that good could come of what appeared to be a most ugly scene.

He opened the heavy wooden front door once again and held the screen door open as they entered without saying a word, filing into the living room, where they all found chairs to sit. None of them took off their coats, which made the silence even more grim and lengthy. Andrew noticed that Arden was particularly agitated, spinning his old leather hat in his hands, and his face was red.

"I really don't understand the nature of this meeting," Arden started in, looking around the room at Vivian, George and Maude Clark, and Bill and Harriet Olson. "You're already aware that the church board approved the reverend's working with the school, and we're quite delighted that he's been able to keep it going for our children in Rebecca's absence. Unless we feel the church is being hurt because he's too wrapped up with the school, he has our heartfelt approval. I've seen nothing that changes my opinion on it. His responsibilities to the church have not been hampered thus far. The elders and deacons are quite pleased."

"But we're convinced," Vivian countered, "that the church is already being damaged, and perhaps the board hasn't recognized it. We've been talking about this among ourselves, and we feel there are a lot of members who don't have all the facts."

"You've only been talking among yourselves, Vivian?" Arden sat forward in his chair. "Or have you been talking with anyone else who'll listen?"

"If you're going to be rude, Mr. Walton, we'll simply take this to the whole church like I originally intended," Vivian retorted. "This meeting with the pastor alone was a concession on my part."

"Fine, but just remember that if you want to go down this road, you better be prepared to face the ruts," Arden warned. "In what ways do you feel the church is being damaged?"

Vivian nodded to Maude Clark, who spoke as if on cue, "The reverend declined our invitation to speak at the women's Bible study, which meets on Thursday morning. He said that his school commitments would not allow it."

"Why would you even ask him?" Arden's voice expressed some surprise. A deep frown cut across his forehead. "You know he's teaching at that time, and you know that the board sanctioned this activity. Those are our children in that school, and that's far more important than your women's Bible study. Let's cut to the chase, here, Maude. Whose idea was it to ask the reverend to come?" Arden looked directly at Vivian.

"I said if you're going to be rude—"

"Did *Vivian* tell you to ask the reverend?" Arden cut into Vivian's objection.

"She did, but I thought it was a good idea, and I was looking forward to it." Maude showed no sign that she was in the wrong. "He's the best Bible teacher we have, and we're paying his salary, so why shouldn't he do it?"

"Maude," Arden said, "you've got more common sense than that. You can't expect him to just leave twenty-three children to do something that any of you women could handle! And just because he's the best Bible teacher doesn't mean he should teach every Bible class in the church. You're going to have to come up with something a lot better than this to get the church board to listen."

"What about the money he's making?" Vivian jumped in quickly. "How can he continue to receive his full salary from the church as well as be paid by the school board? Doesn't that seem like he's pulling the wool over your eyes as a church elder? He can't teach the women's Bible study, but he still draws his full pay while he's doing a second job that keeps him from these services? Doesn't that bother you, Mr. Walton?"

Arden drew in a deep breath and glanced over at Andrew, then returned his gaze to Vivian's heated expression. "Quite frankly, no, it doesn't. He's not cut back in any way from what he was doing, and I can tell you that the board doesn't want the reverend to take over the women's Bible study."

"So where's the money going, Andrew?" Vivian demanded. "Perhaps the church board doesn't care, but we do. Don't you feel guilty about this double-dipping?"

Andrew had listened intently until this point, but Vivian's sudden direct challenge only drew an initial chuckle. Doing his best to wipe a smile from his face, he replied, "Do you actually think that I would choose to pastor a small rural church if my intent was to make money? Our denomination has several large city churches whose pulpits are open. Why would I have to resort to double-dipping, as you say?"

"We want to know where the money's going," Vivian stated again. "I think a lot of church members are talking about it."

"Then they'll just have to keep talking," Andrew replied. "You would say that it's inappropriate for me to ask any of you how much money you make or what you do with that money, and I agree that that is inappropriate. And it's inappropriate for you to ask me what I do with the money I earn. That's between me and God."

"But you're employed by the church, and the church has the right to—"

"No, the church does not have that right," Arden cut Vivian off. "What the reverend does with the money earned from teaching the children is completely up to him. Besides, he's only doing this as long as he's needed. He wasn't seeking it as a second job." Arden stood and stretched his back as if it had a cramp needing to be loosened. "What else is bothering you folks? Bill, you look like something's got your dander up."

"Yeah, it does, Arden. And what does the board think about all the emotionalism that has come into our services? I think it's high time we did something about it. It's getting out of hand." Bill glanced from Arden to Andrew. Then his eyes dropped to his fingers pressed together against each other forming a tent.

Arden responded calmly, "You're going to have to be more specific than that. It would be one thing if the reverend was playing on people's emotions, but that's not the case. The fact that after the services a few people are staying in the pews to deal with God . . . how can that be bad, Bill? And if they're truly dealing with God, it's no surprise that some emotions are displayed. I haven't seen anything that I would define as emotionalism, but I've seen plenty of emotions shown. Can you give me one situation that you felt was wrong or out of line? If so, perhaps you and I could talk with the person involved and hear their explanation of what happened to them. If what is occurring is only emotionalism, I want to deal with it. Emotionalism has no long-term beneficial results."

Andrew cleared his throat and said, "Is that what's really driving this question, or is it perhaps more that you don't like my uncle praying with people in the church?" Andrew spoke in a deliberate manner.

He let his gaze connect with each of the five accusers in the room before he continued. "Vivian has already made it clear to me that she doesn't believe he should be involved in this way."

"I agree with her." Bill didn't hesitate to defend Vivian's viewpoint. "He's neither an elder nor a deacon, and he's just started coming to church. Don't you see how it's getting out of hand?"

"People have asked him to pray for them, Bill," Andrew responded with conviction in his tone. "He didn't seek them out ... and he certainly wasn't looking for a position in the church. He is a true believer in Jesus Christ and has been since he was a young boy. Surely you don't feel only elders and deacons are qualified to pray for people."

"No, but it just doesn't seem appropriate," Bill replied lamely. His fingers continued to form a tent, and Andrew noted they were white from the tension.

"If the real reason is because Harry Regan has a cleft palate and clubfoot and we're not comfortable with that, God help us." Arden spoke slowly and deliberately as to children who are getting one more chance to change their tune before punishment is dished out. He looked down and watched his large fingers squeezing the edges of his leather hat. "God forgive us if we treat him as less than our brother in Christ because he doesn't measure up to the norm physically. That his speech is terribly marred has no bearing on the status of his heart, his rightness with God, or the effectiveness of his prayers. I'm afraid to admit that he puts most of us to shame when it comes to communicating with God ... at least he does me."

Andrew took his turn again. "Vivian, I don't mean to be rude, but I can't help but think that you've been talking to these folks when they come into the store," he surmised. "Why are you so opposed to my uncle Harry? I've gotten the impression that you'd prefer that he didn't come to church—that he's a bit of a blight in the pews of the church. Am I wrong? Do you really feel this way?"

Vivian stared at Andrew for a few moments, then said caustically, "I think everyone was better off when he stayed to home. I can't understand having retards limping around our church and praying for people. What does that say about us? I think it's an insult and embarrassment to the other parishioners and guests."

"I see. And what about Rebecca Ellington?" Andrew pressed. "I take it that you talk a lot about her and Christina at the store as well. Would you prefer that the Ellington women remain at home as well, or perhaps attend another church?"

"We've had conversations regarding our concerns over Rebecca," Vivian spoke up boldly, looking at the other four conspirators. "She played the harlot, and the result was Christina. Time doesn't change the reality of her sin. Now even Christina is coming to church. That is an unfortunate blight as you put it, Andrew. But I suspect there's not much we can do about it."

"Except to slander them at every opportunity you see," Arden snapped. By now his eyes were smoldering with deep anger at the declarations of these longtime churchgoers. "I am utterly amazed at my not having confronted you and your mother long ago. For years the two of you have stood behind the counter in that store and spread stories and ill will about people you dislike. Everybody knows you do it, but no one's had the guts to confront you on it." He took a deep breath and shook his head like one trying to shake off a fly. His glare was no less intense. "Rather than this being an indictment against the reverend here, I declare this is an indictment against you."

"Now wait just a—"

"I've waited way too long," Arden cut her off. "The words you spoke about Harry Regan and Rebecca Ellington are not the words of a believer in Jesus Christ. They are lies to be sure, and if you're spreading them around, this is called slander. Tell me, folks, do you agree with what Vivian said?"

The two couples looked at one another and then shook their heads no.

"But you let her talk you into this?"

Bill Olson stood abruptly and spoke sharply to his wife, "Harriet, let's go home." His eyes sought Andrew's. "I'm mighty sorry that I listened to any of this, Reverend. It was wrong. Everything I said was not the truth of the matter. I guess I knew it before I came. Please forgive me."

Harriet stood, as did George and Maude Clark. Their countenances had fallen, like those of disciplined children. Their voices were shaky as they expressed their regrets to Andrew, then made their way out the front door, leaving only Vivian to continue her crusade. She looked as if she was prepared to start in again, but Arden did not allow her the opportunity.

"Vivian," he stated firmly, "I will not allow the lies and the slander and the gossip you have spread in this community to continue unchecked. Your statements about Harry and Rebecca are sufficient grounds for church discipline, which I will pursue at the next meeting of the church board. Unless, of course, you choose to repent. Do you not see how sinful your attitude is?"

"You're not going to scare me into anything. If—"

"There is neither an intent to scare nor to punish you," Arden continued. "The intent of church discipline is to lovingly confront your sin in the hope of saving your soul. It is the last thing we would ever want to have to do, but given what you've said at this meeting, we must do it. And if we begin the process of discipline, you should be aware that we will also be talking with your mother. If she agrees with you on these matters, I'm very sorry for her . . . and for Lloyd."

Vivian appeared totally oblivious to her wrongdoing. "Is that all?" she snapped, standing up and glaring down at Arden, who was still seated.

"Only that we plead with you in the name of Jesus Christ to repent of your ways," Arden replied. "God loves you dearly, Vivian."

Vivian walked across the room and stopped in front of Andrew, who stood up to meet her. "I could have loved you so much more than she ever could," she whispered hoarsely. "You'll regret the day you chose her over me."

Chapter 26

After Vivian stormed out of the parsonage, and after Andrew regained his composure from the blast of her departing words, he spent time talking with Arden Walton about what to do next. Arden felt the best plan was for him to talk with the other board members personally, and then to call Vivian to appear before the church board at their next meeting, which was two weeks away. Andrew was concerned that Vivian might try something else in the meantime, but Arden didn't want to make it look like a rush to judgment.

Much to Andrew's surprise, the rest of that Saturday was void of any further communication from Vivian or her mother. He was quite sure that Vivian was not going to surrender without a fight, and he was even more sure that Gertie would be alongside her. Nevertheless, all three of the Wilsons were at both the Sunday morning and evening services, and there was absolutely no hint at what had transpired the day before. The three did manage to find their way out the church doors without shaking Andrew's hand, but that was understandable and actually came as a relief to him. The worst possibility for Andrew was that either Vivian or Gertie would make a scene in church.

On Tuesday afternoon Andrew got a call from Doc Anderson saying that one of the church's oldest members, Grant Terrett, had suffered a heart attack and wasn't expected to make it through the night. The family requested that he come, which was hardly a necessary request, for Terrett—who at eighty-seven years of age was the community's self-proclaimed "king of the old folks"—had quickly become Andrew's favorite local character. Andrew had never once visited him without the old man telling a story or two from his pioneering days that the long years had helped stretch into yarns rivaling the tales of Paul Bunyan and Babe the Blue Ox. He would miss their fast friendship.

It was late Tuesday evening before Andrew pulled his car to a stop alongside the parsonage and turned off the engine. He was bone weary and emotionally drained. The old man's passing had gone quietly and peacefully, but he was deeply loved by his family and neighbors, and their grief was sharp. Andrew and Doc Anderson had spent several hours with those who gathered at the house, offering comfort as they could.

Andrew exited the car and was walking around to the front steps of the parsonage when he noticed the entryway light come on in the Ellington house. Christina stepped out onto her front steps and waved at him to come over. "Good evening," he called out, shaking off the tiredness as he walked quickly across the lawn. "Is everything all right? Is your mother—?"

"Mother's better—at least she was today—but you'd better come in for a talk," Christina replied. She stepped back into the house and held the screen door for Andrew.

"Vivian, I take it," Andrew muttered, which he gathered from Christina's look of concern as he entered the house and walked into the living room. He plopped down on the davenport, feeling at home, and proclaimed, "I knew the other shoe was about to drop."

"Can I get you something to drink? You look beat."

"No thanks. I really just need some sleep and then I'll be fine."

"I hear you've been at the Terretts' since late this afternoon." Christina sat down in the rocking chair across from the davenport and tucked her legs up under her. She was wearing a long housecoat of soft gray velour. "I'm so sorry to hear that he died. It was pretty hard not to like old General Grant . . . least that's what we used to call him. My mother used to have him come into school and tell stories from the Civil War days. For years we thought he had fought at Bull Run; then it turned out it was his father."

"I kept wondering if the dark tarnish on his father's sword was actually blood like he claimed," Andrew commented. "He was one of a kind, and I'll miss my chats with him. The funeral's going to be on Thursday afternoon." He rubbed his hands up and down over his eyes, hair, and face, then dropped them down onto his lap. "Now, much as

I don't want to know, what has Vivian pulled?"

Christina looked at him intently, noting how weary he appeared, and said, "Maybe it should wait until tomorrow. It might keep you awake if—"

"No, don't worry about it. Let's get the bad news over with."

"Well," Christina began, "I got a call tonight from one of the neighbors. She said that since yesterday morning Vivian's been talking with everyone who's come into the store and calling anyone else who she thinks might have some church influence. Apparently she's been telling them that she and a few others met with you and Arden on Saturday morning and raised concerns about your receiving two salaries. She also complained that you have been letting things get out of hand emotionally in the church meetings. But she said that neither one of you would listen to a word of it; then you forced the others out of the parsonage and proceeded to threaten her all alone with excommunication if she didn't keep quiet."

Andrew shook his head and closed his eyes for so long that Christina thought he might have drifted off. "That was a much heavier shoe than I figured she'd drop," he finally stated, opening his bloodshot eyes and managing a half smile. "She fights much dirtier than I anticipated. Guess I should have asked you for more specifics from the past."

"This isn't all that Vivian's done, though. It gets worse."

"Marvelous. Tell on." Andrew's hands flew up and out in exasperation.

"She's left town."

"What? What do you mean? For good?"

"Her mother has been telling people since late this afternoon that Vivian left for Minneapolis, feeling driven away by you men, sensing that there was no possible way she could vindicate herself with two men's words against hers." Christina watched Andrew's features appear to crumble. She hurried on to finish her thought before she feared he might finally lose his composure. "Gertie was sure that Vivian would never return to Liberty Center. I can't say I felt too bad, until it dawned on me what she'd done."

"Made us look like the bad guys, then hit the road so she wouldn't have to defend herself," Andrew reasoned calmly. "She walks away like the hero, and Arden and I are the scourge of the earth."

Christina was amazed that Andrew remained intact with this summation and smiled wearily. "With the wounded mother singing the blues at the store."

"And she can sing 'em." Andrew let his head fall back heavily on the top of the davenport. "I'm sure this wasn't Vivian's original plan, but it is a dandy backup."

"I wish you would have listened to me," Christina rebuked gently. "She wouldn't have pushed if I were out of the picture."

"It was just a matter of time," Andrew surmised. "Everything needed to go her way, and the minute it didn't, there was going to be trouble. And she either wins or she leaves. This time she leaves, but she feels like she wins."

"So what are you going to do?" Christina uncurled herself and wiggled her toes back to life.

Andrew groaned and slowly stood up. "I'm going to sneak into the Wilsons' house and tie a thick gag over Gertie's mouth. What else can I do?"

Christina burst out laughing and Andrew joined her. It felt good to release the tension, but it was hardly the response she expected from him. "Seriously," she asked when she could stop laughing, "what can you do? Call a church meeting?"

"Seriously?" Andrew's raised eyebrows produced several lines on his forehead. "I don't know how best to handle all this, tomorrow or whenever. My chief concern right now is getting some sleep. I'm not all that prepared for school tomorrow morning."

"You're not afraid about this?"

"Not at the moment . . . maybe I'm too tired to be." Andrew produced a bit of a smile. "King David said that a good man shall not be afraid of evil tidings: his heart is fixed, trusting in the Lord. I don't know how fixed my heart is, but Arden and I were not responding wrongly to Vivian, of that I'm sure. God can turn her evil tidings around and make something good come out of it. I just hope it's soon. I don't care much for suffering."

"My mother said the same and mostly got suffering."

Andrew was stepping slowly toward the door, but stopped and turned to Christina, who had stood up and was following. His dark eyes sparked and all the tiredness seemed to wash away from his face.

"Christina, if I could become like your mother, I think I'd be willing to endure a lot of suffering. Don't miss what's there. It's precious."

The force of Andrew's words nearly caused Christina to take a step backward, and she felt the truth burning at the edges of her soul. She had sensed the same burning on other occasions when she heard him preach. Once again she found herself wanting to respond and open her heart, but there was still much clutter in the way. She could only nod to Andrew, who turned and continued toward the entryway.

"Andrew," she said softly as he pushed open the front door, causing him to stop and turn around again. "I have an idea about tomorrow. Why don't you sleep in, and I'll take the children for the first two hours. You can finish your preparations, and we'll have simply swapped our time slots. What do you think?"

"Hmmm." A smile crept across his face. "That sounds like a plan. Do you think your—"

"Mother won't mind, and you know that," Christina chided. "Now, you get on home and get some shuteye. See you at school."

"Good night." Andrew gave a sad excuse for a salute and disappeared into the dark.

◆◆◆◆◆◆◆◆◆◆

The next few days for Andrew were a blur of teaching, the funeral, and preparations for next Sunday's services. He did review with Arden the situation with Vivian and Gertie, and they decided to simply not do anything until the upcoming board meeting. Arden had had a talk with Gertie, but it appeared that whatever damage was going to be done had already been done. He learned that most people were skeptical of any story that came from Vivian or Gertie, yet there was no question that Vivian had created an unsettled mood in the community.

It was just a little after three o'clock on Friday afternoon, and Andrew was in the parsonage den putting the finishing touches on his Sunday morning sermon when he heard a loud knock on the front door. He got up and headed through the living room, momentarily dreading that it might be Vivian, and was relieved to find Christina instead. But the look of concern on her face did not dispel all of the dread he felt.

"Andrew, you need to come quickly," Christina blurted out before

Andrew could offer any greeting. "Your aunt and uncle—they're up at the Wilsons' store."

"What's wrong?" Andrew picked up on Christina's tone as he grabbed his coat from the hall tree and yanked it on. "Is Gertie after them?"

"Not yet, but come on, please," Christina urged, taking him by the arm and tugging him out the front door. "I'm afraid she's going to do something to them ... say something dreadful ... and soon."

"What are Aunt Lizzy and Uncle Harry doing in the store?" Andrew wondered out loud, following Christina as she cut across the front lawns to the gravel road.

"They're not in the store," Christina replied. "They're on the concrete walkway in front of the store."

"So?"

"So, they're praying."

"Praying ... as in ... praying?"

"What else is there? The two of them are sitting there praying."

"You're kidding!"

"I'm not kidding." Christina was practically exploding with the pre-posterousness of the situation. "And it's driving Gertie crazy inside. I went in there to buy some things and she's like a stick of dynamite that's ready to blow. Seeing me didn't help things any, I can assure you. Can't you walk faster?"

"You're almost running." A laugh began to push up his throat, but it stopped short of producing sound as he came past a tall hedge of shrubs and the store came into view. The first thing he saw was his aunt and uncle's horse and buggy that was parked at the corner of the store; then he saw the older man and woman sitting right in front of the store on the concrete walkway, just as Christina had said. Several neighbors were gathered at the other corner of the store and appeared to be watching the unusual prayer meeting.

"See!" Christina challenged; then she turned to Andrew and put her hand on his arm. "Seriously, you have to talk them out of staying there. I know Gertie's going to hurt one of them. What if she's got a gun? Or maybe she'll say something that could cause as much damage as a bullet."

"No," Andrew soothed, holding her gaze for a moment, trying to dismiss some of the concern. "Gertie gets worked up, but she's not crazy. I'll try to talk them away from the store."

Andrew and Christina crossed the street and walked straight toward his aunt and uncle. Elizabeth saw them coming and got up to meet them at the corner by the horse and buggy. Harry, however, had his head bowed and eyes closed and was absorbed in prayer. His lips were moving, but no sound was coming from his mouth, which was typical for him.

"Aunt Lizzy," Andrew exclaimed quietly, "what are the two of you doing here? You're creating a scene."

"Andrew, this is our business, not yours, so . . . don't be upset," Elizabeth remarked firmly. Her dark brown eyes were clear and commanding in the late fall sunshine. She quickly glanced down at her watch and said, "We had no intent of creating a problem, and I believe our one hour of prayer is just about over. We'll soon be on our way. Harry needs to get the chores started."

"But why are you doing this?" Andrew questioned, glancing from his aunt to his uncle. "You've got Gertie inside there, ready to lynch the two of you."

"She is on the warpath. I could hear her," answered Elizabeth. "Harry told me this morning that he felt the Lord wanted the two of us to come up here and pray that God would overrule whatever damage has been done in this matter concerning Vivian. I wish he had said he was going alone, for I surely am humbled by this, but I too felt it was the right thing to do. Was I to allow my fear of embarrassment about praying in public to stand in the way?"

Andrew looked into her thin face and had no answer. Who was he to tell her she was wrong . . . or right? "Well, you could have talked with me first," he muttered.

"Why?" she asked. "The Lord didn't talk with you about it."

"Should I get Harry?" Christina asked. She had already gone up the concrete steps and was on the walkway. "Did you say the time was up?"

"Yes," Elizabeth replied. "Tell him the hour is over and we need to get home and do the chores. He'll come."

"Do you know him, Christina?" Andrew looked over at her. "I can—"

"Stay there," Christina said, waving him back.

"She was one of the few kids who ever approached your uncle and tried to talk with him when she was little," Elizabeth explained to Andrew. "She'd always come up to him when she saw him. I had a feeling that she knew what it felt like to be rejected."

"She'd try to talk to him?"

"Every time . . . and she had an amazing way of understanding him. I think the two of them sort of hit it off," Elizabeth answered. "She could get him to laugh."

"You're serious? Why didn't you tell me before?"

"I didn't think it would be of interest to you. Are you and her—?"

"We teach together . . . she's my neighbor . . . she's a good friend . . ." Andrew replied as he watched Christina step up to his uncle Harry and put her arm around his thick shoulder.

As Harry turned his face upward to a smiling Christina, the front door of the store suddenly burst open and slammed inward, rattling the big front windows, and then the screen door flew open. Gertie exploded through the doorway with a broom raised over her head and screamed, "Get away from my building, you idiot!" Without a hesitation she aimed the broom down toward the back of Harry's head.

Christina saw the blow coming but only had time to get her body between Harry and Gertie. The broom struck her in the middle of the back, cracking the shaft in two, and knocked her down onto Harry, who caught her with his weak left arm. Gertie held the broken wooden handle in her hand and quickly moved to strike the back of Christina's calf, but Harry intercepted the blow by catching the shaft with his strong right hand and then jerked it from her.

Andrew raced down the concrete walkway followed by his aunt, but it was too late to stop what had happened. Gertie was so livid with rage that when she saw Elizabeth, she dove at her, but it was Andrew who intercepted her this time. Wrapping his arms around the struggling storekeeper, he simply held her tight and lifted her off the ground.

"Gertie, stop!" Andrew ordered as she squirmed and tried to kick. "Your neighbors are watching, and you've really hurt Christina."

"You can't hurt trash," the woman growled, her dark brown eyes wildly searching around. When she saw the stunned crowd gathered at the corner of the store, she immediately simmered down. "Let me go," she pled, but Andrew wasn't about to let her off yet.

Harry said something as he continued to hold Christina in his arms, and she replied, "No, I'm all right, Harry. Thank you for catching me."

"I'm calling the sheriff," Elizabeth piped up, shaking a finger at Gertie. "You should be ashamed of yourself, Gertie Wilson. I've never seen such an ungodly anger. You try to explain that to the sheriff when he—"

"No," Christina spoke as she gingerly stood up and turned to face her attacker. Her blue eyes were pained from the blow, but she did not flinch as she said, "Let her down, Andrew. Let's not give her the pleasure of another reason to hate us. Let her go."

Andrew set Gertie down and slowly released her but was prepared to grab her if she made another fast move. Both her speed and strength had amazed him, and he wasn't about to allow her to strike again.

"You are white trash!" Gertie spat out the words, but Christina did not back up as the short woman leaned toward her. "You drove my daughter away . . . you and that idiot hunchback. You're both a blight on the church and—"

"Enough of your mouth, Gertie," Andrew ordered, his tone authoritative. "You've got enough to answer to God for today. Don't you dare start speaking about the church you've already defamed."

Gertie bristled and yelled, "The Lord's damnation be upon you!"

When she cried out those words, Harry backed up and kept backing up for several steps; then he turned and slowly limped down the concrete walkway to the buggy. Elizabeth put her arm around Christina and the two women followed Harry. Andrew stood stock-still, shocked into disbelief at Gertie's behavior, then walked away as well.

As he came down the concrete steps to the buggy, Andrew heard Christina ask Harry why he had stepped back from Gertie. Harry mumbled his flawed response as he pulled himself up into the seat of the buggy and sat down.

"What?" Christina asked again, looking somewhat stunned by his answer. "Slower this time."

Harry tried again, squinting hard and speaking much slower and clearer.

"Wow!" Christina exclaimed softly as Harry finished and glanced back toward where Gertie had disappeared into the store. She shook her head and looked at Elizabeth, who simply nodded in agreement.

"What did he say?" Andrew asked.

Christina turned her blue eyes toward Andrew and spoke slowly, "He said he backed up because he thought the ground might crack apart and swallow her up."

Chapter 27

*S*unday morning arrived, and Andrew was still so tired that he fell back asleep after he'd turned off his alarm clock. Fortunately, his inner clock woke him just in time to get dressed and organized for the morning service. But he did not have time to go through his sermon notes one last time, which he always did.

As he crossed the street to the church, he carried the same knot in his stomach that had been there since the incident with Gertie. His legs had actually ached the following day, and the only explanation he came up with for this pain was that it had resulted from his encounter with such extreme rage. Greeting church members as he walked into the sanctuary, he immediately sensed the tension in the air. Everyone in the community had heard about the incident in front of the store, and everyone seemed on pins and needles waiting to see if Gertie and Lloyd would step through the double doors, smile, perform their normal greetings, and press on toward the usual third pew from the front. The way the sanctuary was filling up, though, if the Wilsons arrived too much later, they would find their seats taken.

The fact was that Andrew hoped the Wilsons would stay home, and he had no idea what he would do if they did come and if another confrontation arose. He felt a bit of relief that Arden Walton and the elders were there to intervene this time. The more he prayed about it, though, the less relief he seemed to feel, so he finally surrendered it all to God and tried to push it from his mind.

Sitting down to the side of the pulpit and waiting for the choir to join him at the front, he looked at his sermon notes and thought the words that had seemed so brilliant earlier in the week appeared now to be totally irrelevant. "Seeing Is Not Believing, but Believing Is Seeing" was his sermon title, based on verses eight and nine of the first chapter of First Peter, but he wondered if something more like "Mercy, Omnipotence, and Judgment" might have been a better choice.

He looked out over the gathering crowd. Indeed, there seemed to be more folks than usual. He spotted Christina as she entered the sanctuary. Her deep blue eyes and bright smile met his look, and he instantly felt his own heart surge. Despite his best efforts to restrain his feelings toward Christina, the weeks of working with her and all the things they had shared had weathered him to the point that slowly the strings of his heart were surely thinning to the point of snapping. He wasn't fighting these changes. He had never met anyone like her, and to say that he wasn't falling in love would have been foolishness. He was delighted that she continued to come to the services despite what she had said about her own faith.

The choir joined him, and Eunice, the organist, began to play the prelude music. Andrew glanced around the crowded church again, knowing that the remarkable attendance was in anticipation of something special happening in the service, and was relieved to not see either Gertie or Lloyd Wilson. Lloyd, he knew, would be silent as always if he came, but no one could predict how Gertie might act.

His relief was short-lived. He spotted Gertie as she stepped quickly into the sanctuary, glared up at him through her thick glasses, and came straight down the center aisle. She turned into the very front row and took a seat that was almost perfectly in front of Andrew. Bowing her head in prayer, Gertie was the picture of a saint. That her choice of a different seat was deliberate was without question. Except for the organ music, the sanctuary was absolutely silent.

"Oh God, please help me," Andrew whispered in prayer, wishing he could leave and wishing he had picked the theme on judgment. He glanced toward his uncle Harry, whose head was also bowed in prayer. Gertie and Harry were the only ones with their heads bowed. Every other eye appeared to be riveted on him.

The dreaded moment came when Eunice finished her prelude, and Andrew stood to call the congregation to worship. He lifted his hands for the congregation to stand, and as they did, he spoke loudly the words of Psalm 113: " 'From the rising of the sun unto the going down of the same the Lord's name is to be praised. The Lord is high above all nations, and his glory above the heavens. Who is like unto the Lord our God, who dwelleth on high, who humbleth himself to behold the things that are in heaven, and in the earth!'"

Andrew stared down at the last words, which he had hardly noticed as he had selected this verse to open the service, and was caught momentarily by their significance. An awkward silence followed as he considered them, and the congregation waited for him to announce the hymn. But then he looked up and instead began to pray, "Who . . . who is like unto you, O Lord, glorious in holiness, fearful in praises, doing wonders? To think that you behold the things that are in heaven, we can understand. But to think that you behold the things that are in the earth, we must tremble. How grievous it must be for you to see our hearts stained and impure! To think that you would humble yourself, O Lord, to come and live among us . . . and then, wonder of all wonders, to live inside us! Lord, I tremble before you. Lord, I humble myself as the dust before you this morning. Forgive my sins, purify my heart, cleanse my soul, and cause me to only seek to please you. Amen."

Looking up slowly, Andrew was amazed at how free he felt from the pressure of the moment. He saw Gertie standing tall with her eyes fixed on him, but it no longer bothered him. He then took up his hymnal. "Please join with me in singing hymn number seventy, 'Holy, Holy, Holy.'"

The organist began with an introduction, and the congregation joined in on the first verse. Andrew paused to pray that the words of the hymn would ring true in the lives of the church members, and then he heard the commotion from the front pew. Glancing down, he saw that Gertie had collapsed back into the pew and had started crying. What began quietly soon grew loud and disturbing.

The organist kept playing and many members kept on singing as Andrew quickly came down from the elevated wooden stage and went to attend to Gertie. Her uncontrolled sobbing was heart wrenching. Before he could reach her, she slid from the pew and crumbled to a heap onto her knees. The people around her looked genuinely concerned, but no one seemed to know what to do. Those standing closest to Gertie moved aside as Andrew stepped up to the pew.

"Gertie, are you all right?" he asked, putting his hand on her shoulder as he bent down next to her. When she didn't respond, he turned and asked one of the people nearby to get the glass of water that he had on the pulpit. Gertie's weeping went unabated. She covered her face with her hands, seemingly unaware of Andrew's presence. By the time the organist finished the hymn, not a soul was singing.

Suddenly Gertie pulled her hands from her face, and her eyes slowly opened. Her face was wet with tears that she tried to wipe away. She gazed in bewilderment toward Andrew . . . as if she'd been gone for a long time and was trying to remember who he was. Andrew took her hand and offered her the glass of water, but she did not respond.

"Gertie, tell me what's wrong," Andrew whispered close to her ear. She closed her eyes and her head slumped down against her chest once more. Andrew called her name softly several times. Seeming to respond to Andrew's voice, Gertie slowly straightened and focused on Andrew's face. A short gasp escaped her lips. "Dear God, what have I done?" Her face was the picture of abject sorrow. "I owe you an apology, Reverend," she whispered hoarsely, then paused for a moment as if to collect her thoughts. "I need to say something from the pulpit. Please . . ."

The request took Andrew off guard. His mind was still reeling with what he thought was an apparent nervous breakdown of Gertie in front of an overflowing sanctuary. "Gertie, should we get Lloyd?" Andrew grasped her outstretched hand as she struggled to her feet.

"No, this can't wait for Lloyd," Gertie spoke clearly as she reached down to retrieve a hankie from her handbag. "I need to apologize, and I have to do it now. God began speaking to me even before the hymn, Reverend, and He said I must repent. Please, may I take the pulpit?"

Andrew stared into her puffy red eyes, amazed at this radical turn of events, and felt he had no reason to not believe that she was in her right mind. He nodded his assent, then followed Gertie as she walked purposefully up the few stairs to the pulpit. Andrew sat down in a chair next to the pulpit and noticed that Gertie's hands trembled as she reached to hold on to the lectern.

"I . . . could never . . . convince you of what I've just experienced," Gertie started in. "But that's not so important as what I need to do right now. I have sinned publicly, which you all know about, and I need to repent this morning of the terrible, terrible things I did the other day. I called upon God's damnation toward the reverend, Harry and Elizabeth Regan, and Christina Ellington, and to them I am apologizing.

"And if that wasn't enough, I have spread lies to support my daughter's deception about the reverend and Arden Walton," she continued. "All of these things have damaged, and were meant to damage, these people. Beyond that, the Lord has shown me that I have slandered and created rumors about many, many of you in this sanctuary. I have hurt many of you ... too many over the years to remember ... nevertheless, I need to apologize to all of you for my disgraceful life. I am ashamed that my name appears on the membership roll of this church, for I surely have not lived accordingly. I'm asking for the reverend to forgive me, and I'm asking that every person here would forgive me for my offense to you. I cannot undo what I did, but I am asking you to give me another chance. Please, forgive me."

Gertie let go of the pulpit, and Andrew thought for a moment that she was going to collapse backward. He rose and took her into his arms, and immediately she began to weep again. Many in the congregation bowed their heads in prayer, a few wept with Gertie, and others simply watched in a stunned daze. This was all too incredible to fathom.

When Gertie's weeping again subsided, Andrew said gently to her, "On behalf of myself, I forgive you, Gertie. The blood of Jesus cleanses us from all sin, and His blood was shed for you. And I think I can speak on behalf of the church and say that we forgive you. If we confess our sins, He is faithful and just to forgive us our sins and cleanse us from all unrighteousness. We ... I believe that God in His mercy has intervened in your life. Take His mercy and go and sin no more. Start this moment by receiving Christ as your new life."

Gertie's face was still plastered against Andrew's suit coat, and she simply nodded her head. Someone in the church called out, "We forgive you, Gertie!" which was seconded by others. She pulled away from Andrew, wiped her glasses with the handkerchief he gave her, then stepped back up to the pulpit.

"I wish I was done, but I'm not," Gertie continued. "There are two people here whom I've particularly sinned against." Then she stepped out of the pulpit and walked down off the platform with Andrew following her. She headed straight for his uncle Harry, who was seated at the aisle end of a middle pew.

Stopping alongside Harry, her red-rimmed eyes bulging out at his squinting eyes, Andrew thought it a humorous sight, despite the solemnity of the moment. Every eye in the sanctuary was focused on them.

"Harry Regan," Gertie declared, shaking her head, "I called you a terrible name, and I've said even worse things about you to others behind closed doors. You showed me in front of the store what a fool I've been, and I'm ashamed that I was a big part of why you stopped coming to church all those years ago. I ask you to forgive me, and I know it's asking a lot, but would you pray for me that I might be changed?"

Andrew was at a loss for words. This about-face in Gertie was unexplainable. He was dumbstruck along with the rest of the congregation. But Harry smiled, then suddenly laughed out loud. It was easily understood as a laugh of joy. He swallowed Gertie up in a big hug, his strong right arm wrapping around her, and he muttered something to her that no one understood, including Gertie. Then she pulled away and did the unthinkable, lightly kissing Harry on the cheek, which brought an eruption of cheers and claps.

Looking around, Gertie spotted Christina, who was utterly moved by what she'd seen and heard of Gertie's confession to the congregation and Harry. Christina began to cry as Gertie approached her and reached for her hands, taking them tightly into her own. She spoke brokenly, "I cannot possibly expect you and your mother to forgive me; nevertheless, I'm going to ask. My daughter and I have caused you more grief and pain than anyone else in this room can imagine. I've damaged your reputations and slandered your characters beyond measure. You have no reason to forgive me. But I am asking you, Christina, to forgive me. I can't make it up to you, but please forgive me."

Christina's emotions were in a rugged state. Her tears couldn't be stopped. She stood and looked into the eyes she had long despised and saw the change, but she couldn't forgive as easily as the others. She pulled her hands from Gertie's grasp and tried to wipe away the tears that blurred her vision. Andrew put his arm around her, and she leaned against him as she struggled to say, "My mother . . . is feeling stronger

... and she's dressed. I won't forgive you unless you apologize to my mother ... in front of everyone."

Gertie's composure had returned in an amazing fashion. She wiped away any remaining tears with the handkerchief, smoothed back her hair, and slid her hands down over the skirt of her dress. She blew her nose as quietly and discreetly as possible. Glancing up from Christina to Andrew, she replied, "That's fair. Do you mind taking the church service outside?"

"No. No. Not at all," Andrew responded almost mechanically, still stunned by all that had transpired. Letting go of Christina and signaling for the church to follow them, he turned swiftly and called out as he passed pews on his way toward the entry, "Anyone who wants to join us, put your coats on and come along."

Slowly the church sanctuary emptied out and headed across the road to the Ellington house. Fortunately, it was a sunny morning without any wind, and the temperature was a little over fifty degrees. Christina ran all the way home. It was all too incredible, but she focused on getting her mother ready, trying to provide a logical explanation of something that was anything but logical.

Rebecca wasn't grasping well why her daughter had dashed into the house, had grabbed a brush from her dresser, and was prodding her to get up and move to the living room. Christina was trying to communicate the reason, but Rebecca's sleepy brain couldn't seem to focus fast enough to comprehend. She allowed Christina to maneuver her out of her bedroom and toward the front entry, where Christina touched up her hair and then reached into the closet.

The longer the people waited outside, the closer they moved toward the Ellingtons' front door to be able to hear. Andrew and Gertie came up and stood patiently on the steps.

Soon the front door opened, and the congregation cheered as Christina emerged with Rebecca, who had on her winter coat. Despite whatever damage Gertie and others might have done to Rebecca's reputation over the years, she was deeply loved by most of the church. And after weeks of being hidden away and the worst of the rheumatic fever having passed, it was a great joy for the people to finally see her. Rebecca looked around in bewilderment. She held up her hand to shade her eyes from the sunlight as she gazed over the congregation in disbelief and held on to Christina, overwhelmed by it all.

Rebecca then noticed Andrew and Gertie right in front of her. Their presence brought a puzzled look to Rebecca's eyes. "I don't understand...."

Gertie stepped forward and broke into tears again. "God won," she blurted out to Rebecca. "After all the evil I've done, and after years of your never once returning evil for evil, He brought me down and showed me the blackness of my soul. Rebecca, I know what a godly woman you are, and I know you've forgiven me a thousand times without my ever asking you. Today, in front of all the church, I'm here to ask you to forgive me one more time. I hope to never give you another reason to forgive me, but I've hurt you and Christina countlessly. I am so sorry. Please forgive me!"

The final words were so high pitched they were nearly a squeal, and Rebecca let go of Christina and wrapped her arms around Gertie's small frame. "I forgive you, Gertie," she whispered to the weeping little lady, and Christina reached her arms around both women and said gently to Gertie, "I forgive you, too."

It was a deeply moving scene, and the impact on the congregation could be measured by the stillness of the crowd as well as the looks on the faces of the church members. Andrew was amazed as ever by the incredible events of the morning. He wondered what to do next, but felt he couldn't do anything until Gertie was finished.

Gertie remained in the embrace of Christina and Rebecca for several minutes, then pulled back and turned toward the congregation again. "One more thing," she pleaded, "and you won't hear from me again for a long time. With Rebecca's illness, I've known I should do something to help her, but the hardness of my heart has kept me from it. I'm here to do something about that as well." That said, she reached into her purse and pulled out a ten-dollar bill and handed it to Rebecca, who tried to hand it back, but Gertie was already making her way down the steps and through the crowd.

Andrew felt a bit shell-shocked, standing there with most of the congregation's attention now fixed on him. He rubbed his hands over his face and looked at Christina and Rebecca, who were all smiles and holding each other again; then he surveyed the congregation and said, "We could go back into the sanctuary and I could preach my sermon, but I honestly don't think it's the message you were meant to hear this morning. We've just witnessed a wonderful demonstration of how God can take a very damaged relationship and turn it around by His grace. I think it's the message that God wants us to ponder in our hearts.

"Perhaps there's someone in your life you have hurt or damaged your relationship with," Andrew continued. "Today would be a great day to do something about it. Humble yourself and go and talk to the person. Apologize if you need to, ask forgiveness, pay back the money if you owe it to someone. But don't wait. Do it now . . . while it's on your heart . . . before you close the door again and the walls of separation go up. Then go in peace, and the God of all peace shall keep your hearts and minds in Christ Jesus, amen."

Andrew watched the congregation linger for a moment, then slowly begin to disperse. Much to his delight, and somewhat to his surprise, he saw many individuals pairing up and talking very seriously. It appeared to him that more was happening directly as a result of this one incident than had happened in all the previous church services he had led.

But the most remarkable scene took place at the Ellington house. One of the church members had stepped past Andrew and asked Rebecca and Christina if she could have a word with them. Rather than remain in the cool fall air, Rebecca suggested they go inside and talk. After they went in, a line slowly formed at the door of church members who apparently were waiting for their chance to apologize to Rebecca and Christina. One by one the confessors went forward, extending well into the afternoon, as the simple home in the village of Liberty Center became a haven of forgiveness and reconciliation.

Chapter 28

Christina pulled the schoolhouse door shut behind her and turned to make her way home. As usual, she planned to stop and update Andrew on what she had accomplished with the students that day. During the first week of teaching, she had simply left Andrew a short note each day regarding their progress, which he read when he came in before school started. But she so enjoyed being with Andrew that stopping at the parsonage provided the perfect excuse, and she determined that today would be no exception.

Cutting across the gravel road, Christina spotted Andrew sitting on the front steps of the parsonage. While he gave the appearance of looking down and reading a reference book, she noticed that his eyes were actually on her as she approached, so she pretended to not notice him and marched straight across the parsonage lawn to her house.

"Hey, where you going so fast!" Andrew finally called out as she nearly made it to her lawn. "Don't tell me you're so blind that you didn't see me here."

Christina laughed and turned back toward Andrew. "Oh, I saw you, but you were so absorbed in your book that I thought you wouldn't want to be disturbed. You have a funny way of reading. Your head was down, but your eyes followed me."

"So I was waiting for you," Andrew confessed, displaying a slight shade of red on his cheeks. "So how'd it go? Did you finish grading the history tests?"

"Of course," Christina replied, her demeanor full of spunk and charm as she sat down on the steps next to Andrew. "And we worked on the play this afternoon. If I can just get the Billingsley boy to memorize his lines, the parents will love it. He's the only one who seems less than enthusiastic about it."

"We need your mother to spark him up a bit." Andrew noted again her sparkling blue eyes. "Speaking of Rebecca, how's she been since Sunday? You've had a raft of visitors over there. Makes me nervous that she's going to get too run-down."

Christina tipped her head to the side and pondered her mother's present condition. "No, I don't think so," she spoke softly. "The past three days have been like tonic to her soul. So many people have stopped by—some to apologize for stuff from years ago, others to simply tell her how thankful they are for her and what she did for them at some point in time. It's amazing, and she's amazing. The more I hear from others, the more amazed I am at how wonderful she is. Instead of tiring her out, I'm convinced she's stronger than she's been at any point since she got sick. I think the fever is totally gone, and it's primarily the tiredness that remains."

"That's terrific news," Andrew said as he closed his book and glanced into Christina's face. "Are the people who are stopping by talking to you as well?"

Christina nodded and looked away from him. "Some of them are, but most of it regards my mother. It's been very emotional, though, for both of us."

"What do you make of it all? Obviously, you don't think it's church foolishness. But what do you think of it?"

Christina's blue eyes flashed back at Andrew, then she looked away again. "Trying to pin me down, aren't you?" she said half teasing and half not. "I honestly don't know what to make of it all, Andrew. People I'd written off years ago as hypocrites are suddenly sitting in our living room, crying their eyes out, asking us . . . some are begging us . . . to forgive them. Watching my mother, listening to her responses, what's happening is just so right . . . so true . . . that I can't explain it. If I believed in miracles, which I almost think I do, I'd say this is a real one. I assume you already do."

Andrew whispered a "wow" before he could check the words. "Yes, I do," he replied. "If it wasn't God who was speaking to Gertie, I'd like to know who was. She's like a new woman in the store. People can't believe it."

"It's very hard to believe."

"But it is believable, seeing the new-and-improved-beyond-measure Gertie."

"Yes, it is," Christina replied, looking down the road at a slow-moving car that had just turned the corner and was coming toward them.

"So, what is it that keeps you from believing now?" Andrew pressed.

"Who is that?" Christina asked, diverting Andrew's probing question. "I don't recognize that car."

Andrew looked down the gravel road and said, "Whoa! It's a brand-new silver Packard. There's no one around here who can afford one of those. I don't recognize them. The license is from out of state."

"Oh, my goodness!" Christina shrieked, suddenly jumping up and running out toward the road. "Grandmother!" she cried out and waved. "We live here! Here!"

The car pulled into their driveway and came to a stop just as Christina reached it. Taking the handle of the passenger door, she pulled it open and cried, "Grandmother! I can't believe you've come!"

Grace Adler's green eyes were sparkling with excitement as she stepped out of the car and hugged Christina. "Oh, I've missed you!" she exclaimed, holding her tight. Then she whispered, "Your mother wrote and asked your grandfather to come. He finally broke."

Christina felt her grandmother tremble, and she burst out laughing for joy. Peeking around her grandmother's head, she could see her grandfather sitting perfectly still behind the steering wheel, staring at the house. "Grandfather!" she released her grandmother and leaned into the opened door. "Welcome to our home. This is so incredible. Come on. Let's go see my mother."

William Adler glanced at her and smiled but shook his head. "You go ahead with Grace," he urged. "I'm not ready for this. Just … give me a moment. Go on and take your grandmother in."

"Let's go, then!" Christina grasped her grandmother's hand, tugging her toward the house. "Mother's going to collapse when she sees you!"

"Is she well enough … it's not going to be too much of a shock?" her grandmother asked, hurrying along behind Christina.

"No, her fever's gone. But she'll be shocked all right." Christina suddenly stopped. "Andrew!" she called out across to the parsonage steps, where he was still standing. "This is my grandmother from Chicago! It's another miracle!"

Andrew waved and laughed at the comical sight of the elderly lady with the white hair being towed up the Ellingtons' front steps. "It's a season of miracles," he suggested silently as the two women disappeared through the front door.

"Mother!" Christina exclaimed as she stepped into the living room and stopped to listen. "Mother!"

"Christina, what's wrong? I'm right here," Rebecca's voice spoke from the kitchen; then she stepped into the living room doorway and froze in place. "Oh, dear Jesus!" she cried, her hands flying to her face. "Mother!"

"Rebecca!" Grace Adler gasped as she ran across the room and wrapped her arms around her daughter. "Rebecca! I'm so sorry! I'm so sorry!" Then she burst into tears and moaned. "I'm so sorry!"

"Mother, you know I forgave you years ago," Rebecca whispered into Grace's ear. Tears were streaming down Rebecca's face, but only tears of extreme joy. "No more apologies. You're here, just like I asked you to come. That's all I wanted. You and Daddy. Is he here?"

"Yes, he's in the car," Grace replied, holding tightly on to Rebecca. "When we heard you were sick, he wanted to come, but he couldn't let go of the past. . . . He couldn't forgive you, even though he knows he's the one who needs to be forgiven. But your letter did him in. I'd never seen your father cry until he read that letter."

"I'll go out and see how he's doing," Christina offered, wiping tears at the tender sight of her mother and grandmother finally reunited. "Is he still mad at me?"

"No, Christina, no." Grace glanced up through eyes brimming with tears. "But he's angry with himself, and it's a deep pool of painful regrets. He needs to know that both of you can forgive him."

Christina turned and walked out the entryway and through the front door. She could see her grandfather still sitting in the front seat of the car. Then she noticed that Andrew was raking the leaves on the front lawn of the parsonage.

"How'd it go?" Andrew asked as he set his rake down and walked toward her. "Is your mother all right?"

"Couldn't be better, thanks." Christina couldn't smile any brighter.

Her heart was overflowing. Her eyes focused on the sleek vehicle in the driveway. "It's the next one that's going to be hard. He won't come in."

"Do you want me to talk to him?" Andrew asked.

"No, not yet, anyway," Christina said. "I think he needs a little reassurance from me. We didn't exactly get to the 'grandpa and me' stage, but I know some things I said to him did dent his armor."

"I'll keep praying, then." Andrew reached out and gently squeezed her shoulder.

"Thanks." Her blue eyes were sincere and her smile appreciative.

"You do mean that, don't you?" Andrew acknowledged.

"What?"

"You're thankful not just as a courtesy, but you're actually thankful for prayer, right?" Andrew answered, fishing around a bit.

Christina held his gaze. "After everything that's happened, are you suggesting I might not believe that prayer gets answered?"

"It's possible."

"No, not anymore. Twenty years of my mother's prayers have been answered in that man sitting in his car over there. I know what he was like, and something's happened. I can't explain that away. Right now, I only care that he's there . . . and that I can get him to come inside."

"He wouldn't have driven all the way from Chicago to sit and stare out a car window," Andrew reasoned. "All he needs is your hand in his, and he'll melt like butter."

Christina smiled and put her hand on Andrew's right forearm. Then she said, "You're absolutely right. I can't tell you how much I appreciate your being here. I would like it if we could talk later."

"About—?"

"Guess, if you can," Christina replied, squeezing his arm and then turning to walk toward the car. "I thought you would have figured it out by now."

Andrew didn't move, nor did his eye stray from Christina as she walked in her usual graceful motion across the lawn. It wasn't until she reached the car that he returned to his rake and began to haphazardly heap leaves into piles, giving Christina and her grandfather some sense of privacy.

Christina opened the passenger door and slipped onto the plush front seat of the car without speaking a word. Her grandfather had taken off his leather hat and set it down alongside him on the seat. His large hands still rested on the steering wheel, and his wide shoulders were slumped. The somber expression on his face did not change.

"When I first arrived here," Christina started in, speaking slowly and gently, "one of the first things I told her was that you still loved her. I actually think it's made a difference in her recovery. On some of the long, bad days when her fever was up and every joint in her body seemed to ache, she'd talk about you and what it was like when she was little. It was a challenge for me to think of the two of you sitting on little chairs in her room and enjoying imaginary tea together. Did you really do that?"

William Adler smiled slightly and nodded his bald head.

"She's . . . um . . . waited twenty years to see you, and she really wants you to come in," Christina's voice was pleading. "You can't be wondering whether she forgives you or not. She wrote you about that, didn't she? But that's never been an issue, and you've known that. My mother cannot withhold forgiveness. Her heart would never allow that."

"And what about you?" he asked, finally looking away from the house and into Christina's face. "You know what I did to your mother . . . and your father. I did everything I could to drive him away. And when you came to my office, I set myself to get you out of Chicago and away from our lives. I can't believe you don't hate me. You'd be foolish not to."

"Call me a fool, then," Christina suggested, reaching out her hand and taking her grandfather's right hand in hers. That he did not pull away immediately choked Christina up, and she squeezed his hand warmly. "It's time to bury the hate, Grandfather. It's stolen so much from us already that we can't afford to let it separate us any longer. I forgive you for everything you've done to hurt me, and I'd like the opportunity to get to know you. I've never had a chance to love a grandfather, but you're going to have to do a little better than you've done so far if we're going to make this work. What do you say?"

"I think your father would be extremely proud of you," her grandfather said, tears etching down the stony features of his face. "You have no idea how many times I wish I could have been the one to die in France. If only I had welcomed—"

"But *you* are alive, Grandfather, and my father is long dead," Christina broke in. "My mother loved my father so much that she never even looked at another man, and there were plenty of men interested in her. All she has is you and Grandmother and me. Don't deny her any longer. Please come with me . . . now. She still calls you 'Daddy,' and she's waiting."

William nodded and closed his eyes tightly, squeezing out another wave of tears. He let go of Christina's hand, opened the door, and walked around the car toward the house. Christina did the same and took his hand as she met him at the front of the car. She led him slowly past the living room windows and up the steps to the house.

As Christina opened the front door, he suddenly gasped, "I can't do this!" pulling his hand loose and backing down the front steps.

"You can do it. You have to do it," Andrew piped up, standing at the corner of the parsonage nearest the Ellington house, where he was still pretending to be cleaning up the leaves. "God listens to Rebecca's prayers, and He's not going to let you go until you do."

"Who are you?" William whipped around and snapped, sounding much like the businessman he was.

"Just a neighbor," Andrew replied. "Don't spoil what God's trying to do for you. In your heart, you want this as much as He does."

"Christina, who is he?" her grandfather persisted.

"He's the reverend," she replied. "He's a dear friend of ours."

"You're the one who's been teaching in the school for Rebecca?" William questioned Andrew, who simply nodded as he stepped closer to them. "For free. Why would you do that?"

Andrew laughed and shrugged his shoulders. "Sir," he said, "it's a long time since you've been with your daughter, but I can't believe you've forgotten what she's like. I would do anything within my power to help her, and the little I've done, I count it a privilege. You raised one of the nicest women I've ever met, and I can't let you walk away. Would it help if I went with you?"

"No," William replied with a half smile, "but I appreciate the offer. I'll be all right, and you don't want to watch me. I can already feel it, which is why I backed off. We need to talk later, young man. I've already done something about this school situation."

Christina reached out and took her grandfather's hand again.

When she did, she felt him tremble, and for the first time she put her arms around him and hugged him. He stood like a stone statue, shaking, and tears began to pour down his cheeks again as she held him tight. Then finally he put his long arms around her and hugged her back.

"Daddy!" Rebecca's soft voice spoke from the front doorway, where she stood holding on to her mother. "Daddy, I'm here!"

"Rebecca!" he called out, his voice clearly in agony. Then, with what sounded like a protracted moan, he released Christina and ran up the steps to Rebecca. "Oh, dear God, I'm sorry!" he cried out, clutching her in his arms as Grace joined the two of them and put her arms around Rebecca as well.

Christina stood still for a moment, watching a scene that she'd never even dreamed possible as it unfolded on the front steps of her house. The sound of their crying pierced the depths of her soul, making her want to cry out for their healing. Then she noticed that Andrew was watching . . . and weeping . . . as well, his rake lying on the ground next to him and his arms limp at his sides. She ran to him and hugged him tight without speaking a word, and in his arms she knew that life would never be the same for them again.

Chapter 29

"*I* appreciate your praying with us, Reverend, especially for me," William Adler said from the living room davenport, where he had his right arm wrapped around Rebecca and his left around his wife. "I have a terrible time believing anyone can forgive me, and particularly God. When you spoke the Bible verses, I can't explain the power I felt inside ... like the chains were dropping off me."

"They did drop off, William," Grace assured him, patting his hand. "I can see it on your face and in your eyes, and I can hear it in your voice. Now we just have to keep the chains away ... from taking hold again ... to all of us."

"Only one way to do that," Rebecca said, "and that's by staying close to Jesus. He is the only One who can set us free from our sins, and He's the only One who can keep us free. You can never allow anything to separate your faith from Him and the truth He has shown you."

William smiled weakly and said, "I know how strange this must sound coming from me, but I feel like a man who just rose from the dead."

Grace looked up at him and added, "Like Lazarus after four days. Remember how Martha told Jesus that 'by this time he stinketh'?"

"That about sums me up," William replied, breaking into laughter. "When I paid off Carl Langstan to cut off Christina's lessons, it's hard to imagine reeking any worse than that."

"You did what?" Rebecca asked, sitting up straight. "Christina, you never told me."

Christina shook her head and smiled. "As sick as you've been, you didn't need to know," she said. "Besides, there was plenty more where that came from. Grandfather wasn't smelling so hot when he paid off the police and my neighbors and my landlord to get me kicked out of my apartment. Maybe we should go through the list of things to forgive you for again."

"No, it's way too long . . . and way too ugly." Her grandfather grimaced. "I prefer things as they are right at this moment."

"Earlier you said you'd done something about the teaching situation," Andrew said. "What did you mean by that?"

"Exactly what I said. I've taken care of it," William answered. "On Monday there will be a young lady from Chicago arriving at the train station in Bradford. I've hired her to teach the rest of this school year, with the future to be determined by what Rebecca wants to do next year."

"You can't just—"

"I didn't do this on my own. Actually it wasn't my idea at all," William interrupted Rebecca's protest. "Grace and her neighbor friend, Maria Sikkink, knew this woman from church. She's an excellent teacher, and she's wanted to get out of the big city for a long time. This seemed like the perfect place for her. I told her that if she was willing to come, for one year I would match whatever she'd also be receiving as the regular teacher salary here."

"But that's my only income," Rebecca said. "I have nothing to fall back on if—"

"You don't have to worry about your income," Grace assured her. "William and I have talked about it, and we're hoping that for a time, at least until you're feeling strong again, that you'll let us take care of things. I was hoping, for my sake at least, that you'd consider coming to Chicago for a while. I feel like this may be our chance to put our lives back together. William and I aren't getting any younger, which you might have noticed. Money is not a problem."

"But this is my home . . . and my school," Rebecca replied. "My life is here. I appreciate your offer to help, but I'm not looking to change anything."

"And we're not suggesting that you do," said Grace. "But it could take you months to fully recover from the rheumatic fever, and we've found a wonderful teacher to fill in for you. Don't you think it's possible that the good Lord is giving us back the years that the locust has eaten? That's what my friend Maria said. Why not come to Chicago for the winter and be with us? We even have a room for you!"

Rebecca laughed and squeezed her mother's hand. "Christina tells me that it's exactly the way it was when I left. Sounds like the museum is in need of some updating."

"It desperately needs your help," William said. "Your mother refused to do anything to your room, and I couldn't go in there . . . ever. It was too painful. When I saw Christina in your blue hat, I thought I was going to collapse."

"You did get a little green around the gills," Christina added. "Sort of like you'd seen a ghost."

"I guess I did . . . like Dickens' old Scrooge," he replied. "Rebecca, I can beg if it would help, but I really want you to come home for the winter. I'm . . . ah . . . I'm going to sell my business when I get back. I've spent enough time salvaging what was left of other people's businesses. It's time for me to salvage what I've got left of my life. That starts with you . . . and Christina."

"Just say yes, Mother. It's the chance of a lifetime," Christina urged, easily reading the yearning she saw in her mother's face. "And I'm sure that your dear friend, Edgar Mitchell, will be thrilled to see you. He said the most amazing things to me. Grandmother, I asked him why I should give you and Grandfather a chance at all. Do you know what he said? He said that I had a chance to end the darkness. I didn't know what he meant at the time, but I do now."

"He will be thrilled, and he's a fine Christian man," Rebecca said. "The night when I left Chicago, he took me to the train depot and told me that he was going to pray for me every day . . . every day. I believe he has, and I believe we owe him a deep debt of gratitude. And, yes, I very much would like to return home . . . for a while. The time has come . . . finally."

"It'll give you a chance to consider what you want to do with the rest of your life," Christina added. "You're only forty years old, Mother. Maybe it's time for change."

"What else would I want to do?" her mother asked, turning her full gaze upon Christina. "The saddest day of my year is the day school closes for the summer. If I didn't have my flowers to tend to, I'm not sure what I'd do."

Christina smiled and shook her head. "I don't know that anything should change, but what if you never get the stamina back that it requires to teach? Or who's to say that you're to stay with this school? Maybe . . . there's another school out there for you. Or . . . what if you took some time and explored your writing? What if it's time for you to write the stories that are in your heart? Think of the thousands of people out there who might want to read them and benefit from them."

"No, I'm no—"

"You are a gifted storyteller, and I watched your eyes light up as you read through the manuscript you wrote years ago," Christina interrupted her mother. "You know, and I know, and Grandmother knows, that it's publishable. Think if you were to rewrite it now, knowing what you know. I'm sure that Grandfather knows a way to put it on the desk of a publisher or an editor. I watched him pull a whole bunch of strings."

"I sold one of my buildings to the Morgan—"

"You're getting way too far ahead of me here," Rebecca broke in on her father. "Let's stick with getting to Chicago and airing out the museum."

"Just don't be stuck in a rut, Mother," Christina persisted. "You no longer have to look out for me. You're free to do what you want, and with your gifts, there are a lot of possibilities."

"Christina, you'll come with your mother, of course," William stated. "I'll get Langstan to resume the art lessons and you can stay with us. And you won't have to support yourself with—"

"I'm not interested in studying under Mr. Langstan anymore," Christina said. "If he was so willing to be bought out, I don't want him for an instructor. Every time I'd look at him, I'd want to punch him. Besides, somebody needs to be here to take care of the house."

"I'm sure the new schoolteacher would be more than happy to have a place to care for until she can find a place of her own," her grandmother said. "We truly want you to come with your mother, Christina. If you'd like to set up your own art studio, you can take any room you'd like and have as much space as you want. Perhaps there's another art instructor in Chicago whom you'd like for a teacher. We can pay for it."

"I truly appreciate your offer, and it sounds . . . wonderful," Christina replied, taking a deep breath of air. "I'm just not sure that I'm ready to go back to Chicago. I know it must sound strange to you, Mother. At one time I couldn't wait to leave this village and get away. But it's been good for me to be back here, and I'm not sure what I want anymore. I don't understand how your whole world can change in only a few months, but mine has. Maybe I need time alone to figure it out."

Rebecca nodded and said, "I've often thought back to how drastically my life changed after I left home, Christina. I got here, then the news came that your father was killed, then Grandpa Ellington died, leaving us without any income. Everything seemed so terrible—so unbearable—but God brought good out of the situation. If I had stayed in Chicago, who knows what my life might have been? Think of all the children I've taught here . . . and all the joy I've had doing it. I wouldn't trade it for anything, although I wish a lot of things could have been different."

"Grandfather, do you think the new teacher would mind if I continued to teach the art and music lessons?" Christina asked.

"I'm sure she'd appreciate your help," he answered. "Is that what you want?"

Christina nodded. "I had no idea that I'd enjoy it so much, and the children have made so much progress. I'd like to keep working with them and see how far I can take them."

"Sounds like another aspiring teacher in the family," Grace said.

"She's tremendous with the children," Andrew joined the conversation. "But I thought painting was your life."

"So did I." Christina smiled intently at Andrew. "But I love teaching . . . it's like a whole new world for me, and every day is a brand-new challenge. The thought of painting for a living suddenly seems dull in comparison. I used to love painting just to paint. I'm not sure I could continue to love painting if I did it primarily for the money."

"But money no longer needs to be—"

"Grandmother, I know all about the money," Christina explained. "I've seen your home and Grandfather's business, but I'm not wanting your money. I want to discover this on my own."

"But you'll inherit it all when—"

"I don't want to hear *anything* about it," Christina cut off her grandfather, holding up her hands for him to stop. "For the first time I have the two of you in my life, and that's all I need and want. I don't care if you own the Palmolive Building and every business in it. Let's not talk money or inheritances. Let's enjoy what we have together."

"There's something else you're trying to figure out, isn't there?" Rebecca asked her daughter. "I've watched since you got home, and I've seen you changing. Can you tell us about it, or am I prying again?"

Christina glanced at Andrew, then looked out the front window as she thought about how she might answer the question. Finally she turned back toward them and said, "Yes, I'd love to talk about it . . . at least tell you about what's happened. I hope I don't embarrass you, Andrew, but it especially relates to you."

Andrew smiled cautiously and squirmed a bit in his chair. "Perhaps we should talk privately first?" he asked.

"No, I think it's better if I tell everyone at once," she replied, staring sincerely into his dark eyes and then turning toward her mother. "I've always admired your faith and life, Mother, but you're well aware that I've always despised the church . . . and God. So few people, it seemed to me, lived their lives in a manner that measured up to what they said they believed. It's been so easy to write God off because of them. And He failed us badly, letting my father die, letting you suffer alone, letting us be reproached by church people in this community. I could never love a God like that."

"But that's changed," her mother said, tears forming again at the corners of her eyes.

Christina nodded and choked up for a moment. "It started with meeting Grandmother, which was no accident, I believe. Then there was Edgar Mitchell, whose love for my mother was so evident and whose words were so mysteriously true. He told me, when he saw Grandfather react to the news of mother being sick, that I'd just seen a miracle, and he was right. I had seen it in Grandfather's eyes, and I couldn't deny it.

"Then," she continued, "there've been all the remarkable things that have happened in the church here. If you knew how much I hated Gertie Wilson, or how badly I would have liked to have seen her and Vivian be hurt, and then to have Gertie apologize before the whole church for all the horrible things she did to us . . . it's totally unraveled every argument I've held up to God."

Christina stopped and took a choppy breath, her emotions running deep and her mother's tears running hard. Andrew's hand covered his trembling lips but did not hide the tears cascading down his cheeks. Only her grandfather appeared to be unshaken by it.

"But it was your offer to help us," Christina said, turning directly to Andrew, "that pushed me over the edge. I thought at the time, when you asked me to teach with you"—she gave a short laugh—"it was a ploy on your part ... that all you were interested in was me. I thought you wanted to use it to get to me ... like other men had tried in the past. At first, I didn't feel I had a choice but to go along with it—we needed the income. But I watched you. I watched every move you made. If you had laid one finger on me, I would have walked away. I saw your love for the children ... and I saw your love for my mother and the church ... and I slowly came to believe that you were true to your words. I ... ah ... haven't seen many men whom I can trust ... like you.

"So," Christina continued, turning back to her mother, "God has taken down every barrier I put up to keep Him at a distance ... just like you told me He would do someday. And I find it's just Him and me ... and it's my sins that are the real barrier ... not all the other stuff He trashed. The problem all along has been me. Still, He called and said, 'Come to me, Christina. Come.' So I came to Him this morning and put everything at His feet. He forgave me ... with all my anger and excuses and bitterness. It's gone. I know it's gone, and I know He took it from me. In my heart I sense His love, and I want to love Him back. I'm just not sure what all that means."

Rebecca waited until Christina was finished. Then she quietly slipped off the davenport and from her knees began to extol God in words and tones that made the hair on Christina's arms stand up. She had often heard and seen her mother pray, but she had never heard anything that rivaled this. Almost instinctively, she sank to her knees and quietly thanked God for His great goodness.

Andrew, too, then Grace, and finally William, could not stay seated. Ten knees pressed the hardwood floors, and five voices softly did their best to exalt the Redeemer and Lover of their souls as something of God's glory seemed to pass among them. Time was of no matter to them, though with every passing minute one could easily see God giving back the years the locust had stolen. It was just as King Solomon once said, "I know that, whatsoever God doeth, it shall be for ever: nothing can be put to it, nor any thing taken from it: and God does it, that men should fear before him."

Chapter 30

*I*n the evening darkness, Christina quickly crossed the lawn to the back of the parsonage and hesitated before knocking on the door. She knew that Andrew's car was parked out front and that the lights in the den were on, but as she peered through the window into the dark kitchen, she wondered whether she dared to knock. Then as she raised her hand, Andrew suddenly stepped into the kitchen, turned on the ceiling light, and walked straight toward her.

Fearing that he had seen her or heard her on the back porch, Christina panicked and rapped her fist hard on the door's window. Andrew nearly collapsed backward with shock at the explosion of noise and he gasped aloud "What!" as his hand went to his heart. In the dim light he spotted Christina as she burst out laughing at the comical look on his face, then he shook his head and came slowly to the door.

"We're closed!" He managed to smile as she continued to laugh. He pulled the door partially open and said, "Come back in the morning and perhaps we can find a job for you."

"I'm sorry. I didn't mean to frighten you," Christina said, bursting into laughter again. "The look on your face . . . was perfect. I thought you were going to faint. May I come in?"

"Why don't you go around to the front door?" Andrew asked as he opened the door wide and let her pass. "I was just coming out to the pantry to get some of my aunt's apple pie, and you scare me half to death. Why the back door?"

"Oh, I don't know," she replied, stepping into the lighted kitchen and turning around. "I was afraid that someone might see me coming into your house alone after eight P.M. You know how people talk around here."

"I am aware of it, yes." Andrew followed her into the kitchen. "And it would definitely give folks something to chew over. So, what's up? Everything okay at your house?"

"Everyone's happy and in bed already," Christina answered. "Can we go into the living room? I'd just like to talk for a while."

"Sure." Andrew was completely in agreement with talking while gazing at Christina's shining countenance ... her blue eyes ... her sweet mouth. "You want some pie and milk? It's about all I have."

"No thanks," Christina said as she walked into the living room and sat down in one of the green crushed velvet cushioned chairs. "The last few days people have been dropping by with food, mostly desserts. We ate enough tonight to count for a couple of Thanksgivings. I should bring you over some of the food before it spoils at our house."

Andrew plopped down in one of the matching green chairs. "How'd the rest of the day go? I was sorry I had to leave, but we do have school tomorrow. I'm finding that it's requiring more and more preparation on my part. I hope that this new teacher measures up to your mother's approval. I'm not sure how much longer I can keep up."

"You've been going day and night for weeks now, and nobody should be expected to keep that up." Christina was sympathetic. "I'm so glad that they found this woman, and I'm sure she'll work out fine. It'll be a relief to my mother as well. She dreads how hard you've had to work to keep everything going."

"So, all's well at your house?"

"Beyond my dreams," said Christina. "Unless you knew the story, you could never tell that there'd ever been any separation at all. Grandmother brought along a thick album of old photos that she'd shown me in Chicago. We sat for over an hour and a half just talking and laughing about them. Watching my grandfather today, and seeing what he was like when he was a young father, I have a hard time understanding how he became so coldhearted and indifferent. Sort of scary, isn't it?"

Andrew nodded and said, "Look at Gertie. Aunt Lizzy says that Gertie was the most charming girl around when they were teenagers, but every year after Vivian was born she seemed to get more and more protective and nasty. Every choice we make leads down a road that has more choices. If we go down the wrong road and all the choices are making us worse and worse, it does get scary."

"Andrew," Christina said, leaning forward in her chair and crossing her hands on her lap, "I'm sorry to come over so late, but I felt like I needed to talk with you tonight, and I wanted to wait until the others went to bed so I didn't have to raise any suspicions."

"About what?"

"Well, today when I said I wasn't ready to return to Chicago, Mother asked me what else I was searching for answers for," Christina said. Her deep blue eyes were bearing down upon him hard. "I mentioned that you especially figured into my coming to faith, but you initially looked nervous and said that perhaps we should talk in private first. I thought . . . maybe there was something about it that you wanted to discuss. I didn't mean to put you on the spot there."

Andrew laughed and squirmed in his chair exactly as he had earlier in the day. "I think I could use a piece of pie," he said as he stood up. "Are you sure you don't care for some?"

"No pie for you or for me until we've talked," Christina persisted. "I want to know what you were thinking."

Slumping back into the thick cushions of his chair, Andrew took a deep breath. "Give me a little break here. When you answered your mother, you said nothing initially about coming to faith. You simply mentioned that I figured *especially* in something with which you were still coming to terms. I didn't know you were referring to your faith. But it was an extraordinary story, and I'm delighted to have been a part of it. I haven't been able to concentrate on my lesson preparations all night. Your story keeps running through my head, and your mother's prayer . . . I thought the roof was going to lift off your house. I'll never forget this day as long as I live."

Christina's mouth broke into a bright smile and her eyes searched his face. "I'm sure I'll never forget it either, and the words I spoke about you were absolutely true. But . . . I need to know what you thought I meant."

Andrew pulled himself to the edge of the cushions and rested his elbows on his knees. He looked away and covered his mouth with his hand, staring out through the front windows into the dark night for what seemed like several minutes. Then he looked back at her and said, "I have a feeling I should offer you an apology before I answer. While

I never laid a finger on you, as you mentioned today, I have to confess that being together as much as we've been, I've had a difficult time keeping my feelings toward you in check. While I've done nothing that I've considered improper, there were moments when I was afraid that perhaps my affections were flashing all over the place."

"So when I mentioned you today," Christina pursued, "you thought I was going to tell them that I wanted to stay here to sort out my possible affections for you?"

"I'm really sorry to have presumed so much . . . or to have hoped it was the case," Andrew finally nodded in assent. "I feel like a foolish schoolboy, but there were moments when I thought I read it in your eyes as well. You must forgive me, but you can't fault me for dreaming that someone as lovely and charming as you could be interested in me."

Christina's intent expression did not change. "When did I give you that impression?"

"You are a cruel one," Andrew gasped, shaking his head and shifting positions in his chair. "I'm so embarrassed at what I've just said that I'd like to crawl under my chair, and you have to torment me with asking for details? Please, just forgive me and we can live our lives happily ever after, knowing that once upon a time I loved you and dreamed you might love me."

"How did I give you that impression?"

Andrew laughed and threw his head back against the chair, then his hands shot up as in surrender. He leaned forward and focused his dark eyes to match her stare. "How? There have been times when you put your hand on my arm, and it felt affectionate to me. When you ran over me at first base and I caught you in my arms, I got the impression that you were in no hurry to get up. There were days when you came to school early and watched me with the students, or times after school when we talked about the students and their work. I thought . . . on occasion . . . that there was more to it than just killing time. I thought you enjoyed my company. I certainly have enjoyed yours."

"You said you were in love, Reverend Regan," Christina said. "Do you mean really in love, or is it a fairy-tale love?"

Andrew closed his eyes and chuckled. "It may sound like a fairy tale, but I'm afraid that I fell in love . . . really."

"With an unbeliever. Aren't there rules against that?"

"There are warnings in Scripture about being unequally yoked to unbelievers, yes," Andrew replied sincerely. "I had no intention of pursuing this relationship ... or even mentioning it to you, but that doesn't mean my love for you was any less. Everything about you made me want to love you, and I couldn't stop my affections from overwhelming me. When they mentioned your going to live with them in Chicago, I actually felt a tremendous relief. It—"

"You want me to leave?"

"No, heavens no!" Andrew exclaimed. "My heart sank into my shoes when they said it. I dread the thought of not seeing you every day, and I'd gladly stay up late every night to be spending time with you at the school. But don't you get it? I'm in this too deep. It's incredibly difficult to be around you and not show my affections. In that sense, it would be easier for me if you left."

"Anything else I should know, Andrew?"

Andrew stood up and walked to the front windows where he crossed his arms and gazed out on the moonlit-etched church. "I'm not sure what you want from me," he finally said, turning back toward her. "But there is one more thing. I often wondered, when I first got here, why someone as lovely and young as your mother never remarried. Now I know."

That said, Andrew turned back and stared out the window again.

Christina quietly got up out of her chair and stepped across the hardwood floor to Andrew. She began to reach out to touch his shoulder, but then pulled back and said, "Is it possible, do you think, to fall in love so deeply and yet never have kissed the person you love?"

"Yes" came his answer without hesitation.

"Might a kiss help, though?"

"I suspect it would, but I don't know."

"You've never kissed a girl?"

"I've never kissed a girl I loved."

"But you'd like to?"

Andrew turned around slowly and studied Christina's face. "I would love to kiss her, but she must know that this is no game. My greater desire is that she love me as I love her."

"Which she does, but she would really like to sample one of his kisses."

"Only one?"

"A dozen then."

For the first time, Andrew took Christina's hands in his hands and pulled her to him, then wrapped his arms around her and buried his face against her cheek and blond hair and whispered into her ear, "I love you, Christina."

Christina returned his words with, "And I love you, Andrew," words she spoke with fire and conviction. Then she took his face in her hands and kissed his lips softly, once and twice, then hard and long, almost struggling to breathe. "Whew!" she whispered finally, resting in his strong arms. "That was worth the wait. I think I'm going to like this. How about you?"

"Delicious," Andrew said. "I'm not sure I can handle a dozen."

"Especially when we're standing in the living room window with the whole world watching!" Christina exclaimed, pulling back from Andrew.

Andrew laughed and stepped away from the window and pulled Christina back to him. "For all that you put me through tonight, I'm going to try for my dozen, then you head on home," he said. "We've got some serious talking to do, and I think it's safer to do it in the daylight! I don't trust myself here, and I sure hope you don't."

"If I didn't trust you, I wouldn't be here at all," Christina replied, hugging Andrew. "But ... you're not the only one whose affections can't be trusted. Now, let me pay up and I'll be on my way."

✦✦✦✦✦✦✦✦✦✦✦

Christina closed the kitchen door without a sound and tiptoed lightly across the kitchen to turn off the living room light before she went to her bedroom. As she stepped into the living room, she was surprised to find her mother staring at her from the davenport. "Mother!" she exclaimed, trying to collect herself. "I thought you were in bed. Aren't you tired?"

"I always find it hard to sleep when I hear the back door click shut and think I hear someone walking in the backyard," Rebecca replied, tapping the cushion next to her. "I think we better talk, don't you?"

"Do you have all night?" Christina asked as she walked to the davenport and sat down next to her mother.

"No, but I need to sleep, and I won't be sleeping till you deliver the news. It's Andrew, isn't it? You and Andrew."

Christina's smile gave the answer away before she spoke any words. "How does one go from hating the church one day to falling in love with a churchman the next?" she asked, then laughed softly, taking Rebecca's hands in hers. "Mother, I am totally in love with Andrew, and he loves me! Can you believe that?"

"Yes!" Rebecca exclaimed, shaking Christina's hands, then wrapping her arm around her daughter and holding her tight. "And it didn't happen in one day. I saw it coming. I could see that both of you were fighting it. He told you he loved you?"

"Tonight," Christina answered. "I asked him directly."

"You asked him?"

"I tortured him, Mother." Christina sounded jubilant. "I made him tell me everything before I told him anything. It was beautiful beyond words, although his words were like a poet. And his kisses—"

"You kissed him?"

"Of course!" Christina enjoyed shocking her mother with such delicious information. "What was I supposed to do? We declare our love and then shake hands and say good-night? I kissed the man I love. That can't be wrong."

"In the parsonage you kissed him?"

"Should we have gone outside?"

"No," Rebecca said and laughed, "but it seems so strange to be talking about love and kisses in the parsonage!"

"Unseemly! Scandalous!"

"Very!"

Rebecca and Christina laughed delightedly until Rebecca finally got worried that her parents might wake up. Settling down, she said, "I can't imagine how hard it's been on Andrew to have fallen in love but not be able to show it. It could have ruined his ministry, you realize."

"Which is also why I held back," Christina replied. "I wasn't going to ask him to step away from what he has felt is God's calling on his life, and I knew I presented that problem to him. I think it's been very hard on both of us."

"So what will you do now? If I go to Chicago for the winter, and Andrew's next door, that isn't going to look good."

"What if the new teacher stays here with me until you return?"

"Well, that's a big improvement over your being here alone, but still

... you two are in a very difficult spot. Did you talk about—?"

"Marriage?" Christina cut in. "No. We thought we best talk about that in the light of day. The parsonage was getting a bit warm, you know."

"Yes, I may be forty, but I haven't forgotten," Rebecca replied. "It seems to me that ... given Andrew's position ... and the fact that you've gotten to know each other so well, a short engagement would be appropriate. What do you think?"

"I think the shorter the better," Christina responded, then laughed again. "I'm not sure you should be gone the whole winter, though. Maybe a week is enough."

Rebecca laughed, too, but with some reserve. "I think it's something you need to consider really seriously. I know you'd like to stay and keep working with the children, but right now, this may be more important. Mother mentioned to me that the new teacher is wonderful with music and art. Maybe it would be good if you did come to Chicago and have some time to let this simmer. If it's—"

"It's real, Mother. I have no doubt about that."

"I'm not doubting you, but it might be good to let it simmer anyway. Maybe more for Andrew's sake than yours. And this may be the only chance the four of us have to spend time together as a family. Despite all the good things that happened today, there are still a lot of ghosts to get rid of in our house in Chicago. I think we need one another ... for a while ... to put our lives back together. Wouldn't it be nice to close this chapter with an ending that we're all happy with? Drive out all the darkness, as Edgar put it so well."

Christina nodded reflectively, not liking the thought of being separated from Andrew, but appreciating the clear ring of truth in her mother's words. "It seems," she spoke softly, leaning her head against her mother's shoulder, "that we've lived our lives in the shadow of a secret, which has finally been exposed to the light. I never want to go back there ... into the shadows. Will the light actually get brighter than this, Mother?"

"Oh yes," Rebecca said. "All you have to do is walk in it, Christina. The darkness ... and the shadows ... have no place here. The light shines in darkness, and darkness can never overcome it."

Epilogue

Christina discovered that her mother was absolutely right that she come to Chicago with them, as hard as it was to say good-bye to Andrew temporarily. It came as a complete surprise to her that it was her mother who needed her in Chicago more than anyone else. Had she thought it through, she would have realized it wasn't just a matter of "airing out the museum" as they joked about, but for her mother it was truly a time of coming to terms with a past that indeed was dark. For the first several weeks, anything related to Christina's father renewed a grief in Rebecca that time and distance had not eliminated.

But as the old calendar was replaced with a new one dated 1938, in the warm Adler mansion on a frigid, blustery Chicago winter day, the light finally burned its way through Rebecca's grief and it truly became a time of healing. Once again, laughing and singing echoed through the rooms of the old mansion, and joy danced in an old man's heart every time he saw his daughter and granddaughter. He walked away from his business life and never went back. In the spring, gardening with his wife would make him forget whatever delights he had found in possessing defunct businesses.

Much of the winter, Christina was busy painting portraits of her family. One of her mother, one of each of her grandparents, and one of her mother and grandparents together. Fortunately, the winter months had many sunny days, providing her with an abundance of light and countless hours talking with her loved ones while she painted. The result, as you might guess from all the love and care she put into the portraits, was four remarkable canvases so stunning in their essence that people could stand and look at them for long periods of time and still feel as though they hadn't seen everything there was to see. Carl Langstan would have approved, had Christina been willing to let him look at her work.

Twice during the winter Andrew took the train and visited them in Chicago. Stuart Anderson filled in for the pulpit duties and—not to Andrew's surprise—was a major hit. The news of Andrew and Christina's engagement had been received with great delight in the community, and the church was anxious for the announced Easter wedding. The quiet sort of revival that the church had enjoyed throughout the fall continued on, week after week, with more people repenting and more conversions, which kept Andrew busy with follow-up work and discipling. Gertie ran the Wilson General Store quietly and retold her story to all who asked . . . and many who didn't ask.

Andrew and Christina's days together in Chicago were whirlwinds of delight. From touring the city with Edgar Mitchell at the wheel of the limousine to late-night dinners at some of Chicago's finest restaurants, courtesy of Grandfather Adler, the engaged couple went from early in the morning to well past midnight. On one of his visits, Maria Sikkink and her senator husband threw a big dinner for them with a houseful of rich and influential people who were acquaintances of her grandparents. Each visit concluded with a painful good-bye at the railroad station.

William and Grace Adler seemed to grow younger as the winter weeks edged toward spring. Even the hard exterior that William had built up through years of practice on the job softened with time. He could smile easily and talk easily and relax easily, and it wasn't long before he got talked into helping out with the church's soup kitchen. By spring he was working on some plans to retrain workers who'd been displaced by machinery in their factory jobs. Grace took it all in, enjoying every moment, never again to collapse in a bundle of tears in the entryway as she had on Christina's first visit to the mansion.

With her grieving days behind her, in mid-January Rebecca went back to work on her manuscript, revamping nearly every sentence. Although the rheumatic fever was long past, she did have to rest often, and she wondered if her teaching days were behind her. She found that she loved recreating the story, and when she had typed the last sentence, she had at least a dozen more stories in her head that she was ready to write. The publisher she sent it to, who did not in fact know William Adler or have any connections to him, so loved the story that he signed Rebecca to a six-book contract with manuscript deadlines every six months for three years. Rebecca, who enjoyed her days in Chicago despite the bittersweet beginning, longed to return to her home in Liberty Center and set up an office in the largest bedroom upstairs. Its tall windows would provide a profuse amount of sunlight and its view of the countryside promised to be the perfect place to write her stories.

Finally the spring robins reappeared and snowbanks melted into oblivion. Rebecca and Christina returned from their dark brick mansion to the humbler accommodations they called home. Emily Manley, the new schoolteacher, had moved out a few weeks before the Ellington women came back, renting a tiny house in the village that had stood empty most of the winter. In shortened bursts of energy, Rebecca soon had her garden in tip-top shape, despite the lack of care it had received during her sick days the previous fall.

A few days before the wedding, Andrew's family arrived from Michigan and unpacked their suitcases in the parsonage. William and Grace Adler made the long drive from Chicago again, promising that they would return home by rail and that the shiny silver Packard was the wedding gift they intended to leave behind. They also had insisted on financing a big church dinner after the wedding, with the best meat Harry Regan could carve from one of his prized Herefords. Grace had spent the last two months sewing Christina's wedding dress, which turned out so dazzling that poor Andrew looked undone, even though he had managed to buy himself a fine new suit.

It was unheard of to have a marriage ceremony after the traditional Easter morning service, but Andrew wanted it that way, and being the pastor of the church, who was going to object? The morning started cloudy, but by church time the sun was radiant and spirits were high. A local Lutheran pastor, whom Andrew had become friends with, came to conduct the wedding ceremony, which also raised a few eyebrows. But most unusual was the small bridal party. The maid of honor was Rebecca Ellington, whom Christina easily considered her best friend as well as her mother. And the best man was Harry Regan, with his thick shoulder muscles bulging out of a black suit coat that almost made him look handsome. He'd never bought a suit in his life, but his sister Elizabeth had insisted that he get one in honor of Andrew's fine day. Elizabeth, of course, had the dinner crew in high gear, and it promised to be the finest spread of food ever served in the church.

Christina was so beautiful in her long white dress that they feared her grandfather might burst into tears from the front of the church. He had done so when she first modeled the dress, and he was quite certain he would do so again. If he started weeping, the photographer was worried that he would wreck the family portrait. Christina would carry a large bouquet of fresh flowers from her mother's garden, and when those were combined with Christina's natural beauty and elegant dress, Andrew found he could hardly breathe when she walked down the aisle toward him. He was happy to have Harry standing behind him, just in case he fainted.

The wedding ceremony was short and sweet. After the vows were said and the rings given, Andrew kissed Christina for an unbearable length of time according to Aunt Lizzy, but most of the folks who were gathered seemed to enjoy it. Even Gertie Wilson started clapping, although her husband Lloyd managed to resist any urges he might have had to get demonstrative. Vivian Wilson did not attend, but no one expected her to.

Andrew and Christina did not leave Liberty Center for their honeymoon, although Andrew was given a week off from his pastoral duties. With his family taking off for Michigan late in the afternoon after the wedding, the two of them were quite content to have the parsonage to themselves. The winter's separation had done nothing to diminish the intensity of their initial passion, and had it been winter, Andrew was certain all the windows in the parsonage would have steamed up. Christina preferred that he not talk about steamy windows.

Rebecca never did return to teaching school. Emily Manley, though not Rebecca's equal, was a fine teacher who cared deeply about her children, and Rebecca took it as God's way of opening the door for her to write. And her writing opened another door that Rebecca had always said she'd never go through. The publisher of her books, as it turned out, was a widower who fell in love with more than just her books, and over a two-year period did his utmost to win her heart. Being one of the most charming men Rebecca had ever met—besides just being really nice and a fine Christian—Jacob Bolton eventually persuaded Rebecca to wed and come to Chicago. Saying good-bye to Christina and Andrew was very hard, but the chance to be close to her elderly parents, and even closer to the man whose love had eventually swept her off her feet, won the tug-of-war.

Andrew and Christina enjoyed the first four years of their marriage in Liberty Center. Two healthy little boys were born to them during that time, delivered by Doc Anderson, of course, who had delivered Christina and just about every other baby in the county surrounding Bradford over the previous thirty-five years. The church in Liberty Center grew in numbers and in depth, which was enormously satisfying to Andrew. Christina managed to teach piano lessons and voice lessons to a handful of eager students from the community, but the babies occupied most of her time.

After the bombing of Pearl Harbor, Andrew felt a new call from the Lord. As much as he wanted to join the thousands of young Americans taking up arms to fight, he sensed that God wanted him to take up his Bible and be a chaplain to men who were about to put their lives on the line for their country. Christina desperately hated the idea, but she knew in her heart that Andrew was in God's hands and that he was being called to a higher mission that she could only pray about. And pray she would, night and day.

Aunt Lizzy and Uncle Harry hated to see them leave as well. They loved the baby boys . . . oh, how the two of them loved the babies! Fortunately, there were two babies to love; otherwise, they would have had to share time. Harry also adored Christina. No one understood Harry better than she. Their grief was sharp in saying good-bye. But both Elizabeth and Harry had their newfound involvement in the church, which they served faithfully all of their lives, and that helped comfort them in their loneliness.

At her grandfather's invitation, Christina and the boys moved into the dark brick mansion in Chicago for the duration of the war. That put her close to her mother again, which was a joyful reunion, and she and the boys would be a tremendous comfort to her grandmother. A year after Andrew left, in the spring of 1943, her grandfather died in his sleep of a heart attack. To be alone, as Grace often said, in that big house would have been extremely difficult. She had a hard time sleeping and found a special consolation in holding the youngest child in the night.

Andrew did not make it home for over three and a half years. First, he was in North Africa, then in Italy, then in France and Belgium. He saw it all, from the absolute worst of the war's horrors to the most glorious heroism one could ever imagine. He befriended many, prayed with countless of the army's bravest and most scared, buried more men than he could stand, and somehow survived himself. A dent in his helmet from a German bullet served as a constant reminder that he'd be fortunate to ever see Christina and the boys again.

But he returned the victor, coming home to a wife who was even lovelier than he remembered, and to his sons, who were six and five and didn't know who he was. The brick mansion proved to be a great place for them all to get reacquainted, but soon they were off to a new church in a small suburb of Seattle, Washington. It seemed that every person there was a Norwegian or a Swede, that most of them were commercial fishermen or builders, and that they were just as stubborn as people said they were.

It wasn't long, though, before they fell in love with the people in their community and church, and it started all over again. First, an unlikely soul coming to repentance, then another, and their voices attracting others to the beauty of the good news. Then a third baby came along, a beautiful little girl who managed to coax a lonely grandmother and great-grandmother to board an airplane and fly across the country to see them. And so the family grew ... and the church grew ... and great was the grace that was upon them.

Christina Ellington, now Regan, refused to live in the past, but she never forgot her past. She had a way with children, especially fatherless children, that blossomed into a lifelong ministry. It was as if she had special radar that could spot them and pull them out of a crowd, and she had a way of teaching that addressed the needs of their hearts without making a big show of it. Andrew won the adults, and Christina brought in the children.

And, yes, she never stopped painting, but never for money. She filled their home with canvases of expansive snowcapped mountains and towering pine trees and then found pleasure in portraits of mothers with their newborns. Whatever else was happening around, she always had her paintings to help bring a fresh perspective to the world. She never stopped painting, and she never stopped giving.

Rebecca's words proved true. The shadows never returned, for the light had come.

FROM GIFTED STORYTELLER LANCE WUBBELS

Change was sweeping through the land... and through their lives!

THE GENTLE HILLS is the dramatic and delightful story of the Macmillan family during the era that redefined the nation.

For Jerry Macmillan, the Japanese air strike on Pearl Harbor compelled him to join the throngs of American men who immediately volunteered to go to war. But he and his wife, Marjie, had no way of knowing how the war would change their lives forever.

From the heartrending challenges of keeping their farm in the Midwest, to Jerry's dramatic survival when his aircraft carrier is sunk, and his return home to face calamity, the gripping story of the Macmillan family unfolds.

Through the challenges they face on the homefront, Marjie and Jerry find their faith and fortitude tested to the limit.

They had answered the call of their country, but how will they respond to a call that transcends flesh and blood?

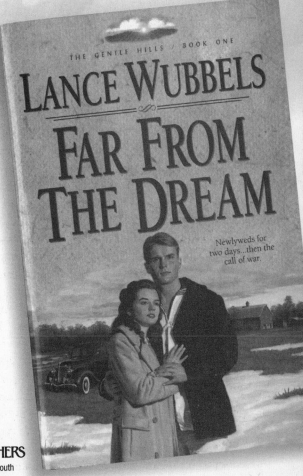

THE GENTLE HILLS
Far From the Dream
Whispers in the Valley
Keeper of the Harvest
Some Things Last Forever

BETHANY HOUSE PUBLISHERS
11400 Hampshire Ave. South
Minneapolis, MN 55438

www.bethanyhouse.com